CRUEL

PROMISE

KETLEY ALLISON

DEAR READER

My lovely reader, this is not a book for those wishing for Prince Charming. There is no redemption here.

POTENTIAL TRIGGERS:

Tempest is, and stays, a villain. There is one scene that could be considered dub con (dubious consent), so please be advised.

There are also many references to witchcraft and the occult (but this is <u>not</u> a paranormal romance).

If this sounds like a story you would love to get lost in, please continue reading! If you prefer your men to understand their bad ways and repent for it, then ...

Stay far away from Tempest.

Turn the page to enjoy Tempest and Ardyn's fall into an obsessive love story.

TITAN FALLS STUDENT PLAYLIST

Let Me Hurt - Emily Rowed
Boyfriend - Dove Cameron
The Motto - Tiësto, Ava Max
Cigarettes - Juice WRLD
Infinity - Jaymes Young
Toxic - BoyWithUke
For Tonight - Given
Where's My Love - Acoustic - SYML
Love Story - Sarah Cothran
Playground - Bea Miller

Find the rest of the playlist on Spotify:
https://geni.us/cruelpromisemusic

1

ARDYN

It's one thing to use protection to keep people out of your home, but it's a whole other effort to use that protection to escape.

"The dove is in her bedroom, boss," Barry, my security detail, also known as my ride or die, mumbles into the discreet microphone on his wrist.

I can't currently see him, but I can picture his stance and the following fifteen minutes of routine checks he'll go through before nodding to himself, tapping my closed door thrice with the pads of his fingers (he's the superstitious sort), then rotating one-eighty until his back is against my door, crossing his arms, and remaining in place until my alarm goes off at 5:30 a.m. and my weekday routine begins.

My phone chirps, drawing my attention. With half an ear to Barry's movements, I lift it from where I'd flung it on my bed and read the message.

Mila: Have you broken out yet?

My stomach leaps at the words. Mila's helped me plan this moment meticulously since we heard the words *black tie secret auction* three weeks ago. My parents, of course, would never let me go to an event unsupervised, never mind one held at midnight. The thought of going hadn't even crossed my mind until Mila caught my eyes with her green ones, the sharp slant of them adding to her mischievous wink the instant she realized I'd heard the whispered conversation in Manhattan Elite's cafeteria hall, too.

Mila's wanted to be my bad influence since she met me, and this was her moment to shine.

Not yet, I texted back, annoyed at the way my thumbs were already shaking.

C'mon, Ardyn, you're sneaking out and going to a party. You should be an ace at this by now if you ever got up the nerve to try since enrolling in junior high. Which you didn't. Wimp.

It's my internal voice talking, but the longer it goes on, the more it absorbs Mila's playful cadence. *It's no biggie. We'll steal some champagne and flirt with older men, and you'll be home before Barry turns into a pumpkin!*

Mila: Hurry!!! They shut the doors at 12:30.

I check the time on my phone. 12:06. *Shit.*

"I can do this," I whisper, smoothing down my pajama shirt and straightening the hem of my plaid shorts.

Hermione makes a low-pitched mewl in response.

"I didn't ask for your opinion," I say to her, then wince once I realize where she's decided to curl up.

The black silk gown Mila lent me currently acts as my cat's bed, despite it being laid carefully on the corner of the mattress.

"It's a king-sized bed, Hermione!" I whisper-screech. "You literally could've chosen anywhere else!"

Hermione slow-blinks in reply.

Hissing under my breath, I carefully nudge her fuzzy white butt aside and pull the dress from underneath her. She swipes out in warning, and I nearly choke on my swallowed cry as I try desperately to save the silk from catching on her unsheathed claws.

I stumble back on weak knees, clutching the fabric to my chest.

A light knock follows. "Everything okay in there, Ardy?"

I blow out a tense breath. "Yes!" I reply, glaring at my cat. Then I remember what I'm supposed to do. "I mean—no. I'm feeling ... I'm not feeling very good..."

I wilt onto my knees to give my voice a true wobbly effect. Hermione looks on in disdain.

"Do you have a fever? Should I come in?"

"No, I'm-I'm indisposed. I've been throwing up in the bathroom and trying not to let you hear me." I cringe in embarrassment, then guilt, at how easy it is to gain Barry's concern. He's more a father figure to me than my actual one.

"Oh, Ardy, what can I do? Should I call your parents?"

"Absolutely not." I bite back the panic at the possibility of my parents coming home from their banquet and sending *them* into a round of alarm at the thought of something being wrong with me.

Guilt burrows further into my chest. They've never gotten over what happened to me six years ago, and here I am, using the concern of people I care about just to go to a party...

My phone buzzes nearby.

Clover: What's with the radio silence? Where are you guys? I'M HERE!

Mila: Currently waiting in the bushes for baby dove. I'm doubting she'll show.

Me: You know I'm on this chat chain, right?

Mila: Then spread your wings and flyyyyyy!

. . .

I anxiously chew on my cheek, making it harder to frown at the screen. Mila's always using my codename against me. I'm sure she thinks it's hilarious because our other friend, Clover, always laughs, but I hate hearing it from my friends' mouths almost as much as I despise listening to it every night—*the dove's settled in her bedroom, boss*—my father's version of "good night, sweetie," I guess.

Of course, I'll never tell them that. I have so few friends as it is. I don't want to aggravate the ones I do have.

And something tells me if I chicken out tonight, I'll never hear the end of it.

"Um, could I have some miso soup, maybe?" I ask Barry while remaining on my knees. Belatedly, I realize I'm still holding the dress against my chest in a way that will absolutely wrinkle it. Standing, I shake it out while sending panicked glances at my door. It's not like Barry could barge in here. Well, I suppose he could since he has a master key for emergencies—but he never has.

"Sure. I'll call down to the kitchen."

"I don't want to be a bother to Frances. Could you maybe go down the block and grab some?"

A few seconds of silence. "You know I can't leave this post."

"It's only for a second. It's not like I'm going anywhere." *Lies. Utter lies, Ardyn!*

"I'm sorry, Ardy, but I can't. I'm sure Frances would be happy to make you a quick cup."

"Never mind. It's probably best I stick to water, anyway.

I'm, uh, I'm going to try to sleep now. If you could please not have anyone disturb me…"

"You want me to call for delivery? How about that?"

"That's all right, Barry." The whole point of asking for something, according to Mila, was to lower suspicion. For who would try to sneak out while wanting your guard to come in?

Barry grunts. "I'm not gonna leave you up here to suffer, Ardy. Give me two minutes. I'll warm you up some broth in the microwave and be right back."

The swell of excitement battles with remorse. "Oh, you don't have to—"

"Don't let me second-guess this. I'll be right back."

"If you could just leave it outside my door!" I say before his shadow moves under the crack. "I-I really want to try to sleep."

"All right. I won't disturb you."

The dress is damp where I'm clenching it. This thing'll be ruined by the time I put it on. My phone buzzes again, its incessant vibrations telling me to get a move on.

I scamper around my four-poster bed, stuffing the silk gown in a tote bag I find by my bedside table and plucking whatever makeup brushes and compacts are closest on my vanity, sending them tumbling into my bag, too. Oh, and a hairbrush.

It's black tie, sure, but the art is the most important and should be on display more than the guests. This is how I reason with myself as I toss the bag over my shoulder and pad over to the door, pulling it open and peering through the small crack.

The coast is clear.

I creep through the opening on my tiptoes. "Don't be a narc, Hermione. Remember who feeds you," I say over my shoulder, taking one last look at my (Mila's) setup.

I've put pillows under my covers in the shape of a body, as every teen movie I've seen does, but Mila swears it works. With the years Barry's had to trust that I'll be in the places I say I will, she had no doubt I could pull it off. The pillows are a plan B. Barry's unlikely to open the door after I've asked him not to, now that I'm a "woman" and have to deal with "private needs."

As a kid, it was easy for him to order me around. He has a son my age and took to the job with aplomb, teaching me soccer, sneaking my favorite gummy worms when Mom wasn't looking, and trying his best to appear more as a friendly uncle than a guy with a gun.

Until puberty happened.

The morning I first got my period will be one to put in *both* our never-to-be-accessed memory vaults. My parents tend to travel a lot and go to frequent functions. My father's the founder of his hedge fund firm, and my mom is a top-level executive there. When they are home, they work with international clients and are often in their home offices with strict no-access policies. That left Barry with the task of prying the truth out of me when I woke up with cramps, went to the bathroom, then let out a bloodcurdling scream when I saw what was in the toilet.

Barry broke down the door with his gun drawn. So there's that.

The hallway's clear, and with my shoes hooked in my fingers, I pad down the Persian runner and to a side door leading to the servant's quarters back in the day. We live in a nineteenth-century brownstone in the Upper West Side. It's dark, creaky, ominous, and covered in ivy. A beauty to behold in the daylight but a crouching, sentient shadow at night. I use its beast mode to the best of my abilities and stay close to the shadows as I creep down the narrow stairs, avoiding the ones that moan the most. I'd tested out my escape route more than once—okay, twelve times—since Mila and Clover convinced me that this was the night to taste freedom.

The staircase leads down two floors. Once I reach the bottom, I peek past the corner and into a darkened hallway. A few security men are patrolling the brownstone, but like every executive protection, they have shifts. I'm banking on that switch occurring at twelve fifteen, leaving me a small gap to push the side door open, squat/run to the side gate, and hop the iron fencing into the neighbor's bushes where Mila apparently awaits.

I make it to the fence, and I'm mid-hop when my shirt catches on one of the iron spears and rips, sending me sprawling face-first into the dirt.

Damp soil clumps in my mouth, stifling my groan.

"You made it!"

I look up to a furtive shadow moving toward me. Her

face comes into the golden light cast by the streetlamps as she helps me up.

"I can't believe you actually did it," Mila says as she helps me brush off the dirt. "You're a rebel bitch in ... plaid? What are you wearing? Where is the dress I gave you?"

I lift my tote, stained in parts by the neighbor's garden.

Despite hiding in bushes for over half an hour, Mila looks like she just drifted out from her salon and spa appointment and got lost finding her chauffeur. Her open leather jacket can't disguise her black dress that flows down her torso but cinches at the waist. A small slit at the hem shows off even more of her tanned, toned legs, and her wavy, sun-soaked hair cascades across her shoulders, absorbing whatever light the night has left to give.

The running joke is that we look a lot alike. That is, if I saw the sun, gave my hair any attention, and stopped talking to my cat. Other than sharing the same coloring, dimensions, and height, we're as different as cream and cottage cheese.

While a little put off by Mila's personality, Barry understands why I'm drawn to her. He's the one who taught me —the louder the people you're with, the less you'll be noticed.

Mila cringes at the sight of my bag. "I mean, I suppose the dress is better protected there than here. On you." She gives me a dubious once-over. "Whatever. The point is you made it out, and none of the Matrix men have followed you over the fence."

"I know I don't look great, but I was running out of

time, and I figure we can pop into the restaurant on the corner, and I can use their bathroom to get ready," I offer, following her out of the terrarium my neighbor's helpfully created to shield us from view.

"No worries, I have us covered."

I squint at her suspiciously. "How? We have less than fifteen minutes to get to the auction, and we can't let any of our drivers know what we're doing in case it gets back to my parents." I left my phone in my room because of the obvious tracking apps my parents have put on it. "Should we call a car on your phone?" I've never been allowed to take the subway, but its sordid appeal lends itself to the kind of night I'm having. Might as well go all in. "I'm pretty sure the 2 train is around here somewhere..."

"We're not down *all* drivers." Mila straightens once we reach the sidewalk. Grabbing my hand, she leads us farther down the street.

I skid to a stop on my socked feet. "Mila, no one can know what we're doing. That was the deal. You can't tell anyone. I swear, my dad has electronically bugged all the sidewalks in Manhattan—"

"Relax, baby dove. Clover and I figured it out."

The mention of *Clover* and *driver* said so close together has my spine stiffening. "No."

Mila spins to face me, arching her brow. "What do you mean, no?"

"Not him."

Mila's answering smile is closed-mouthed, slow, and too much like Hermione's.

"Shit, I'm right, aren't I?" If we weren't still so close to my house, I would've screeched it at her. "Why, though? He's the worst. A complete asshole."

Mila turns toward the cross street, pretending she can't hear me.

"He'll be the first to narc on me to my parents, and you know why? Because he's amused by misery. He feeds off watching other people suffer. It gives him the energy required to operate at maximum dickhead speed."

"What are you, a Miami cop? Who says narc anymore? And anyway, he won't say a word to your parents because that would mean he'd have to care about your outcome, and that guy cares about nothing, especially you."

Mila doesn't mean it the way it sounds. I know she doesn't. Yet the sting comes, small and sharp. She's salty from the way Clover's older brother has dismissed, ignored, and completely deleted every move she makes toward him. And Mila's tried everything.

Heck, even I don't know why he hasn't given in. Mila Hernandez is tall, highlighted an exquisite blonde, naturally tanned, and gorgeously trim. Eyes skate to her in every room she walks in, especially men's. Women can't resist her prowess, tracking her movements with attraction and jealousy.

I'm used to operating in Mila's shadow. Come to think of it, Clover's, too. But something about this guy makes his dismissal hard to swallow. Probably because I don't even get that much from him. I'm less than a ghost, not even requiring the close inspection of a mite on his bedspread.

Since I was nine, I've been trained to be invisible. I was able to accept it until I met *him*. He was a gorgeous, witty, charismatic boy who made friends with everybody and had every single girl he came across becoming stupid for him. Including me. I was obsessed with watching him, amazed at his easy confidence and a little light-headed every time he unleashed a smile. Never at me, since I was usually hiding somewhere in the shadows stalking him, but always nearby.

And I hate myself for it.

A black car rolls up to the curb, anything but covert. Due to Barry's love of cars, I can immediately tag this one as a Lykan Hypersport. Rare, only seven in the world, and of course this dude owns one of them.

The tinted passenger window rolls down, taking my bedraggled reflection with it.

In its place is a silhouette who melts out of the luxury interior's shadows, his angles cutting through the dark as seamlessly as sharpened weapons.

I gulp.

Yes, for nine years, I was able to accept being invisible.

Until I met Tempest Callahan.

2

TEMPEST

Never in my life would I have considered driving my Lykan to be an annoyance until right now.

Her low roar turns into a purr when I coast to a stop at the corner of 76th and Columbus in front of two girls who've completely fucked up my night.

The first idiot, I expected. Clover's friend Mila struts to the curb, jutting her hip out and curving her smile like I'm a john about to give her the *Pretty Woman* moment she's been waiting for. With her loud laughter, try-hard outfits, and pay-attention-to-only-me vibes she gives off every time I come across her, I don't know what my sister sees in this friendship, but who am I to judge.

The other one, though, she catches my eye as I roll the window down, prepared to give them a good *fuck you* glare for not having the wherewithal to figure out a ride on an island that's literally famous for its transport systems.

Ardyn Kaine.

The sequestered princess of Manhattan, a mystery to most and an enigma to any man who tries to get to know her. She's the quiet, wallflower type and therefore of no interest to me if not for her title: the only child and heiress to Kaine Industries. Now *that*, I'd love to fuck.

I look past Ardyn in search of her bald, heavily bearded shadow and don't find him anywhere.

Oh, I see. Bad girl.

I go back to her, smiling. "Did you fall headfirst out of your tower, Rapunzel?"

Ardyn scowls at me through the streaks of dirt on her face.

Mila steps in front of Ardyn before she can respond, not that she would. "Thanks for picking us up, Tempest. You got us out of a real bind."

Reluctantly, I slide my attention over to her. "I'm sure."

"That's a two-seater."

My brow jumps at the small, tentative voice behind Mila. "I've been told there's plenty of room for two on my lap, yes."

Mila laughs, though I'm anything but funny.

Ardyn steps out from Mila's shadow. "I meant your car."

"I know what you meant." I offer another slow smile, the one that made her stumble and scrape the tops of her toes once she realized who rolled up on her. *Your fault for not wearing shoes, princess.* "There's plenty of room for three."

"Totally!" Mila agrees, too loudly. We've gained enough

attention from pedestrians with the type of car I'm driving. I don't need to add more by having them think I'm picking up a hooker and a runaway.

"I can sit in the middle," Mila says, bending to open the passenger door.

I hit the auto lock button.

She glances through the window at me.

"Ardyn's in the middle." I don't voice it as a question.

"But—" Mila looks back at her friend, then at me. "Why?"

"She's thinner."

Mila's mouth drops open. I suppose that was crass of me, but I'm not suited to reading people's feelings and have no desire to find the insight.

Had Mila been on the other side of that comment, she would have preened underneath the praise despite the barb aimed at her friend. In this case, the line between Ardyn's brows only deepens as she folds her arms and stares down at me.

I admit, when pitting these two against each other, Mila should be the clear winner. *Should* be. She has the glorious body, flawless skin, and expertly injected lips. Natural or not, they'd be adept in bed. But I've always been drawn to broken things, wondering what caused those fractures and if I can stick a finger in them and crack them further.

Ardyn, the sweet creature, stands on this curb in ripped pajamas with dirt stains, tangled hair, and ... leg. A lot of leg underneath those wrinkled shorts.

"Whatever," Mila bites out, then jiggles the handle again. "Can we just go?"

"Don't let me keep you," I say dryly, disengaging the lock.

The Lykan's door opens in the opposite direction of regular cars, surprising and confusing Mila further. Ardyn doesn't react, simply stepping around Mila and reluctantly sliding in beside me.

"Hello, princess." I greet her with a wretched smile.

Her thigh brushes up against mine, and I'm almost positive she shudders at the contact.

Grinning, I lean back in my seat. Maybe my night isn't shot to shit after all.

Mila follows, pouting as she gets comfortable and shutting the door behind her.

I rev the engine, the roar echoing down the street and well into Central Park. Mila bites her lip and wriggles in her seat, sensing another chance to turn me on by flattering my car and, therefore, my big dick prowess. Ardyn remains as stiff as the bodyguard who trails her every move, with her ratty canvas tote covering the tops of her legs as if she's afraid I'd try to pry them wide open and slide my hand through her pussy.

The thought brings a foreign stiffness to my jaw. I quell the urge to bite the frown off her face, but not before I suck her taste into my mouth. *What would she taste like, I wonder? Poisoned apple? Tart cherries?*

"Where to, ladies?" I grit out.

"Clover didn't tell you?" Mila says.

"Only that I was to pick you two up at this location and be discreet about it." I splay one arm to indicate the obnoxiously loud rumble of my car. "Clo always tells our family what a wonderful listener I am."

"You could've really screwed up our plans if anyone we knew saw this," Ardyn pouts.

"Oh," I say with awed wonder as I turn into traffic. "She speaks without permission. Signal the guards."

"I know how to speak my mind," Ardyn retorts. "I just choose to do it to people who deserve the attention."

I mime being stabbed in the chest. "Ouch."

She shakes her head in annoyance in my periphery, arms folded and staring straight ahead.

"Sweet plaid, by the way. Am I taking you to a lumberjack event or a maple syrup-eating contest?"

"To Bowery and Third," Ardyn answers as if I were her taxi driver and doesn't react to my quip. Rude.

"The East Village. Boring. Why?"

"There's an art auction I'm interested in."

"Doubly boring," I muse as I take us out of the Upper West Side.

At Ardyn's response, any intellectual interest I have in her wanes. Art is pretty, I suppose, in the eye of the beholder and all that. Technology interests me more, especially Kaine Industries' usage of mathematical and statistical modeling to predict how an investment will perform. Ardyn likely knows nothing about it with her head in the clouds. Coupled with how high her father keeps her above the city's comings and goings, there's a lack of proper oxygen, too.

Too bad. I would've enjoyed digging into her brain matter while convincing her to pop open the buttons of her shirt. I wonder if she's as dirty underneath her clothes, too.

Ardyn continues, "Rumor has it a Rembrandt is going up, along with rare artifacts from the Chinese Dynasty and a never-before-seen Roman sword. I'd've thought ancient civilization would appeal to you, Tempest."

"Why?" One of my favorite games is predicting an insult before it comes because it usually annoys the shit out of the person trying to sling it. "Because I'm a Neanderthal?"

"No because it's where the most violent form of human conquering occurred."

I risk taking my eyes off the road to look at her. Assess her.

My vision's wide enough to notice Mila leaning forward, taking in our exchange with a none-too-pleased expression. "Wherever we're going, I doubt you'll get in looking like that, Ardyn."

Ardyn twists to her friend. "I tried asking you to let me use the restaurant's bathroom to get changed."

I take the next turn with a sigh. *Let her?* How can this girl be so intriguing one second and so disappointing the next? "How about this: *I'll* grant you permission to get undressed."

Ardyn swivels, her hip batting against mine again and

sending a zing of pleasure to my groin. "Excuse me? Where do you propose I do that?"

"Right here. In this car."

The whites of her eyes grow more visible in my periphery, and I chuckle. Mila scoffs as she looks out the passenger window. "Ardyn would never."

"Just ... drop me off at a Starbucks or something."

"And risk someone seeing you?" I drawl. "C'mon, princess, everyone here knows you're hanging out in public by a thread. The minute your old man drops a pin on you, you're dead meat. Why risk further exposure before you see the impressive sword you've been waiting for?"

There are so many dick innuendos in my sentence, even I have trouble stomaching my words, but the simple joy in her expression of disgust makes it all worth it. Fuck, she is all too easy to rile up. And I'm taking way too much pleasure in it.

Ardyn's mouth works. "I'm not ... I'm not getting changed with you next to me."

"I'll be a good boy." To demonstrate, I keep my eyes straight ahead and my hands at ten and two on the wheel. No way does my posture communicate how much the ache in my cock grows at the thought of Ardyn taking off her clothes so close by.

Sweet, innocent, and completely untouched. I'm dying to take in the color of her nipples. Pale rose or deep scarlet? What color would they turn if I tongued them hard enough?

It's always the forbidden fruit that tastes the sweetest, I rationalize as Ardyn fidgets next to me. That's the only reason I've taken on a sudden interest in this wisp of a girl who barely speaks above one decibel.

Mila rolls her eyes. "Ardyn is as proper and upper-crust as it gets. There's no way she'd even bare a shoulder to you, Tempest."

Ardyn glances at her best friend, her forehead wrinkling like she's torn between rebelling against Mila's point and proving it.

"You only have so much time," I say, coasting into the second lane on the West Side Highway. To enunciate my point, I press on the gas.

Ardyn's head falls back. Mila and I have the joy of a headrest. She doesn't.

She drops her chin forward and glares at me. Oddly, I don't think it's because the increase in speed bothers her.

"Fine," she mutters, digging through her tote.

She pulls out a flash of shining black, shaking it a few times as if that'll make it suddenly formal-worthy again.

"Christ, have you ever been outside your fortress before?" I ask her. I've never seen a woman so blasé about her designer gear. I gain a modicum of respect for her, but it's not enough to prevent a sneer in her direction.

"Eyes on the road," she snaps.

Amazing how she's so sassy with me yet so capitulating to Mila.

"Yes, ma'am."

"Don't worry, baby dove. I'll make sure he doesn't creep

on you." Mila angles in her seat, but her slitted eyes are on Ardyn.

I dismiss the intricacies of their relationship with a shrug. If I'm to make it through this ride with Ardyn stripping next to me, I have to key into the whole "chauffeur" thing and not the "sister's best friend" thing.

Ardyn starts off shy, experimenting with her top button before the whites of her eyes move to me like this is some kind of test.

Fuck, it is. It's not every day I'm next to a woman who takes her shirt off and expects me *not* to touch her.

Like the Boy Scout I lied that I am, I keep my gaze forward, counting the painted traffic lines in an effort to stop the growing bulge in my pants.

Ardyn moves to the next button, then the next. After what seems like the most painful cocktease strip ever, she shrugs off her shirt and passes it to Mila, who takes it with two fingers and drops it in her footwell.

Sadly, I'm only able to see a flash of cute, pert globes before she slips on the top half of the dress.

A subtle, closed-mouth smile lifts my lips as the answer presents itself. *Pale pink*.

She pauses after she hooks the top of her pajama shorts.

"Problem?" I ask mildly.

Ardyn doesn't answer. Instead, she stares into the passenger floorboard, where she and Mila share space.

Understanding dawns, and a low growl of approval sounds in my throat. Ardyn's head snaps toward me as if she heard it.

"Afraid to straddle the gearshift to give yourself more room?" I ask.

"Don't look," she whispers.

It's said so brokenly and with such a shaking tremor that my hands involuntarily clench against the wheel.

Rumors ricocheted around Clover's school since Ardyn enrolled last year. I've just graduated from a different boarding school, and even I heard how Ardyn had become faceless at the age of ten, isolated and homeschooled until she suddenly appeared as a junior at the most prestigious private school in Manhattan—the one Clover attended. After the shit that went down at my supposed elitist academy in Rhode Island, there was no way my parents could enroll Clover there and save any face. Four years above her, I didn't pay much attention to Clover's high school drama, but it was hard not to fall prey to the whispers of the ghostly heiress floating through Clover's halls. She's heavily guarded and in the permissible company of only two friends, Clover and Mila. I'm confident this is the most rebellious Ardyn's ever been, and I'm happy to assist her in it.

As long as she's not stupid enough to get caught.

"I won't look," I assure her. I'm shocked at how kind my voice sounds. And that I'm telling the truth.

Ardyn seems to believe me because she lifts her hips and slides the cotton down, bunching her knees to her chest to unhook them from her feet. Her white panties stay on, but I'm true to my word and don't risk a peek. I can't be punished for what goes on in my periphery, though, so focused that I nearly swerve into the lane next to ours.

Someone leans on their horn, bringing me out of my sidelong trance.

Mila screeches.

Ardyn dives for my chest.

I stiffen under her sudden warmth, though I return to our lane with ease. Her nails dig into my sides as the smell of mixed earth and gardenias floats into my nostrils.

Nobody touches me without my permission. Under most circumstances, I would fling a person off—even a chick—and growl at them never to do so again unless I ask them to, adding the promise of murder into my glare.

With Ardyn, for reasons I've yet to figure out, I don't.

Thankfully, she does the work for both of us before I'm forced to say anything. She flings herself off me as quickly as she pressed her body to mine, straightening with haggard breaths and wild eyes.

"I'm sorry," she pants. "I was—I'm not used to loud sounds like that."

"It's fine." I sound out the words as if I'm talking to a spooked animal. "Nothing bad will happen with me at the wheel."

Mila *harrumphs*. "Yeah, you've totally proven that. Try not to get us killed, please."

I'd mostly forgotten she was here.

"Nice moves you got there," she mutters to Ardyn before folding her arms and glaring out the passenger window.

"It wasn't intentional," Ardyn whispers in reply. I'm

tempted to tell her that it's a-okay to tell your friends to fuck off once in a while, then decide that it's not my damned business.

Ardyn pulls her dress down to her ankles, our makeshift lapdance at an end. There's no reason to have these girls in my car any longer and a hell of a lot of reasons for me to get back to my plans for the night, which was to meet my boy Rio at his chosen club where I could select my liquors and my ladies for the night. None of them would be innocent. Therefore, there's no chance of them whispering brokenly in my ear, giving me a new awareness of the more sensitive parts of myself I'd thought I'd killed off a while ago.

My GPS blips her 200-feet warning, and I roll us to a stop in front of one of those hipster museums with clear glass windows and all-white walls showcasing their latest subjective masterpieces.

I stare at the entrance a little too long as the girls rustle beside me, grabbing their shit and readying to exit. It's a strange place to host the rare artifact kind of auction Ardyn described, but what the fuck do I know? All I remember about ancient creations were the ones that decorated the underground tombs of my high school academy, and that shit is *long* buried in my gray matter.

Mila opens her door (the correct way this time) and exits without so much as a finger flutter.

Ardyn shifts into the open space but pauses with her tote back on her lap. "Thank you for the ride. And for being decent about my whole getting dressed thing."

I tip my chin in acknowledgment without looking back

at her. I can't peel my gaze from the art house, and I'm having trouble figuring out why. It's crowded, both inside and out, with women in long gowns and men in suits, most with a champagne flute in their hands. I spot an open bar in the back, and the few labels I catch showcase top-shelf liquor. A few clusters and cliques break off from the crowd and pause in front of large colorful paintings, musing over the art.

Clover's red dress parts a group in black as she heads to the door, waving as she spots Mila. Everything looks on board.

"You sure this is the place?" I ask Ardyn.

"Yeah. Why?"

I work my jaw. "Have you ever been to an auction before?"

"No, but my ... contact ... says this is one of the better ones."

Then I finally get it. "Where's the shit?"

"The what?"

"The artifacts you were wetting your panties over. I don't see them."

"Oh. The auction's happening in the basement."

I finally spare her a glance. "Does that seem like the usual to you?"

Ardyn shrugs. "I doubt they want to showcase such priceless pieces to the street."

"Yeah. I guess you're right." But I'm unconvinced. And suspicious.

My phone brightens the interior between us, and I

glance down. Rio's using shouty caps, probably shit-faced, asking where the fuck I am.

Good question.

When I don't fill the car with more chitchat, Ardyn fidgets in the bucket seat.

"Okay. Well. Bye."

"See you," I say, flicking two fingers in salute.

These girls have been attached to the hip since they were fifteen. My sister's not an idiot most of the time. Safety in numbers. They'll be fine.

I get a nice visual of Ardyn's ass as she slips out of my low-riding car. She stumbles on her heels as she stands, cursing under her breath as she shuts my door with a light *click*.

She's the most elegant, doe-eyed, fawn-legged creature I've ever seen, and I can't take my eyes off her as she rounds the front of my car, steps up to the curb, and joins the other two with a wobbly gait.

A gust of wind picks up the tendrils of her long, sand-brown hair and those floating strands imprint the remembrance of her clutching my chest and smelling like freshly turned earth.

Her sharp cheekbone is exposed, milk-white in contrast to the moss green of her eyes. I find myself tracing the elegant line of her neck and the angle of her collarbone, wanting to mar that flawlessness with bite marks.

As if she can sense my thoughts, Ardyn shivers.

I smile in the darkened interior, showing teeth.

In a surprisingly thoughtful move, Mila shakes off her

jacket and helps Ardyn into it, her lips moving a mile a minute as she talks Ardyn's ear off.

Mila's interruption is enough to shake me out of my trance and gun the engine, drawing their gazes once more.

I lift my fingers from the wheel in a *see ya* gesture before spinning it to move back into traffic.

The girls head into the art show, linking arms and settling the strange wriggling in my gut.

A flash of movement on the road catches my eye. I slam on the brakes.

The limo that almost took one of my headlights stops parallel, blocking my exit.

Snarling, I push open my door.

This fucking car nearly clipped mine, and I swear to fucking God—

A guy in a cheap suit gets out of the driver's side, opening his passenger's door as if I weren't parked at an angle in an attempt to leave.

"Yo, what's your problem?" I clip out as I lift out of my car. "You colorblind? Blinker-averse? Able to pay for the million fucking dollars in damages I'll bury you in if you hurt this beauty?"

The chauffeur ignores me, retreating when a lithe, older gentleman peels out of the passenger side, straightening his Armani lapels and catching me with hooded black eyes.

"Tempest Callahan," he says in a low, throaty voice. "I wouldn't think this would be your type of function. Now, your father I'd expect. Or your mother. How are they, by the way?" A glimmer of a smile hits his lips. "And your beautiful sister. How is she?"

Fuck.

Fuck me.

I don't answer him.

I pivot, pushing through the crowd in search of the girls so I can get them the hell out of here.

3

ARDYN

A guy that lean should not be coated in that much muscle.

I can't shake the thought of how Tempest felt under my hands for the entire walk from his car, to the curb, to the sidewalk, to my friends...

He was poured, hardened concrete as I gripped him. Unyielding beneath my soft skin, pushing against my bones. It was so distracting that I couldn't remember why I swung to him in the first place, not until Mila's scream reminded me that he nearly killed us in a high-speed collision.

Was it an adrenaline rush for him as much as it was for me? The slightest undulation of muscle played under my palms like he was reacting...

"Jesus, baby dove, you're shaking." Mila's voice sounds out right beside my ear. She shoulders off her leather jacket and tosses it around my shoulders before I can protest—not that I would. She's right, just not for the reasons she thinks she is.

I can't still be attracted to Tempest Callahan. He's a stupid unrequited crush from childhood. A jerk. A charlatan. Certainly not someone appropriate to care about when I've never been with a man before.

He's the type who would break me before he'd bury me.

"Earth to Ardyn. Is the nightlife too much stimulation for you?" Mila waves her hand in front of my face.

My nose twitches with irritation before I school it into a serene smoothness. Mila risked a lot to get me out of my home, and she continues to do so by staying at my side despite the very real risk of no less than five Town Cars screeching to a halt in front of the art showcase, my father leading the battalion.

Instead of snipping at her that I'm fine for the millionth time, I say thank you for the jacket and turn to Clover, her thick black hair, so like her brother's, loose and falling to her elbows. But that is where their similarity ends. Where Tempest's eyes are a wintry green and his skin glacier pale, Clover's kind copper eyes and warm, freckled arms open wide as she approaches us. "You made it! I was so worried I'd be alone in this place."

Her chin lowers along with her voice as she completes our triangle. "You should see some of the people who are here. I swear I just saw Zeke Aiden pass by."

I lift my brows in awe. I'm no stranger to binge-streaming on my laptop, and after a brief hiatus, Zeke Aiden's resumed his character in my favorite show.

An engine revs obnoxiously behind us. We all turn, none of us surprised to see Tempest give us the barest of acknowledgments before attempting to swing into bumper-to-bumper traffic.

"Leave it to my brother to save the night," Clover says as she loops her arms through ours and steers us to the entrance. "I wasn't sure if he'd do it. He's so disagreeable when it comes to offering assistance to other people."

"That's putting it mildly," I say.

"Tempest was the perfect gentleman," Mila adds, talking over me. "Ardyn had to strip down to her granny panties in his car, and he didn't even peek at the peep show."

Clover wrinkles her nose. "Ew, Mila. Please don't talk about my brother and my bestie's boobs in the same sentence."

My lips pull to the side in embarrassment. With all of us facing forward, Clover doesn't see. Add *he's my best friend's older brother* to the list of why not to be attracted to Tempest.

"It's not like she has that much to show," Mila jokes. "I bet Tempest is used to eating more than pancakes for breakfast."

Before my mouth can fall open, Clover cuts in with, "Again, *ew*, Mila. I'd rather not know what he eats. Ever. Even after I'm dead."

I talk past the swell of hurt in my throat. "Can we stop talking about me and move on to the amazing artifacts we're about to witness?"

Mila rolls her eyes, saying, "I really wish you'd stop watching history shows," but gamely speeds us up and through the doors, opened for us by two staff members wearing all black.

"Good evening, ladies." They don't ask for our invitations. We were probably assured entry solely through the use of Clover's last name. When busting out of home supervision, it helps to be friends with Manhattan's second most powerful family when you're prevented from using your own.

Clover slows near the coat check, operated by a glamorous woman with a neck as long as a giraffe and wearing a deep V-cut black dress.

"Do you want to check your coat?" Clover asks me.

I shake my head, pulling Mila's jacket tighter around me despite my cheeks heating dangerously. *The better to hide my still-hard nipples from pressing up against your brother.*

"I can give her this, though." I hold up my canvas tote, making Mila cringe.

"Whoa, what happened there?" Clover takes stock of the various dirt stains and the tail of my pajama shirt hanging out the top.

"I had a *Mission Impossible* moment."

Clover doesn't ask for further explanation, one of the many reasons I love her so much. She takes the bag from me and plops it on the counter in front of the woman, who sniffs in distaste. I pretend not to see it and turn my back on her, taking in the space.

A lot of white space with splashes of colorful, impressionist canvas pieces. Marvelous, but not the reason we came. "Where are the stairs?" I ask Clover after she finishes at the coat check.

"This way."

Clover takes her hand in mine, and Mila squeezes my other one. Whether on instinct or as a form of protection, they always put me in the middle, and I'm instantly at ease. Between these two, I'm comforted, alive, and safe, feelings I can never truly find when I'm alone in my bedroom with Barry stationed at my door.

Whatever happens and if I get caught, I think, *I'll remember this moment when I'm happy and free with my friends.*

"Hey," Mila says, drawing my attention. "I'm sorry for how I acted in the car. Tempest ... gets to me, you know? I'm not used to being denied such a prime cut of meat if you know what I'm saying."

Laughing, I release her hand and loop my arm around her shoulders. "I understand."

Mila wiggles close. "I love you, girl."

Me, too.

This is just like Mila, to be frustrated with her one moment and in love with her the next.

Clover leads us behind a fake wall, jutting out from a real one and housing some abstract pieces with violent slashes of red and black paint. A man dressed in all black hovers near an all-white door, a stark yin and yang.

All three of us offer innocent, doleful smiles while Clover reaches for the handle.

He scans all three of us with a shrewd look before giving an infinitesimal nod that allows Clover to push open the door.

The hallway leading down is black. A plastic string of LED red lights outlines the stairs at our feet. No wilting flower, Mila takes the stairs first.

"C'mon!" she says over her shoulder before disappearing from view.

My hand involuntarily clenches around Clover's.

"This is normal," she assures me. "Auctions like this, they don't like the average Joe to know about it, so they make it super intimidating."

I nod, though my internal alarms are screeching.

Clover gives me a light tug, and I follow her into the basement.

4

ARDYN

The difference between upstairs and down is like night and day.

Where the art display was pure white—painfully so—down here is endless black. Nothing adorns the walls save for a darkness so deep, the shadows refuse to compete. A select number of pot lights line the ceiling, dimmed to their lowest setting, spotlighting the rows of wooden chairs in the center, all facing a nondescript podium draped in black velvet.

"This is wild," Mila whispers beside me. The atmosphere has lowered even her to muted tones.

Shoes clomp down behind us, and fifteen or so patrons mill around the chairs, conversing in hushed voices.

The air is thick. Like I've stepped into a void sucking up precious oxygen.

"Hey. You okay?" Clover's face smudges into view.

"Yes. I, um ..." Rapid breaths follow my words. "I didn't know it'd be like this."

It's like a bag's been shoved over my head. No, a cloth pillowcase. A black one. Thick cotton. The stale scent of mothballs.

I can't breathe.

"Ardyn?" A hand tightens around my arm, jostling me. "You good? People are staring."

My knees turn weak. The suffocating blackness creeps into my vision, unsatisfied with just eating the walls.

"I-I have to ..."

"I told you this was a bad idea." I hear Clover murmur over my head to Mila.

"Omigod. I think she's gonna be sick."

"No, it's—I'm fine." I try to straighten, realizing I've doubled over.

"Bathroom's that way—" Clover begins, pointing behind the podium, but I don't wait for her to finish or help me in that direction.

I bolt.

In a rush of gluttony, the shadows swallow me whole.

I run down a darkened hallway, using the feel of the walls to give me a sense of direction. The sounds of the basement auction room quickly fade away, leaving only my panicked breaths for company.

I thought I could do this. I thought I was over this.

I won't let the whimpers escape.

Swallowing, I slow my steps and control my breath the way my trauma therapist taught me. *In one, two, three, four, and out, one, two, three, four...*

My heart keeps drilling into my ears, but my chest feels less tight, the walls less close to me.

I don't know how much of the corridor I've traveled or if I took a few corners along the way. As my mind clears, the panicked claws retreat, leaving gaping holes of time and distance.

This sometimes happens when the panic attacks take possession. I lose substance, though I'm physically the same. I haven't succumbed in years.

Voices draw my head up—close but not coming closer. A low, baritone drawl utters clipped syllables. Another one —also male—responds with a higher, faster pitch.

Straightening from the wall, I creep closer, unable to resist a distraction occurring outside my head.

Dim light arcs across the floor ahead, coming out of a door not fully shut. On silent feet, I creep closer, the muted, urgent words between the men taking shape.

"Why are you doing this? I've been nothing but loyal to you."

"It's the only way to fast-track my position and get out of the fucking purgatory he's kept me in!"

"We moved up the ranks together, caro amico. How could you betray me like this?"

"Because nothing is more important than the family."

"You speak of family when you hold a gun to my head?

What do you know of family, brother, when you're willing to kill your own?"

I gasp, then slap a hand to my mouth to stifle it. Yet my feet remain rooted. My fingers tremble.

"It wasn't supposed to come to this," the man with the supposed gun says. *"I did everything he asked. Killed who he wanted. Trained who he commanded. Yet still, he keeps me a Vulture."*

"Why now? So you could properly frame me for stealing the Roman sword? I'm sorry to disappoint you. Maybe it's the simple explanation that you weren't cunning enough to properly disguise your plans from me. I knew it would come to this, so I came prepared. You're caught, Miguel. The ruse is over. My men are outside."

I dare bend to the side and peer through the space between the door and its frame. My stomach curdles, my heart lurches, and my brain bombards me with decade-old images—facing the barrel of a gun, screaming at the *click* of the trigger. *"Do as I say, or next time this will be loaded..."*

The threatened man switches tactics. *"Please, brother. Don't end it this way."*

"Turn around."

Through the crack, I spot a suited man on his knees, his hands raised in surrender, a handgun pressed to his forehead.

The thick-veined hand clutching the gun jerks, causing the man on his knees to flinch, his dark lashes fluttering.

I inch farther to the right, where the hand becomes an

arm clothed in dark navy. Then a broad shoulder, thick, tanned neck, and a copper swirl of thick, medium-cut hair.

Then I reach his eyes.

Black craters nestled in a heartbreakingly handsome face. So pale, it's as if his blood refuses to travel any farther than his neck, lest it turns into blue ice in his cheeks.

His features are hardened, even, cold, and emotionless.

"All it'll take is one phone call, and my men—our men—will break down these doors and drag you to the Cosa Nostra. Miguel, you know what happens then."

"*I said* turn around."

The threatened man doesn't. The thick, black curls on the back of his head tremble. "If you choose to kill me, brother, then you'll have to look into my eyes as you do it—"

BANG.

I don't control my intake of breath in time—a squeak of noise as I cover my mouth with both hands.

The threatened man flops to the ground, a gaping, bloody wound on the back of his head. The man brandishing the gun, Miguel (oh God, I shouldn't remember his name) glances up, catching me with depthless, demon-held eyes before I jerk back from the door and run, run, *RUN*.

My chest walls lock together like prison bars, preventing any thoughts from escaping and releasing harmlessly into the air. Past and present are trapped in my mind. They mingle, flashbacks and flash-forwards, the gun killing the man and the gun used on me, the binds on my wrist and the threatened man's held above his head, both of us facing down black eyes, coal hearts, poisoned souls...

I have to make him pay somehow.

You're his most precious item, and you're mine now.

You're going to frame me for stealing the Roman sword?

We're family.

You're his family.

Please, brother.

Please, sir, just let me go home. Please, please, PLEASE, I'll do anything!

I sprint through the halls as blindly as I entered them, footsteps echoing in my ears. I can't be sure if they're real or in my head. All I know is what I saw—what I remember—and that I must escape this maze of nightmares before I'm caught and stare into the eye of a gun again.

My breaths are so hard as I run, so heated, that they must be turning into steam in the air, clouds of panic I must break through until I can find a door, an exit, an escape—

"Oof!" I slam into a hard torso on my next turn that doesn't bend against my sudden weight.

Hands clutch my arms, digging so thoroughly, the hard leather of my jacket does nothing to quell the shocking pain.

"Where the *fuck* have you been?" A voice rains down on my head.

Glancing up, I notice sharp cheekbones piercing through the hellish shadows, emerald sparking through the skeletal hollows of his eyes.

Tempest.

"I—" I gulp, then in turn clutch under his arms, my nails poking into his skin through the thin cotton of his shirt. "I saw—there was..."

I snap my head around, convinced this Miguel will be the next to materialize with his weapon aimed at the center of my back.

"Wait, hold on." Tempest's hold loosens. He releases me with one hand, using his finger to steer my chin back to him. He bends ever so slightly to meet my eye. "Who did you see?"

Somehow, my mind snags on his question. Later, I'll call it my survival instinct. "How ... how do you know I saw someone?"

Tempest's jaw tics, but he holds my stare. "A lot of shit goes down in these types of auctions. Did you know these are black market goods?"

"What?"

He lowers his eyelids. "Thought so. I've already directed my sister and Mila to get the fuck out of here. They told me they lost you, so I was tasked with locating you. Lucky me, here you are. Are you being followed?"

"I don't know. Yes. He saw me. I think he saw me."

"Who did?"

"A man named M—"

"Tempest? Are you insisting in addition to your non-invitation to also meddling backstage?" a disgruntled voice calls from a close distance away. "I'd much rather you fuck with my clientele and convince them to open their wallets with your infectious, if misdirected, charm."

Tempest angles his head toward the call. "Shit," he mutters, then comes back to me. "Get out of here. Now."

"Who is that?" I send a panicked glance over his shoulder. "Are there more of them? He said there were men stationed around the building—"

"There's an entire infestation of them, princess. Take the emergency exit before you're discovered. It's in the holding room where they've been carting in the works to be sold. I've called you girls a car to take you home. Meet them at the north entrance."

"But—"

Tempest gives me a not-so-gentle shove to the side. His hand disappears from my arm, and in its place is a tingling, aching feeling from being held by him too long and not long enough.

My heart kicks up in speed. When Tempest had me, the pounding in my ears had stopped. I could hear and see, and I wanted to tell him everything. To curl up into his unforgiving chest, convinced there was a safe spot for me in his arms.

How could that be?

Tempest turns to face the voice, his profile sharp edges and porcelain flawlessness. He risks glancing to the side, at me, his lips curling into a hiss. "*Go*, princess."

But is he safe? My eyes dart to the place where Miguel could appear at any moment, then to the opposite end where the other commanding voice came from. Tempest is blocked in on both sides. *What if this third man has a gun, too?*

Tempest's eye twitches as he waits for me to make a move.

"I can't leave you," I whisper as bravely as I can.

Tempest breaks off our stare to look skyward, his chest heaving on an aggravated sigh. Then he moves so fast, his contact with my chest barely registers before I'm flying into a room and sprawling onto the floor, the hem of my dress close to floating above my head.

The door slams shut behind me.

I scramble upright, my knees and palms burning from scraping against the concrete floor.

An uneven horizon looms above me, sharp tips and smudged faces. Weapons, golden treasures covered histories of bloodshed, paintings of long-dead artists whose works are more coveted than the human flesh that created them.

I'm convinced Tempest shoved me into a room of my nightmares.

Get ahold of yourself. Clutching the collar of my jacket, I inch forward through the shelves of artifacts meant to be auctioned off to the highest bidder. After purchase, these beautiful, violent works will likely never see the light of day, finding their homes in the basements of private wealth and lonely display cases.

A looming, fossilized head of a raptor, its cretaceous teeth appearing razor sharp enough to bite into my throat, is the last thing I see before I find the exit, pushing against the metal bar and stumbling out into the night.

5

ARDYN

The sidewalk shines like oil, slippery with recent rain, the air moist and thick from evaporated storm clouds. Streetlights cast their golden reflection into the puddles, shattering into a thousand tiny droplets when I sprint through them.

I'd flown out the side of the building, and it takes me a minute to get my bearings, even as I run away. I end up on the corner of Bowery and Third, bowing forward and clutching my knees to catch my breath.

Did the man named Miguel follow me? Is Tempest shot? Has he taken my place as a sacrifice?

I must staunch these thoughts if I'm to make it all the way home. *Like a coward.*

Father was right. I should stay in my gilded cage. It's where I'm safe, looked after, and shrouded from the worst of human society. There are no Tempests there to swell my heart and awaken my bones, daring me to risk danger.

"Ardyn!"

Clover's familiar voice comes through the dull ringing in my ears. I right myself as she approaches, concern shining through her dark lashes.

"Are you all right?" She grabs both my hands. "You ran off, and we couldn't find you. Tempest promised he'd get to you. Did you see him?"

I nod, squeezing back. "Yes. He's ... I saw something, Clover. Something I shouldn't have, and I'm afraid he's paying the price."

Chloe's eyes darken. "I wouldn't worry. He's no stranger to scary situations. He'll be fine."

My brows tighten. "You don't understand. The man has a gun. He-he *killed* someone."

Instead of freaking out—like I would, did, will for the next century—Clover's expression shutters even further. She drags me away from the corner and to the curb. "Then we have to get you out of here."

"Clover, did you hear what I just said? Your brother could be facing down a *murderer*."

"I heard you." Her throat bobs as she looks out to the road, searching through the row of parked cars and onto the busy street. "He's been through worse. What's important is to get you back home and pretend this night never happened."

"You're hilarious." I pull my hand out of hers. "We need to call the police."

"No cops."

I jerk my chin back. "Are you out of your *mind*? I can't

pretend I was never here! Someone died, Clover! I don't care if he was some kind of-of criminal or if we're exposing a black market auction, we have to do something—"

"*Shhh!*" Clover's eyes spark to life as her head whips toward mine. "Do you want to attract more of those kinds of men? Keep your voice down. I *knew* this was a terrible idea." She turns back to the row of cars, scanning them with more desperation.

"Hey, ladies!"

"Speak of the source herself," Clover mutters, crossing her arms as Mila approaches.

She stumbles on her heels with a silver flask clutched precariously in her hand. "Apparently, we have to leave early. Lame-o. But look! I scored us a roadie." She holds up the flask as if it were an auction piece. "This should salvage some of the evening."

I stare at her but say to Clover, "Mila has no idea, does she?"

"About as much of a clue as you," Clover answers. I jolt at the change in her tone, containing a clarity or an aware-ness I'd never heard before. *No, she sounds like her brother.*

The realization makes me retreat from her and a little closer to Mila. A part of me still believes there's safety to be found in ignorance.

Mila squints at me. "You're looking ghostier than usual. Here." She unscrews the cap, then shoves the flask in my face. "Drink up."

"I don't—"

"Do it." The cold metal rim smacks against my lips.

Bitter, burning liquid fills my mouth. On instinct, I swallow it, wincing as the fire travels down my throat. Within seconds, the savage burn turns into a pleasant thrumming in my veins. I grab the flask from Mila, who squeaks in surprise, then smiles as I gulp down more.

"Just what we need, depositing her back home drunk and terrified." Clover rolls her eyes while she pulls out her phone. "Where the fuck is the car Tempest promised? I might as well order our own."

"Terrified?" Mila cocks her head. "Why would anyone be scared? Did you see how many hot men were in there? Why are we leaving? Ardyn didn't even see what she came for. That sword thing, right?"

"Oh, I saw it," I mumble, remembering its bronzed decay in the darkened holding room.

"Huh?"

"Miss Callahan?" A man in yet another suit climbs onto the curb, signaling to us.

"Finally." Clover takes my hand and pulls me toward him, but I yank mine away.

"I'm not a child," I say. "I can walk on my own."

Mila claps me on the back. "Thatta girl. I knew you'd claim your independence one day. Gimme."

I hand her back the flask. She shakes it with a frown. "Damn girl, how much did you drink?"

"Enough to forget," I say, my voice dropping a few decibels as the images return. Thick hair. Scarlet blood. Pieces of skull. Emerald eyes. Oh, God. I think I might throw up.

"Not with my jacket on, you don't." Mila grabs my collar

and peels the jacket off my shoulders as I fold over and gag into the street gutter. "This is a classic Tom Ford."

I allow her to pull it the rest of the way off, coughing on the salted, acidic spit.

"She better not puke in the car," the man says. "It's just been reupholstered."

"If she does, I'll pay you triple." I hear Clover say. "Just get us out of here."

"You got it. She need help into the car?"

Clover answers with a clipped, "No," before she hoists me at the hips and assists me into the Town Car. Mila follows, slipping on her jacket and pocketing the empty flask.

I don't end up vomiting anything but my own terror, and I slip into the middle seat with shaking, sweaty limbs as the nausea subsides. I'm getting away. Everything will be fine. There's no way that man could know me. Father ensures I'm never in any photos, not even class pictures.

In any case, Barry will protect me. All I need to do is return to him.

Both Mila and Clover huddle close to me as the man slips into the driver's seat and smooths into traffic. Mila requests he play EDM hits from her phone and whines until he increases the volume to obnoxious levels.

Clover looks like she's close to jumping out of the car window to escape the noise, but I don't mind. It helps drown out the pounding in my head, and the gnawing worry that I left Tempest back there, doing God knows what.

The thumping bass drives into my spine, vibrating along my limbs and hardening my bones like a tuning fork. Mila bops along to the music, her arms flying as she mouths the words and urges us to join her.

"C'mon, guys!" she yells. "This is meant to be Ardyn's night! We can't end it with frowns!"

Her enthusiasm is infectious. She doesn't stop until she nudges a small smile out of me, and soon, I'm singing the words with her. I can always rely on Mila to put a positive spin on things. Plus, I want to feed off her pleasure in the small things. The big things can wait.

Clover remains stiff-backed beside us but endures the incessant climb of our dance moves. She shakes her head at us. "What did you guys drink?"

"I slipped a little Molly in!" Mila cries out, then shrugs and laughs.

I pause in my gyrations. "What? I'm drugged?"

"Mila!" Clover balks. "Are you crazy?"

"Yep." Mila smiles. "Girl needs to live a little. She's been wound up tight since she escaped her tower."

Clover responds, "Mila, sometimes I wish you weren't so fucking clueless—"

"Actually, this makes it easier to put the monsters away," I add as the car's interior turns into bright neon.

Clover's mouth twists into a worried frown as she studies me.

"There's a door in the back of my head," I explain, though she hasn't asked a question. "It's where I lock the monsters in. And they can't get out. Not if I don't let them.

And tonight … tonight… wait, did I see something bad tonight?"

"The fuck?" I think I hear our driver say.

"Spare us the lecture, old man," Mila says. "We didn't do drugs in your car."

But he's not glaring at us. He's staring through his rearview mirror at something behind us.

Mila's arms are entangled with mine, my hair catching on her wrist bangles, but I turn my head to see out the back window. Flinching, I scrunch my eyes shut at the glare of headlights.

Clover turns, too. She frowns.

The driver does a hard left, smacking me into Clover and sending Mila into a fit of giggles.

I laugh with her, the world going fuzzy at the edges like I'm living in a ball of cotton candy. Oh, this is *so* much better than what I witnessed back there.

What did I witness, anyway?

All I can remember are bright, vicious green eyes, the color of a royal jewel, the kind you'd have embedded into the hilt of a lethal, ancient sword...

Where were we? An art thing? A show? A broadway play? It must've been an *avant garde* production because most plays don't involve such a realistic display of violence...

"Shit!" The driver makes another hard turn, slamming me into Mila this time.

We both howl with laughter.

A small part of me, that survival instinct, registers the

pure terror on Clover's expression. Her hand smacks against her window while her other clutches my bare thigh, keeping her upright.

"*Drive faster!*" she screeches. "Don't let him—"

I lurch forward so violently that the seat belt cuts into my skin, instantly fracturing my pelvis and crushing my internal organs.

Glass shatters. Deafening screams burst my eardrums, coming from Clover, Mila, the driver, *me...*

Metal crunches, squeals, and twists into impossible shapes with us trapped inside.

My last thought is that *the shadows have caught up to me* before I'm consumed by utter blackness.

6

ARDYN

Tick. Tick. Tick. Tick.

It's a comforting percussion in the background as I lay back on a stack of pillows in my bay window and open my favorite author's newest release, fanning the pages with my fingers and releasing the pleasurable smell of freshly printed paper.

My nostrils twitch, then itch at the smell permeating my room.

This isn't the smell I'm used to. I frown at the gasoline's sweet and sour scent but continue to bask in the early morning sunlight, turning my cream pages yellow and tinging my skin in a warm golden hue. I draw my knees up...

They don't move. I try again.

I draw my knees up.

I DRAW MY KNEES UP.

Why can't I move my legs?

My head suddenly feels swollen, pressure building at my forehead and clogging my ears. It becomes hard to breathe.

My eyelids feel dragged down by anchors. It takes an inordinate effort to crack them open, and when I do...

I wish I hadn't.

The world is upside down.

My fingers twitch as if reminding me they're dangling over my head. The movement sends a shockwave to my brain, and I slam my palms to the roof of the car, pushing myself off the ceiling, and-and I don't know.

I unclip my seat belt in a bid of misdirected logic, sending myself crashing through gravity and landing in an upside-down heap. Warm skin and strange fabric gets in my way—not mine. I'm blocked in by two people. Two friends. *Two bodies.*

"Mila? Clo?" I croak, lifting my head and pushing tangled hair out of my face.

A groan sounds out to my right. Clover's eyes flutter as she hangs by her seat belt, her arms dangling limply.

I scan her, searching for any mortal wounds with my amateur eye. I can't see anything except a small trickle of blood at her temple, collecting in her ear. There's also a nasty gash along her arm, but it's since clotted. Relief coats my voice when I say, "Hang on. I'm gonna check on Mila."

I twist as much as I can in the cramped space until my cheek hits something hard. A shoe. The bottom of a heel.

Mila's feet are in front of my face, and at first, it makes

sense because we've been in an accident. Our car rolled, so we're all in positions we shouldn't be.

Until…

I note that her upper body has been dragged out of the broken window. She was wearing her seat belt, wasn't she?

Yes. Yes, she was. We all were, which is probably why we're still alive.

Mila's alive, right?

Panic sets my nerves on fire. Where I didn't feel pain, I now experience fire, but I pull myself to the side of her legs to get a better look at her.

Maybe she regained consciousness before me. Perhaps she tried to escape to find help, then stopped halfway because … because…

"Mila?" I whisper, my voice coming out hitched and unsure.

I shake one of her legs. Her entire body moves with it.

"Mila?" I try again, scooting up beside her.

She's lying facedown, her hair splayed around her head in a tangled spiderweb design, her luxurious blond dampened to a murky brown.

"When you wake up," I say, clearing my throat, "you're going to be so pissed at how your hair looks."

Mila doesn't respond. Or move.

"Mila?"

Blinking, I search the area around us, keeping one hand on Mila's strangely cold leg. It's then I spot our driver out on the road, his neck twisted at an odd angle. He faces me with enlarged eyes almost popped out of their sockets. His tongue hangs out of parted, sagging lips, swollen and purple.

I swallow back a scream.

"Ardyn?" Clover asks behind me.

I slide backward. "I'm here. Are you okay? Can you get down?"

"Am I ... am I the wrong way, or are you the wrong way?"

"You are. Here." Without warning, I unclip her seat belt, and she crumples to the ground.

"Ow. Oh, my God, *ow*."

"Sorry." It's becoming hard to talk over my pounding heart. As time passes, my vision clears, and I don't like what I see. "We're in a lot of trouble."

Clover blinks and looks around. "Shit. Where's Mila?"

"She's sleeping."

Clover slides her gaze back to mine, holding steady. "She's what?"

"Right here. Sleeping." I gesture behind me to Mila's shoes, both tilted at unnatural angles. "The accident must've been too much for her, so she's taking a nap."

Clover peers around me. Her face pales, and her throat bobs before coming back to me. "Ardyn..."

"It's okay," I assure her. "Sleep is a wonderful escape. It makes you forget all the bad things."

"Ardyn," Clover whispers with more urgency. "Ardyn, *wake up*."

"What do you mean? I'm awake. I'm here."

"No, you're not." Clover's eyes fill with tears. "I don't

know how you survived your kidnapping, I don't know what you witnessed at the auction, and I don't know what was in that flask you and Mila chugged, but you know what I do know? I know Mila's dead."

I shake my head in response, sharp and painful. "Stop lying."

"She's dead, Ardyn, and so's our driver."

"No. *No one's dead.*"

"We need to call for help."

"She's not dead, Clover! She's right here!"

"Ardyn. Ardyn, look at me—"

"No. *No!*" I scramble until I'm splayed on top of Mila's legs, shaking the life back into her.

"Ardyn, she's lost too much blood. It's too late—"

"*Nooooooo!*"

7
TEMPEST

TWO YEARS LATER

Fucking freshmen week.

The fourth time around, it's not any easier to deal with.

Hordes of them congest the road in front of the quad, crying, hugging, or dismissing their parents altogether while younger siblings paint the car windows with drool, wishing they were old enough to leave home and take up residence in three-hundred-year-old buildings with creaking stairs, slanted floorboards, and enough history in the walls to choke the living while they sleep.

I've always been drawn to the haunted and macabre.

As one of the smallest, most prestigious colleges in

North America, acceptance is rare and hard-won for those lucky enough to attend.

If it weren't for having to welcome my little sister, I wouldn't have left the solitude of Anderton Cottage, the smallest dormitory at Titan Falls University. It's nestled comfortably in the woods, shrouded by evergreens and fir trees so thick, it's impossible to tell day from night, unlike where Clover's chosen.

Clover is moving into Camden House, a thankfully all-girls dorm that gets about one-third of the females enrolled at TFU. It sits at the top curve of the main quad, basked in sunlight from its large windows and blindingly yellow walls. I left her door open as we carted in her boxes and suitcases, sunshine following us in the form of fourth-floor chatter, excitement, and a general annoyance to my ears.

"That all of it?"

"Gee, Tempest, contain your excitement." Clover flops onto her twin bed, the springs creaking under the slightest weight. I eye the scratched cherrywood headboard and matching dresser with distaste. At Anderton, we're allowed to move in our own furniture. Here, they're forced to use the same items as in the Brontë sisters' day.

"Aren't you glad I'm here?" she asks, folding her arms under her head. The long, puckered scar on her right forearm flashes out from her T-shirt with the movement. My eyes dart to it, then away.

If Clover notices, she says nothing and instead lets her head loll until her attention falls on the bare mattress across from her.

I say, "Yes, I'm glad, but don't be upset I didn't bring you a cupcake in celebration. Where's your new roomie?"

Clover, being Clover, is about four hours late in setting up her room. Orientation begins in twenty minutes, where I'll bid her adieu and slip *far* away from the freshies' nervous trek around campus. If one timid female wanders away from the group, so be it. I'll be waiting in the woods to greet her.

Clover shrugs. "Ardyn'll be here soon, I'm sure."

My chin snaps to attention. "Ardyn Kaine?"

"Are you acquainted with any other girls named Ardyn?" Clover arches a brow.

I frown. "I thought she was locked in her fortress for the rest of her miserable life after..." I greatly dislike trailing off, but when it comes to my sister and her accident, I can't help but linger inside the spaces between words. The mere thought of what she endured fizzes my nerves. Clover is the one blood relation I care about and the only woman I'd ever take a bullet for. Too bad I was so busy cleaning up Ardyn's mess that I couldn't protect her.

That thought curdles my veins.

After the car wreck, Ardyn was sequestered by her family so quickly, I had no time to blame her or rage at her like I wanted to. Such an innocent, *stupid* lamb, scuttling around where she shouldn't, involving herself in misdeeds likely to kill her.

"She's changed, Tempest."

I reluctantly return my attention to Clover. "Last I heard, she had a breakdown she couldn't recover from."

Clover rolls her eyes. "That's the story her family fed to the press so they'd lay off."

"What's changed, then? I'm shocked she's allowed two feet outside her door, never mind rooming with you at a university in a different state."

"She's eighteen now. Ardyn can make her own choices." Clover sits up, rifling through her pet carrier-sized purse. "She's going against their wishes, which is super rebellious of her. I'd think you'd respect her for it."

"Two people were killed that night," I say calmly, though inside, I'm on fire.

"Three people," Clover corrects.

"If you're to believe Ardyn's story, sure, someone at the auction also died, but after her nervous breakdown, everything she says is hard to believe," I lie. "And no third body was found."

Clover blows out a breath in relief when she finds what she's looking for, pulling out a deck of tarot cards.

I sigh. "Not this again."

Clover flicks her eyes to mine, identical in color and temperament. "*This* could've saved Mila's life had I known about it before."

"Magic doesn't exist, Clo, any more than the man at the auction who was supposedly executed."

Clover's stare doesn't waver. "You cling to your beliefs, brother, just as I will cling to mine." She shuffles the deck, then lays out three cards facedown on her bed. Sadly, I know enough to understand that each indicates past, present, and future. "Now, *am I making the right decision to have Ardyn room with me?*"

I massage the answering growl wanting to rip out of my throat and scowl at my sister instead.

Two things could've happened after the accident—Clover could have exiled all mage-like reminders from her life, finding them too hard to stomach after failing to save Mila (and technically, she lost two friends that night. Ardyn was also swept away by her father and bodyguard, and as far as I knew, the two never spoke again), or Clover would immerse herself so deeply in the supernatural, like readings, ghost hunts, and seancès, that she'd separate herself from reality and become convinced she could protect herself and everyone else she cares about with the guidance of the psyche. Unfortunately, she's chosen the latter.

I chew on the inside of my cheek as she mutters over her cards. "You were bullied at your high school for being a witch. Why are you asking to start this all over again?"

Chloe's lips pull in, likely to lob an insult or a demand for me to GTFO, but we're interrupted by a light tap on the doorframe.

I lift my head, refusing to turn to the door. "Don't bother unpacking your shit. You're not moving in with my sister."

"Tempest!" Clover scrambles off the bed. "You have no right to say that to her."

I look at Clover and shrug. "I sure as fuck do. *She's* the one who changed the course of history by doing dumb shit at the auction house and forcing the three of you to leave early in a car not driven by me, not your card spirits. If it weren't for her—" Now, I spin on my heel, readying to add the weight of my unsettling, piercing stare to the hate in my words, but once I do…

It's like being punched in the gut.

Meadow-green eyes stare back at me, with the lightest touch of the sun shining through gold-flecked shards. Her gilded brunette hair cascades in soft waves down her shoulders, parted in the middle and framing her heart-shaped face, as snow white and flawless as I remember. She's grown curves in the past two years, and breasts, her body molded under a sculptor's hands so exquisitely, the T-shirt and jeans she wears do an injustice to her beauty.

Ardyn's thick, auburn-tinged lashes plummet, allowing me to regain my point until she opens them, and I'm again enraptured.

My jaw clenches.

"Mila would still be alive, and you wouldn't be so scarred," I finish saying to Clover, but I'm unable to rip my stare from Ardyn's.

Ardyn moves inside, pulling a simple roller case behind her. "Nice to see you too, Tempest."

Her voice is huskier than I remember, heavier with experience outside the four walls of her bedroom.

As she passes me, I get a whiff of gardenias and soap, slamming me back into the memory of our last car ride, minutes before she ruined both our lives.

It's enough to wake me the fuck up. "What did I just say, princess?"

If my voice turns her veins to ice, she's a *very* good actress because all she does is cant her head toward me, nailing me with that guileless green again. "You asked me very nicely to leave, and I'm responding very nicely that I'm not going anywhere unless Clover wants me to."

Clover pivots to her bed, then grabs a tarot card and waves it in front of my face. "See? The Judgment card, Tempest. It means self-reflection. Evaluating ourselves and our actions. This is how the future answered my question, and it very aptly includes Ardyn."

"I don't give a fuck what your playing card says, Clo. I want you *out*." I stab a finger in the air toward the door. "If you don't get your own ass out of here, Ardyn, I'll pick you up and toss you out myself."

Ardyn steps up to me. She has the gall to *step up to me*.

She looks me in the eye, parts her full mouth, and whispers with sweetened breath, "I dare you to touch me."

Her deadened gaze has Clover backing up a step while my brain whirrs with this new information.

My first instinct is to cup her breasts and squeeze, lick, and bite them until she moans for me to touch her again, down low, and taste her innocence. My fingers twitch at the idea, and my nostrils flare like I can already smell her sex.

The air is thick with it.

She inches closer, tipping her chin up to maintain her glare, her chest almost bumping into mine. The carnal urge to grab her ass cheeks, spread them, and pound my ownership into her is so overwhelming that my body shudders with the effort to keep myself in check.

"You'll find I'm a lot less easy to tame," she continues in a soft voice, "than the last time we met."

Her beauty may fell me, but her words don't. "Shouldn't we report you to the university's psych department?"

The Ardyn I knew would've shriveled under the insult, her eyes welling with tears.

This one—she doesn't blink. "That depends. Has anyone reported you for mutilating forest animals and burying them in the woods outside your window?"

One corner of my mouth twitches with a reluctant smile. "Been keeping up with my comings and goings, have you?"

"I know a lot more about you than you think, Tempest."

My grin sours. Searching her eyes, I can tell she's dead serious. The thought of Ardyn 2.0 knowing my deepest secrets is unsettling at best. She has to be bluffing.

"Jesus, you two." Clover comes between us, dissipating the heat in the air and turning to me. "Ardyn stays. Not only do the cards deem it so but I also do."

I don't respond, all too aware of Ardyn's stare digging into my cheek.

Clover throws her hands on her hips. "You can leave now."

After a beat, I flick my gaze to Ardyn. "This isn't over."

Her lips quirk. "This hasn't even started."

The fuck does that mean? "You want to stay at TFU? Fine. But your daddy's money can't protect you from my determination to protect my sister. You're bad luck, princess, and I'm going to be on your ass for your entire stay."

When Ardyn *still* doesn't flinch, I grab Clover's arm, raising it high. She screeches and bucks in my hold until my grip grows so tight that she stills.

"See this?" I say to Ardyn.

She doesn't remove her gaze from mine.

"Look at it," I say. "*Look at it.*"

Ardyn's jaw works, her teeth grinding together. She blinks. A muscle in her cheek spasms.

Right when I'm about to dig my fingers into the soft pillows of her cheeks and force her to look, her eyes slide to Clover.

"This scar is from you. Clover's mutilation is because of *you*. You're ignorant, and a coward all rolled into one. And Mila's death is—"

"Don't you dare say it."

I chuckle. Ardyn's venom will coat Clover before it ever reaches me. "Mila's death is on you, too."

Ardyn's lips peel back from her teeth.

Another laugh escapes. "God, it feels good to say that after being unable to scream it into your face for over two years."

She lunges.

My jaw drops open in shock. Clover yanks her wrist out of my slackened hold, shouting something indecipherable as Ardyn unleashes an animalistic cry and goes for my throat.

Clover grabs Ardyn by the waist just in time. She yells over her shoulder, "Get *out*, Tempest! You're such an asshole!"

I raise my hands in mock surrender, walking backward to the door where a collection of freshmen stand, gawking. "Gee, your institution stay has worked wonders, Ardyn. It's too bad I despise you—you'd be a wildcat in bed."

Ardyn nearly topples Clover with her desire to get to me. A few freshmen scatter, the rest fleeing when I spin and saunter out the door. In no time, Ardyn's meltdown will spread through the freshmen and all the way to the upper-classmen's ears, shaping into rumors and morphing into an attack. It suits my plans perfectly, which is why I'm able to walk away with a jaunty swagger, whistling as I pass shocked faces and rapid-fire texts as news of TFU's latest psychotic import spreads.

I chalk the lump in my chest up to indigestion from Anderton Cottage's kitchen, where the cook is ancient, and our meat is mostly jerky. It has nothing to do with seeing Ardyn's classical face again and reigniting old feelings ... and memorialized oaths.

Not even two months ago, I was assured Ardyn couldn't remember any of the events from that night. The trauma, coupled with the Molly in her system, made any recall unreliable if she had even that much. My sources confirmed her version of events was spotty, at best, intermixing with the kidnapping she endured as a child so thoroughly that authorities couldn't tell one from the other.

I believed the explanation. I'd still stand behind it if it weren't for the way she looked at me just now.

Fuck, if she remembers what happened, who was executed, and who did it, *everything* I agreed to in order to keep Ardyn and my sister out of it is at risk. I was forced to make a deal with the devil after I sent Ardyn away that night, and I've been under his thumb ever since—committing his dirty deeds, collecting information for him to use, and handing him his victims on a silver platter.

If Ardyn remembers...

After all my efforts to keep her alive, it'd be a shame to have to kill her.

8

ARDYN

Clover approaches me cautiously with a steaming cup of tea in her hands.

We're in the deserted common room at Camden House. The rest of the freshmen on our floor are headed to orientation, beginning in the center quad. I'd never intended to go, but I was surprised that Clover hung back, too.

"You shouldn't have to stay back for me," I say as I settle into one of the worn velvet armchairs by a window.

"Please." Clover waves me off. "Why would the witch of Titan Falls leave the girl from the asylum all by herself?"

I manage a small smile. "We've always made a great pair."

"We have." Clover settles in the armchair adjacent to mine. "I've missed you, Ardy."

"I know." I take in a deep breath. "I've missed you, too."

"So…" Clover wriggles in her seat, keeping her hands

carefully placed around her mug. "Do you want to talk about what happened, or…?"

I blow over the rim, buying time. I always knew it would be hard to see Tempest again, and Clover for that matter. What I didn't predict was how easy it would be for him to get under my skin. I'd spent months in a private clinic with psychologists possessing expensive, pristine degrees who would explain to me on a loop, *"What happened wasn't your fault,"* and *"We need to balance the serotonin in your brain,"* or *"If you stick to our prescribed regimen, you'll feel better."*

I'd armored myself with pills, meditation, and group therapy. It gave me the capability to call Clover after almost two years of silence and admit to her what I'd been gearing up for since the first day of signing into the clinic. *"I'm going to college, and we'll see each other again."*

TFU was our top choice. The three of us. I felt like it was a disservice to Mila's memory to completely abandon the plan, and I was happy to see that Clover thought the same.

What I didn't explain to Clover over the phone, though, was that I was tired of the therapy, and I wanted to know if my world would truly end if I just stopped listening to those cushy medical degrees and forged ahead on my own path.

So here I am, in college against both my parents' and my doctors' wishes.

If they'd been here to witness what Tempest had unearthed so seamlessly, I'd be carted off again in no time.

Clover stares at me over her mug, waiting patiently for an answer.

I clear my throat. "It's taken a long time to get to this point."

"I understand. I was there when you … well, at the accident."

Nodding and swallowing hard, I push the images of a facedown, broken Mila from my mind. "I wasn't prepared for your brother's hatred."

"Mm." Clover wrinkles her nose, settling back into her seat. "To be honest, I wasn't prepared, either. I had no clue he felt that way about you. He's always been a helicopter older brother, though. What he said is more about him than it is about you. I hope you know that."

The cruel curve to Tempest's lips as he spat poison flashes into my mind. I hurl it away as quickly as I did my last memory of Mila, but not for the same reasons. Tempest brings about a heat, an endless burn in my belly that flames into my chest and scorches my heart. After all this time, even with his most recent words, he still unleashes an inferno in my soul.

It burns. It decimates. It should turn me to ash, yet here I am, discussing him over tea with his sister, a girl he would light *me* on fire for to protect.

My lips uptick at the thought. One of the many reasons I shouldn't be attracted to Tempest—he shares way too many traits with my father. Overprotectiveness, casual aggression, and a quick-tempered flare whenever he feels he's been wronged.

"You look good," Clover says, redirecting my thoughts.

I smile. "For an asylum girl?"

She laughs softly. "Hey, don't I look good for a witch?"

"You do," I agree. "What have your readings said about me lately?"

We both know it's true. While I was gone, I envisioned many moments of Clover hunched over her tarot cards, making sure I was okay. It's why I love her. It's why I'm back. *Not just for her brother,* I assure myself. *And also for the truth.*

"Nothing but good omens," she lies. I let her. I also allow her to change the subject. "I'm hoping I'll get some time to truly explore the grounds. So far, Tempest refuses to allow me entry into Anderton Cottage."

"Why?" Though I know the answer.

Clover leans forward, whispering conspiratorially. "That's where it all started. You remember the true story of TFU's foundations, right?"

"How could I forget? It's all you'd talk about. Mila threatened to—" I swallow my words.

Clover blinks but doesn't miss a beat. "Can you imagine if I actually find the ritual room? I'm convinced Sarah Anderton's grimoire is hidden in there."

"It's also believed there are cat skeletons in the walls," I say, "And the skulls of the children she helped execute."

"I don't remember telling you that."

I pull my lips in, then pop them out. "I've done a lot of reading lately. You don't have to protect me anymore, Clo. I'm okay hearing this stuff."

Clover squints at me like she's not entirely convinced.

I sigh, disappointed in myself. My confrontation with Tempest has only convinced Clover to treat me like a fragile eggshell again. "Sarah Anderton, born 1690. She built her covenstead on the highest point in Titan Falls, where she would cater potions, poisons, and abortions to the American elite. She also had a daughter, greatly deformed, probably because she imbibed in her own potions from time to time. Her name was never written down and remains unknown. That daughter became her apprentice. They operated under the radar until three prominent women were arrested for poisoning their husbands, and it was traced back to her. Sarah and her daughter had their tongues and fingers cut off before their hanging because of all the elite clientele they'd accumulated. If they spoke or wrote a word, those elites would have to be executed, too."

Clover regards me with owlish eyes. "Dude. You said that so smoothly I kinda want to start a coven with you."

I shake my head, laughing under my breath. "I've had a lot of time to read and do my research."

"And you still came here, despite TFU's gory history. Even after experiencing so much violence yourself."

I could always rely on Clover not to beat around the bush, and I was grateful for it. Too many people handle me with kid gloves. I'm convinced that's what made me so vulnerable and stupid that night. So open to execution myself. I vowed never to be like that again.

I suppose, in a way, I'm grateful for Tempest's handling of me, too.

"You came here, too," I say. "And Tempest has been a TFU student for four years."

She nods. "This place calls to us. Tempest doesn't talk much about his boarding school days, but he's lasted into post-grad, so the hauntings can't be that bad."

"Or he just yells at the ghosts to shut the fuck up or to make themselves useful and read him the final exams."

We both laugh.

I sober. "We've all come from violence in some way or another."

Clover follows suit. "I have a confession to make."

I perk up, all ears.

"Tempest thinks I've come here like a good little sister so he can keep a close watch on me while I study English lit and become nothing but a light fixture like our mother, but I'm tired of paying for the consequences of *his* mysterious trauma. Really, I want to major in occult studies. Walk in Sarah's footsteps and understand what made her so drawn to dark magic." She snorts. "What do you think my brother will have to say about that?"

"I won't tell. If you don't tell him that I'm here to discover my own truths, too."

A chill falls over the common room, filled with scarlet velvet, ornate golden frames, and paintings of the forested Titan Falls landscape and the Victorian era elite. Book-shelves line our backs with a large window between us, and we both look out at the afternoon sky. The sun shines its rays through the glass and over our skin, but Clover's arms carry goose bumps the same as mine.

"Are you still convinced you saw a murder that night?" she asks quietly.

The night Mila died comes to me as mismatched puzzle pieces my brain has trouble managing. Flashes of cruelty and the slick smell of blood. The *flash-bang* of a silencer and one too many broken skulls.

"No," I say to Clover, despite the image of a crumpled man appearing on the backs of my eyelids sometimes when I blink. "I've long since accepted that it was all in my head. He wasn't real."

Clover's answering grin is relieved and bright. She reaches a hand out, and I clasp it.

"We're going to have a great freshman year together," she says over our connected fingers. "Reunited at last."

I squeeze back a little too hard.

9
ARDYN

My violent ghosts slink back into their shadowy graves when classes begin.

Freshman orientation week goes by easier with Clover by my side. I'm both relieved and nostalgic at how seamlessly she fits next to me regardless of the time we spent apart. There remains a Mila-sized gap between us, but we fill it with quiet evenings in the common room and midnight tarot readings—between my nightmares where Mila hovers at the foot of my bed with a broken neck and the driver, Max Stelton, pleads to me with bulging eyes—when the rest of the dorm is sleeping or out partying. Neither of us drinks much. At least, not anymore. It also comes as no surprise that we haven't made any friends outside of each other.

The first Monday of classes is as sunny as the week proceeding it. It'd be hard to believe the university was founded under such darkness unless you're someone like me who understands that the brighter it is, the longer it takes for the deadliest creatures to take their naps underground ... gaining their strength.

The crowded TFU quad contains students hurrying along the sidewalks or reclining against the thick oaks in the center, stretching their legs on top of freshly mowed grass. Our modern wear of button-downs, jeans, and skirts clashes with the centuries-old stonework buildings, but nothing is as ancient as the tree-topped hills with skyscraper-sized evergreens bowing under the wind, their spiked branches whispering to their neighbors.

The STEM building across the quad is closest to the lake. Yes, lake. Flat, placid, and as black as onyx. There are no waterfalls in Titan Falls. Perhaps Sarah Anderton named it thus to pique the interest of America's nouveau riche—the business tycoons of the 19th century, searching for gold and progress as she lures their wives with her ancient apothecary.

I stroll through the thick mahogany doors with iron hinges bolted to the stone doorframe, taking my time admiring the exposed mixture of wood and brick halls and thick maroon carpeting. Students flow by like I'm nothing more than a rock in their babbling brook, uncaring of their surroundings or their privilege in moving from place to place without being watched.

They don't know what it's like to be swallowed by white, covered in it, ingesting it in the form of pills, staring at its walls, and sleeping under its bleached cotton.

After that kind of experience, the color black doesn't seem so bad and scary at all.

My arms swing out, testing the roominess and freedom to twirl if I wanted to. I wouldn't care if I knocked a few others out—I'm walking untethered. I could run, skip, do cartwheels, and no one would put me in a straightjacket.

As an irresistible grin crosses my face, I get a few strange looks and judgment-filled eyes. Word's spread about my "delicate state," in thanks, no doubt, to Tempest. I meet every open study with a flat-eyed gaze, daring them to say something. None do. They all slither away and go back to the safety of their newfound friends.

I wish Clover were with me, but her classes are mainly in the literature and classics building. Her mention of occult studies interested me, so I dropped calculus and joined hers last minute, but other than that, we have completely different schedules. I'm staying within my interest in art history, clinging to my dreams of becoming an art restoration or museum specialist. Father has long since given up on my capacity to rule his empire, and while it brought Mother to tears, she also understood that I was much too fragile to hold such a heavy title.

I'm not fragile. Just disinterested. Give me old artifacts over cutthroat business associates for company any day.

What amazes me is that even after my kidnapping, they thought they still had a chance to mold me into what they wanted. But add a dash of a deadly car accident, and I was a lost cause. My parents were furious that I snuck out, relieved I survived, and determined to put my shattered mind back together. Barry was fired, and my unreliable mental state got me committed. When I was released (against medical advice), I swore to my father I was ready to attend a small university, sequestered deep in the Appalachians where even his most notorious enemies wouldn't bother to get me. My parents allowed me to go so long as I never left campus. I'm sure they've hired security around somewhere, discreet enough so as not to "upset" me.

I do wonder about Barry. I hope he and his son are doing all right.

My business class is at the end of a long hallway, the door open and inviting. Classes at TFU are deliberately small, held around a long, rectangular formal dining table or a circle of cushioned chairs like we're just having a chat in a library. In this classroom, two walls are lined from ceiling to floor with shelving that holds row upon row of faded leather spines. I wouldn't be surprised if there were a ton of first editions in here. My fingers itch to check.

I control myself and go to one of the last available seats at the dark wood table, pulling out my chair. I'm between a girl with a messy ponytail and glasses and a guy with cropped hair and a crooked nose. As I sit, I wonder how they'd describe my physical appearance. Dishwater blond? Red-rimmed eyes? Vampire skin that starts cooking under the sun?

As the girl watches my descent into the chair with a curled lip, I'm tempted to murmur, *I don't burn, I sparkle, bitch,* but keep my mouth clamped shut. I've already made it clear I'm not making friends. I don't need my mother descending like a concerned vulture, pecking at anyone's innards for daring to ostracize me.

My back faces the door, so I don't see the last person to come in. They shut it with a resounding *click*, so I assume it's the professor.

The person strides behind me, the disturbance in the air playing with my loose strands. Cinnamon, cloves, and a sharp pine scent lingers in my nose, so intoxicating that at first, I don't wonder why it's so familiar.

A stack of books slams at the head of the table, gluing me to the back of my chair and snapping my chin up.

"This is your required reading, kids. Professor Rossi doesn't play. If the size of these textbooks makes you want to piss your pants, now's your chance to drop out of Titan Falls and run home with skid marks—"

Tempest cuts off abruptly when he meets my eyes.

My mouth goes dry.

A mere stare from Tempest Callahan sucks all the energy out of the room, tunneling it into one source: me. I can't look away, but I'll burn alive if I don't.

He blinks, and his hold breaks.

My chest collapses on an exhale.

"As I was saying," Tempest continues to the rest of the class, "Professor Rossi expects the first ten chapters to be read by next week. That information is essential for your upcoming project."

Tempest doesn't preface *project* with *group*, but I hear it nonetheless. I want to shrink in my seat at the thought. A mere week at TFU, and I'm as much an outcast as the one year I spent in high school. Tempest's efforts weren't even all that much—an offhand comment here, a nod of confirmation there—and I was turned into the university's asylum girl, a person whose brain fell apart when she let her best friend die and almost killed his sister, too.

"Um, excuse me?" A dark-haired girl across the table raises her hand. She bites her lip under Tempest's attention, her fingers trembling ever so slightly when he answers with a curt, "Yes?"

Gag me. The girl can barely get a question out without a *will you have sex with me?* undertone.

"Can I ask who you are?" She smiles, dimples flashing. "I'd like to put a name to a face."

As *if* she doesn't know who Tempest is—everyone on campus does. Girls, boys, nonbinary people. Every single person wants to get into his pants. I'm horrified to realize I can't blame them.

He's viciously beautiful, all dark edges and marble hues, as perfectly at home among priceless books and old-fashioned furniture as he was in the cold, modern building on Third and Bowery. Tempest is a chameleon, a salt-water changeling. He adapts to any environment, a feat I've wished I could master for my whole life.

"Sorry I'm late." A roughened baritone cuts in with a sweep of cold air as the classroom door opens and shuts a second time. "Ah. I see you've all met my TA for the semester. He's one of my top fourth-year students and is an excellent source of information if you're ever having an issue in my class. However, I don't recommend you use him until you are utterly, irrevocably desperate." A dark chuckle follows his words.

Coldness seeps into the back of my neck, ice trailing down my spine.

"For if you need Mr. Callahan's advice..." the professor continues. He rounds my chair and comes to a stop beside Tempest. "It means you've exhausted all chances of excelling in my one basic tenement of business—become an expert at the subject before any of your peers."

Tempest's gaze skates back to mine. I keep my face devoid of all emotion, as embedded in stone as his. My fingers are loose as I grab my pen and flip open my simple black notebook. My breaths are even as I start jotting down notes.

My cursive is illegible.

I tip my chin up under Tempest's scope, blinking innocently before turning my attention back to the instructor, famed for his Build Your Business Empire lectures and whose biography is easily accessible online.

"Welcome, new students. You're in for quite the experience."

Professor Miguel Rossi smiles.

IO

TEMPEST

She can't know.

She can't fucking know.

My blood *pops* under my skin, bursting bubbles of lava that singe through my nerves. Of all the buildings on campus, I didn't expect Ardyn Kaine to occupy mine.

Rossi scrapes his chalk across the blackboard, old-school among all the laptops facing his back—all except for Ardyn, that is. She dutifully jots notes with pen and paper, appearing unbothered and attentive.

She can't know.

I go through the appropriate motions as Rossi's teaching assistant, handing out papers and glares on cue, until the hour and forty minutes are finished and Rossi dismisses the class.

It felt like one hundred and forty years.

Keeping Ardyn in my periphery, I pack up my own shit, swinging my leather crossbody over one shoulder. She's not hard to keep a steady gaze on. Despite her stint with plastic trays with peas and carrots, she's still a fucking bombshell with lips I could feast on and an ass my grip could leave divots in and a nice, red mark of my handprint behind.

The image makes me adjust my satchel until it's at the front of my pants. Whatever it is with this girl—my paranoia, her delicious curves, her godforsaken *presence* on my campus—I need to shake it off. Now.

"Callahan. Stay behind a minute, would you?"

Rossi asks the question with ease, busying himself with stacking spare handouts. His attention spears through his thick hair as it falls across his forehead—snake eyes through the grass. And they're trained on Ardyn.

To her credit, she doesn't give either of us a second look when she leaves the room, her long hair sweeping against the small of her back.

As soon as we're left alone, Rossi whirls on me. "What the fuck is she doing here?"

"I was asking myself the same thing."

"I thought you'd taken care of it." He doesn't bother to disguise the deadly warning in his tone.

"I did."

"You sure you offed the right girl?"

I give a curt nod. "You stood beside me while I did it."

Rossi breaks our stare off, turning instead to the closed door as if Ardyn were still standing under it. "Dammit, I couldn't tell then, and I sure as fuck can't differentiate them now. I'm relying on your judgment."

"They're my sister's best friends," I respond calmly. "I

have no doubt who nosed in on your business that night, and she's not your problem anymore."

"Will this one be?"

I lift my chin in thought. Outwardly, it might seem I'm debating between the colors of black and blue. Inwardly, I'm a raging storm. *If Ardyn had kept away, this wouldn't have become an issue. If my sister knew how to keep her mouth shut, I wouldn't be in this position. If, if, if.*

None of it matters anymore because here I am, having to clean up their fucking mess. *Again.*

"I'm trusting you to ensure that girl doesn't turn into a problem," Rossi says. "We chose this location for a specific reason—privacy. If the boss gets one tug from a loose end, we're the ones who'll pay."

"I understand." My voice sounds level and confident even though I'd love to lob an accusation right back at him. *If you weren't so trigger-happy and butthurt over a personal grievance, none of us would be in this position in the first place.*

I don't dare. With all his slicked-back, debonair attitude that makes undergrads wet their panties and a voice that has them begging for him to read them sonnets, Rossi is not a man to be messed with on his good days. He turns into an utter demon on his bad ones.

"We allowed your sister on campus at your insistence," Rossi continues. I allow a tic of annoyance in my cheek to come through.

Rossi sees it. Instead of a dark scowl in response, he laughs softly, clapping me on the shoulder. "Relax, youngblood. Clover Callahan is under your protection, and a lucky girl she is because the things I'd like to do to her—"

I whirl on a snarl, hooking his throat and slamming him into the bookshelf.

Rossi should break my neck. He'd have every right to after I laid hands on him, as our oath so states.

He releases a choked, delighted laugh under my hand. I release him with a pissed-off growl.

"There's the temper you've been hiding. I was worried you left it back in the city over the summer. Use it. I won't touch your sister, but I make no promises about the new girl. Make sure she's as innocent as she appears to be because I don't believe in coincidences."

"She's a Kaine. It won't be so easy to clean up that kind of mess." *And you're not fucking touching her,* I almost bite out. If anyone lays a hand on her bare skin, it'll be me.

His dark eyes shine like black marbles. "Worth it, in my opinion."

Rossi would do anything to keep that night a secret from our superiors. Even torturing and killing a broken heiress.

Fuck, just when I thought I was out of the woods, I have my work cut out for me.

"We have a new target coming in tonight." Rossi spins on his heel and lifts his suitcase from the parquet floor, settling it on the table and opening it. "I assume you've cut out the time to be there." He chuckles at his own joke.

Hell, any girl stupid enough to fall for this man deserves the pain that comes with it. The same can be said about me.

I'm Rossi's protégé, after all. Molded to fit into his shadow with perfect, deadly precision.

"I'll be there," I confirm.

"Good." After sticking the papers in, Rossi snaps his briefcase shut. "You're dismissed. I expect you'll have confirmation that the girl is a nonissue by the time you see me again."

I nod, wasting no time getting out of there. He doesn't give me instruction as to how to get that confirmation, not that I need any. I know what I have to do.

Rossi's fury follows me outside like charred ash and smoke, mixing in with mine until I can't tell rage from reason.

I'd had it under control. The girls were unconscious, the car a mangled tin can on the side of the road, and under Rossi's panicked eye, I pointed at the one who saw him kill one of our own. I was so green back then, coming from one body of criminals and being forced into another. All I could think of was saving my sister. After ensuring Clover was alive (there was no way I could order Rossi not to hit the car that housed his witness, not unless I'd chosen for my sister and me to die at a later date), imagine my surprise when I was consumed with an insatiable urge to save Ardyn, too. So I lied. I'd told my mentor it was Mila Hernandez who saw the whole thing. He didn't argue with me, considering Mila was in the leather jacket he'd described—*a blond chick in black leather, FIND HER*—too good to be true, in my esteemed opinion.

Mila's fate was sealed in the same shitty way mine was when I thought I'd escaped the worst society had to offer.

She was still alive when I'd snapped her neck.

The sound of her strangled pleas, clogged with blood filling her throat and gut-wrenching terror, haunt my ears as I prowl the campus in search of Ardyn. This is her fault. I'd set us up perfectly and what does she do? Stumble into the lion's den like a fluffy, stupid rabbit.

Ignoring the girls stepping into my path—"Hi, Tempest!" "Are you coming to the party tonight?" "Do you have a date?" "I'd love to show you what I can do..."—I break through the overly-perfumed clusters, willing to stop for one woman only.

I find her on the other side of the quad, about to step into the arts and literature building.

"Where you fucking belong," I mumble, zeroing in on her sun-bleached strands. It must've been said with a good amount of wrath because the one girl dumb enough to follow me squeaks, then scuttles off.

"What were you doing on my side of campus?" I ask under my breath, my eye on the back of her neck until I'm but a breath behind her.

Her hand stills above the doorknob like she senses my presence.

Ardyn turns—

I lash out, grabbing her by the upper arm and dragging her to the side of the building.

She stumbles after me, too shocked to protest until she suddenly howls, "*Hey!*"

I slam my palm against her mouth and press her against the bricks. "The next words out of your mouth better be *yes, Tempest, do me harder* or *your dick is so big, but I'd love to dislocate my jaw to blow you* because as far as anyone else is concerned, I've taken you to the side of the arts building to fuck you senseless."

I thought I'd lighten the mood by adding a wink, but all she does is narrow her eyes at me. Her lips move under my palm, slickening and heating my skin, and my face breaks out into a smile when I figure out she's trying to bite me.

"Looks like the asylum's taught you a few things, huh?"

My hand falls from her mouth. She topples forward at the unexpected release of pressure, but rights herself. With a scowl, she asks, "What do you want, Tempest?"

"Easy. I want to know why you think yourself smart enough to attend a business class."

"You didn't have to drag me around a building to ask me that."

"Well, you know how much I love my theatrics." I punctuate with another wink. Most girls would melt under one deployment, never mind double. Honestly, it's so easy to extract information from students whenever Rossi wants it that it's almost gotten boring.

Ardyn sets her jaw. "Because it interests me."

I hum under my breath at her lack of puddling at my feet. In the past, all I had to do was look sideways at her, and she'd be wet for me.

"Come on, princess, we both know you'd love nothing

more than to rescind your relations to Kaine Industries entirely. I caught you going to *art class*."

"So? Can't a girl have multiple interests?"

"Not you."

"Why not?" Her eyes glitter within the shadows the cascading ivy casts over us, their leaves trembling against the parts of her they touch. Ardyn's in an oversized cream sweater and cutoffs, and these fucking plants act like they're touching a goddess.

I grab her more forcefully above her elbows. She yelps, struggling in my grip. Her expression ranges from outrage to hurt to confusion since my actions aren't matching my playful tone. "Because you are just rejoining society again. You can't do too much to that sensitive clump of mush in your head too soon, right? Rossi's class is too difficult for you. It'll send you into a nervous breakdown faster than the car wreck that killed your best friend and scarred your other one."

Her eyes flash with astonished hurt.

Exactly, princess. "Drop it."

She wriggles out of my hold. Her back presses into the brick, crushing the pieces of ivy that so adored her a few seconds ago. "I don't have to listen to you."

"Then listen to your shrinks. I assume they didn't want you to bust out so soon?"

Her lips thin, telling me everything I need to know. "I'm not your sister. You can't just boss me around whenever you feel like it."

"No, that's your bodyguard's job, right? Tell me, did you

ever reward him for his efforts?" I mime jerking off with one hand in the air, tonguing my cheek. "Give him a blowie or two?"

She bursts forward on a guttural growl, smacking her palms against my chest and shoving me. "What is *wrong* with you?"

I sway under her push, laughing. I'd missed being this entertained.

"Seriously, what is it with you, Tempest? Did your daddy hit you too hard that one time?"

My laughter dies on my lips.

"You don't know shit about me, princess. I'll let it go this time, but the next time mention of my father crosses your lips, I'll be kind enough not to rip out your tongue along with what's left of your pathetic soul."

"Your soul is about as good as mine," she spits. "You think I'm some sheltered, sensitive child who can't handle the real world. That might've been true in the past, but it's not now. I can take any class I want. Go to any college I'd like. And ignore dickwads like you who think they rule the world. This campus is just as unrealistic as the institution I've come from. Your *theatrics* wouldn't last a second outside these walls."

Oh, how wrong you are. "I'll fail every single one of the papers you submit."

Instead of snarling, she cocks her head. Squints. "Why is it so important to you that I drop the class?"

"Because I can't stand the sight of you. I thought I made that clear when I announced to your entire dorm how apeshit you are. A lot of them are afraid you'll smother them in their sleep, you know. I believe a few calls to parents and alumni have gone out about it."

Ardyn flinches. I'm an expert at aiming where it hurts and coating it in sweet venom while I do it, and Ardyn is no exception. What bothers me is the small prick I feel in my chest when I do it to her.

It's like poking a wounded bird on the ground with a stick. A baby that's fallen out of her nest much too soon.

"You can bring up that night all you want, Tempest," she says quietly. "It's nothing I haven't thought of, on repeat, in my nightmares and outside of them. Nothing you can say will make seeing Mila's body and lying in her warm blood any worse."

"Oh, really?" I arch a brow and step into her space, elated when she shrinks within my shadow. I stare down at the crown of her head, murmuring, "What about my actions then? Do they scare you?"

She raises her head until she meets my eye, her nose brushing under my chin. It causes a *zing* of friction and a snapping of nerve endings. The wind has the audacity to add to my electrocution and waft her scent into my nostrils.

Without retreating, Ardyn says, "*You* don't scare me anymore."

I snarl in her face.

She rises to her tiptoes, getting into mine and showing me just what a big, bad girl she is now.

I snag the back of her head and crush my lips to hers.

If Ardyn thinks she can toy with her enemy and win, I'll show her she'll succeed in nothing but her own torment.

She cries into my mouth, a parting of lips that grants me the perfect opportunity to capture her bottom one between my teeth and bite down.

Her surprised cry turns into a garbled scream as a metallic tang bursts into our mouths, coating my tongue and heating me, giving me life. Ardyn struggles within the iron of my arms, but she's not going anywhere. Not until I prove to her what a mistake she's made in tangling with me.

I'll frighten her so badly that she'll want nothing more than to run to her daddy and never return.

I push her against the brick, the ivy wilting and dying under our friction. While sucking on the wound in her lip, I sneak a hand between us, finding the hem of her shorts and slipping under until I cup her sex.

Wet. Jesus, she's *wet*.

Her sobs turn into moans. Were they ever sobs in the first place? Ardyn's mouth begins moving with mine, her tongue breaking through my rows of teeth and thrusting against mine, like she's fucking my mouth.

I hate her. I resent everything she represents, the role she plays in my past, and the new future I'll have to craft because of her ignorant presence, but I'm hard.

I'm so hard for her that I wish it were my dick and not my fingers digging under her panties. Ardyn reaches for my collar, pulling me in closer, writhing against my fingers.

My dick strains against my pants. I'm tempted—no,

desperate—to tear her shorts off and take her against this building like she so clearly wants me to, but this was meant to humiliate her. I'm supposed to show her who is in control. The next time we crossed paths, she was supposed to piss herself at the sight of me, afraid I'd do worse.

Ardyn pulls at my wrist, her nails collecting skin, urging me deeper into her shorts, begging me with her actions to stick a finger into her, maybe two, or three, or four.

I want to. Jesus *fuck*, I want to—

I tear away from her, wiping my mouth with the back of my hand.

Ardyn slumps against the wall, panting, her lips smeared in bright red. Her blood. *My blood*, I realize as I notice the streak on my hand. She got a nip or two in.

Her head falls back against the wall. Shockingly, her stare is steady against mine.

I'm the first to break our trance, bringing my fingers up to my mouth and sucking the first two in up to the knuckle.

I wasn't graced with being inside her, but enough of her juices were flowing that her taste explodes on my tongue, a sharp sweetness that could only come from her.

"You can't handle me, princess," I say, my voice grittier than I'd like. "Consider that your last warning."

She pushes off the wall. "And consider me a permanent student at Titan Falls. I'm not going anywhere, Tempest. Now, if you'll excuse me, I'm late for class."

She walks off.

Ardyn fucking *walks* away from me as if we hadn't just tried to tear each other's mouths off our faces.

"Huh," I say as I watch her go. Perhaps I'm not giving her as much credit as I should. This new Ardyn, fresh from the funny farm, withstands more than usual.

Time to up the ante then. Scaring her off will be more fun than I anticipated.

I'm about to turn away when I pause halfway and peer closer at her retreating form. I grin at her loping gait.

And the slight limp she's acquired from her thighs rubbing against her swollen clit.

II

ARDYN

What can you do to tame a beast?

You soften under him. Make him believe you're not a threat. Coax and cajole and...

Turn into a wanton mess because you desire him just as badly as the hardness poking into your belly tells you he does, too.

The walk to my next class does funny things to my insides ... and outside. Tempest ignited something in me previously forgotten. I've been so immersed in planning and proving that my nervous breakdown wasn't a result of mental fragility that I'd let my stupid childhood crush on Tempest slip into oblivion.

The rush of it coming back coupled with the rise in pleasure he induced—I'm shocked I make it to my seat without bringing myself to orgasm simply by walking from point A to point B.

Pulling out my books helps. Throwing myself into the

routine of setting up for medieval history and architecture centers my mind, and slowly, painfully, the memory of Tempest's hands on me dissipates, though the heat he left behind will linger for hours.

The lecture goes by without issue. I take an insane amount of notes, focused solely on the syllabus and not the tickling at the back of my brain. It feels like eyes are on me, a certain, burning stare that can come from only one man.

Except he's not here.

I turn around anyway, convinced he's standing in one of the dark corners, arms crossed as he watches me endlessly.

Of course, I'm greeted by an empty wall. Tempest's classes are all in the STEM buildings. Along with his professor, whose name is so familiar...

I squeeze my eyes closed.

Too much trauma, my therapist said, *can lead to fantasies where you are in control instead of becoming the victim.*

I'd responded, *But I wasn't holding the gun. I wasn't the man on his knees—the victim. If I made this up to feel in control, why am I on the outside looking in?*

Did you get away?

I ... yes. If you consider waking up in a car wreck an escape.

The therapist nodded. *Then indeed, you were in control in a way you weren't when you were kidnapped. You couldn't get away from those men, but you escaped from this one.*

At that moment, I knew what I'd experienced wasn't true. I accepted that my nightmares containing Mila's screams in my ears, her pleas to live, weren't real, even though when I regained consciousness in the car, all was silent, and Mila was already dead.

Somebody murdered my friend and covered it up.

And my friend was wearing the same jacket I'd worn when I saw one man kill another in cold blood.

I'd been so sure until everyone convinced me I wasn't.

Like now. A random professor shouldn't bring up these feelings of *wrongness*, like if I only thought hard enough, clarity would surface.

Chills race down my arms as I pack up my bag and head down the hall to my last class of the day. The arched windows showcase graying skies and the mountain trees straining against a strong wind. A storm is brewing, and it's not all inside my head this time.

The occult studies room impressively clings to the eighteenth century like the rest of campus, with its domed stone ceiling and four small archways into darkened library alcoves with books stacked sideways and vertically on their wooden shelves. A long, mahogany table sits in the center with room for twelve creaky wooden chairs. An unlit hearth frames one table head, its mouth black with ash. One small window allows pallid light to shine on the table's surface, old lamps rimming the room doing the rest.

The table is almost full when I arrive. I spot Clover immediately, sitting dead center and patting the vacant seat beside her once she notices me.

Clover doesn't waste time with a greeting. "I'm so glad you got in! Professor Morgan's classes are impossible to snag. He won't even allow students to audit."

I offer a small shrug as I scoot in next to her. "Lucky, I guess."

To be honest, I don't know how I got a spot. Someone must've dropped out, and I thought nothing of it.

Clover's voice lowers as the other students quiet down. "He's tough but fair. No course syllabus. He prefers to keep us on our toes, and I'm *praying* this year he lets us do a topic on the Anderton family. Is it wrong I also want to fuck him?"

I choke on my own spit.

Clover smacks me in the middle of my back, swallowing back her laughter. "Am I that surprising? It's clear we have a lot to catch up on, Ardy."

"Good afternoon, class." Professor Morgan waltzes in, younger than I imagined in a pin-striped blazer and black-rimmed glasses. Like Clark Kent, if he were a librarian, complete with a Superman body under all that tweed. After clearing my throat a few times and blinking back tears, I straighten.

Clover folds her hands in her lap, ever the good student who wants to sleep with her professor. Last I'd seen Clover, she and I were virgins together. Sex wasn't much on my mind these past years, but the same can't be said for Clover. It seems I've missed out on more than just friendship.

Tempest's lingering imprints on my skin turn to fire. The way he shoved his hand down the front of my shorts, his cool fingertips searching for heat and finding it wet. His threats in my ear turning into shivers down my neck, the promise of his hardness leading to my desperate urge to spread myself for him, in public, a virgin for the taking...

"We'll begin with our first subject: ghosts."

My fingers seize around the pen. An ink splotch forms on my paper, growing tentacles. A few of my neighbors groan with boredom.

"One of the most culturally universal phenomena and older than witchcraft, spanning thousands of years. A tablet from ancient Babylon contains instructions on exorcism. The ancient Greeks called them *phantasma*. Even the Bible touches upon it. While Jesus never comes out and confirms their existence, he *does* admit he's not one when his disciples see him walking on a lake. Tell me, does anyone here believe in ghosts, restless spirits, or strange apparitions?"

Less than half of the class's hands go up. One of them belongs to Clover, who elbows me to participate. I keep my arm stubbornly at my side. One becomes touchy about admitting to believing in the inexplicable after being committed for it. It takes a few seconds, but Clover gets the hint and twists her lips in apology.

Professor Morgan's eyes light up. "I do love a divided classroom. A lot of you have taken my class in hopes of dissecting witchcraft in Colonial America. Specifically, occultism in Titan Falls."

After confirmatory head nods, Morgan comes between two students across from us, leaning his palms on the table. I notice the tops of his hands and fingers are all stained with ink. Tattoos of strange symbols.

"They're runes," Clover whispers in explanation beside me. Or more sighs it lovingly.

"You're a violent bunch, and that's okay because the occult, the rituals, can be nightmarish indeed," he says.

His dark brown eyes seem to target me when he says it. Only me. Clover catches my hand under the table and squeezes. Hard.

Morgan lifts himself off the table, tucking his inked hands into his pockets. "Don't worry, we'll get there. For now, your first essay is this: two thousand words arguing the existence—or nonexistence—of spirits in the modern era. Cite parapsychology, occult sciences, superstition, what you will. Just prove to me what *you* believe to be true."

Clover shifts in her seat next to mine, whispering excitedly as she jots down Morgan's instructions word for word, "This is *so* my fucking vibe."

I look down at my notebook, blank except for a spreading ink splotch.

"I want to get a sense of your arguments," Morgan continues, "your sense of self within the curiosity and demonic wonders of our modern age."

I wonder if I can write about personal demons. Mila's screams. A shattered skull from a bullet. My unnamed victim, haunting me until I find them justice.

A textbook snaps shut beside me. I jolt, blinking.

"He's amazing, isn't he?" Clover says breathlessly, rising from her chair. "Do you think he was checking me out?" She gestures down her body, clad in a black scoop dress, knee-high combat boots, and heavy silver necklaces, all complimenting her raven hair. "I dressed my goth best, just for him."

I scan the room, surprised to find everyone packing up and dispersing. Morgan's already exited.

Shutting my blank notebook as inconspicuously as possible, I rise with her. "I'm more interested in what Tempest'll do when he sees you."

"Ugh, don't bring my brother into the subject of seduction."

I pull my lips in, surprised I allowed them to betray me. I may think about him nonstop, but I don't want Clover to know that, *especially* while we're discussing the art of seduction like she said.

He's just too damn good at it.

"You're telling me," Clover agrees, pulling her books to her chest. It's then I figure out I said it out loud. "If Professor Morgan shows any interest in me whatsoever, I will make it my life's work to get under him, regardless of how many of Morgan's family members Tempest threatens to kill. You're lucky, you know."

"How so?" I follow her out the door.

"You got to live over two years Tempest-free. He doesn't give a shit what you do so long as you don't cross paths with him. Oh, how I wish I could be you."

That guy cares about nothing, especially you. Some of Mila's last words float through the murky depths of my mind.

But this is not Mila, and it's not two years ago. I'm no longer a girl who tears up when she's told her crush doesn't like her back. "Does Tempest really blame me for our accident?"

His words to me said *yes,* but his actions ... my belly flutters at the remembrance.

Flutters then sinks as I force the facts forward. Tempest shouldn't matter. Only proving I'm not some weak, fragile princess does.

"He's always had a misplaced sense of justice. One thing is for certain, though. He always needs someone to blame," Clover says as we stroll down the hallway.

As fast as campus becomes crowded in the mornings, it turns deserted after the last class of the day. Strange, considering there's nowhere else for students to go in the middle of the mountains.

Clover stops me with a gentle hand on my arm. "It's not your fault, Ardyn. Whatever my brother says, he doesn't mean it. Tempest is just angry he wasn't there to help us. That he—"

"—sent the car to get us," I finish for her. "If he wants to blame someone, it should be himself for sending that particular car to pick us up. We wouldn't have been on the road at that exact moment in time."

How I wish it could be Tempest I'm confronting and not Clover. Next time I see him, I'll tell him this. I will.

"Don't tell Tempest that," Clover responds, reading my mind. For the first time, I notice how pale her cheeks have become. "It'll only make him want to come after you."

I feign indifference. My bones thrum at the thought. "I'm not afraid of him."

"You should be. I am."

"Miss Kaine?"

Both our heads turn.

Professor Morgan stands at the door to his office, farther down the hallway and where the sunlight can't quite hit through the casement windows. His lenses shine but illuminate nothing.

"Could I see you for a moment?"

"Um. Sure." It doesn't matter how much time I spent in an institution. I'll always hate being singled out by an authority figure.

"You bitch," Clover teases, a smile crossing her face. "Put in a good word for me." She nudges me forward. "I'll see you in time to get ready for the party."

It's all the impetus I need to be reminded of the kick-off party held at the all-boys dorm, Meath Row, or what our dorm calls *Meat Row*. It also serves as enlightenment. The campus is so deserted because everyone's getting ready in their costumes.

Enough silence passes between the three of us that it's grown uncomfortable. I clear my throat. "Okay, yeah. See you soon."

Clover nods, then tosses her hair, fluttering a wave at Professor Morgan. "Bye, Professor!"

"Goodbye, Miss Callahan," he answers wryly, then beckons me over. "In my office, please."

He turns and is seated on the other side of his desk by the time I enter and shut his paneled double doors, the old wood soft under my hands.

I turn toward him and nearly lose my breath.

I'm faced with a skull.

Morgan follows my line of sight at the shelving above his head. "Ah, yes. The skull of Sarah Anderton always scares the bejesus out of my students, even the ones most atheist." He smiles. "Please sit. I promise, simply because she is surrounded by occult materials doesn't mean she'll materialize in front of us."

I feel my throat bob. Before I can even think to stop myself—"Clover would die to see that."

"Not you, I take it?" Morgan's handsome smile slowly wilts. "I apologize. That was insensitive of me. After what you've been through, I doubt jokes at your expense are much appreciated."

I stare at him. When I don't peel my back off the door, Morgan adds, "I'm well aware of your history, Miss Kaine. In fact, I approved your late entry into my class due to it. Not to be confused with favoritism, of course. You must pull your weight like all the others, but I thought you might be a special case, what with your background."

I blink. "Clover Callahan went through the same thing I did. Did you give her a preferential pass, too?"

Morgan cocks his head, surprised, maybe, at how strong my voice sounds while my body still trembles. I don't like the dark, and I don't like being alone with pieces of a real skeleton. *So sue me.*

"Clover seems to have adjusted after your unfortunate accident slightly better than you. Or denied it better."

My brows jump at his presumption. "What does any of

what we went through or how we handled it have to do with your occult lectures?"

Morgan shrugs, unperturbed by my defensiveness. He leans forward to light a candle on his desk. Enough light filters through the two casement windows behind him, but with so much dark wood and scarlet fabrics like the carpet and curtains, maybe a single candle is needed.

"I've called you in here to make sure you're comfortable with the materials we'll be covering. You appeared uneasy at the mention of our first topic, and I wondered if I'd made a mistake by allowing you in the class."

"I'm fine." Even if I'm not, I have the overwhelming urge to lie to him. I'm so tired of being treated like I'll break at any second. "It was unsettling at first. I'm happy to put in the work, though. I want to be in your class."

"That's wonderful to hear." He smiles again. "Do you believe your friend haunts you? The one who died in the accident?"

Again, with his presumptuousness. I at last move away from the door, but it's to unlatch it and get out of here. "If that's all you need, I'll be leaving now."

"By all means," he says behind me. "I look forward to reading your paper."

I don't respond. Instead, I burst into the darkened hallway, my footsteps silenced by the thudding of my heart.

12
TEMPEST

"You're both fucking assholes!"

Corporate executive Desmond Cartwright writhes against the chair, its scarred wooden legs scraping against the dusty concrete floor.

"I'll ruin the lot of you! You fucking animals—"

Desmond's head snaps back from Miguel's direct punch to the mouth.

Blubbering, Desmond's head falls forward, blood dripping from the corners. He snarls, his teeth stained red. "You think that's all it'll take? You idiots are fucking cowboys. Running wild up here, no rules, no laws, when you're just brainless muscle following orders ..."

Miguel's fist crashes into the side of Desmond's face. Desmond coughs, spits, and the small *clink* on the ground tells me he's lost a tooth or two.

With the shirt sleeves rolled up, Miguel turns to me. "This guy honestly believes he's going to leave this chair."

I bring my attention back to Desmond, sending him a droll look. "I didn't think this would need to be explained, but..." I gesture to his bound hands and feet locking him into a seated position. "You're a little tied up at the moment."

"Why, so a kid like you can rough me up?" His eyes dart to Miguel, a bright, shining white against his ballooning bruises. "Is this some kind of initiation for him? To get into your club?"

Miguel chuckles, a low, ominous sound that dissipates as quickly as it leaves his mouth. "He's well initiated, Cartwright. You're not here for that."

"Then what?" Desmond hocks a ruby-red loogie onto the floor in a heavy *splat*. "Is it money? You want more? I got it, Miggie, you just gotta—"

"You have loans coming out of your future children's—no grandchildren's—asses. The shares you've invested are in the toilet. You promise us money? Your promises are about as good as what you've just stained my floor with."

"Then give me time! I can ask for more loans."

"The banks want nothing to do with you. Even the teenage venture capitalists want to forget your name. You're out of time, Cartwright."

"No!" Desmond's eyes flare. "Wait!"

Miguel jerks his chin at me. "Finish him off."

I push off the wall, coming out of the shadows in two leisurely steps.

"People will look for me!" Desmond cries, his chair

squealing as he pushes against the ground with his bound feet to get away. "My wife! My business associates!"

Miguel tucks his hands into his pockets, lowering his chin but watching me with alertness. His white collared shirt remains pristine, despite the multiple blows he landed against Desmond's face. My collared shirt is black like my pants. I wonder if Desmond has made the connection yet.

"You vacation here a lot, don't you, Mr. Cartwright?" It's always good to refer to them with respect before I gut them. It allows them to grasp a level of superiority, one last modicum of the throne they once sat on before I swipe the rug out from underneath them. "With your wife and her parents. The Valley is gorgeous, isn't it?"

"S-Stay away from me, boy."

I take another step closer. While doing so, I pull out a circle of wire from my pocket, capped on each end with a wooden stick. "In fact, you've been quoted multiple times in the press on how much you enjoy the seclusion here. This is your happy place. You especially enjoy the hiking trails. Sadly, this time, while you're enjoying the luxuries of a five-star vacation, you will have wandered those same woods at the wrong time." I widen my eyes at the last word, appearing somewhat maniacal and gleeful. Desmond flinches at the sight. "This time, you're confronted by a wild animal. A cougar, a black bear, it doesn't matter, so long as your family remembers you with a gasp and a hand to their heart as they dissect what your last moments must've been like."

I snap the garrote taut with both hands.

"You don't—you can't! I have the money." In a last desperate plea, Desmond's eyes land on Miguel's. "I swear it!"

"Oh?" Miguel responds dryly as I walk a lazy half-circle around Desmond. "Where can I find it, Cartwright?"

"In my safe deposit box. With-with … in Virginia. My wife's jewels, jewelry she inherited from her grandmother, it's in there."

Miguel arches a brow. "Is it worth 1.5 million?"

"N-No, but it's at least half. I can come up with the other half in a month or so."

Miguel raises a hand for him to quiet. Shockingly, Desmond does. "It's too late for that. Our orders were to receive you, get what information we could out of you, then bury you. I don't see a reason to digress now, do you, Tempest?"

"No, sir."

"You won't get away with it!" Desmond screeches. "This day and age, there is forensics! Testing! You'll be caught and sent to the chair!"

Now it's my turn to laugh. "You assume there will be enough of you left to study."

Desmond's jaw drops. He tries to spin to face me, but I've moved behind him.

I smile. "Bye, Dezzie."

Desmond doesn't say anything else. He can't because the garrote fits so perfectly around his neck, the wire digging into his skin until it pops, warm rivulets of his blood decorating my hands.

He struggles, obviously, but with his hands bound behind the chairback, all he can do is wriggle and kick at the air, his face turning puce and his eyes bulging.

Tipping my head forward while his is dragged back, we meet in a sort of mismatched gaze, one on the upside, the other going down to hell. As for which one is which, I'll let you decide.

Miguel approaches Desmond's front, flicking open a knife.

"Finishing him off before I can have my fun, are you?"

The voice comes from the stairwell, followed by unhurried steps. In the dim light of the unpolished basement sconces, it's hard to make out the person they belong to, save for that trademark drawl that makes undergrads drool and the male-inclined faculty stutter whenever he enters their offices.

I let out a peevish grunt while the top of Desmond's head digs into my belly.

Miguel pockets his switchblade and steps back from Desmond. "Where've you been, Hunter?"

Professor Hunter Morgan comes into the dirty light filled with kicked-up dust and debris. "I was held up by a rather pretty new addition to my classroom."

My blood turns cold. I can't be sure who he means, yet my instincts are never wrong, and they're whispering that he refers to one of two women. I release the garrote before

Miguel even utters the words, "Release him for the moment, Tempest."

"Sadly, I had to let her go due to this outstanding appointment." Morgan finally looks at Desmond, gasping and pleading with sweat streaming down his balding head.

"Who is she?" I ask.

Hunter peels his eyes away from Desmond and to me. "Hmm?"

"The pretty addition." I don't care that Hunter's a higher-up, and my tone comes out demanding. "Who is she?"

"I believe her name is Ardyn Kaine." Hunter's brown eyes spark with delight. He folds his arms with an expression that says he knows perfectly well what her fucking name is. And he's imagining her naked.

I ball my fists until they shake, the wire cutting into my palm. Mixing my blood with Desmond's should disgust me, except I'm too busy thinking how best to get Ardyn out of this prick's head without decapitating him.

"You call dibs on her, Storm Cloud?" Morgan's question drips with amusement. He's truly delighted over the nickname he's given me and uses it every chance he gets, considering I can't do anything about it.

Yet.

"No," I grit out, "but if anyone else touches her, I'll use my admirable skill set on their face before moving to their quail-sized balls."

Hunter responds to my quip with a lopsided grin.

"You've met her, too, under similar circumstances, haven't you?"

I'm prowling toward him before realizing I've tightened the garrote in my hands again. Miguel stops me by throwing a firm hand against my chest. "Easy, Tempest." He adds under his breath, "He's the boss's son. I'm not saying he gets a free pass, but mutilation over a woman is a no-go."

"Fine," I hiss. If I can't initiate a dire situation with our internal affairs, I'll settle for a warning. Just one. "You don't touch her."

"And why not?"

I'm aiming for calm. I truly am, regardless of the coppery tang to the atmosphere, driving my cravings for a lesson in blood forward. "Were you the one who got to look down on her, her life in your hands as you decided whether she lived or died?" The image of Ardyn unconscious and dangling, her hair cascading onto the car's ceiling, and her palms laying flat in benediction as I weighed the option of whether to kill her or Mila is easy to call forward because I haven't forgotten about it since. With a tenth of a second's calculation, I noted Mila wearing Ardyn's jacket, Mila crawling out of the tipped-over car, Mila's glazed-over eyes catching me standing over her ... that part wasn't hard to put onto a scale. She had to die. But when I was finished with Mila, there was Ardyn to contend with, so innocent, at the wrong place at the wrong time, her dark lashes fluttering as she was about to come to. Would she be wise enough to stay quiet? Were the drugs in the flask I'd paid an usher to give to Mila, known to pressure her friends, enough to make Ardyn's memories hazy and unreliable?

I'd decided to roll the dice. I wasn't ready for the reclusive, mysterious princess to be removed from this world.

"No, that was me who had the honor," I say to Morgan, "who became her god when I decided it wasn't necessary to kill her just yet."

"Or her devil," Miguel inputs mildly.

I acknowledge his statement with a tense nod but do not take my eyes off Hunter's. "You don't get that power. Nor will you take it from me. I made an oath to protect this Outfit, and at present, she is not a danger."

Hunter's eyes narrow. Miguel emits a warning hum in his throat aimed in my direction.

"Why would she become a danger?" Hunter asks. He says it with mild disinterest, but I'm not enjoying the way his fingers are playing at his thighs like he's calculating the odds. "You killed the right one, didn't you?"

"Our Manhattan affairs don't concern you," Miguel interjects. He then sweeps his arm toward our latest subject. "Tempest does not make mistakes. You've been sent to our turf to learn from us, Hunter. Now, may we focus our attention on the more immediate concerns, please?"

"Talk more about this girl," Desmond adds desperately. "She sounds like a threat. More of a danger than I am."

"Ardyn Kaine is my concern." My gaze travels from Desmond to Hunter, before finally landing on Miguel. "*Mine.*"

"Yes, yes," Miguel agrees tiredly. He adds for Hunter's

benefit, "I've tasked Tempest to maintain reconnaissance over the girl. So far, she is nothing to us. I'd like it to stay that way. That means no meddling on your part, Hunter."

A muscle tics in Hunter's jaw. He wisely stays silent.

I don't believe in his acquiescence for a second.

Hunter unclips his cuff links, rolling up his sleeves to expose more ink. "Then I suppose we'll move on to the more pressing issue."

I catch Miguel's annoyed glance and answer with a crooked, wry smile. *Fucking nepotism.*

Hunter scans the basement. There isn't much besides the chair Desmond squirms in, a vintage chest, and an old, cracked apothecary cabinet that's sat here about as long as this place has existed. "Where's my blade?"

I pretend to inspect my cuticles. "Where you last left it, I assume."

"It's impossible to find anything in this dank, dusted-over, windowless basement."

"I would've figured you'd be familiar with it, considering it mirrors your soul."

"Boys," Miguel warns. "Focus."

Hunter spares a moment to glare at me, then stalks over to the cabinet, opening one drawer after the next. "Aha!" He holds a blade the size of a kitchen knife up high.

"Wh-What is that for?" Desmond asks.

Miguel grumbles, "We don't have time for this. Allow Tempest to finish him off, Hunter."

"Alas, I cannot do that." Hunter graces us with a wicked

grin. When he deploys it on Desmond, Desmond moans. "Please. *Please* give me the time to pay you back."

"We gave you plenty of time and options," Miguel says. He gestures to Hunter in a reluctant *go-ahead* motion.

Hunter moves, his polished knife glinting at the hilt where rubies were laid over a century ago. A ritual knife belonging to one of the witches utilizing this basement in the 1700s, Hunter's been over the moon since he discovered it nestled in the folded hands of a witch skeleton on the mountains. He's a freak, this one, and not methodical like I am. Incontrollable. Combustible. Partially why he's here under our tutelage.

Desmond releases a high-pitched whine as Hunter leans over him, dangling the knife. "You're going to wish Tempest was faster in his administrations." Hunter pauses to swipe some of Desmond's blood pooling at his neck. "Now that I'm here, I require an extra step. Your death is not enough for me. Oh no, I must also have your soul."

"What the ...? You fucking ... you fuck..."

"Mm." Hunter straightens, popping a bloody finger in his mouth and sucking. "Poor man, you will never see the afterlife. None of my father's victims do once I'm done with you. It'll be trapped here, in this room with all these dead, restless witches, for the rest of your miserable eternity."

Desmond starts to cry.

"Tempest? The salt, please."

"I'm not your fucking servant." But I do retreat a step so as not to be caught in the spray of blood Hunter's about to unleash.

Miguel rubs at his face, begging for patience. "Jesus fuck, do as the man asks so we can get out of here."

Sniffing impatiently, I pull a bag of salt from under the stairs. "Do you think this is kosher or Himalayan pink salt?"

"Fuck you." Hunter's not looking at me as he says it. He beckons it over eagerly with his hand. "Pour a circle around us."

"Dude." I look at Miguel. *Are you fucking serious?*

Miguel, the bastard, nods his assent.

Fuck me. I get to work making the damn psycho a circle.

"Don't close it until I'm back inside it, Storm Cloud."

While I'm spreading salt and planning where to dump Hunter's body so nobody will find it, Hunter moves to a chest in the corner. He pulls out a maroon, moth-hole-infested cloak that he throws around his shoulders, then rifles around for something else.

With his back to us, Hunter affixes something onto his face, then slowly turns.

"What the fuck is he doing?" Desmond asks. "*What the fuck is he doing?*"

Bored, I glance over at Hunter, then roll my eyes at the spectacle.

No wonder Desmond Cartwright's shitting his pants.

Hunter's donned a goat skull for a mask, framing it by pulling up the hood to his cloak. With clasped hands, he returns to Desmond, and I happily finish his exfoliation circle behind him.

Hunter says to Desmond, "See, these boys prefer to cut out their victim's heart *after* they're dead to send to my father as proof. But me? I must cut out your heart while it's still beating. Oh, I *know*," he says with pretend empathy over Desmond's wails and pleas. "Grizzly stuff, but please be quiet. I have to recite an incantation while I do it…"

I stop listening when Hunter strikes the center of Desmond's chest, his stained work shirt blooming with red. Desmond unleashes a bloodcurdling scream.

I massage the back of my neck. Check my watch.

This better be over with soon. I have a party to get to.

13

ARDYN

Clover finishes knotting the satin tie at my waist, then steps back to admire her work.

"Perfect," she says, spinning me by the shoulder until I face her. "Absolutely gorgeous."

"I don't know..." I pull at the ivory satin as if I can give my hips more room simply by yanking at it. "It's a little tight for the eighteenth century, don't you think?"

"Girl, it's a college-themed eighteenth century. I doubt the women burned at the stake for being witches wore lingerie, but I guarantee you'll see some tonight."

"All you've guaranteed is that I can't breathe." I didn't come to Titan Falls prepared for costume parties, so Clover chose from her closet and dressed me a corset mermaid gown with gold thread sown through the satin and a basque waistline. My boobs are also squished into a V-neckline with tiny spaghetti straps. "Why are we going again?"

"Because there will be cute boys." Clover winks, then spins to her closet to get dressed in her "witch" costume. "Besides, someone has to show them how it's done."

I try to sit on my bed while Clover gets ready until the boning in my bodice threatens to stab me. I straighten.

After twenty minutes, Clover emerges from our bathroom clad in a feminine version of a men's ankle-length velvet tuxedo coat, complete with a top hat. Underneath, she's donned a high-collared lace neckpiece, a red-sequined corset, and black fishnets, capped off with thigh-high leather boots.

"Whoa. Clo, you look fantastic."

"I know." She grins with scarlet red lips. "So do you. Mostly because I dressed you."

"No argument here." Laughing, I take her elbow, and we saunter out of our room together.

Clover had the decency to allow me to wear my Chucks underneath the dress, so we both walk without issue from our dorm to Meat Row.

If I didn't know how to get there, all we would've had to do was follow the pounding music and raucous laughter, becoming louder and messier as we cross through the middle of the quad. Some students who got started too early lie on the rim of the fountain in the middle, limbs dangling in the water, while couples make out and fondle each other beside them.

"God, I missed this," I say as I watch a guy trip over nothing and splash into the water.

Clover squeezes my arm. "If you ever want to talk, you

know, about what you went through or how these last years were like ... I'm here for you, Ardy."

I look over with a sad smile. "Thank you, but I'd much rather forget and try to live in the present."

"I don't blame you." She goes quiet within a cacophony of drunken hollers and high-pitched screeches. I'd ask how the faculty let us get away with such an obvious underage party, but I'm guessing the $200k yearly tuition from each student speaks for itself.

"Hey, um, do you know if any professors come to these things?" I ask.

Clover responds with an amused hum. "I doubt it, but I'd love to see Professor Morgan in costume. Can you imagine how sexy he'd look in breeches? Oh, my *God*."

I laugh.

"Which professor would you want to see in a waistcoat, hmm?" Clover elbows me.

Her bony nudge tickles, and I laugh harder to cover up my immediate conjuring of Tempest in eighteenth-century finery, no shirt needed. Just the breeches, his chiseled muscles shining after our hard day's fuck...

"Holy shit, you *are* thinking of someone!" Clover says, skipping with glee. "Who is it? Oh, my God, Ardy, tell me. Who?"

The vision of Tempest coming up to me with that dark look in his eyes, ripping my bodice in two and biting down on one of my breasts won't leave the backs of my eyes. So I panic. "Uh-uh-Professor Rossi. Have you heard of him?"

Clover scrunches her brows. Then to my horror, her

forehead smooths, and a smile pulls at her lips. "I've seen him. My brother's a TA for one of his classes. He should be goddamned illegal. That Mexican-Italian heritage of his, those dark looks, and that solid body ... you have good taste for someone who hasn't been out much."

I press a hand to my belly in a desperate bid to quell the seasick sway Clover's words cause. *If she only knew the evil lurking inside him.* With a hysterical edge to my voice, I say, "I thought you wanted Professor Morgan, not Rossi."

She laughs. "Why can't I have both? It's my fantasy. Don't worry, I'll share."

We crest a small rise, Meat Row coming into view with students spilling out of it and red Solo cups littering the path. Clover pulls me through the entrance.

Meath House is structured in much the same way Camden House is, in the early American colonial style of high ceilings, a central chimney, and exposed oak beams. This one is three stories tall with a wide open space on the first floor. People drape across the heavy furniture that would probably take ten of these boys to move. Thus, the couches, tables, and chairs have become awkward centerpoints for beer pong and hookups.

"I think the kitchen's through here." I hear Clover say. She keeps my hand in hers as she yells over the music and drags me through the gyrating crowd toward the back of the house.

We're clearly the best dressed here. Or we've arrived too late to see everyone's costumes how they were supposed to be seen. Unbuttoned shirts, wrinkled lace dresses falling off shoulders, and pretend witches screeching and smacking at guys who pretend to throw them into the fireplace.

"Is that supposed to be funny?" I watch in horror as a girl's ruffle skirt nearly goes up in flames.

Clover pays it little mind. "Just because we go to school with a bunch of rich kids doesn't mean we go to school with a bunch of smart kids. There we are!" Clover points at a large bar table in the center of the kitchen, as thick as a butcher's block. Rows of liquor and beer bottles fill its space. Clover peruses quickly, finding two unopened cans of Coke. "I'm parched."

I accept the can, drinking along with Clover while I peruse the space.

She seems to read my thoughts. "We won't stay long. I just figured we haven't participated in college life much, and a part of me was curious about what it'd be like."

"How is it measuring up?"

"I think I'd be happier curled up in our common room reading tarot cards."

Me too, but I don't voice it. I'd wanted to enroll in college to break out of isolation and forge my own path, no bodyguards, no parents, just me, entering society too old and too innocent. If I gave in to Clover's subtle invitation to leave now, then I can basically seal my fate for the rest of my undergrad. I'm supposed to enjoy the experience, make friends other than Clover, and pretend I belong. I need to make that happen.

"C'mon." I steer Clover out of our convenient hiding spot in the kitchen. "Why don't we keep exploring?"

She shrugs. "If you say so. In my opinion, the fun part of getting ready is over."

"Agreed, but we can't live out the semester in the common room with a bunch of old books."

"Why not? I bet they have more interesting stories than..." Clover points her chin at a guy pounding his chest with a T-shirt reading *Witch, please* while his pilgrim-costumed friend funnels vodka into him. "Whatever that is."

"True enough, but—" I pause. Since when did I become the positive one in our relationship? My therapist would be proud. If it weren't for the screams closing in on me, becoming less jovial and more sinister the longer I linger, and the smell of sweat, alcoholic fumes, and too much perfume invading my nose. "You know what? Sure. We came. We saw. Let's go."

"*Yes.*" Clover pumps the air. "I'm pretty sure we came from that way."

The instant she points, someone booms over the speakers, "Listen up, undergrads and overachievers! The burning ritual is about to begin! Follow me if you're desperate for some good luck for your first year at TFU. If you'd rather play the odds without the dead witches on your side, then good luck to *you*."

A smattering of applause breaks out, with a few people breaking off from their groups and following the boy with the microphone out the back door. "What's he talking about?"

Clover makes an annoyed sound under her breath. "A

blasphemy of witchcraft. Titan Falls seniors and post-grads initiate freshmen by—you know what? My explaining it isn't nearly as appalling as seeing it for yourself. Come on."

She pulls at my elbow, merging us into the line of undergrads leaving Meat House. "I don't need to see it. I don't even believe in this stuff. I thought you wanted to go home."

Clover shakes her head. "The more I think about this, the better it is for me to be there, so I can cleanse the area and close the circle so malevolent spirits aren't stuck here."

"I'm sorry. Huh?" But I allow Clover to lead me into the woods. Makeshift torches light a well-trodden dirt path. They're not strong enough to break through the black of the forest behind them. "Are you going to make me regret leaving my private facility?"

Clover responds with a thin-lipped smile. "Unlike these heathens, I respect the witches of the 1700s. They practiced paganism and had gentle spiritual practices and didn't deserve to die. Now, these assholes want to commune with them as some kind of sick entertainment."

I eye the trees surrounding us as they become more untended and wild the deeper we stumble. "Where are we going?"

"It's not obvious? We're headed to where the Andertons died."

My heels drag into the dirt, forcing Clover to slow. "Why the *fuck* would I want to go there?"

"Excellent question. I'll take an answer from either of you two morons."

I come to a complete standstill at Tempest's voice, like melted dark chocolate sliding down his throat.

Clover releases me, crossing her arms and grumbling under her breath, "I swear he's inserted a tracking device under my skin."

"No need, sister." Tempest steps through the underbrush and directly into our path. "Whenever I wonder where you are, all I have to ask myself is, where is the witches and wizards pretend-play happening? And there you are."

"Have you added *original* and *creative* to your sociopaths-seeking-sociopaths app yet? Because I really think you should."

Tempest folds his arms over his chest. The siblings don't realize how much their obstinate postures and pissed-off facial tics mirror one another's.

Me, I try to melt into the shadows so Tempest doesn't aim his bad mood between my eyes.

"Get back to your dorm, girls."

Clover rolls her eyes. I'm tempted to cross my arms in defiance, too, if my body weren't so confused about what to do. My core undulates with his presence, flittering and throbbing at the remembrance of his fingers. My stomach is taut with nerves, bolstering itself in case he pounces. Fear slithers down my spine at the encroaching forest and lack of witnesses.

But I'm with Clover. I shouldn't feel so afraid and desirous with her by my side.

"We're not children," she says to him. "Why don't you

scuttle off to the crypt you crawled out of so we can get on with our night?"

Her words highlight his appearance, an aspect I hadn't studied when I was so focused on his face. Tempest wears all black, his silhouette so comfortable in the darkness that it's hard to tell the forest from him. His face is pale, yet his angular cheeks are flushed, and the hollows of his eyes caved in with spent exertion.

When he shifts, the black fabric shines.

My eyes narrow.

Tempest catches my study. "Do you speak, or have you lost your voice along with the rest of your senses?"

No part of me moves except for my eyes. They flare at the sight—looking back, seeing ski masks, blood spray, my screams ringing in my ears as scissors are flashed in front of my face. *Snip, snip. They want proof of life, sweetie. Which part of you should we send to your daddy?*

Then Mila as she drags herself out of the destroyed vehicle. *No. No, please!* as the silver gleam of a—watch?—comes down before hands wrap around her throat.

"Hey. Princess." Tempest snaps his fingers in front of my face.

I recoil. Gasping. Blinking.

Tempest watches my recovery with an arched brow. "It's time for your puppy to go back into her pen, Clo."

"She's not a pet." Clover comes up beside me, shouldering forward enough to defend me from her brother. "If you weren't so narcissistic, you'd realize Ardyn is working through a lot."

"You'd think they'd teach 'don't wander into a dark forest after experiencing a mental breakdown,' but what the fuck do I know, right?"

And there it is.

I step out from under Clover's shadow. "What is it you truly want to say to me, Tempest?"

He points in the direction where everyone else has disappeared. "There's no gingerbread cottage waiting for you back there, princess, but there is a fucking witch."

I let my head fall back. "Not you, too."

"Please. I don't believe in that shit, but what they do in there, how TFU kids decide to start their year, is nothing you want to be involved in. You can't handle it."

"Who are you to tell me what I can and can't handle?" I ask at the same time Clover interjects, "Oh, so you're all protective now? What do you care what Ardyn does?"

Tempest finally tears his low, shining gaze away from mine. "I care about what *you* do, Clo. She can have a meltdown right at my feet if she wants, but I'm taking you back to your dorm. It's not safe."

Clover laughs. "It's a bunch of kids nicking their thumbs and dropping their blood into a chalice they light on fire on top of a tree stump. It's not unsafe. It's banal."

I stare at Clover. "*That's* what you're trying to get me to witness?"

"Clo's right to think so. With your history, you'd faint at the sight of a paper cut," Tempest drawls.

That does it. "You're one to talk! You're lecturing us

covered in-in—" I storm up to him, digging my pointer finger into his chest. "That's blood, isn't it?"

He offers a crooked grin. "Taste it and find out."

I drop my hand from his chest, disgusted.

But I don't step back, and neither does Tempest. Heat curls between us, unseen, tangible, and alive. A strange feeling, curling like smoke, stretches out from my middle and reaches for him.

Tempest surveys me with hooded eyes. Holding his gaze, I suck in my lower lip.

Not with the goal of seduction—I have no idea where to begin with that. I'm just … quivering underneath his gaze.

Tempest's attention darts to my mouth. When he returns my stare, his pupils are dilated.

I hitch in a breath.

He blinks. "Morgan's leading the burning tonight, and I'd rather the two of you fuck off."

The air turns frigid between us. I'm able to distance myself, returning to reality with an uncomfortable *pop* in my ears.

Later, I'll know what to call it: a resurfacing after drowning in his rippling black waters.

Clover pipes up behind us. "Professor Morgan?"

Moment over, I shake my head at Tempest. "You couldn't have said it better."

Tempest's brows crash down. "The fuck that's supposed to mean? Clo?"

But Clover's already dashed down the path, halfway to Morgan by now.

Tempest curses.

I pull in my lips, stifling my amused grin.

Tempest catches it anyway. He glares fire at me, then catches me by the elbow, dragging me forward.

"Hey! What is with you Callahans and your preferred mode of transporting me? I can walk by myself, you know."

He growls while stalking forward. "I'd rather you be on a leash, so I guess we both have to be disappointed. You are not to leave my side until we find my sister. Understood?"

"No."

Tempest grinds to a halt, whipping around and pressing his chest into mine so suddenly that I stumble back. "I will only repeat myself once: understood?"

If it weren't for his continued hold on my elbow, I would've tripped on my ass. Yet I have the irresistible urge to retort, "You've made it clear you're not responsible for me, so I'll go wherever I please, thank you."

Tempest dips his head until his face fills my entire horizon. "I should let them eat your heart."

My mouth hangs open.

He takes advantage of my stunned silence, dragging his thumb across the front of his shirt while his mouth curves into a cunning grin.

Tempest releases his grip on me. My arm throbs where he touched me. I rub it while backing away. "Thank you for listeni—"

He catches my lower lip, pulling it down with his thumb. When it returns to its place, a metallic tang hits my tongue.

Sickened horror leeches into my face. "Oh, my *God*, what is that? *Who* is that?"

Tempest smiles, this time showing his teeth while he casually turns away. "Better the devil you know than the one you don't. Stick with me, princess. You're too tempting of a prey."

He disappears around a thick tree. Spitting, wiping my mouth with the back of my hand, I race to catch up with him.

"I'm not afraid," I say to his back.

"No? You should be. You've had enough warnings to last my lifetime, which means it's not a fucking long one."

"I told you—"

A scream cuts off my argument with bloodcurdling finality.

14

ARDYN

The shriek dies into faded laughter, joined by multiple others. It takes a few seconds, but my heart crawls out of my throat and returns to its natural place.

"You mind?"

I tear my attention from the clearing where students' silhouettes intermingle within the ring of flame-lit torches, tilting my head up to Tempest. His preternatural gaze cuts through the darkness better than fire.

I don't know what to say when I'm caught under his gaze, like a butterfly whose wings flap helplessly under a magnifying glass.

His stare turns into slits. "Mind letting go of me, oh fearless one?"

I jolt, then stare at my hand. It's curled around his bicep like a lifeline with my chest pressed against the back of his arm. "Oh. I didn't realize. Sorry."

Tempest takes his time returning his stare to the clearing. I'm desperate to know what he thinks when he studies me like this, so quiet and slow, but I don't dare voice it. Mostly out of fear that I won't like his answer. *You're pathetic, princess. Go home and be afraid of the dark under the safety of your bedcovers.*

He jerks his chin toward the crowd. "They're starting the cutting ceremony. Freshman girls inevitably freak out, and the immaturity level of the boys in getting the girls to scream is truly astounding. Come on." Tempest strides ahead. He doesn't bother to see if I've caught up. "I want to find my sister, then get the fuck out of this mess."

Tempest stalks into the open space, the closest bodies scattering at his sudden invasion. A few girls trip over their own feet, then summarily pause once they see who it is, their eyelids turning heavy, their lashes fluttering as they bite their lips.

Possessiveness or fights over property have never crossed my mind until I find myself lifting my skirts and racing to Tempest's side, proving to these girls that he's—

What? Taken? By me?

Hilarious.

Yet I move to him. With him. And glare at anyone who decides to appreciate him while I'm by his side.

This is idiocy. Tempest has no interest in me, but I don't want anyone else to have him, either. Here, in this fiery clearing with drunks and partiers and strange, witchy rituals, I especially want him near.

Tempest halts. I'm so focused on other people that I ram into his back.

He gives me his profile, lips quirking in amusement, but otherwise, he remains stormy and pissed off as he scans the area for Clover.

"The fuck is she?" he mutters.

Clover's dressed in mostly black, which doesn't help us at all, but I gamely look through the undulating bodies, flames dancing on their exposed skin.

I'm distracted in my search by a huge tree stump in the middle of the crowd. A shining golden cup is placed in the middle, the ring of jewels sparking against the firelight.

Clover wasn't kidding. They're really using a chalice.

A cloaked figure hovers closest to the stump, his pale hand peeking out when he reaches up to beckon someone close. People shift into a line of sorts, waiting their turn.

I watch as a girl with auburn hair and heavy eyeliner approaches the cloak, stopping on the opposite side of the tree stump. His other hand lifts, brandishing a polished silver blade. It looks old. An ancestral part of me recognizes it as a hunting device—deadly and devastating.

The cloak straightens his arm, laying his other palm flat for the girl to clasp. She reaches forward, taking his hand. He rotates her wrist until her palm faces up, too.

I'm huddled close to Tempest, but step away from him, drawn closer to the ritual, curious.

A jaw cuts through the cloak's raised hood. Full, pink lips move in a foreign undulation. Latin, maybe.

The girl nods, smiling back at her friends, but her

mouth has a nervous twitch. She keeps her hand in his.

"A true spell has two facets." Tempest's voice comes from behind me. "The first half focuses on collecting the power. Centering it and filling the object, or the person, to be at their strongest. And the second half..."

The blade comes down, cutting through the center of her palm. Her blood pools around the cut. I watch, rapt.

"The second half," he repeats softly, "focuses on releasing that power."

She cries out, then laughs with shining, watery eyes as he turns her wrist and small droplets of her blood hit the chalice.

"This is a spell?" My voice barely registers above a whisper.

"Does this interest you, princess?" Tempest's velvet rasp hits the top of my ear.

I clench my hands at my side, refusing to give him the satisfaction of answering in the affirmative.

"Which part?" he asks quietly. "The pain of the cut or the pleasure of being included in something? I bet it was lonely in your white tower."

I feel more than see him move behind me, his fingers dancing along my upper arms and drawing me back, away from the center of the crowd.

For some reason, I move with him. Do my feet betray me by trusting where he leads, or is self-preservation kicking in, wanting to disappear into the fringes before the cloak notices and wants some of my blood, too?

"Who is that?"

"You know him as Professor Hunter Morgan," Tempest answers. I didn't realize I'd asked the question out loud. "I'm familiar with him as the biggest cum-stain on campus. But so long as he's busy slicing into co-eds, my sister can't approach him. We'll keep an eye out for her right. Here."

He draws me to a halt by allowing my back to hit his chest.

I gasp. Something hard nestles into the small of my back. Hard. Firm. Thick.

Tempest tightens his hold on my upper arms, preventing my escape.

My heart rate quickens. "Wh-What is this place? This spell?"

"You've heard of the Anderton mother and daughter. Killers who needed to be killed. Souls whom the colonists wanted to suffer eternally. Each year an alumni calls on Sarah and her nameless daughter to assist in whatever a student desires. Straight A's, attention from the hottest guy, bigger tits, a more memorable pussy..." Tempest's hands move to my shoulders, massaging idly. I hate to admit it feels *so* good. "To be touched where no one has ever touched them before."

I stiffen, despite the tendrils of shivers he spreads from my neck to my toes.

"Spells are pesky fuckers, though. They require exact incantations. Precise times. And, of course, sacrifice." His voice drifts closer as he murmurs, "What do you think that girl is willing to sacrifice for an easy A?"

"What they're doing is twisted." Honesty bubbles up to

the surface a lot easier than parsing through the feelings Tempest elicits with his fingers. "Taking the memories of tortured women and spilling blood for their own gain. What the Anderton went through, I can't bear to imagine."

Listen up, little girl, you do as I say, or you lose an ear. You scream, we take part of your tongue. You whine, and I'll go after your hymen, see if I give a fuck.

"You would know better than most," Tempest surmises. At this point, he's massaging a brick wall. I press my lips together in hopes my anguish stays where it is. Far away and buried under other people's medical degrees and pharmaceutical therapy.

Tempest continues, "You've experienced two tragedies and, in my opinion, possess more sacrifice in your pinky toe than whatever that chick has to offer."

I'm stunned at the unexpected compliment if that's indeed what it is.

"What would you ask of the Anderton women?" he asks.

"Nothing." I move to twist away, but Tempest doesn't allow me to budge. "I want nothing from this place."

"I beg to differ." His fingers dig into the soft parts of my shoulders. "Why have you come here, princess?"

The lie slips out easily. "To be with Clover. I've missed her."

"And?"

"To get the type of education I missed out on."

Tempest presses harder. I wince, but I won't give him what he so clearly wants. Begging. Capitulation. Pleading.

"There are better schools. Easier ones. You didn't need to sequester yourself in the mountains to obtain an Ivy League diploma."

"None of them have Clover. She's my best—she's the last friend I have in the world."

His grip loosens, but not by much. Maybe he believes me. I'm speaking mostly the truth.

"You're part of the reason my sister nearly died that night."

Tempest can't see my face, but I keep it blank regardless. It helps buffer the words coming out of my mouth. "It was an accident."

"What was?" Tempest's question contains curiosity, naturally, but also a cutting edge.

"The car. The driver, I mean. He swerved to miss a pedestrian and—"

"Is that all you remember?"

"I can still see Mila."

"How?"

"Lying still. Not breathing. Covered in bl—" I hitch at the memory. "Blood."

"Anything else?"

"Clover waking up. Asking me what happened, and then I ... I couldn't answer her. I wasn't me anymore. I was —I was ten again, but not with those men. Somewhere new. Foul. Another terrible place where girls die and men murder and nobody wins."

Tempest clucks his tongue. "The world is cruel, princess. It's why I will never stop asking you to slink back into your tower, cuddle up to your father, and bathe in the protection of his four solid walls. Don't for a moment think that this university contains your salvation."

"I would never. But I am jealous."

I'm as shocked at speaking the truth as Tempest is at hearing it. "Jealous of what?"

"Clover. How she's adapted to this new life without Mila and how untraumatized she is by it all."

Tempest's fingers move to my neck, stroking. I don't find them soothing. I'm certain he's exploring my delicate tendons, wondering where best to squeeze.

"Appearances are about as misleading as magicians," Tempest says. "There's something about this pathetic display of showmanship that winds me up tight." Tempest's voice travels over the top of my head. Low with bass.

"Is it the drawing of blood, do you think?" he muses. "Or could it be how you look tonight, so sparkling white and innocent among all these amateurs? Hmm."

Tempest draws in a breath. *Oh, my God, he's sniffing the top of my head. Scenting me.*

"*Fuck*, you smell good," he growls. "Fresh flowers within the ruptured ground. A full bloom among seedlings."

He grinds into the small of my back. I have trouble breathing. Instead of recoiling, I relish the sensation of him, so close to my core yet so far, creating an ache inside me that I've never needed filled before.

Causing confusion. Coaxing heat.

I squirm on my feet, staring forward and keeping my body stiff as a board. I don't know what's happening. I thought Tempest hated me or, at the very least, was annoyed by his little sister's best friend. Fragile, pathetic, stupid.

"I can hear your thoughts, you know," he mutters close to my ear. I close my eyes, shivering. "You're much too hard on yourself, princess, when I can be hard enough for us both."

My lips part. It's almost impossible to keep staring forward and pretending deep interest in the next boy who steps up to Professor Morgan, offering his hand and guffawing at the sight of the knife. "Yo, you think this'll get me the train of chicks I want for Christmas?"

"I don't enjoy being distracted by you, especially at this moment," Tempest mutters over the dumbass. I try to whirl on him, to demand he let me go home, but he holds me rigid in front of him, grinding against me casually like he's testing out my worth.

"I-I don't want this."

Tempest chuckles, his hot breath playing with the strands of hair at my nape. "You tell me you're not afraid, yet here you are, trembling at the mere sensation of my dick up against your ass."

I search desperately for what a cooler, more confident girl would say in my position. Tempest always brings out the worst in me, those insecure nuggets that I'm not good enough, that I'm stupid and deserving of my fate.

"Against my *costume*," I correct him. "Your dick is up

against my thick, multilayered dress that barely feels your little—"

His hand moves from my arm, and in the seconds it takes to go from left to right, he's undone the zipper at my back.

"No!" I clutch at the front of my gown, terrified he's about to expose me in front of *everyone*.

His resultant laughter contains true glee. *I hate him. God, I hate this man.* "Relax, princess. I'm not about to show anyone my prize. Not one fucking soul will see you the way I do. Ever."

Tempest's hand moves into my dress, flicking against my underwear and diving under the straps.

"Tempest—" I gasp.

"Why do I love the way you say my name?" he muses into my neck. He tastes the line of my nape, then behind my ear. His words become tangible when he whispers them at the shell of my ear, their meaning cascading down my body in shivers. My head drops back, close to his beating, black heart. "I have more important things to do. But I don't want to do any of them until I've got you out of my system."

"I ... don't..."

"Finish your sentence, princess. You don't what?" His hand drifts across my hips, then spreads flat against my stomach to pull me tighter against his chest. No, against his —his—*you know.*

I'm hyper-focused on Tempest's pinky finger and the sensation of it going down, past my pelvis, into my pubic hair.

"There are people. Someone will see." My voice barely has sound. It's mostly breath and a whole lot of panting.

"If anyone decides to tear their eyes away from Morgan's fucked-up Satan circus, that'll be the best day of my life. Until then ... hmm." Another finger wanders in with the first, finding my folds. "If I were you, I'd be more concerned that if you can't fit my fingers in, you definitely won't be able to fit my cock."

Horror almost chokes me. "You can't. You *wouldn't*."

I might as well have dared him. Tempest slides one finger in as easily as parting through silk. I'm wet for him. If I'm honest, I became wet the instant he peeled out of the shadows and into my path.

Yet I'll never admit it.

"Do you want to know how many of my fingers it takes to become the size of my cock?"

My knees give out. I'm held still purely by Tempest's determination to unravel me.

True to his promise, he slips another finger in, then another, before stroking in and out and thumbing the most sensitive part of me to take it along for the ride, too.

"Te-Tempest..." I breathe out. My eyelids feel heavy. My tongue is like butter against my teeth. I'm electrified and soothed all at the same time, and my instinct to meet his thrusts happens instantly.

"There's a good girl," Tempest says into my ear. His breaths are harsher. His words raspier. "Decadent, sweet, and all for me. You have no idea how much I needed this after tonight."

"Don't stop." My attention's tilted to the stars as I fall back against him, his fingers dancing expertly into my core.

He slips another one in.

"You're tight." Tempest curses. "Fuck, the idea of fitting my dick into you right now ... You'd scream, cry, then beg for more."

"And you?" I hitch out, gyrating with him, so close, so *close...* "What would you do?"

He laughs, tight and uncomfortable. I'm not the only one wanting to come. "It's a lot to take, isn't it? Imagine the whole of me inside you, princess." Tempest bites my shoulder. Instead of yelping, I moan. "Oh, good *girl*. You like the pain I bring you. The promise of sex."

"Y-You didn't answer my question."

"I don't have to when it's perfectly obvious I'd fuck you until you passed out. That's how much I want you."

The idea of Tempest actually wanting me, the *revelation* causes me to bite back a loud moan, but the spread of butterflies in my middle won't allow me to stifle such beauty.

I buck against him. My hands move to where he's nestled his arm under my dress, and I hold him there. I hold him so I can ride him.

Tempest's breaths are shorter. Brutal. My hair blows against my cheek with every sharp exhale of his. Someone cries out, another cut to a nameless palm. "I want to time your pleasure perfectly with their pain. Ready, princess?"

"Yes." I couldn't deny him if I tried.

"I can't hear you."

"I'm ready."

"Ready for what?"

His torture is endless. Tempest lets me keep his arm against my stomach, but his fingers are still.

My answer comes out in a desperate flow, words tumbling, breaths cutting out. "I'm ready for you. I want all of you. I don't care who sees."

Tempest makes a sound low in his throat, and thank God, his fingers resume their exquisite stroking. He slows when another approaches Morgan, then quickens when the blade is drawn high.

"Watch the knife. Witness the cut," Tempest breathes. "When you come, I want your eyes to be on the blood that falls from their skin. Do you understand me?"

"Yes." I'm nearly begging now. "I won't look away. I won't—"

My heart's given wings when the orgasm comes, taking flight while the rest of my body stays behind and dissipates into the ground. "Oh my—oh my—"

"You cry out with *them*," Tempest demands. "You don't get any pleasure without the spilling of their blood."

The why of it, the reasons Tempest wants this, I don't care to know. Not anymore. Not like this. Maybe later, when my sanity comes down from the clouds, but until then, I'll do whatever he wants so I can keep this feeling for eternity.

Another girl screams when she's tackled by a guy wearing a ...

I drop my chin, awareness dripping through my ecstasy like poison. "Is that an animal skull on his face?"

"Welcome to Titan Falls." I hear the smile in Tempest's voice. His fingers dig into my sensitive flesh, curling and pinching. I wince, but I'm too flushed not to love it.

Tempest digs his thumbnail into my clit. This time, I cry out in pain.

He removes his hand and zips me up with the ease of a salesperson assisting someone in their changing room. Tempest comes around to my front, making sure I see his shiny fingers. And the specks of blood on his thumb.

He sucks them one by one, keeping our eyes locked until he reaches his thumb. "Those idiots can have their witches and risk their luck with black magic. What I'm getting is so much sweeter." Tempest exposes his tongue, then drags his thumb across it, collecting my juices. My blood. "I have your innocence, princess. And I'm going to do with it whatever I please."

I have to internally talk myself out of agreeing with him, the fugue of the most intense orgasm of my life rendering me weightless, pliable, and *his*.

Tempest bites the pad of his thumb, his grin crooked and irresistible. "Your greatest mistake was enrolling here and putting yourself back on my radar. You were better off without me, Ardyn Kaine." He reaches out to stroke the side of my face. My lashes flutter at the contact. "It's too bad you'll have to lose a crucial piece of yourself to realize that."

Tempest walks backward, then turns, roaring over the crowd, "Clover! Get the fuck out here. We're going home."

And I'm left to collect the pieces of myself Tempest scattered all over the decaying forest floor.

15

TEMPEST

"We have to get rid of her."

Miguel's office door bangs against the wall from the force of my entry.

"Oh?" He doesn't look up from his papers as I spread out in one of the wingback chairs in front of his desk.

I force myself to say her name. "Ardyn Kaine is a problem."

It's risky to mention her to Miguel—again—and draw continuous attention to her, but after last night's party, I'm left with little option.

"For whom?" Miguel raises his gaze enough to stare pointedly at my tapping foot. I force it still.

An unwelcome voice adds behind me, "If her attendance at our university pisses you off so much, why didn't you kill her along with the friend when you had the chance?"

My upper lip twitches. I stifle the urge to leap over my chair and bang his forehead against a stack of books.

"How nice that you're here, Hunter," I say, gripping the armrests. "I was sure you'd be nursing the tits of some co-ed while asking her to wear your goat mask this morning."

"Ah, if you knew me at all, Storm Cloud, you'd know I jacked off over three of them last night before they licked my cum off each other's bellies."

Miguel curls his lip in distaste. I mime blowing my pinky and sticking my tongue in my cheek, to which Miguel holds up his finger in warning. Why *I* get reprimanded while this asshole behind me prances around with his small dick and big mouth is beyond comprehension.

"How much longer is this prick in our lives?" I ask Miguel.

"For about as long as it takes for you to be a big boy and tell a girl to *weave you awone.*" Hunter adopts the pitch of a toddler, and this time, I give myself full permission to bolt out of my seat and ram him against the bookshelf.

Snarling, Hunter aims a punch at my kidney, which I dodge, then land an uppercut to the back of his neck.

Hunter sprawls to the floor. I quirk my lips in satisfaction. Then he ruins it by rising from the ground, cackling. Fucking cackling.

"You're a sick motherfucker," I say, stepping over him. I fix my cuffs, then resume my seat.

"And you are both immature burdens on my otherwise satisfactory life," Miguel says dryly as he watches the tussle. "Can I ask why the two of you are ruining my morning coffee break?"

"I'm concerned over my comrade's loyalties," Hunter says, smoothing his slacks. "Storm Cloud didn't participate in last night's ritual. He was too busy trying to fuck damaged goods."

A wildfire spreads from my gut to the backs of my eyes. I'd like to roast Hunter where he stands and use his ribs as my pitchfork. "Call her that again, *think* about her one more time, and I will personally ensure you meet one of your coveted Anderton witches after I carve out your—"

"*Enough!*" Miguel's roar cuts between us. Rising from his seat, he slams his palms into his desk so resolutely that the paperweights rattle. "I did not sign on to be your mother hen to prevent you two from pecking each other to death. You're meant to be above all this. I rotted in hell for *years* to become this, and you two have the gall to insult our ethos and shit all over our traditions, and for what? To see who can piss the farthest?"

Only Miguel possesses the power to shut me up. The veins in his arms bulge with temper, a particularly big one making it to the center of his forehead. It's no secret within our Outfit that Miguel worked his way up from the streets —first as a messenger, and then, once he'd proven himself a cold-blooded killer, to a soldier who fucked up, was exiled to this university, and then ultimately paved his path to the current lieutenant of the Vultures. We're known in our circle as cast-offs and mistakes. Still, we've made infamy by picking at the bones of our enemies and feasting on their rotted meat by leaving them as messages for our future targets to see. After witnessing how far Miguel would go to protect his men, I have no doubt in his capabilities to exact particular and immediate punishment.

I don't come from the streets, but I've emerged from another kind of filth. Dirty money, a twisted father, and an initiation into a cult in high school that would make even the goat fucker over here blush.

Miguel has earned my respect, a moniker very few individuals claim. In the few short years under his tutelage, he's become more of a father to me than my own. It's for that reason alone that I shut my mouth and allow Hunter to run his.

"I don't get distracted," Hunter defends. "Unlike Storm Cloud. You want me to gut, mutilate, and kill? I'm your guy. A pretty lady doesn't factor into it. I can fuck and fulfill my duties all day. It's why I can so easily see that *you*"—he points at me—"need a serious wake-up call."

"That is my decision to make," Miguel warns. "And as yet, Tempest does not require it."

I give a curt nod in thanks.

"Though I do agree Tempest's lines are currently blurred."

I pull in my brows. "Excuse me?"

Miguel leans back knowingly, folding his arms across his chest. "Your sister. You didn't want to leave her as the only remaining runt of her tiny litter of friends and left her one to play with instead of cleaning up the mess entirely.

Well, son, now you must endure the consequences, as any effort on my part to expel Miss Kaine from the premises will be openly studied by the higher-ups."

"How so? We beat and torture assholes on campus with no problem. Why can't we get rid of a girl?" I ask.

Miguel cocks a dark brow. "Ardyn Kaine has an impeccable academic record. She comes from a family of great wealth and influence." After what must be a surprised look on my face, he adds, "Yes, I've looked into her, considering both our reactions when we learned she was here. Unless you can get her to quit, she's staying, and I am none too happy about it."

I roll my eyes. Sometimes, he plays the role of an obnoxious professor too well. Hunter rocks back on his heels, but whether it's gleeful or frustrated, I'll never know. I try not to read too much into the body language of ritualistic psychopaths.

"Her gap year hasn't prevented her from keeping up with her studies," Miguel continues. "It seems the part of her brain housing cognitive skills wasn't too affected by your implosion of her reality. I can't very well ask the chancellor to remove Miss Kaine with all this"—he taps a thick folder at his righthand side—"in her favor. You'll have to get creative, Tempest."

"I'll force her out."

Miguel chuckles. "Do what you will. Just don't involve the Outfit. Am I making myself clear?"

I grunt an affirmative.

It's not enough for Miguel. His eyes narrow. "Do not,

under any circumstances, put into question what happened that night. I've granted you enough leeway by condoning the continued protection of your sister. A year is a long time to have passed, but it's not enough. It never is. If by some measure, more information was passed between the dead girl and the two remaining girls, then I can't promise their lives won't be snuffed out, too. Your priority should be protecting the Outfit, Tempest. Hunter is not wrong. Your sister has too much of your heart as it is. Don't lose the rest to a mistake."

My hands curl on the armrests, my right one dry and sticky from my saliva and *her*. "I never said anything about developing feelings."

"Could've fooled me."

I snarl at Hunter. He grins in response. "Listen, I'm the first to approve of dirtying up a cute girl. But I saw how you looked at her last night. You'd best leave it at that."

"Just what I need. Advice from a warlock." I push to my feet, visibly thrumming with the urge to unleash my frustration.

"We're watching you, Storm Cloud."

"Correction, *I'm* watching you," Miguel says while leveling a silencing glare at Hunter. He crosses his arms and, while standing, creates an imposing figure. One that's supposed to remind me who's in charge.

When in life will I ever make independent decisions? I wonder idly as I head to the door. When one boss is destroyed, another takes their place. Fucking cockroaches, all of them. Ones I'm sadly forced to work under.

"Aw, is our meeting over?" Hunter asks. Whether he realizes it or not, he's mimicked Miguel's posture of crossed arms and a stiff back. Yet his lean, tattooed form will never measure up to Miguel's muscle and my scars.

"For now," I say. "Sadly, you've given me an idea."

"I have?" Hunter's eyes light up. "Yippee. Do I get to participate?"

I palm his chest and shove him out of the way. "No."

"Be discreet, son," Miguel says.

I make no promises and slam the door behind me.

I think of Anderton Cottage as a deliberate outcast. It doesn't sit with the rest of the buildings at TFU. Instead, it's nestled in the forest fringes at the base of a mountain. Getting to it isn't as easy as most students' jaunts from their dorms to their classes. The pathway to it is curved, wild, and always dark from the copse of trees, refusing to let enough sunlight in for flowers to grow.

Some say the permanent decay of the forest floor is because of the Anderton witches' constant spells to keep trespassers out of their business. Others argue the rotting trees and blackened, slime-coated leaves already existed, and the Anderton women knew a proper home base when they saw one.

When the two witches were killed, a nobleman bought up the land and gifted it to his wife to do as she pleased. She chose to create a college-aged school for all the colonial men drifting onto American shores. One would think, with a bountiful number of men to conquer, the witches would be forgotten, but of course they weren't. Rumors of hauntings, discoveries of old bones, animal and human, and the constant smell of strange herbs mixing with death pervaded campus, alluring the curious and frightening the aristocrats. When women were permitted an education, those stories only grew. Women have always been the most curious and entirely cunning when figuring out men's secretive shit. The first class of women at TFU found the Anderton Cottage, tucked away and overgrown like it was desperate to be forgotten. The next wave of women were the unfortunate ones who discovered the hidden rooms.

Nowadays, Anderton House is a dorm of sorts for people like me. Post-grads, TAs, visiting professors. Anyone lucky enough to be clueless about its history or purposely present to devour its violence can stay within its walls. There are five bedrooms, one of which is mine, and that's what I'm aiming for when I step through the stone cottage to find it blissfully empty.

"Hey."

Fuck. Almost empty.

"What's up?" I lift my chin in greeting while dumping my bag on the ground by the front door.

Rio snuffs out his cigarette, flicking out the open window before leaving his perch and coming over. "Why do you look like someone stole all your weed?"

"Hunter."

Rio doesn't need anything else to decipher my meaning. His mouth twists in sympathy. "The turd."

Rio is as familiar with Hunter as I am. In an unfortunate twist of fuckery, Hunter lives here, too. It's only the luck of the draw that our schedules are the opposite of one another's.

"Can I help?" Rio asks as he follows me up the stairs.

He doesn't trail me like a puppy. Riordan Hughes is the one true friend I have left, more of a brother than a best buddy. We've gone through a lot of shit together and are likely to experience more. While the rest of our group was smart enough to escape this life after boarding school, Rio and I fell back into it. The familiarity of violence was more comforting than the foreign effort it took to become normal. Who could thrive in that life, anyway? We were born in violence, taught to manipulate before we made it out of diapers, and held knives with more precision than writing tools. I'm not meant for better or more.

I've long ago accepted I'm destined to destroy. It's really too ironic that the one time I was kind, it's come back to bite me.

"Miguel gave us a talking-to," I explain as we traverse the second floor. My room is the last door, dead center at the dead end. "Nothing I haven't sat through before."

"I thought last night went fine." Rio ambles past me once I unlock my door. The room is sparse, containing bare essentials like a bed, desk, and wardrobe. It's the only one with an en suite bathroom. Hunter tried to suffocate me with a pillow the first night so he could snag the room, but too bad for him, I don't sleep. I only pretend to since it convinces people I'm as human as they are.

"Cartwright was an easy kill," I admit and stretch out on the bed, folding my arms behind my head and staring at the stone ceiling where cracks grow into obvious fractures. "It was the party afterward. That black magic ritual shit that makes Hunter constantly want to jerk off."

"Yeah, sorry I missed it."

Rio isn't apologetic at all. He's the quieter one of us two, less snarky and more internal. He prefers the solitude of a haunted forest, whereas I actively go looking for who I can piss off next.

"Ardyn Kaine was there," I confess, focusing on the ceiling. Maybe if I follow the cracks, they'll lead me to another option.

"Does that mean Clover was, too?"

I break my focus to glance over at him with a frown. Nobody mentions Clover and gets too far in life. "I take it you remember who Ardyn is, then."

"Sure. Clo's best friend. She was in the car when you delivered the hit."

Rio doesn't know that I chose to save Ardyn and killed Mila instead—no one fucking does. Until I have an answer for it myself, I'm keeping that deadly secret locked down, even from my brotherhood. As a Vulture, Rio's aware of that night, and while Miguel kept the reasons behind my orders on lock, the Vultures are up to date on kills. Miguel's boss allows him to seek out personal vendettas. What he did to earn that trust I can only speculate on, but

I guarantee it's because Miguel proved his worth in a glaring act

Rio moves to my single window, though there's not much to stare at. The trees are so gnarled and overgrown, there's no view, and shockingly, I've decided against a professional landscape of the place. "That night's always stayed with me."

"Why? You weren't even there, man." I resume my glare at the ceiling.

"They were girls. She was just a kid. We don't usually go after that gender or that age group."

"You don't go after it at all." I lift on my elbow, studying him closely. Rio is our scout and investigator all rolled into one. Not that he's too soft-hearted for kills—I've seen him slice and dice like the rest of us—but he's just plain smarter than many dudes who try to beat us. He sets up the time and place, delivers the targets, and we do the rest. "Do I have to remind you never to question Miguel Rossi?"

"So you're saying if he ordered you to kill Clo, you would've?"

I push off the bed, the rumble in my throat growing in intensity. "I've had my share of tussles this morning, but my dance card isn't full yet."

Rio doesn't back down. His dark, shaggy cut matches the dark brown of his eyes, becoming one with this place about as well as I stand out. I half-believe if I try to punch him, I'll only hit shadow.

He persists, "So why'd you do it to her friend? Why'd you break Clo's heart?"

"Why the fuck do you care?" Rio is the sole person who could ask that question and wake up tomorrow.

"Because she's your blood, man, and what's yours is mine to protect, too."

My shoulders relax. Slightly. I take a beat, collecting my thoughts because it's not in me to tell the whole truth. It never is. "I know what that girl saw, and it was enough to make me agree to Miguel's orders." I gruffly turn away from Rio's questioning stare. "That's all you're getting out of me. Go away and let me sleep. I've had a long fucking night."

"I'll go. When you answer one more question."

"Fuck me," I groan, falling face-first on the bed.

"If this shit was all sorted a year ago, how was your night ruined by this chick? Why does Ardyn Kaine still matter?"

Because she's better at hauntings than these goddamn witches. Because I can't leave her alone. Because when I saw her dressed in white, all I wanted to do was mark her up and make her mine.

Because I saved her.

Rio doesn't wait for me to answer. "You get this way when there are loose ends, Tempest. I'm not enjoying the panic button my brain is pressing right now."

"You want somewhere for that binary head of yours to go, snag me my laptop. Help me break through a few firewalls and get all the information I can on Ardyn Kaine's childhood kidnapping."

Rio cocks his head.

I sigh. Alas, I am still the sharpest one out of all these

fucking tools. "You can help me with my master plan." I fall back onto the bed, re-folding my arms behind my head and pretending these past few minutes never happened. "I will break Ardyn Kaine for the second time and get her committed for good."

16

ARDYN

Rain plinks against the window, the white noise rush of it flowing through my ears and into my dreams.

Rolling to my side, the down comforter wraps around me like a cocoon. I'm warm and safe, drifting through dreamscape images within the healing arms of sleep.

Mila's hair is wet with blood.

Her neck doesn't look right—her head at an odd angle.

Footsteps. Unhurried. Black military boots coming to a stop at her shoulder.

What are you doing? Help me. No. Please!

I'm in a chair. Bound. A sack covers my head. My feet don't touch the floor. They dangle uselessly until I lift them for a kick. Rough laughter follows. I'm grabbed by the ankle and pulled, the chair legs squealing alongside my screams.

I'm smacked across the face.

Behave, and we won't have to kill you. Be a good girl, and you might like what comes next.

I bolt upright in bed, clutching the covers under my chin. The rain comes harder, the soothing plinks sounding more like smacks against the windowpane like someone is trying to get my attention. To get through.

I scrunch my eyes shut.

Breathe in one, two, three...

After a few agonizing minutes, my labored breaths slow. I'm able to open my eyes, my vision adjusting to the darkness, and to calm myself, I take inventory of my room.

A simple dresser. The twin bed I'm sleeping on. The door. *Always locate the exit.*

Clover shifts on the other side of the room. She's on her side, facing the wall and sleeping soundly.

The darkness doesn't scare her. She covets it, even worships it. After experiencing the same thing I did, losing the same friend, she's managed to keep her peace.

My cheek tickles. I swipe at it, and my fingers come away wet. I curl them into my palm, biting my trembling lips and telling myself that our journeys are different. Clover's experience wasn't compounded by a past abduction. She was under the protection of unconsciousness a lot longer than I was in that car.

Why can I hear Mila's screams, and she can't?

A *bang* jolts me where I sit. Clutching the covers tighter, I instinctively twist toward the sound coming from the window.

A tree branch. That has to be the sound. Maybe thunder,

too. Or someone dropped something next door. Any number of things that don't involve sinister intent.

I'm in school. Safe in a dorm surrounded by cameras and mountains. Clover's right beside me.

Clover was also beside me when Mila died.

Moonlight travels through the window's glass, speckling my white comforter and whiter skin with the raindrops' black silhouettes. I count them to calm myself—I don't want to wake Clover and have to explain and make her worry. The last thing I want is for her to wonder, like a lot of other people here, if I can handle the pressures of college. Worse, I don't want her thinking I can't tolerate being away from my parents, my bodyguard, my *tower.*

I count to ten before I notice an oddity. An unnatural gap between drops and the odd, jagged rivulets that come after.

I glance back at the window.

Then scream.

Clover shoots up from bed. "What? *What?*"

With a trembling finger, I point at the wet handprint on our window, being cut into pieces by heavy rivulets of rain.

I swear it's steaming, the print so hot and evil, it lingers long after it should have dissolved.

"Ardyn, I don't—I don't understand what you're pointing at. The window? Outside?"

"Don't you see it?" I whisper.

"See what?" Clover slides out of bed, pressing a hand to her chest. "You're scaring the Jesus out of me."

"Someone was here."

"In our room?" Clover stands, her delicate hands clenching into fists. "Where? Did he sneak under the bed? Come out, *pervert!*" She roundhouse kicks her bedframe.

It'd be hilarious if I weren't so beside myself with terror. "No. Outside. They're outside."

Clover rises from her quick crouch to check under her bed. "What?"

"The—the hand—" Is long gone by the time Clover glances over. "There was a handprint. Someone was looking through the window. At us."

Clover gives me a wary stare but gamely steps to our singular window and peers out. "We're on the third floor. I don't know how someone could scale the flat exterior unless you saw Spider-Man."

She doesn't mean it the way it sounds, yet her statement sends a flare into my chest, that sick, poisonous spread feeling of not being believed.

"They must've climbed up a tree." My explanation comes out sharper than I intended.

Clover doesn't flinch, nor does she turn away from the window. "No ... I don't think so. There aren't any branches close enough to bear a person's weight. This part of TFU is pretty well manicured, too. Ardyn..." She turns.

I shift until I give her my profile, unable to take being fully under her anxious scope.

She asks gently, "Was it a nightmare, do you think?"

I shake my head. "I was wide awake. There was a bang at our window, and I looked over and saw a handprint! It was big, like a man's. Four fingers, one thumb, and a palm."

God, it's like I'm trying to prove it's a human instead of something supernatural. I press my lips shut, refusing to further make a fool out of myself.

"Actually, you're not the first to see something like that." Clover moves from the window to my bed, perching next to me and rubbing my thigh.

"You don't have to humor me. Maybe it was a bad dream." It sure as hell was *not*, but I've long since learned not to press an issue that no one else believes. Especially when they're wearing scrubs.

"Do I look like the type of girl to humor people?" Clover arches an ebony brow, resembling her brother to such an extent that I force myself to control my inhale. "It's been happening for decades, students reporting seeing unexplained handprints. On windows, doors, walls, sometimes in blood, other times in water. They say it's one of the Anderton witches' spirits marking you for death."

It's enough to get me to raise my head. "Is this meant to make me feel better?"

She laughs, squeezing my thigh. "Yes. No. Probably. None of those people who claimed to see those prints died."

"How do you know for sure?"

She pats my leg. "I'm more in the know of TFU's dark history than you are, so take my word for it. It's superstition, and something assholes like me enjoy using to terrify unsuspecting students."

I slide my gaze to the window, gnawing on my lower lip. The ghostly shape is long gone, replaced by more *splats* of broken raindrops.

"Tell you what, come with me into town after our classes today. There's a New Age shop I'd like to explore, and we'll collect ourselves a few crystals to purify and protect our room."

I screw my face up. "I don't believe in that stuff."

"I didn't think so, either, but you were sure taking my Anderton curse to heart a few seconds ago. What'll be the harm? Maybe it'll even help you sleep better."

"I know what I—" I stop myself. This is the mantra of my life. *I know what I saw.* It's a lonely statement, one I've learned not to employ unless desperate, and with Clover, I'm not.

"If you believe you can help me with voodoo, who am I to stop you?"

She smacks me lightly on the outer thigh. "Healing crystals are *not* voodoo. Look." Clover pulls at a chain on her neck until a glittering, pink crystal bar encased in a circle of small diamonds emerges from under her T-shirt. "Rose quartz. I have this on me at all times. It's meant to promote love, healing, and sucks out any negative feelings that weigh you down."

I stare at it suspiciously as it glints within her fingers.

"Do you see me having nightmares and becoming terri-fied of third-story windows?"

I pull my lips to one side. Clover has a point. Wasn't I admiring her peaceful acceptance of a traumatic experience a few moments ago, too?

"Fine. I'll go with you."

She smiles, her face somehow beaming through the

night. I bend around her once she stands to rifle through my bedside drawer. "Until then, I'll take some Xanax."

Usually, I'm averse to my pills, considering I had them shoved down my throat involuntarily for months. But my need to fall back asleep and not be haunted by old memories reshaping my dreams outweighs my principles. I shake two tablets out of the bottle and dry swallow them both.

Clover watches my movements quietly. Probably thought she could heal me so much better if given the time to work me over and convince me that becoming one with nature is better than any chemical.

Maybe she's right. I have nothing to lose except for the one trait I fought like hell to regain—my sanity. A part of staying at TFU is to show everyone that I'm fine. If that means learning Clover's Wiccan practices and letting her fuss over me until she's satisfied I won't speak gibberish to her again, then fine. I'll do it.

It's not her I'll have to act my best in front of.

It's her brother.

I know what I saw.

After getting ready for the day, Clover and I split off in front of our dorms. My walk to class is more of a trudge, my brain a hard mix of grogginess from the Xanax, twitchiness from my nightmares, and paranoia from what I'm now terming "the Hand." My attention is scattered but aware, diving from side to side and clocking anyone who walks too close to me.

No one pays me any mind, most wearing headphones or beanies to drown out the rumbling gray clouds. The quad is wet and smells like dead leaves and smoke as stragglers drop their cigarettes and head into the buildings at the last minute.

I make it into the business building before it starts to drizzle again. Sadly, my hair did not make the trek undamaged. The electricity in the air from held-in lightning frizzed my ends, and I pull the scrunchie from my wrist and tie it into a low, messy bun as I take a seat in Rossi's class.

Rossi isn't late this time, walking in right behind me. His confident footsteps release lightning into my spine. I have to coax myself down from the ceiling, internally berating my lack of poker face.

Knock it off. He's just a professor.

"All right, folks, I have your first papers right here." Rossi pats a stack of stapled and spiral-bound essays once he reaches the head of the table. He scans everyone seated. I can't help it—when he reaches me I hold my breath, otherwise chanting at myself to stay blank, calm, and blasé. My worries are unfounded when his disinterested gaze glides past me and to my neighbor, cataloging me as any other student.

He's handsome. I'll give him that. All cut cheekbones and sharpened jaw. His eyes are like dark chocolate. Not the kind that melts, but the kind of chocolate bar you leave in the fridge so long, it becomes hard and brittle with a white, frosted cast over the sweet bitterness. Miguel Rossi also has height on his side and broad, intimidating shoulders that his suit jacket can't quite contain. I can see why Clover thinks he's sexy—the silver wings of hair at his temples and his brown-black waves held back from his forehead like he just casually scraped it back with his fingers. A few lines on his forehead and crinkles around his eyes make him seem mature and experienced, not old.

"I must say, I'm impressed with most of you," Rossi continues, his rich baritone captivating all pronouns in the class. "I read every paper, and Mr. Callahan took a second pass, deciding on the grades."

Two damning words snap me out of my study of the man. *Tempest* and *grades*. A light sweat grows under my arms, nerves warring with fear as Tempest enters the room with a folder tucked under his arm.

He's dressed in a casual black tee and dark denim and is smaller in stature than Rossi with paler skin and shrewder eyes. Yet ... my gaze falls on him and doesn't move, even while Rossi goes on about skill levels and what he expects from us.

I really should be writing this down. I'm adept at lists, often planning out my days weeks in advance. What else is there to do when you're locked in a room, either in a mansion or a facility?

My fingers don't move for my pen.

Tempest slides in next to Rossi, his head down, his expression tense. A piece of hair falls onto his forehead. He impatiently shoves it back.

His eyes dart up.

I was so busy staring at his fingers and how he buried them in his thick hair that I'm caught red-handed, my thoughts as clear as the flush on my face.

Those fingers were in me. Stroked and collected and pleased.

Those surreal green eyes do not contain an intensity. Just a flatness, like a shark's. Alive enough to approach a fish and snap it in half with the barest of bite.

I swallow.

"Tempest? Mind handing out the papers?"

Tempest breaks our stare. I can breathe. *I can breathe.*

He strolls around the rectangular table, starting on the other side and slowly, painfully, fanning through the papers in his hands before laying them in front of the right person. Rossi begins today's lecture, but between the sorting out my brain has to do with Rossi and watching Tempest take a lap slower than the elderly patient who paused in my hallway at regular intervals to clip his toenails with his teeth, I'm having a tough time paying attention.

The girl across from me sees her grade laid out before her, then crooks her finger at Tempest. He bends down, bringing his head close to hers, and they murmur together.

A swell rises in my throat. It burns. Makes me feel sick. And it's completely foreign to me. It's only when Tempest looks up, catches my expression, and smirks that the swell boils down to a piece of coal in my stomach.

After fifteen minutes, or maybe the entire ninety,

Tempest stops behind me. His scent is the first to catch my attention. Heady, cinnamon-like, and cut with rain. He steps close to my chair. I don't have to turn around to sense his proximity. A heat sizzles between my shoulders, the small hairs at the back of my neck and down my arm standing with unseen electricity in the air. It's like Tempest bottled the lightning from the bloated clouds outside and uncapped it behind me, striking me stiff. Overstimulating my senses.

The rustle of papers at my back is louder than it should be as well as the slide of my essay onto the table. His arm brushes the top of my shoulder. I have to close my eyes at the rush of feeling, a mixture of awareness and fight-or-flight. I did neither the last time we saw each other.

I submitted.

Cold air hits the side of my face. Tempest has moved on. I slump in my seat and exhale any electricity Tempest may have left behind.

Then I see it.

Honestly, I shouldn't have missed the glaring, fat red D-minus on the corner of my pain-staking essay that I worked hours on. I blink once, then twice, hoping I'm hallucinating.

"That ends our class. I expect you to be prepared next week when we begin our analysis."

I stare at my paper, unmoving. Students pack up around me, and I register laughs and groans of disappointment. No one says a word about their grade until Rossi leaves.

I don't have anyone to talk to about my grade, so I just keep staring at it. Even as the last student leaves. Even when Rossi supplies a curt, "I expected better from you, Miss Kaine," before leaving.

"Problem?"

I'm able to peel my gaze from my essay and to the head of the table where Tempest sits in Rossi's seat, his legs crossed at the ankle on the table and his arms folded behind his head, exposing the hard lines of muscle under his biceps. That piece of hair has flopped onto his forehead again.

Not even his unnerving good looks can distract me from my horror.

"This is a D."

One corner of his lips curves. "A D-minus, actually."

"Why?" I carefully place my palms flat on the table on either side of my essay. As if I can defend it better by protecting it.

"It's obvious, isn't it? Your paper sucked."

"My *paper* is above-average and contained every point necessary to prove my argument."

Tempest tongues his cheek, bored. "Correction: your essay was bland, uninspired, and as I somberly informed Professor Rossi, contained direct quotes from Wikipedia."

I fly to my feet. "That is *not true!*"

Tempest grins. "There she is."

This is exactly what he wants. My meltdown. My useless frustration over his misplaced power move. And I'm falling right into it. "Why do you feel the need to screw me over at every turn?"

"Why do you feel the need to stay here *despite* my

fucking you over at every turn?" Tempest leans forward, folding his arms on the desk, peering up at me like I'm a curious bird watching him from a tree branch. "I fuck you on the inside," he continues quietly.

Heat builds under my skin. Humiliation clashes with sweet remembrance.

"I fuck you on the outside. I'll keep fucking you in all the ways that count, princess, until you fucking leave this school."

"I won't do it." I hold my arms rigid at my sides.

Tempest's amusement vanishes. He stands, leaning over the table. "This isn't the place for you."

"You don't get to make that decision for me." *I'm tired of people telling me what to do.*

"Don't I?" Tempest angles his head. "Tell me, how did you sleep last night?"

I can control my breathing, but the numbing in my face, the rush of blood to my cheeks, gives Tempest all the information he needs.

He smiles with the devil's satisfaction.

"There are two reasons people come to this school," he says. "The first because they're lucky enough to get in and claim an exclusive, private education." Tempest rounds the table toward me. The backs of my legs hit my chair, and the scraping sound that follows only fuels his desire to scare me.

"The second," he continues, a soft, beckoning lilt to his tone, "is because they want to see if all the ghost stories are true. The hauntings, the horror, the torture. Do you hear the screams through the trees, princess?" He stalks closer. *Scrape, scrape, scrape* of the chair legs as I retreat. "Are you privy to the ghosts that scratch their nails across walls and imprint their death faces on fogged glass? I'm told Sarah Anderton's frozen expression is a particularly traumatizing one. But you'd know all about trauma, wouldn't you?"

"You're sick," I manage to say through trembling lips. "All I want to do is get my life back. Get the education I deserve. I'm not hurting you. I could be invisible to you if you'd let me."

He's close enough to drag a finger down my cheek. Cold, calloused, and too close to my lips. "That is the opposite of what I desire."

The back of my head bumps against the wall. Tempest corners me, one palm resting against the wall beside my head and his thumb dragging across my lower lip.

He dips his head, and I'm able to see the flecks of gold in his green eyes. Fool's gold. There is no true shine within him. "If the other night taught you anything, it's that I like to toy with you. You'll continue to be my plaything until the day you can't take it anymore. Plenty of schools would take pity on a sad story such as yours. You don't need TFU to get a decent education."

"Clover's here."

"*I'm* here," he growls. His hand moves from my mouth to my chest, cupping my breast through the thin fabric of my shirt, flicking my nipple.

I gasp, arching instinctively.

Tempest leans into my ear. "Where you go, trouble

follows." *Flick.* I swallow a moan. Tell myself not to close my eyes. "The night Mila died should've proved to you we are not meant to be a group of friends."

And just like that, ice water splashes over the heat.

"You left my sister and me in peace for two years. We had a wonderful life without you."

Tempest pinches my nipple. Hard. Yelping, I grip his wrist to pull him away.

He palms my sore breast and pushes me into the wall. Not violently, but firmly, as a warning. "Keep it that way. Don't make me go through all this effort to show you what you already know: you're not strong. You never were."

Hot tears gather in my eyes, blurring Tempest into a cruel painting. An artist with a savage hand created him. "You have no idea what I've fought for. I'm not crazy. I didn't hallucinate that night. You have no idea who—I know what I—"

"What?" Tempest peers closer at me, a firm line to his lips. "You know *what,* Ardyn?"

The door to the classroom swings open, a large body filling the doorway. "Tempest? You coming?"

I sag under Professor Rossi's calm voice. An irony, for sure—relaxing under the interruption of someone else who makes me uncomfortable. But when faced with Tempest's cruelty, it's the lesser of two evils.

Rossi looks between us, suspicion turning his eyes into slits. "Everything all right, Miss Kaine?"

Tempest steps back, shoving his hands in his pockets

like he hadn't been using them for seduction and sadism. "Ardyn had a question. I was answering it."

"I'm sure. Don't let this boy intimidate you, Miss Kaine." Rossi's hand drops from the doorknob. "He's one of the smartest students I've ever had the honor of teaching, but he also has a very stupid way of showing it sometimes. Come with me, Callahan."

My eyes widen as Tempest does what Rossi asks without question. After an insult like that, the Tempest I remember would be snarling by now and threatening Rossi's job. My attention lingers between them, as if trying to find the thread that connects them.

"You're fair game now, princess," Tempest says through the side of his mouth as he passes. "Don't say I didn't warn you."

It's not until the door shuts behind him and I'm sure I'm alone that I allow my knees to give out and curl up into my knees, ashamed and confused, my nipple throbbing with pain and...

... need.

17

ARDYN

How can I hate a guy but want him at the same time?

It's not daddy issues—I don't think. My father's been overprotective for most of my life for justifiable reasons. I've never felt a lack of love from him or my mother. They're busy, successful people running an empire, and their daughter is self-sufficient enough not to need constant attention.

Well, not anymore.

Tempest toys with my idea of independence and what it means. He wants me to believe I'm weak enough to run home and hide under the safety of bodyguards and walls.

Doesn't he know? None of those things keep me safe. *Nothing kept me safe when it counted the most.*

He's decided that mixing pain with pleasure will terrify me. What a mistake. He's making me realize that pain *can* be pleasure, a mind-blowing revelation not even my thera-pists could come up with to accelerate my treatment.

Pain doesn't have to control me.

I can oppress the fear of it with the expectation of releasing it in the most beautiful way.

And *oh*, how it would piss Tempest off to know he's fueling me, not draining me.

With a small smile on my face, I find Clover waiting for me at the center fountain, sitting on the octagonal lime-stone while water spouts behind her, scrolling through her phone.

She catches sight of me once my shadow falls over her screen. "Oh! Hey! You ready?"

I nod. I'm actually really excited to leave TFU, go into town, and explore somewhere new. Just don't tell my parents.

"How were your morning classes?" Clover asks as she hikes her bag over her shoulder and stands.

"They were okay."

One thing about Clover and my relationship—during the years of knowing her, we never talked much about her brother. I watched him all the time, observed him with heightened awareness with every glimpse I saw of him, which wasn't much. He was at boarding school in Rhode Island, and Clover and I went to a private school in Manhattan. It was only the summers, maybe one or two since he didn't often come home, that Tempest sightings changed the course of how I crushed on a boy forever.

"I'm proud of you for sticking with the difficult classes,"

Clover says. We're taking our time down the pathway through the manicured lawn and to the student parking lot behind our dorm. "With all you've been through, I wasn't sure if—omigod, do you even want to talk about this? I'm sorry. I won't bring it up if it makes you uncomfortable."

Clover appears honestly embarrassed as she glances over at me, hooking her thumbs into her bag's straps on her shoulders and digging them in.

I rest a hand on her tense upper arm. "It's okay. You're the only person I'd want to talk to about it."

"Yeah." She sighs, looking down at her shoes. "I want to be honest with you, too. When you left after ... after Mila..."

I nod, letting her know she doesn't have to finish that sentence for me to understand.

"I was all alone. Yes, my brother was there, and my mom tried, and they threw a bunch of trauma therapists at me, but it wasn't the same as talking to someone who'd been through the same thing. God, this is so selfish of me. I'm not trying to say you weren't there out of choice because I know what your parents did and how fast they locked you up. I'm saying, I'm just trying to say..."

"That you were lonely," I finish for her softly. I pull her hand from the strap, keeping it in mine and squeezing tight. "I understand, Clo. You don't have to mince words with me or treat me like fine china the way everyone else does."

Except for your brother, who actually wants me to break.

Clover's expression clears. "Yes. Lonely and grieving. I wanted you beside me to process Mila's passing. So badly."

"If it helps, I missed you just as fiercely."

She looks over and smiles. "It's nice to hear you say that. It really is."

I study her profile. Serene smile, flushed cheeks, confident walk. But like recognizes like, and her pain of loneliness much like mine. "A lot of those years were out of my control. This year, I want to take it back. I want to *live* in ways I've been stopped from doing. If part of that means talking to you about that night, then so be it. I haven't forgotten. I don't want to forget. I wish Tempest would understand that."

"Tempest gives you a hard time because anyone else's happiness in proximity weakens him." Clover pats me on the arm. "He can really be an asshole, but if you accept it and ignore him, he'll move on to another unfortunate soul."

I don't think so. What Tempest and I have is undefinable and addictive. A frightening mix.

I shrug, though I'm oddly annoyed Tempest could move on so easily. Strange, considering I'd love for him to stop terrorizing me, but I don't want him touching anyone else the way he does me.

I can't reconcile the pit in my stomach with the swell in my heart every time I think of him. I can't freaking do it.

Clover directs us to her car, an Audi sedan. I'm sure Tempest brought his car, too. Funny, considering there's no need to leave campus or have luxury cars in the mountains, but the elite do what the elite do.

She drives us through Titan Falls' gates and into the narrow forest roads, cresting and descending at a pleasant pace. Unlike her brother.

Jesus. Stop thinking about him.

"What's on your mind?" Clover asks while staring straight ahead.

"Hmm?"

"Your hand." Her eyes dart to my tapping fingers on the car's door before going back to the road. "You composing something over there?"

I laugh it off, then tuck my hand firmly under my other one. "I get nervous leaving familiar places," I lie. "I've never been into town before."

"Oh, it's great! Cute little shops and cafes, some boutiques. I'll take you to lunch after we browse a bit, and you'll be comfortable in no time."

Clover chatters away about the small town. I listen with one ear tuned in while focusing on the woods outside my window, the dark patches spreading over the sunlight like ink splotches against white paper.

The trees thin, and the roadway widens until we reach a large wooden billboard shoved into the ground declaring, *Welcome to Titan Falls, where our kindness is our strength.* Clover parallel parks on a sparsely populated street. When I exit the car, I can hear the nearby shop shingles creak in the wind.

"Come on. It's just over here." Clover motions me to her side of the street.

We walk half a block past wooden façades and streak-free windows containing everything from antiques to vintage clothes. Every display is free of stickers, open signs, or help wanted ads.

It's all so pristine.

And deserted.

"Where is everyone?" I ask. Clover's a few paces ahead of me, eager to explore the New Age shop.

"It's a workday. Probably everyone's out ... working," she says over her shoulder.

I hum in unconvinced agreement. I haven't even seen a shadow of a person or a moving car since we got here. Everything seems frozen in time, at a different date. Another century, even.

A flash of movement catches my eye. Ironic, considering I was just thinking the place was as deserted as an old Western film. I glance toward it, not thinking much until the flash turns into a face.

Two eyes framed in black. Mouth covered; neck encased. Balaclava.

I choke on my breath. Familiar heart palpitations follow, a panic attack in the making.

"Clover..." I whisper brokenly.

She doesn't hear me.

"We're here!" Clover halts and grabs my arm, power-walking us to a shop named *Sarah's Apothecary*.

Clover pushes open the door, our entry announced with a sweet tinkling of bells.

The sound jars me out of the growing rush in my ears. I blink, centering myself by taking in the new surroundings.

The sharp scent of incense, hand-sewn dream catchers hanging from the ceiling, a spinning postcard stand by the counter, crystals, jewelry, candles, and statues ranging from pregnant women to erect wooden penises.

That's enough to jolt me into reality.

It's nothing. I didn't see him. It's a trick of my imagination.

"Can I help you?"

A woman in a pale lavender flowing skirt and bright red curls swishes out from behind the counter, her beaded curtain clacking as she strides forward.

Luckily, Clover speaks for us. "Yes, hi! We're here to grab some crystals, mostly, but also to explore."

"Take your time." The woman sweeps out her hand with a kind smile. "I love getting new customers. You're from the university, I presume?"

We both nod. My movement catches her attention, and she stares at me for longer than is polite. I offer a stiff, uncomfortable smile to let her know I've noticed. She blinks, her pleasant smile back in place. "I'm Mariana. Do let me know if you have questions."

"Thank you," Clover says. She jerks her chin over to the crystal basins hanging against the far wall. I find my feet again and follow.

Rows and columns of sparkling, frosted, and matte crystals fill my vision. I read the handwritten placards as Clover runs her hand along them, purring with happiness as she touches the pastel rainbow.

Lapis Lazuli, Black Obsidian, Carnelian, Turquoise, Fuchsite, Blue Topaz...

"How do you know which ones do what?" I ask her.

"Practice and patience." Clover smiles at me. "Here."

She plucks out a purple and yellow crystal. "Amethyst and yellow jasper. Healing and happiness."

I accept the crystals, and they clink gently together in my palm. "How do I use them?"

"Put them in your purse, by your bedside, under your pillow. Anywhere you want to amplify those senses."

"So like, I can get a twenty-four seven feeling of happiness?" I joke.

"It can't hurt."

Clover collects a few crystals for herself, and we head to the counter together.

Mariana doesn't shift as we approach, her hands folded in front of her and her stare direct—like she was watching us the entire time.

"Found what you were looking for, I hope?" she asks.

I shake myself out of it. There's nothing suspicious about her. It's my mind again, turning into a trickster, making me question my senses.

"We did!" Clover says. "My friend and I have classes to get to, but I'd love to come back and look at your Wiccan and pagan collection, if you have one."

Mariana pauses in opening a paper bag to deposit our crystals. "Indeed, I do, behind me." She gestures to the beaded curtain she initially entered from. "Not many people show interest in that section, especially around here, so I keep it hidden while the more tourist-friendly products are out in the open."

Clover nods in understanding.

"You're welcome to explore any time you'd like."

Mariana finishes bagging our items. "That'll be fifty-two seventy—"

"Your shop is named after Sarah Anderton," I say.

Mariana glances over at me, unhurried. "Yes. I don't enjoy exploiting her history, mind you, but one must pay rent, and the seasonal visitors love the macabre, I'm afraid. Are you familiar with her?"

Mariana holds my stare, her expression benign, but I tense, my teeth clenched together.

"My brother lives in her old cottage," Clover interjects, hopefully to lighten the mood.

"Ah, yes!"

I let out a breath when Mariana's attention returns to Clover. "That area is absolutely *rich* in energy. Does he feel it?"

Clover shrugs noncommittally. I doubt Tempest feels much.

"You know, I wasn't going to say anything, but..." Mariana worries her lower lip, then glances back at me. "Now that you mention someone close to you lives in the Anderton home ... you possess the same energy as that cottage. Are you aware of that?"

Clover turns to stare at me, too. I shift uncomfortably. "Um. What kind of energy is that?"

"Well—this is why I didn't want to say anything, but ... I sense a darkness in you. A blackened aura, if you will. You've been through tribulations, much like Sarah Anderton."

Make a sound, and I'll cut out your tongue. Fight me, and

I'll cut off your fingers and send them to Daddy...

"I-I never tried to poison anyone like she did," I say lamely. "And I'm not interested in witches the way Clover is."

Mariana smiles. The edges of it don't reach her eyes. "I've made you uncomfortable. I apologize. Allow me to make it up to you by offering you this. Free of charge."

Mariana reaches behind her, rummaging through boxed items she has yet to display. As she does, I catch movement behind her beaded curtain.

"Are you alone?" I blurt out.

Clover gives me a warning look.

"Uh-huh," Mariana says without turning. "Off-season, there isn't much reason to have extra hands. I'm sure you've noticed the lack of pedestrian traffic outside—"

A ski mask with penetrating dark eyes cuts through the beads, the decorative lines knifing through the nightmarish image into a carving of beauty and ugliness. Light and dark.

I stumble back, knocking into a display case of incense burners and dried herbs. Some packages burst open as they fall to the ground, scattering their scents and intermingling them in a way that, according to Clover's face, is horrifying.

"I'm so sorry!" I bend down to scrape up the mess but end up making useless piles on the floor. I can't help but look behind Mariana again to see if *he's* still there or was ever there in the first place, afraid of either option.

"It's not a problem. It's okay, really." Mariana comes from behind the counter and kneels beside me, bringing the calming scent of something sweet, musky, and completely unlike the smoke in my nightmares. "Accidents happen."

"We can pay for what we ruined," Clover says. She bends in front of me, squeezing my wrist in solidarity as she does so. I'm so thankful she doesn't scold, berate, or humiliate me, but why would she? She's my friend. She's not Mila. I'm the one who left her, not the other way around.

And here she is taking half-responsibility for my mess.

"I'll pay," I correct gently. "Again, I'm so sorry."

"Darling, I can feel it, too." Mariana lays both hands on my shoulders. Normally, I shy away from a stranger's touch, especially after Mariana showed such over-familiarity with me after only a few seconds, but her weight steadies my panic. Centers me.

I meet her eyes.

"I was going to offer you this." Mariana releases one of my shoulders and pulls a black stone from her dress pocket. "Black tourmaline. Keep it with you, for it blocks psychic attacks."

"I—I don't—"

"Shush, now." This time, Mariana's smile reaches her eyes. "Whatever you want to call it, whether negative energy or someone wishing you harm or simply wanting to be at peace while another is in turmoil beside you, this will keep you safe."

I find myself closing my fingers around the shining, jagged black crystal.

"You two should go. You'll be late for class. Don't worry about this. I'll clean it up in less than two minutes."

"Are you sure we can't pay?" Clover asks.

"Positive. This is a place you can come to and learn how to defend yourself." Mariana looks at me as she says it. "Do you understand?"

I nod, even though utter confusion ripples inside my head. I don't believe in this stuff. I'll never think that crystals can protect me. Yet I can't unsee what haunts me every day.

Clover and I stand at the same time. As nice as the shop owner is to us, I have the overwhelming urge to *run*. It's like my leaving campus has thinned the already fragile thread between my past and a safe space I can call home. Like I'm out in the open now, and my demons who'd once thought me lost can now track me.

"You might have a kindred spirit in Sarah," Mariana calls as we move to the door. "I suggest, instead of the gaudy horror shows students put on and the complete disrespect most use it for, you use that place to contact her, center yourself."

To my horror, Clover looks intrigued by this until I smack her to get moving so we can get out of here.

"I don't have anything in common with a murdering witch," I say as Clover pulls open the door. *And I will never go to that cottage because of the man who now guards it.*

Mariana responds, "You don't know what she went through, much like no one truly understands your struggles, either, sweet child."

Her gentle, closed-mouth smile is the last thing I see before I firmly shut the door in her face.

18

ARDYN

Clover decides to argue the merits of Mariana's points all the way home.

"It's like she read right into you. I've always wanted to learn how to do psychic readings," she says as we enter the university's gates. "Maybe we should hold a séance at the cottage. With enough cajoling on my part, Tempest'll let us use his room."

"God, no." It takes a metric ton of mental weight to prevent myself from covering my ears. "For so many reasons, *no*."

"Okay, so we won't contact Sarah. What about her daughter, though? Aren't you intrigued that her name has been erased from history?"

An angry thought pops into my head. *Next, you'll be asking me to use a Ouija board to contact Mila.*

I'd never hurt her like that and say it out loud. Instead, I argue, "Mariana probably recognized us from the news. Our families don't exactly stay out of the press." I focus on picking my cuticles. "God knows they like to point out that my kidnappers have been paroled every anniversary of my abduction."

Clover sucks in a breath. I never talk about the two weeks I spent locked up, unable to speak for months after the ransom was paid and the exchange was made. My therapists practically had to pry my mouth open with pliers to get me to talk about when Mila was killed, too.

"All Mariana did was take advantage of open information about me and refer to it as 'darkness.' No kidding."

"Forgive me for saying this, but your reaction in store after she spoke to you ... what was that about?"

A drop of blood beads at the corner of my thumbnail. I curl my finger to stop it from picking further. "I thought I saw something. It had nothing to do with her."

"What did you see?"

Out of everyone in my life, I should be able to confess the truth to Clover. She wouldn't judge or consider calling my parents. She's the only safe person I have left. "I saw a face. In a ski mask."

"Seriously?"

"Behind that beaded curtain thing. It's nothing—probably a play of shadows. I've already dismissed it."

Clover slides her gaze over to mine before going back to the road. "I agree it probably wasn't real."

My stomach sinks at her ready acceptance of my hallucination. Just Ardy being Ardy, who probably needs her meds increased.

"But Ardyn, that's where she said the occult books were. If any angry spirits would exist, *that's* where they'd be. You probably saw a manifestation of evil in the shape it wanted you to see it as. Your greatest fear. Don't you see? An exorcism is needed."

I can't help it. I scoff, then relax my features and scold myself to listen to her. Clover deals with my shit without complaint.

"You've tried everything else, haven't you? Why don't you humor me and let me do what I'm good at to help you? All you'll lose is time, and hey, maybe you'll even feel better after a good cleanse."

I try to see my friend's side of things, I really do. This is how Clover has decided to deal with Mila's death through the mystical and divine. I don't blame her since my coping skills aren't exactly stellar, but sometimes Clover gets ahead of herself. I'm reluctant to shout, *I've had enough dark rooms and terrifying encounters, thank you very much*, which would shut her up in a second. But then she'd feel terrible, and I'd feel bad and we'd both be awkward with each other until one of us says something stupid again.

It's an unnecessary and predictable segue that I don't need to make us take, so I let Clover ramble on about the benefits of spirit summoning until we part ways at our respective classrooms and I don't see her until the evening.

She tries to coax me into a study session with a group

she's met in her literature class, but I decline, preferring to spend my night in the common room skimming through one of the many thick hardbacks it has on its bookshelf.

Camden House empties early, the girls choosing parties or late night study sessions at the library rather than staying inside on a gorgeous, cool night. I'm elated—it means I have the common room to myself when I descend the circular staircase and walk into the carpeted interior with lines of books and old wingback chairs for company.

To add to my preferred atmosphere, I light a fire and drag a chair closer to the golden flames. It's stunning how TFU allows working fireplaces despite the very real correlation between drunk people and fire hazards, but I have to assume it's the outrageous tuition proving its worth.

I'm happy for the lax rule because I get to hear the cracks and pops of a warm fire while curling up on a chair in my favorite leggings and sweatshirt, reading an early copy of *Wuthering Heights*. Heathcliff kept me company for years when I didn't have friends and the chances of finding a boyfriend were zero. He'll be fine company tonight.

Half an hour into my re-read, I find my eyes dragging across the page until my attention focuses more on the fire than staying in Yorkshire. Mariana's inquisitive gaze seemed to assess my skeleton more than my skin.

Setting the book down, I dig through my hoodie's front pocket and pull out the three stones. Amethyst, yellow jasper, and black tourmaline. Purple, yellow, black.

I wonder if Mariana or Clover thought to question giving me the exact colors of a bruise.

Using the chair's arm, I lay them out in a perfect row, suspended for a moment within the subtle glitter of flame against crystal. They're beautiful. Mesmerizing. But rocks can't protect me.

A sound draws my head up.

Curious, I lean forward to see past the open doorway and into the hall that eventually turns into the front foyer. The overhead lights are on motion detectors during the night, but the side windows give me enough streetlight to see the bare floors and slashes of moonlight through the dark interior.

Shadows have no eyes, yet I feel like they're looking at me in the high corners of the ceiling.

I debate staying close to the fire where it's light and warm versus sprinting up to my room where I have a lock.

Another sound whips my head to the right. Like shuffling footsteps.

My heart skitters in its cage.

On my left, a dragging, clanking noise, like heavy chains being pulled across the floor.

"Nope." I clamp my lips shut and leap from the chair. No ghosts of TFU's past are visiting me tonight.

Whether it's my imagination getting the best of me or one of my dorm-mates returning to screw with my head doesn't matter—I'm out of here before my fear takes over, and I can't tell real from the past anymore.

Don't let it get that far.

After one deep breath, I sprint for the hall, aiming for

the staircase that'll take me up high, into the shadows that will either protect me or swallow me whole.

My exhales are scattered, my eyes wide and darting. Despite all this, I'm not prepared for strong arms to swoop around my middle and drag me into the dark.

"N—" I start to scream. A gloved hand clamps down on my mouth.

So I bite.

Kick.

Do everything I did when I was ten years old, even though it was useless, even though I was so small.

No, no, no!

"Shut her up!" growls a voice close by. Deep. Resonant. Terrifying.

"I'm trying—she's squirming—fuck, she's like a squirrel!"

I don't stop screaming. My throat is raw with the effort, my jaw aching while I fight against the hand that holds my mouth. I wiggle and jab—using all the self-defense skills my mother demanded I get the instant I "returned to good health."

None of it works.

"Jesus," a gruff, impatient voice growls. "Let me do it."

A man, dressed all in black, steps in front of me, his face obscured by a ski mask.

My past coming back to haunt me.

The tremors start at the base of my spine once I catch sight of him. Travel up my back, down my limbs, and paralyze my mind as the fear takes control. *NONONONOTAGAIN.*

He cocks his head. "We're back, little girl."

I yowl, high and animalistic, tears bursting from my eyes.

There's a prick in my neck and a swirl of nausea in my belly before everything goes black.

19

ARDYN

Put the girl over there.

Too loose. You need to tie her up tighter.

No, not like that. Grab her. Harder. There you go.

Don't cop a feel—focus on restraining her and covering her mouth! Then you can grope her all you want.

The rotting, dank scent of mildew hits me first. A sharper, metallic smell comes next, and the ancestral part of me recognizes it as the lingering stains of old blood.

With a sharp gasp, I jerk my head up. Unable to see. My lashes scrape across the fabric as I regain my senses and blink, blink, blink.

"Hey, little girl. You're awake."

The guttural voice slithers into my left ear. I snap my head toward it.

"You might be a little groggy. Here. Drink this."

Something wet hits my lips, and I recoil. Spit it out.

The voice *tsks*. "Bad girl. You should do as I say. Otherwise, you'll be punished."

Do as we say, little girl, and you won't get hurt.

"I ... who are you?" My voice is brittle and light compared to his.

"Don't you recognize me, sweetheart?"

A sickening shiver runs down my spine, sinking into my stomach and roiling what remains of my dinner. "I don't know you."

"You do. We *found* you," he sing-songs.

A sharp sting of dread clears the nausea. "We?"

"Me and two of my friends. You remember us, don't you? Although, you were younger then. More impressionable. More malleable."

There's a scrape of feet against the floor, like someone is uncrossing their legs. Wood creaks. Something flicks. A lighter, maybe? A match?

Fire.

"What do you w-want with me?" My tone takes on the edge of panic. It's only through my focused breaths of *in, out, in, out* that I'm able to maintain control.

"Our ransom wasn't enough last time."

"No," I whisper. "You were caught. You're not to come near my family or me ever again..."

"Hmm. We didn't get the memo. Feel this."

The same man—the only man—who's been talking to me (*where are the others?*) stalks forward with heavy footfalls. My blinks turn rapid, though I can't see a thing. Blindfolded.

The footsteps stride behind me, to where my wrists are bound around the chair back I'm seated on. Softness brushes the tips of my fingers, and at first, I curl them inward. Away.

"Come on, don't you want to pet her?"

Her?"

The soft downiness presses harder into my tied hands until I register the sticky wetness. I hiss in a breath.

"What did you call this thing? Hermione?"

My heart surges into my throat. "*Hermione?* No, you didn't! You couldn't!"

"Oh, I fuckin' did." He lets out a cruel laugh. "Why did you name her that, anyway? Shouldn't it have been Hedwig?"

At my distressed moan, he adds, "Because she had white fur, and so did the owl. Get it?"

"*Fuck you!*" the shriek bursts out of me without warning, without control. It lashes out of my throat with barbs, burning a pathway of hate.

He chuckles. A long whistle between teeth responds from another section of the room.

"She has some pipes on her than when we last had her."

Another voice. A different male. *Oh God, what's going to happen to me?*

"That furball is a warning to you, sweetheart. You listen to us. You do as we say, and you may come out of this with all your limbs in tact, unlike your poor pussy."

I ask in a scratched tone, "How much do you want? And what makes you think you'll succeed this time?"

A dark chuckle follows. The presence behind me moves to my front, and I hope, with all the good that's left in my life, that he doesn't bring my childhood pet with him. *Hermione is meant to be safe at home. She's too old to travel. Mom was meant to be taking care of her. How could this happen? How could I have let my guard down so much?*

I can feel my mind slipping, and I grapple to get it back. To stay present. They can't do this to me a second time.

Something pricks under my jaw, and I flinch. The tip of a knife. Laughter spirals through my ears, layered with different voices. There really are three of them, and one of them just blew in my face like I'm an animal in a cage.

My chest turns to fire when both my breasts are gripped and squeezed to a painful, wrenching level.

The initial voice comes closer. "We don't want money this time, sweetheart. We want to send a message. With *you*."

He twists my nipples, and I cry out. My stomach has dropped out from under, dread and horror taking its place in the center of my body, and I'm freaking out, I'm freaking out, I'm going away, I'm going, I'm gone...

"You're naked, sweetheart. Did you realize that yet? And you're all ours."

... and then I smell it.

Him.

And I return, knowing exactly what this is.

20

TEMPEST

"What about this pussy? Is it dead, too?"

My voice has taken on a grit I'm not entirely used to—thick with restraint and heavy on discomfort, as I talk to Ardyn, naked and exposed.

No man—not Rio or Hunter—was allowed to touch her during her transport into my basement. Hunter tried a little grab-ass when I hoisted her over my shoulder after Rio pricked her with his good stuff, and daddy's boy got smashed in the face because of it.

I'm not above ruining the features of the boss's son. If Hunter didn't know that, he's aware of it now. He didn't dare try again.

We took the back way behind the girls' dorm to Anderton Cottage, through the woods and hidden from outdoor partiers by the thicket of trees as we traipsed on by, just a trio of dudes with an unconscious girl draped between us. We got her into the cottage's basement with little fanfare since I threatened to bite the ears off anyone who tried to assist me in stripping her bare, then propping her up in her seat, her pert breasts on display and her (to my delight) shaved pussy spread before me. I zip-tied her ankles to the chair legs and pulled her arms behind her and tied those off, too. My dick strains against my pants as I look down on her now, but if I'm to be brutally honest with myself, it's been hard since the moment I came up with the idea to mirror her kidnapping and scare the shit out of her. It's only been in these recent seconds that I've realized I'm enduring blue balls not just to terrify her into leaving this school, but because I *want* her.

Her rose-colored nipples bounce with her ragged breaths. A sheen of sweat coats her skin, sparkling against the fine lines of muscle on her torso and the soft, blond hair of her thighs. Ardyn's cascade of hair is a mess, poofing up like a mushroom top over her blindfold, which should be comical, but all I want to do is yank it out, wrap it around my knuckles, and use it as reins to ride her from behind.

I pull away from her breasts, full and ripe in my cruel hands as I squeezed and twisted until she cried out. I'm so absorbed in her—Ardyn's scent, her body, her *terror*—that I forget where I am and who I'm with.

After asking about her pussy, I decide to check for myself by swiping a finger down and through.

My finger pauses at her clit. I stiffen in shock.

She's slick. *She's fucking wet right now.*

That can't be right. Frowning at her, I dip my index

finger all the way in to the knuckle, then dragging it out before plunging it back in.

Ardyn writhes beneath me, and I wait for the sobs, the familiar cries of *please, stop*, or *I'll do anything*—any number of the last words I've heard since accepting a lifetime career in the Vultures—but I get none of it.

Instead, she moans.

Ardyn bites her lower lip, then arches her hips to accept me deeper.

"Yes," she whispers.

The fuck?

Ardyn should be terrified. What is she playing at?

It sickens me to say it, as this is the one line I draw with tortures and kills, but Ardyn's got me all twisted up. "Is this what you remember we did to you as a little girl?"

She curves her hips into my finger *to get a different fucking angle.*

A growl leaps into my throat before I can contain it. As punishment, I stick in all four fingers, painful for a virgin and excruciating for a dry one.

Except she's not dry.

Ardyn's lips curl inward on a sharp inhale. I've pained her.

A satisfied smile pulls at my lips. I still have the upper hand. Not that she'd ever be given a chance to outplay me.

"Have you forgotten?" Ardyn asks, lifting her hips. My fingers grow hot inside her. She clenches around them like a perfect vise. Exactly like those suction vagina toys Hunter pretends he doesn't play with. "I've spent a year in an institution. Alone. Lonely. With only my fingers for company. I've missed this."

My arm jerks of its own accord. Pushing deeper into her.

She hisses in a breath.

"Careful what you say next, sweetheart."

"I've missed *you*."

Me? You mean the fucking piss-wipes that kidnapped you as a kid and held you for their entertainment for weeks?

I read all about her ordeal. My gift with computers allows me a shit ton of access on the dark web and boring legalese memos and police databases. The reports, the investigation, the pre-trial papers before a plea deal was made—I absorbed everything in full detail, what they did to her. How they threatened, stripped, and laid her bare, starved her for days, fed her water from a dog bowl, and made her sleep in rat shit.

And she still *wants* these guys?

No, I'm not buying it—

My dick sure is, though.

I'm so turned on, it hurts, and there are two other men in this room who very much shouldn't be.

Looking at Ardyn's wet, plump lips and hearing her moan—I realize I don't need backup. I never fucking did.

"Goddamn, she's up for it. When do we get a turn?" Hunter asks. He's off to the side, close to the apothecary chest with itchy fingers. All he wants is to take out his ritual gear and throw us an orgy as the Goat King.

I sneer at him with my hand still very much where it should be. "She's mine."

Hunter angles his head, his eyes gleaming along with the apothecary jars behind him. "I thought we agreed—"

"Plans change. Go upstairs and keep a lookout for partiers who've strayed too far from where they belong." I glance over at Rio, who stands at the base of the stairs with his arms folded bodyguard style, yet even he can't disguise his slack-jawed surprise as he listens to Ardyn hump my hand.

Rio responds with a curt nod. He's heard me, yet he keeps staring toward Ardyn, at her perfect body, stark white against this dimly lit, cobwebbed room. Pure beauty against filth. Her long hair flows down almost to her tied hands. Her shoulders are so wrenched back, her breasts are pulled up, the nipples hard and wanting from my sharp ministrations earlier.

"Dude," I bark.

In less than a second, I've decided no one is allowed to look at her that way. Like she's hot and bothered for them.

Rio jolts. "Sure, yeah. Hey, you, get over here," he adds for Hunter's benefit, wisely refraining from names. I can't be so certain about Hunter, and I'm glad when he stands to attention and strides over to Rio. Not before licking his lower lip at the sight of Ardyn as he passes.

"I will beat your face in so fucking hard you'll think butterflies and bees are the same goddamned species," I hiss.

Hunter's brows go up, and he covers his mouth in mock fear. He has a death wish. He must.

Rio storms over, grabs Hunter by the back of the neck,

and throws him toward the stairs. Hunter responds by ducking out of his grip and uppercutting Rio in the jaw.

"Yes, *Nick*, yes..."

Motherfucker. My stare returns to Ardyn, squirming and slickening my fingers to a concerning degree.

"Take it outside," I warn the two idiots, then quickly return to more important matters. "What the fuck did you just call me?"

"That's your name, isn't it?" Ardyn whispers. Her head lowers, then centers on me. She's blindfolded, yet she regards me like she can see exactly who I am. No, who *he* is.

"I know my fucking name," I rasp. The names of her abductors are Terrance Smith, Michael Krakowski, and *Nicholas* Brewster.

I guess clarity comes at a price.

"Do you remember more than you claim, sweetheart?" I ask softly. Gently. Like a prowling cat approaching an unsuspecting mouse. "Are you a dirty liar?"

It's meant as a whisper of warning. A slithering notion of what's to come. Most of my victims piss their pants at this point. Ardyn, however, smiles. Tentatively, like she's unsure just how deep into shit she's stepping, but she's committed to the stink.

Brave girl.

Brave, *stupid* princess.

"I've been thinking about you, Nick," she coos. "And how the last night we spent together, you weren't able to ... you know ... but you tried. And you promised you'd come back to finish what you started. I'm so glad you have."

She's shitting me. I pull my fingers out, ashamed to say I stare down at her, fucking gobsmacked.

"I'm so relieved you sent the other two away. It's always been you and me. I've been working so hard to play the victim, just like you asked. To disguise our relationship through trauma and amnesia. Everyone believed me. Do you know how difficult it was to get my parents to let me come to Titan Falls? It took a year of full commitment in a glorified insane asylum. You owe me, baby. You owe me big."

I work my jaw. Clear my throat. Glare.

"Take the blindfold off," she begs. "Let me see you again. I've missed you so freaking *much*, baby."

That's fucking *it*. With jerky motions and a full-throttle temper threatening to boil over, I unclasp my belt, pull it through the loops, and toss it aside. She hears the sound, her head moving to and fro to follow, employing that enigmatic grin as she does so.

"You're playing me," I say, yanking my pants down and tossing them aside, too. "You were squealing for mercy a few minutes ago."

"Because you killed my cat," she pouts.

I focus on the dead wild rabbit I made Hunter scavenge for before going back to her. Ardyn's blind, but I curse myself for allowing that much of a tic to come out.

"And," she adds, "you always said I had to put on a show for your comrades so as not to arouse suspicion."

"I did, did I?" The question comes out choked and rough.

"Yes, baby."

Ardyn's fucking around—I know it. She has to be. Maybe she believes turning the tables on her latest abductor will give her the kind of advantage she could never obtain as a kid, I don't know. Or she's calling my bluff and using her skills to see if it's the real Nick Brewster who has her or an imposter.

I don't much care since I'm at pushing people to their utmost limits before I break them in half.

"You wanna play, sweetheart?" I croon while stroking my dick. "Let's play."

Ardyn's running her mouth, but it's no secret she's still a virgin. If she wants to push me into proving I'm "Nick," then so I will. She'll be a sobbing, snotty mess when I'm finished.

Ardyn's breathing changes. Labored and short. I wonder if she hears it, too.

I stand between her spread thighs, her ankles shackled to each chair leg. She couldn't escape if she tried.

I yank her hips up.

Ardyn yelps, her arms bracing against the back of the chair and her shoulders wrenching painfully.

"You're in perfect alignment with my cock, sweetheart." I dart my tongue out at the sight of her glistening pussy. "Do you still want me to give you the pounding I promised you as a little girl?"

Ardyn doesn't respond. Her delicate mouth twists before she pulls her lips in, biting down hard.

She's going to say no.

And I'm going to take it anyway.

Ardyn whispers something.

I cock an ear to her. "What's that, sweetheart?"

"Y-Yes."

My eyes widen, and my body is in full accord. I plunge into her without further thought, ripping through her barrier and burying myself to the hilt so ruthlessly that I buckle over halfway and groan in pleasure.

Ardyn cries out, her thighs stiffening and her entire body fusing into solid bone. Tears leak out from her blindfold.

I don't feel any remorse. "I warned you, sweetheart."

"I … I…"

I expect the pleas to start. The begging, the sobbing, the drool and the snot. She brought this on herself, though. Don't poke a bear and all that.

"Don't stop, Nick."

Nope. Not happening.

I slam my palm against her mouth to prevent further utterances of *Nick* and take what I'm due for suffering through this botched fuck up of a plan. If Ardyn really did make a love pact with the shithead, if they really were due to meet when he got out, I will find him and destroy him, but until then, I'll own and then destroy *her*.

Ardyn Kaine, the sweet girl who reluctantly flashed me her white cotton panties in my car.

The stupid innocent who witnessed a murder she had no business stumbling into.

The unconscious beauty who I couldn't kill.

She's here and not as dumb as I thought. *And whether it's all a show, she's willing to stomach this farce and give me her virginity.*

I've already claimed ownership over her life. Why not take her innocence, too?

I pull out, then slam back in. Her body jolts, and her pussy clenches. She's so tight and wet, I'd like to come here and now, but there's too much dirtying up to do.

I draw away again and drop her hips, her bare ass slamming against the wooden chair in surprise. Without warning, I grab her jaw, digging my fingers in her cheeks to get it to loosen, then shove my dick in her mouth.

She gags at the force, but I've pushed so deep into the back of her throat that she couldn't bite down if she tried.

"Stick your tongue out," I grit out. "You'll take me in without vomiting all over yourself."

Ardyn does as I ask.

I shouldn't be shocked at this point for so many twisted reasons. The things I've done, the violence I've witnessed, the loves I've personally taken from families.

Ardyn Kaine has me shook.

She's meant to be the innocent one, the sweet and fragile bird who can't quite unclip her wings. Yet here she is, taking my cock in two holes, blindfolded and bound, without complaint.

Who the fuck is she?

She moans, drawing me back to the pleasure of her face and the tears cascading down, the wet sucking sounds she makes.

Drool clings to my shaft as I withdraw, then plunge, withdraw, then plunge. She grunts, but her tongue slides, accepting my girth and attempting to stroke it.

The fuck. Thefuckthefuckthefuck.

I'm about to come but I pull out just in time, backing up a few steps and catching my breath.

The vision of her from this distance isn't any better. The wood beneath her pussy is damp. Strings of drool hang from her chin. Her hair is mussed, and the blindfold slightly askew.

I wrap my hand around myself and squeeze. She's fucking gorgeous. She's fucking mine.

"Did you taste your blood on me?" I rasp. "How did you enjoy your virginity taken so suddenly and brutal?"

Her throat bobs. I think she might cry again, but no, not my Ardyn. "I-I want to taste you."

I ask slowly, continually stroking, "You want to taste my what?"

"Your cum."

This girl, this woman, this stranger, will be the end of me. "You don't mean that."

"I like it when you dominate me, N—"

I rush her and clamp a hand on her mouth. "Don't you dare say it."

She mumbles something underneath my hand.

"You want to call me anything, it's master. Sir. Sire. I don't give a fuck. Just not that."

Ardyn nods. I debate removing my hand, then rethink it and instead use my other to cock her hips up once more.

My dick slips into her like she's already forged its shape. I lose myself in her heat. My hand stays over her mouth as she garbles something between moans, but I'm not focused on her pleasure. She's shown me enough as it is—for this *Nick*.

It's time for me to take, and I slam into her with enough force to leave bruises. I tilt the chair until I'm at the perfect degree and can go as deep as possible while she's made immobile.

Her small hips try to meet my thrusts. The only movement she makes as I bring myself to the edge and explode inside her so thoroughly that she'll be leaking cum when she hobbles out of here.

If I let her go.

The chair's front legs slam to the ground when I release her and back away, hands on my hips as I heave and regain breath.

Ardyn pants, too, and I give her the once-over with a wry smile. That was the biggest orgasm of my life and I didn't even have my sex partner as a witness.

"Good girl," I say now. "For giving it up to me so easily."

"You're welcome," she murmurs, struggling slightly against her bindings. I bet she's hurting now. I stretched her like a used hair tie.

"... Tempest."

My entire body goes cold.

21

ARDYN

While reading fairy tales as a small girl, I always believed in the prince. I never once considered my virginity would be taken by the villain.

My heart is on fire as I stare into a black void, my sole memory of first having sex consisting of hearing, touch, and smell. It should feel like I've lost a crucial aspect of my first time, except all those senses were amplified, like the stretch from Tempest's dick and the taste of his pre-cum mixed with the metallic taste of my blood... those are sensations I wouldn't have fully appreciated if I were distracted by his pretty face.

And he fucked me. I was fucked by Tempest Callahan.

The man himself storms over to me and rips the blindfold from my head. His turquoise eyes burn into mine. I make sure to match his ire with insolence.

He stands before me in full glory, naked and pristine,

lines of tendons, bulging muscles, and a sweat-drenched torso highlighting his glorious six-pack.

Maybe I was wrong. Seeing him take me probably would've added to the entire experience.

He unclenches his jaw. "When did you figure it out?"

In pure Tempest fashion, it's not a question but a demand.

"About the time you smacked my breast," I reply. "You stepped too close. I could smell you."

Tempest's brows fuse for a moment before he schools them back to normal. "I don't wear any cologne."

"You've smelled the same since we were young. Cinnamon, cloves, pine."

Tempest regards me like I have three heads even though he's the one who just had sex with me while I'm naked, blindfolded, and tied to a chair, calling him another man's name. "In all my experience, not once has a person identified me by my *smell.*"

I give a one-shouldered shrug—as much as I can—in partial agreement. "You represented all the things I couldn't get while trapped inside."

His lashes twitch. He's having trouble processing what I'm saying. I'm not surprised. It's not every day a guy like him is bested by a delicate woman.

"Can you untie me?" I ask him.

Tempest's lips thin, but he leans over and breaks the zip ties at my wrists. Just like that. It's unnerving how strong he can be. A disquieting notion comes over me—Tempest was probably being *gentle* with my handling this entire time. In his mind, anyway.

After unbinding my hands, he straightens.

"What about my feet?"

"Not yet." He crosses his arms like a naked, still-hard god lording over his latest virgin sacrifice. "Explain yourself, Ardyn."

Tempest is intimidating as all hell. I do my best to disguise my reaction. "You're the one who should be explaining to me why you kidnapped me from my dorm and brought me here."

"Because I felt like it," he snaps. "Your turn."

"Bull. You wanted to freak me out and turn me into the hollow shell I became after Mila—" It hurts to even finish the sentence. "Do you know how perverted that is? To pretend to be the men who took me intending to mess with my mind enough to send me back to a facility?"

"You wanna talk perverted? How about asking the guy who abducted you as a kid to *fuck* you?"

"I knew it was you the whole time!"

"Did you?" he scoffs. "I've seen a lot, princess, but I've yet to see a performance like the one you just put on for *Nick*. You made plans with him, huh? Where were you gonna meet him? Was he meant to take you like this, strip you bare, and live out your rape fantasy as a full-grown, shaved pussy adult?"

I stand. It's difficult with my ankles strapped to chair legs, but I do it. "And if I was?"

Tempest jolts. He doesn't expect that.

"You don't have any idea what I've been through this last year," I barrel on, "and the amount of work it took to get me to this point where I feel stable and strong and independent. You haven't bothered to know. All you've done is yell, intimidate, and touch me in my most intimate places to scare me into leaving. If I wanted to reunite with my kidnapper, then that's *my* prerogative. What isn't your right is to take me and use me and tie me up in this—this *basement*. You know why?"

"Oh. Do enlighten." Tempest sounds bored by my very existence.

"Because I'm your sister's best friend. The only one she has left since her other one was *murdered*."

He goes still.

"So if you don't give a shit about me, how about you think of the one person who actually gives a shit about you?"

I notch my chin, satisfied I've gotten to him until he eats up the space between us and shoves me until I slam back into the chair.

Tempest's scowling features darken my vision. "Too bad for you, princess, Nick wasn't the one who fucked you. *Nick* isn't the one who claimed your pussy and your mouth, and *Nick* isn't going to be the one to ever touch you. He'll lose whatever limp dick he's managed to hang onto during his stint in prison if he ever tracks you down and tries. That clear?"

Thank God. I don't voice it. My quivering muscles give Tempest the answers he needs, anyway.

"You're a sick chick. More twisted than I gave you credit for," he continues. "Wanting a man who treated you worse than a farm animal. That's how you like it, huh? Trussed up like a pig? Spread like a mare?"

I can't contain my flinch at his words.

He hooks his hand under my jaw, forcing my chin up. "Sacrificed like a little lamb?"

Tempest feels my answering swallow against his wrist. He smiles. "I'm worse."

"What are you?" I ask through the pressure on my throat. "What is this place?"

"Your nightmares and jagged memories are heaven compared to this."

Tempest kneels between my knees. His thumb goes to my clit, and I gasp.

"I'll do you a favor," he says while looking up between my legs. "I'll suck out your juices, blood, and my cum, and then I'll send you on your merry way, back to my sister, and I'll leave it to you to explain to everyone else you fooled the loss of your fragile, sweet image and what a dirty, bad girl you've become."

"I—"

He pulls at my hips in the same spots he left bruises on earlier, his mouth suctioning onto my pussy and tongue darting out before I can so much as say *wait*.

The pleasure is so instant and consuming that I forget that my hands are free. When I do remember, I should use them to yank at his hair and unglue his lips, but I can't. I won't. Instead, they tangle against his scalp, pushing him deeper, turning his tongue into a dick as I toss my head back and moan.

"I'm exactly who I claim to be," I say through a sigh. "You, on the other hand…"

I let my head loll to the side, taking in the old, lopsided shelving on one wall with colorless pots and vases.

Tempest swipes a circle inside me, then bares his teeth against my folds and digs in. I jerk, but, unable to lift my legs, I squeeze my thighs against his face instead, keeping him there, driving him deeper.

I'm supposed to be sore. Swollen and tender. If only my body wanted to listen to my brain.

Tempest presses in, tonguing and lapping me up just like he promised, and I whimper.

Blinking, I attempt to return to my assessment. Rows of jars. Some ripple, others are opaque, and the rest … move? Bugs? Frogs?

I don't know. I don't care.

Yes. Yes, I do care! I have to.

My nails curl into Tempest's blackened chestnut hair, the silky strands tickling my skin.

If I had to guess, I'm at Anderton Cottage, underground perhaps, in a basement or bunker. There are streaks on the ground, discerned with the help of what little light shines from the corner lamps. Chains hang on the wall over Tempest's head, ending with cuffs. A wooden contraption leans against the corners, its sharp edges poking out of the shadows like joints from a forest creature's limbs…

"Ardyn," Tempest demands.

I drop my chin, meeting his eyes.

"What are you doing?" he asks with glistening lips.

"Trying to answer who you really are," I admit through heady breaths.

Tempest reaches up and clasps one of my breasts, squeezing possessively. "I'm a man who wants you to beg, not to learn."

His thumb flicks over my hard nipple before he digs his nail in. I exclaim, whimper, and squirm.

Satisfied, Tempest resumes his meal, burying his nose inside me as well as his mouth and focusing on my clit to the point of causing uncomfortable ecstasy. My motion is limited, and I can't escape the endless sensation. It builds so fast that the orgasm bolts through me and leaves me wanting.

Tempest isn't done, and he brings me to another explosion, then another, within minutes.

The chair is soaked under my bottom, against his chin. I'm loose and limbless, barely able to hold my head up.

Vaguely, I hear Tempest get to his feet. He uses the tops of my thighs as leverage as if his legs have turned to jelly, too.

There's a *snick*, then a tug at my ankles as he swipes through the zip ties with a blade.

"Get up."

Leaning forward, I brace my hands on the chair's arms, rising with effort. I'm a sore, swollen puddle. Never in my wildest dreams did I think this is what losing your virginity looks like.

I don't want to admit how much I loved it.

Once I've fully straightened, I open my eyes in time to register Tempest's hand gripping the back of my neck and propelling me forward. My feet fight to keep up with my upward momentum until I'm slammed against the concrete wall, my cheek pressed against the cold, rough surface.

Tempest growls into my ear. "You don't speak of tonight. Do you hear me?"

I nod, though his fingers squeeze the tendons of my neck to the point of excruciating pain.

Is he ashamed of this? Of what we've done?

"You don't have to worry about me saying a word." I force the words out of my stiff jaw. "Because this is the last time you'll ever touch me."

His grip spasms against my nape. "Excuse me?"

"You want me to leave campus? Well, I want you to see me every day, realize what you had, and that you can't get it back."

I'm pretty impressed with my ability to sound so sure while Tempest bullies me against a wall. The idea came in haphazard fragments, gaining momentum the longer he took to ravish my body. He could've come in two seconds, satisfied himself, and left me tied to a chair. Instead, he did the opposite. Pleasuring me, enjoying bringing me pain before erasing it with ecstasy.

My past has taught me a lot. I was ten when trauma became a permanent fixture in my mind, but I learned how to watch, learn, and stay alive.

And this is how I'll do it now, save for how much I'll

suffer by not experiencing Tempest again. However, I'll die a happy girl if this is the one sexual experience I'll remember.

My confidence takes a nose-dive when a sharp sting blooms against the tip of my bum.

"Is that what you think is going to happen, princess?"

The knife. He didn't let it go.

I cringe, half of it squished against the wall.

Tempest releases my neck, and for a stupid second, I think *I'm free* before the same pressure builds against my anus, cutting and sudden.

I scream, my hands slamming against the wall alongside my face.

He didn't just stick a knife inside me. *He didn't.*

Whimpering, I force myself still, some part of me acknowledging the more I move, the more damage it'll cause.

Then there's a wriggle of movement deep inside me.

Tempest rasps close to my ear, "Never forget who is in charge here."

There's a release of pressure, then it pounds back into my anus. I realize it can't be his knife because it's starting to feel ... good.

"It's my thumb, princess." Tempest chuckles darkly. "The tip of my switchblade is still on the small of your back, right up against your ass crack."

He shoves his thumb back in. Unwillingly, my bum arches into his hand.

"That's right," he says, his voice taking on a low, velvet tone. "You're mine, whenever I want, however I require it."

"No." But I moan the denial.

Something clangs far away—Tempest tossing his knife. He lines his hard dick up with his thumb, replacing the small pressure with a larger one.

"I won't be craving you, Ardyn," he rumbles, deep in his chest. His hot breaths send goose bumps trailing down my back. "You'll be craving *me*."

A blast of cold air comes between us. I have time to push off the wall when a black cloth covers my vision and tightens around my neck.

"Time to go home."

Incredibly, I'm not afraid of this new blindness. It's not like before. It's nothing like it was when *they* had me. The men from before. Tempest is in charge, and I'm okay with it. *Holy crap, I'm* okay *with it.* "You're going to drug me again?"

Tempest laughs softly. "Nah. You can walk on a leash this time."

A flutter tickles my belly, but I keep that small excitement on lockdown. I still want some authority, and he's not going to hear me beg for him to do more intriguing, sexual things to me. Not in the current state I'm in. I doubt my body could take much more, as much as I'm curious.

Soft fabric brushes against my bare breasts, perking them up. Tempest lifts my arms by brushing his hands under, then up, his barely-there touch raising my small hairs and heating my center.

He pulls my tank top over my arms and head, straightening it against my torso with gentle, caressing movements, doing the same with my underwear, leggings, and sweatshirt, lingering on the parts he hurt the most, brushing them sweetly.

Like he's savoring, healing, and worshipping my body.

Completely at odds with his previous behavior and the total opposite of his harsh words. My lower lip slackens in confusion even though he can't see it, and I can't see him.

I'm desperate to know what he looks like right now. Is his expression as shocked as mine? Does Tempest want to touch me the way I've dreamed of touching him?

I'd like to honor him the same way. Run my hands down his muscular torso and bury them in his hair. Caress his cheek.

Before I know it, I'm doing exactly that. The pads of my fingers catch on the stubble on his jaw before he rips out of my hold.

"There. You're clothed."

My lips quiver before I say, "But—"

A loud whistle cuts through the air, and I jump from the sound. Multiple footsteps follow, coming down the stairs.

"Take her home," Tempest says.

"Sure."

I recognize the voice as the more serious of the two men I've yet to put names to.

"Don't go out of your way. I'm headed in that direction. I'll be her happy escort," the other one says.

"No." Tempest's tone holds no room for argument. "You're never to touch her. You can look at her since there's no choice in the matter, and I love the idea of you pining over what's mine, but if you so much as knock your hand against hers, I'm coming for you. Got it?"

Tempest's warning isn't even directed at me, and I'm trembling. The other guy, however, responds lightly, "We'll see what the boss says about that."

"You do that," Tempest snaps. "See how well it works out for you without a tongue."

"All right," the serious one cuts in. I track his movements to stand between Tempest and me. "I got her. I'll get her home safe."

The one with a death wish adds, "Did you get all you need from her? Sadly we weren't allowed to watch."

Relief lightens my chest at the confirmation that it was only Tempest and me, and there weren't cameras pointed at us or peepholes the guys could jerk off through.

"Not quite," Tempest answers curtly, "but it's enough for now."

"Interesting," the jokester croons.

"Touch her and die," Tempest reminds him. "You. Take her out of here."

"Got it."

A hand clamps down on my arm, and Tempest snarls. "With this."

"Oh."

There's a jangle, then the distinctive scent of leather as a belt is looped around my neck.

"I *like* this," the jokester says.

The more he talks, the more recognizable his voice

becomes. I tilt my ear through the fabric in an attempt to jar the memory loose.

"Take it all in, asshole, because this is the most action you'll get from her," Tempest says.

"Yeah, yeah."

I'm jerked forward, Tempest's belt transforming into a leash, just as he promised. Sadly, it's not him tugging me up the stairs, through another floor, and out into the forest. I try to impart the different scents to memory and the unique sounds. Anything to guide me back to a place where everything changed.

The man leading me doesn't say a word during our trek but gently touches the backs of my knees to guide me over rocks and other debris. His guidance isn't as brutal as Tempest's would've been, and for some reason, I'm disappointed by it.

We come to an abrupt stop. The sack is pulled off my head from behind and I'm pushed forward through a clearing, disoriented and gasping.

Enough instinct remains for me to spin around and try to catch the face of the man who pulled me through the trees. Still, nothing remains except dark clusters of shadows, made jagged and sinister by bare branches and drying leaves.

I spin on my heel, steady and sure, and see Camden House up ahead. Its multiple casement windows emit soft golden light into what I now consider a haunted forest.

And not by witches.

On a sigh, I begin my short walk to the front door. Now

that my sight has returned, my other senses have dulled, all except for one. Feeling.

The throbbing between my legs intensified with my stumble through the trees. It's uncomfortable and obvious what's been done to me—that this time when I was abducted, my greatest fear has come true. I was kidnapped and raped.

Except I *wasn't*. Tempest dropped me in the middle of one of my most traumatizing experiences and reshaped it into a twisted dream.

Tempest has been a fantasy of mine since I was a little girl. My kidnappers are a recurring nightmare of mine since I was ten. Combining the two has given me a sense of bravery. Of control.

I sneak into my room without much sound, finding Clover snoozing in her twin bed, facing the wall with her hands tucked under her chin. I'm eager to do the same.

Two reflective glints of yellow on my bed catch my eye. My shoulders tense, fear fusing my limbs together. What has Tempest left for me, now?

A small meow comes from the same direction. My knees nearly buckle at the sound.

"Hermione!" I whisper, running to the edge of my bed and collapsing in front of her. "You're here. You're okay!"

She purrs into my hand, her belly turning into a motor boat of pleasure. My heart swells at the feel of her soft fur, alive and unharmed. This was the one unforgivable move Tempest could've made, and he didn't do it. He didn't kill my baby.

Burying my face in Hermione's fur, I let her catch my tears. How is it possible to be thankful, scared, and horny, all for one man? How is Tempest able to manipulate emotions so damned well?

There's more to Anderton Cottage than a history of witches. Tempest uses that basement for something other than what he did to me tonight. He made it clear who was in charge down there. Him. But I'm too tired to ruminate on it, choosing to catalog it for later and sleep on it instead.

After washing up, I slip into my cool sheets, wishing for the heat of Tempest's exhales between my legs again. Hermione curls up against the backs of my legs.

For the first time in almost ten years, I fall asleep without any nightmares chasing me awake.

22

ARDYN

Tempest isn't in class the next day.

To say I'm disappointed is the understatement of the century. I'd gotten myself all worked up before sunrise, flitting around the room and waking Clover, who is *not* a morning person, while I tried to make myself look perfect. Hermione's grumbles sounded a lot like Clover's before she moved from my bed and curled around Clover's head. Clover showed no surprise when our new roommate purred into her face.

I was thankful my friend fell back asleep while I debated between nude and rose lipstick. First off, I didn't want her to see me looking so pathetic. The still inexperienced part of me also wondered if she could tell if I had been de-virginized just by looking at me.

By her brother.

I press the rose lipstick too hard into my lips, smearing it onto my skin.

At some point, I'll have a lot of explaining to do. For now, I'm saved from it by Clover's nocturnal sleep schedule.

I'm not sure what I'm doing, wearing perfume and putting on a cute yellow sundress, other than that, I want to please him. There's a constant, hopeful niggling at the back of my head that if I'm a good girl, Tempest will want more of what we did last night.

Primping and priming took a lot of effort, so it's not surprising when disappointment lands like a brick in my stomach when the seat beside Professor Rossi's stays empty.

Rossi dismisses the class. I'm ashamed to admit I daydreamed through most of it, so I keep my eyes down as I pack up my books and laptop.

"Ardyn, stay behind a minute, would you?" the professor's voice, soft and gradual like a rising tide, flows into my ears.

Most co-eds at TFU swoon whenever they receive Rossi's undivided attention. For reasons I can't decipher, I shudder.

Those same girls hood their eyes with envy before taking their time exiting the classroom, hoping Rossi will ask them to stay, too. He watches, blowing through his lips sharply when at last, the door closes behind them.

"Please, take a seat," he says to me, casting his arm out to the chair adjacent to his.

I'm reluctant to leave my chair, strategically chosen in the middle of the table, but I can't think of an excuse to stay there. I slide my books over and sit, almost knocking knees with him.

Rossi's dark eyes watch every jerky move I make. When I finally still and fold my hands on my lap, they're alight with amusement. "Do I make you uncomfortable, Ardyn?"

"Not at all." I try to laugh it off. There's no use explaining to my professor that I have unpredictable episodes of reliving past trauma with strangers. I want to earn my grades, not have them gifted through pity. "I'm just worried I might be in trouble."

He smiles, the skin around his eyes crinkling in that handsome way all older men seem to know how to use. "For what?"

"Um—my paper last week. But if you'll give me a chance, I'd like to argue my case. I don't think Tempest was being fair simply because I offered a different argument than what he's probably used to—" I clamp my lips shut before I continue talking myself off a cliff. It's almost laughable, wanting to be good for Tempest but throw him under the bus at the same time. I'd like to blame my parents for this. *Do you see how far social isolation has gotten me, Dad?*

Rossi rests back in his seat, his smile thinning. "You and Tempest Callahan have a past, do you not?"

"Oh, I wouldn't say a big one." My shrug almost hits my ears. I am a *terrible* liar. "He was mostly annoyed by me. I'm friends with his little sister."

The mere mention of Tempest's name from someone else's lips makes me wriggle in my seat, the soreness from last night transforming into a reminiscent throb. I do my best to hide it by clenching my thighs together.

Rossi's attention darts from my face, to my lap, then back again. That only makes me want to squirm harder under his scrutiny.

"You don't have to play it off," he says kindly. "Tempest was there the night you lost a good friend."

I wasn't expecting the professor to come right out and say it. I nod tightly.

"I would say that leaves quite the impression on a person."

"It does," I admit.

"Tempest has said little about that night, but I do believe he tends to take out his frustrations in ways that aren't always wise. Your paper, for example."

I push my brows together. "Tempest wouldn't lower my grade because of Mila's death."

"Of course not." Rossi waves me off like I was the one who mentioned such a preposterous theory. "What I mean by that is, I believe almost losing his sister that night affected him in ways he's yet to understand."

I'm not sure what to say, so I bite my lower lip instead. I'm not current on social norms, but I suspect this isn't the normal course of student-professor discussions.

"Tempest may be releasing his frustrations on not being able to protect the three of you by being over-zealous in other areas of his life."

Now I'm getting uncomfortable. I cross my arms over

my breasts, afraid my hardening nipples will betray just how over-zealous Tempest has become.

"Like grading students," Rossi continues, "and coming up with almost impossible topics to write an essay on. Would you agree your relationship with Tempest has changed since your friend was killed?"

I swivel my head to the door before thinking.

"I'm making you uncomfortable." Rossi clears his throat. "I apologize. I'm only trying to understand my TA. He's become like a ... son to me, and your paper, in particular, caused me some concern. You're right, Ardyn. Your essay was pristine. I asked you to stay back to try to understand what would have prompted Tempest to grade you so low, and I perhaps mistakenly related it to your interactions with him last year."

The sincerity in Rossi's voice slackens my arms, and I rest them back on my lap. "You might not be wrong. I was taken away so quickly that I forgot how it could've affected the other people there. Like Clover and Tempest."

Especially Tempest. I've spent most of my time worrying about Clover. Tempest is always so flippant and unaffected that I'd never thought to question how he might've absorbed Mila's death and blamed himself for it. It makes sense, too. My therapy sessions sometimes consisted of misplaced blame. Could his anger toward me be explained by that?

Rossi leans forward, propping his elbows on the table and folding his hands underneath his chin. "Do you remember much about that night?"

He has to tone of seasoned therapists, soft and unsuspecting. Open and sincere. But unlike the safe space they created for me, I'm shying away from him instead. "So many people have asked me that question. Police, my parents, doctors. All I remember is glimpses of us driving, then waking up next to—her."

Rossi nods sagely. "You and your friends had taken MDMA that night."

"How do you know that?"

Rossi's almond eyes widen. "I apologize if that was too forward. It was on the news, and because it involved my top student at the time—Tempest—I remember small details like that."

"Right. I'm sorry." I stretch my lips nervously, hoping they're shaped into a smile. "I don't enjoy talking about that night, mostly because I'm frustrated at how little I remember."

Rossi reaches over and pats the top of my hand. There's nothing sexual about it, and he doesn't linger improperly, but I'm not comforted by it.

"I understand. Thank you for opening up to me." Rossi withdraws his hand. "You've given me more answers than you think by discussing this with me. I'll have Tempest change your grade."

"Thank you." It's all I can think of to say. Rossi offers me a placating smile, like I've almost reached his target but didn't quite make it, and I have the overwhelming need to correct my course. My doctors would call it anxiety-related people pleasing. I call it survival in a world I haven't yet come to understand. "I do have a feeling about Mila's death, though."

Rossi pauses in stacking his papers. "You do?"

"Yes, I can't quite explain it, but ... her death didn't seem natural."

"I'd think not." Rossi lowers his chin, his expression forming into the one I most despise. Pity. "You were in a violent crash."

"No—I mean, yes, we were, but, her neck…" I shake my head, annoyed with myself. "I'm sorry. I shouldn't have brought it up. Her death was ruled an accident, and enough time has passed that I should accept it by now."

"You don't think her death was accidental?" He asks it carefully like he's approaching uncertain territory.

This is why I don't bring it up. Because people think I'm crazy, especially if they've researched all there is to know about my past, and I'm certain, with Tempest's help, that Rossi does.

"Never mind." I swipe my books off the table and stuff them in my bag. "I shouldn't've brought it up."

"No, I'm intrigued, Ardyn. What do you mean by—"

The classroom door bangs open. Both our heads swivel to the sound.

Tempest stands in the doorframe, dirty, bloody, and bruised. My brows shoot up in surprise while Rossi notices Tempest's presence with mild distaste.

"What," Tempest asks tightly, "the fuck are you doing?"

He aims his glare at me.

23

TEMPEST

The air in this room is thin, and I inhale it with a low whistle.

Ardyn sits diagonal to Miguel in a ridiculous yellow dress dotted with white flowers. Her posture is so immaculate. Her breasts are pushed up, rising and falling with her nervous heaves of breath. My eyes are drawn to those perfect mounds like she's deliberately entrapped me before I get a hold of myself and go back to her face.

Big mistake because now I'm staring at rosy lips that beg for natural lip plumper. My dick concurs. And remembers.

"I asked you a question," I say to her. There's a deathly warning in my tone that wasn't there a second ago. Probably because I didn't expect to see her so close to finishing up Miguel's last assignment in the basement. If it weren't for his gruff voicemail demanding I see him immediately following the execution, I would've showered, glowered into my mirror, and come up with a distinct excuse to never stick my dick in Ardyn again.

Leave it to Miss Innocent to insert herself into my plans dressed in a damned sweetheart dress that silently begs me to rip to shreds.

Miguel smirks, reading the room, and I scowl while keeping my gaze locked on Ardyn's.

She blanches but opens those perfect lips and answers. "Professor Rossi wanted to talk to me about last week's essay. The one you graded."

I raise a brow. "If you have a complaint, you should have brought it to me instead of wasting the professor's time."

Miguel pushes to his feet. "It was my idea."

That gives me enough pause to change my point of view from Ardyn's angelic glitter to Miguel's cunning stare. "Oh?"

"It was an unfair mark, Tempest. You must know that," Miguel says.

I lift one shoulder. One corner of my lips pulls up.

Ardyn sees my half-smirk and glares, crossing her arms under her breasts and pushing them up further.

"I thought it prudent to discuss your prior interactions with her to decide for myself if there remains any bias between you two."

My attention steadies on my mentor. "Why would there be bias? I barely know her. My memories of Ardyn consist of annoying moments when she and Clover wouldn't shut up."

Ardyn's shoulder blades hit the back of her chair like she was slapped. I hurt her by saying this, by virtually telling her that last night was as banal as my memories of her. It's for her own good. She doesn't need a guy like me in my life.

It's better to frame it that way than by pondering whether I need a girl like her in mine.

"That may be true," Miguel defers, "but your actions toward her indicate otherwise. I felt the need to gently question her on your tragic night together, which Ardyn graciously allowed."

My stare grows sharper. An unyielding tingle spreads against the base of my spine in warning. "Why would that be? I drove up after the fact. Rescued the girls from the rubble."

"Mm." Miguel nods like I make a good point. If I didn't have so much respect for the man, I'd lunge over the table and strangle him. *What is he playing at?*

As if sensing the shift in mood, Ardyn pipes up. "It doesn't matter. It's like I told Professor Rossi. I'm not able to remember much, so I doubt whatever ... animosity ... you might have toward me relates to my recall of how Mila died."

Her last sentence strains her vocal cords, choking her. It urges me to throat punch Miguel for forcing Ardyn to push the image of Mila's corpse forward in her mind before I remember I did the same thing to her last night. Worse, even. I forced her to relive her ten-year-old self. Then fucked the fear out of her.

I roll my shoulders back. Stare at the ceiling. Anything to quell the writhing beast inside me demanding protection of the damsel.

"I don't have animosity toward you," I say now, pinning Ardyn to her seat with a look. "I just don't think you belong here. You can't hack this class, and you will hardly get through your freshman year intact, what with your documented history. If you have a problem with how I'm proving that to you, that's your issue. I'm merely doing my job." I slide my heated gaze to Miguel before adding, "And I do it well."

"That you do," Miguel murmurs. I have no idea if this means he's lowering his flag. If I have to guess, he's not.

"Come with me, Ardyn," I say.

Ardyn startles.

"My sister's looking for you."

There's no room for argument. After one last glance at her professor, she rises and lifts her bag.

God*damnit,* her dress barely covers her ass.

My glare practically tattoos itself between her thighs as she walks over, intelligently keeping enough distance between us that it would take obvious effort for me to grab her by her braid and drag her out.

"Thank you for the talk, professor," she says before inching out the door and past my immobile frame.

I ready one more glare in Miguel's direction. "I'll take her to Clover, then return."

I'm impressed at how mild that came out.

"Whatever you want, Tempest." Miguel's lips tilt in

amused derision. "I got what I needed from you, regardless."

My eye twitches in my otherwise frozen expression. I shut the door with a sharp click before rounding on Ardyn. "Move."

Ardyn jumps at my tone but turns and tries to match my strides. "What the hell was that about? And why do you look like you just crawled out of a grave?"

"*That* is between Miguel and me, and how I look is none of your fucking business."

Ardyn's jaw tightens. "Tell me where Clover is. I'd rather not be led around by you while you throw a mysterious fit."

I whirl, getting so much in her face that she darts back. "If I were truly to lead you, it would be on a leash, which we both know you enjoyed last night." I tug on my belt loop. "Care to have me use this again?"

"No because you passed it onto your buddy like I was nothing," she heaves into my face. "After what you—what we—you couldn't be bothered to escort me back to my home."

I stiffen at her unexpected honesty. "I received a call I couldn't ignore. And don't you ever get it twisted. I would *never* put you in the hands of somebody I didn't trust completely to keep his hands off you. He took you home just fine."

"So now nobody else is allowed to touch me? Because I'm *soiled* now?" She scoffs and, shockingly, shoves my shoulders. Her vigor surprises me so much that I actually allow her to move me. "You knew exactly what you were doing. And when it came time to explain yourself, you didn't care."

"I never do."

"Well, *I* care." She points at her chest. "About you. And what we did. It mattered to me. I'm not going to let you ruin it by barging into my meeting with my professor and manipulating my GPA and-and stomping all over me like *You mine now, me Tempest take to cave with stick.*"

I can't control it. A laugh shoots out of my mouth. Incomprehensible, considering I just finished decapitating a man who buried his family in gambling debts and offered to sell me his daughter to save himself while Rio held him down. It's just, she looks so cute and angry, like a perturbed anime doll, the very one I dirtied up mere hours ago. It's like she put herself through the laundry while we were separated, hoping to come out clean, but the filth of me stayed in her mouth.

I get out, with choked restraint, "What did you just say?"

"Do I have to spell it out? You treated me like a caveman would last night and right now. I refuse to be yanked around by you any further. So tell me, where's Clover?"

"In your dorm."

Ardyn releases a drawn-out sigh. "You're unbelievable. Goodbye, Tempest."

I allow her enough of a lead to watch the ruffle of her dress bounce against the backs of her thighs before resuming my walk.

She glances over her shoulder, perturbed, and picks up her pace.

I could match hers easily but prefer the view, so I linger behind as she cuts through the quad, past the fountain, and makes it to the stairs of her dorm.

Her hand raps against the banister. She asks, without turning, "Why are you following me?"

"I'm making sure you make it home safe."

Ardyn spins, nearly toppling off the first stair. Honestly, this girl. "I believe I asked you nicely to go away. Do I have to reach your level of cruelty for you to get the message? *Fuck off*, Tempest."

I'm impressed with her word choice since I'm sure she rarely lets curse words malign her precious tongue but press forward.

"Let me get this straight." I lean up against the banister, close enough to catch a whiff of her ambrosia perfume mixed with the sweat of her frustration. I fucking love it. "You're angry with me for not escorting you home last night, and you're pissed at me now for walking you home from class today? Make up your mind, princess."

"I'm mad at you for *existing*, Tempest," she spits.

We've drawn a small crowd, and if Ardyn took enough of a cleansing breath to notice, no doubt she would shrink like a flower and scuttle through the doors praying for an invisible cloak. I've made her mean, and meanness begets confidence, so here she stands, a warrior princess with flushed cheeks and a hate-filled gaze, bearing down on me with the might of a titaness.

I smile, rather impressed with myself for drawing this out of her.

She takes it the wrong way. Obviously.

"You don't get to choose my friends, concoct my grades, and haunt me until I leave, okay?" she shouts, her melodious voice trembling. "I'm choosing my destiny now, and *no one* but me gets a say in how I live my life. If I want to stay at TFU, *then I fucking will!*"

I cock my head. "You'll have to grow some massive brass balls to withstand my plans for you, then."

"Do your worst!" Ardyn throws her hands up, the rest of her face catching the color of her cheeks. "Don't you get it? My nightmares have already happened. My worst fears have come true. There is nothing you can do to worsen my existence, so just get out of my face and bother some other unsuspecting girl who will break in half at your whim."

I narrow my eyes. For a minute there, I enjoyed pissing Ardyn off so much that I'd forgotten about my purpose and the seriousness of Ardyn's meeting with Miguel. My shriveled heart unfurls, filling with the toxic smoke it needs to keep beating.

I say in a low voice for only her to hear, "Be careful what you wish for."

Ardyn misses the hint entirely. "I'm not kidding, Tempest. You've proven your point. You can screw me over in any direction, but I—"

I grab her by the crook of her elbow and "help" her up the rest of the stairs.

She gasps, our small audience retreats in stunned

shock, and I force her through the doors, some bystanders tripping over their feet to get out of our path.

"What are you doing?" Ardyn cries. "You can't just force me places! People are watching. You'll be reported—"

"Let them." I push her up the inside staircase, her dress slinking up her thighs as she resists me. Any higher, and I'll bend her over right here. Let's see them report that. "If you'd move with your own legs and deposit yourself in your room, I wouldn't have to shove you up there."

I say it with such logic that fury reddens her stare. "I'm going there anyway. You don't have to force me."

"Not fast enough, clearly." I poke her between the shoulders in a reckless attempt to distract myself from what I truly want to poke her with. "Scoot."

"You're insufferable," she bites out as we resume our climb. "An asshole. An animal. A snake."

I answer in a bored tone, "I've been called all of the above and worse. Get inside."

She grinds to a halt in front of her door, her back smacking into my front.

Ardyn releases a sharp exhale, and I know she feels the evidence of our stimulating argument.

"Clover's in there," she breathes. "We can't. I don't want her to know."

I reach around her and push the door open. "You think I do?"

Ardyn instinctively presses into me as if she's afraid of what my sister would do if she caught us standing together in a doorway. I suppose Ardyn's right to be afraid. Clover has all the dark art materials she needs to curse my dick for eternity. But she's had every opportunity to do so, and she hasn't yet.

"Clo's not here," I say over Ardyn's head, then push her inside.

Ardyn trips over the carpeting, righting herself with an oath sounding surprisingly close to what Clo might ultimately curse me with.

Ardyn turns to face me, digging a frustrated hand through her ruined braid. "Why am I surprised? Of course you lied. Why did you want me here then if Clover didn't?"

"We need to talk." I shut the door, then lean up against it in case Ardyn gets any ideas to scurry past me.

"Why?"

"I want to know what Miguel said to you."

"I repeat: why?"

"He had no right to question you about that night."

"A lot of people don't, but they ask anyway."

She stares at me dead-on. There's a tight pinch in my chest at the levity in her expression. For the first time, I picture her within white walls, drugged emotionless, and sitting across from a white coat peppering her for details about her kidnapping, her friend's death, and her life.

For once, I'm exhausted for her.

Putting myself in someone else's place isn't a natural habit. I roll my shoulders back to rid myself of the foreign warmth.

"What did Miguel want to know?"

I ask it casually enough to not raise her suspicions.

However, when it comes to Ardyn's tragic past, I doubt she suspects anyone who pries.

"The usual." Ardyn lifts a thumb to her mouth, chewing on the nail. A nervous tic I haven't seen from her before. "What I remember, if I've recalled anything since, if it's affecting my ability to function at present or in the future." Her eyes slide back to mine. "Why do *you* want to know?"

"I deserve to know why a professor wants information on my sister and her friend."

"Isn't Miguel Rossi your mentor? Superhero or something?"

I snort. "Or something. You sure that's all he wanted?"

"Yes. Why wouldn't it be?"

Miguel's interest isn't shocking. Ardyn was a liability that night and she could still be now. My worry stems from *why* Miguel thought it necessary to pry into Ardyn's mind, even if it was the tiniest bit. It makes me wonder if he doesn't believe her, or he doesn't believe me. Neither is a positive outcome.

"Why are you learning underneath him, anyway?" Ardyn asks, resting her slender hands on her hips. I watch the movement, remembering how hard I gripped that waist and envisioning the bruises I left blooming under that dainty yellow dress. "Last I saw you, you were close to graduating private school and primed to take over your family business..." She trails off, but prediction is what I do, and I mentally fill in the rest of the sentence for her. *Just like me.*

Invisible needles prick my throat when I answer. Discussions about my father and subsequent entry into this world are never a happy priority. "There was an unfortunate event just before graduation. My father decided it would be best for me to pursue another avenue before taking charge of his company."

Ardyn tilts her head, her dark blond waves swishing against the smooth skin of her shoulder. The one part of her remains untouched and unsullied. I lick the inside of my lower lip, wanting to end this conversation and bite her there instead.

"So he made you become a teacher's assistant? That doesn't make sense. You're too smart to be cloistered in the middle of nowhere living in an old witch's cottage. Your skills are wasted learning business when you could already be running it. Unless." She scrunches her nose in thought, an irresistible garnish to her do-gooder wardrobe. "Is this a punishment? What a dumb move on Mr. Callahan's part. I remember how everyone in my father's circle talked about you. You could've tripled your family's equity by now."

Her sincerity wraps around my chest and squeezes, causing my heart to twitch with an uncomfortably strong beat. Rubbing my chest with a filthy hand, I crack a smile. "Was that a compliment that just left your pouty lips? C'mon, give it to me more, baby. You're turning me on."

Ardyn frowns, her curiosity swallowed by annoyance. "You know what? Forget I was ever interested. Your father probably dumped you here because you're insufferable. You can leave now."

My smile widens. "But we're just getting started."

"We're not. You've tried your best, but I'm still here,

attending TFU, cozying up to your sister, and generally trying to improve my life, unlike you."

My grin fades at the edges. "You think that was my best, princess?"

"Do you have more planned for me than forcing a reliving of one of the scariest moments of my life? What's next before you realize I'm not going anywhere, Tempest? Will I find myself upside down again, next to a murdered friend?"

My vision darkens at the same time, and my struggling heart sends its keening throb into my ears. "What did you just say?"

Ardyn's mouth works. The stained pink long since faded with all the chewing she's done. "I'm—I just meant that it's not like you can orchestrate a natural cause of someone's death beside me. If you want me running scared, I suppose a dead body will do it. After what you did to me last night, I wouldn't put it past you—"

"Shut up."

The force of my demand acts like a lashing against her face. Ardyn reels back in shock.

"I'm going to use your shower now. And when I come out, you better be dressed in something different than that virginal fucking dress because if you aren't, I'm going to waste the effort of getting clean and split you with my cock again."

Ardyn sucks in a breath. Pink splotches her cheeks.

"You're right, princess. I'm not above pulling the filthiest shit imaginable and don't you fucking forget it." I point my index finger at her in warning before I saunter into the en suite bathroom in an attempt to hide the urgent pounding going on in my head, the same word playing on a loop.

Murder, murder, murder.

There's no way she could know. Ardyn was out like a light when I made my decision and turned Mila's off for good.

As I turn on the spray, my brain reminds me that I got lucky once when Ardyn woke up and didn't remember what she saw. It was helped along by a doctor I blackmailed to confuse and derail her if any memories came to light, but she's out of the safety net of an institution now, and Miguel has his eyes on her. If Ardyn ever starts to recall the truth behind Mila's death, there's no way I'll dodge that bullet again.

And in my life, luck is just another word for laziness, and I am *not* fucking lying down for this.

24
ARDYN

Tempest doesn't close the bathroom door.

Like an idiot, I stand in the middle of the room, stunned into silence.

Nobody talks to me like the way he just did. Well, nobody but my abductors, and back then, I was a kid with the barest grasp of bad words.

But Tempest, he took those bad words and caused a buildup of heat between my legs, so intense that I'm afraid to move.

I'm not supposed to like it when I'm insulted, and I'm certainly not allowed to enjoy the way Tempest manhandled me last night. Like I wasn't fragile. Like I was a rag doll meant to be pulled apart and left to fend for myself. No one does that with me—Ardyn Kaine, the fractured heiress.

Tempest pulls off his shirt in one smooth motion, the muscles in his back tensing and flexing. Scratches mar one flank, four perfect curves like someone clawed into his skin, in pleasure or in pain.

They're not from me. My nails are too short and bitten to the quick to mark that kind of territory.

The thought of someone else, another woman, gaining access to his bare skin makes that heat at my center unfurl into the small of my back, spreading its tentacles and strangling my insides. That he could've done it between his dismissal of me and seeing him now turns that strangulation into sickness.

I was blindfolded then, covered and bound. He could've already had those marks on him. Same with the small bruise at the back of his neck and dirt stains all across his back, as if he allowed a woman to ride him while he bucked on the forest floor behind his cottage, rutting and sweating under a full moon.

The hair at the back of my neck rises as a foul taste enters my mouth. I have the vague notion that this is what jealousy must taste like until all my thoughts scatter like a spooked flock of birds when Tempest drops his pants.

He's not wearing underwear. A perfect, melon-shaped butt appears out of the stained denim, smooth and unmarked compared to the rest of him. He stretches his arms over his head, his back cracking and torso twisting before releasing a satisfied groan and dropping his arms to his side.

My mouth goes dry.

Tempest steps into the shower, and I peek at the shadow of his balls and his impressive length. A clear glass panel separates the shower from the rest of the space, fogging up with the intense temperature of the spray. I'm drawn to the steam, my steps wide but tentative, as I approach the bathroom. Then before better sense gets the best of me, I step over the threshold.

Flashes of his body come through the condensation, his arms going up to his hair and the thick ropes of muscle undulating under his skin. He tips his head back, his striking profile set in perfect relief as his hair flattens against his head.

I don't know why he's decided to shower in my dorm room, but I'm starting to wish he'll never shower anywhere else again.

Tempest turns his head, his eyes blazing at me through the fog.

He says nothing, simply waiting for me to speak.

My lips part to make up some excuse, though it's obvious why I'm here. What I'm doing.

It's pointless to try to say anything. I'm trembling, my belly's quaking, and my bones are liquifying the longer I remain under his stare.

I know what he wants. What he told me to do. With shaking fingers, I give him what he desires.

My thumbs hook under my straps, and I pull them down. My dress, the simple cotton that it is, flows freely with gravity once I release them.

I'm left in a simple strapless white bra and underwear, but under Tempest's scrutiny, I'm wearing a see-through scarlet teddy.

I gulp.

Tempest dips his chin, slowly stepping out of the spray and out from the glass borders. I can see him clearly now at the entrance to the shower, droplets running down his nose and cheeks and collecting at the base of his sharp collarbone.

He crooks a finger. "Come here."

I go to him with shallow breaths until we're almost toe-to-toe. His hand, wet but hot like fire, clamps down on my shoulder and spins me. I gasp at the sudden movement, my breath cut off when he halts me with the same hand.

We're both looking in the mirror across from us, fogged over, but our forms discernable. His face hovers over mine. I'm able to study the arctic tundra of his expression before his hands start to move, unclasping my bra, the worn cotton falling to the floor at my feet.

He does the same to my underwear, hooking the hem and pushing down until they fall. The brush of fabric against my thighs makes me shiver, and I tilt my head against Tempest's chest until he grasps both sides of my face and forces me back down.

"Look at yourself," his voice rumbles into my ear. "And don't stop until I give you permission to do so."

I pull my lips in and clamp down with my teeth, used to discipline but so unfamiliar with it when it's used as a sexual weapon. One that I *want* aimed at me.

"You're sore, princess," Tempest says next, then tongues the shell of my ear. I release a soft moan. His dick responds, pulsing at the small of my back. "Because of the pounding I gave you last night. My cock was too big for your tight cunt then, and it'll be excruciating now. Isn't that right?"

When I don't respond, he bites down on my lobe. I cry out, then moan, "Yes. You're right."

"Do you still want it?"

I'm so in the throes of him that I can barely register his voice. My back presses into him, desperate to feel his length, like it'll prove he's as throbbing for me as I am for him. "I ... I don't know."

The heat from his body dissipates as he moves away, and I swallow down the whine for him to return.

"I'll make it easy for you then," he says. I don't turn to face him and instead watch his reflection. Tempest's eyes, so green and vibrant in reality, have become the center of a mist-coated storm.

I'm so lost in them that I don't see his arm whip up until it's too late. His hand clamps around my throat, and my head slams against his firm chest. His other hand moves down, *down*, until he cups my center, stroking and spreading the pool of wetness that I've been adding to since the second he threatened to spread my legs again.

Tempest angles his lips until he speaks into my ear again. "Which kind of man do you want? This one?" He squeezes my throat. "Or this one?" He inserts one finger into my folds.

My chin is forced up. I'm pinned against him, but my writhing is instantaneous, angling for him to go deeper.

"Because I promise you, princess, I can't be both." He

nips at my ear, then licks. Pain, then comfort. "You have to choose."

"I want ... I want you," I breathe out.

"I'm only one man." He sucks on my earlobe, then spits it out with a *pop*. "I'm confident I'm not the kind of man you dream about. The one who would finger you gently after a firm fuck to make sure you're sweetly satisfied after, or the kind who would hold you tenderly and allow you to fall asleep in his arms." He strokes. I sigh. Tempest circles my bundle of nerves and my hips follow suit, a kitten trailing after her new owner.

An intense, burning fire spreads from my core while air constricts in my lungs. My body starts struggling before my mind catches on that he's strangling me. That he's digging his thumb into my clit so hard, the sensitivity has turned into my nerves fraying.

"I'm *this* guy," he growls, talking as low as he did before but with a distinctive, ominous undercurrent. "The one who will gladly hurt you while he gets off on his own plea-sure. The asshole who loved to make your first fuck about being held against your will, and the guy who will happily fill you with his cock while you scream."

I'm clawing at his forearms, but they're cinderblocks against my body. My hips buck to get away from the too-intense flare he's forcing my clitoris to endure, and my eyes feel like they're about to bulge out of my head.

Tears fall.

My voice bleats.

And he flips me around and slams my back against the

shower tiles, only releasing me enough to readjust his grip. His hand splays against my throat again, his thumb finding its mark within my folds. He knees one of my legs up and out of the way, spreading me open.

"Do you want this man's cock again? Huh?" His eyes take on the color of nuclear war. Neon green. Toxic.

He lifts his hand on my throat enough to slam it back down again, cracking the back of my head against the tile. "I asked you a question. Am I the guy you want?"

I choke on the snot nestled in the back of my throat.

"Say you want me to stop, that you want to go home, and I'll let you," he rasps. "Forget this shit, forget this campus, forget me."

"Y-Y—"

Tempest relaxes his grip enough for me to speak.

"Y-You told me to take my dress off," I gasp out.

His top lip curls up. "You don't want access into my world, baby."

"I want you."

I've wanted you since I was a little girl. I had a taste, and I can't stop thinking about it. You're an addiction I can't break. You've fractured my nightmares into tiny, insignificant pieces.

Of course, I can't say any of that to him, not in our current state. Not ever.

He wouldn't let me, anyway.

Tempest licks his bottom lip, a mental war going on behind his eyes. He removes his hand from my throat.

I suck in a grateful inhale, bowing over from the exertion.

I'm lucky Tempest gave me enough time to do that because in the next instant, my back is flush against the wall again, and he's thrust into me, keeping his thumb where it is.

Digging hard, too hard, into my nerve center.

If I thought I experienced an inferno before, now I'm in hell. His girth is too thick for the rawness he caused last night. I picture blood leaking out of me as he plunges so deep, his balls tighten against my folds.

He presses his thumbnail into my clit, and I shriek at the tearing sensation.

"This is me," he says, his face close to mine. "This is the man I am, the one you want."

With a trembling jaw and a million thoughts telling me that he's right, I still clench around his dick in answer.

Tempest's lips twitch like he can't believe what he's feeling. He strokes a finger down my cheek, catching the tears. "Fuck, baby, you don't want this."

I clutch at his shoulders, digging my nails in. Wishing I could scrape across his back the way his other marks clearly could.

"All right," he murmurs, brushing his lips near mine. "All right, you win," he repeats, then pulls out and slams back in.

I mewl, the pain overriding the pleasure, yet the pleasure somehow proving its continued presence by offering me precious *zings* of ecstasy between his torment.

With every thrust, he twists his thumb like a screw, hammering me, hurting me, yet bringing me comfort, too.

Tempest holds me with his free hand, pressing his cheek to mine and assuring, "I got you, princess. Ride it out. It's okay. I'm right fucking here with you."

I moan, cry, and tangle my hands into his hair, the sensations too much, too many at once. I'm dying, but I've never felt so present. Tempest's warm, wet body is glued to mine, his breaths panting in my ear as he buries himself inside me, again and again, unstoppable and grueling.

The orgasm is abrupt, the burn from Tempest's agonizing ministrations to my clit almost too much for me to notice its build inside me, but when it comes, oh ... *God*.

I'm flying. I'm bursting like brilliant fireworks in the sky. Tempest croons, "Come with me, princess. Oh, *fuck*, yes, come with me."

Tempest swallows my cries with his mouth, attaching his lips to mine and refusing to let go until we've both stepped off the ride.

He lowers his head into the crook of my neck, heaving. Sliding my hands up the slick skin of his back, I hold him there, catching my breaths, too.

Tempest hauls me up in one swift maneuver and spins us until I'm under the spray, his dick still nestled inside me as I wrap my legs around his waist.

Without saying a word, Tempest resumes a slow in and out, small but pleasurable as he slides through my swollen folds. He runs his mouth down my neck, the water cascading onto our heads, dripping over our faces, leaving marks with his teeth as he nips and bites.

This isn't meant to give me another orgasm. An ancient part of me knows that. This is him leaving his mark on me.

He lowers my legs, setting me onto the tiled floor and slipping out of me at the same time. I emit a small whine at the feeling of emptiness, one I immediately recognized as forbidden and tried to swallow. Tempest's eyes dart to mine, then away, as he bends to pump soap into his hands, lathers it, then coats my breasts with warm suds.

I let him sweep and caress my body, leaning into his firm hands and purring under the circular massages he gives at the perfect spots—between my shoulders, on the meat of my thighs, my butt. He doesn't stop until my entire body is cleansed, including my hair.

We do it in silence, his reasons for not speaking continuing to be a mystery, while mine are not to ruin this surprising, tender moment.

When Tempest turns me toward the spray, he squeezes the tops of my shoulders, and a cold, brief wind takes its place.

I turn my head sharply, both afraid and certain of what I'll see. He's left the shower, dragging a towel quickly over his body and tying it around his waist.

Pressing my hand to the glass between us, I say, "Let me do the same for you."

He glances over sharply, snagging my gaze through the condensation. "No."

Tempest bends to collect his soiled clothes, steals one of our laundry tote bags, and disappears out of the bathroom. Through the beating spray, I hear the door click shut.

Depleted and more than a little weighed down with disappointment, I shut off the tap and step out. It's then that clarity decides to dissipate my rebellious cloud, pointing out all the things that could drive Tempest away.

The row of medications on the vanity.

His sister's clothes, books, and childhood stuffed animals tossed onto her unmade bed.

Hermione, a reminder of the sacrifice he didn't make, lolling around in the middle of the room, watching our entire show while plotting world domination with benign, golden eyes.

If Tempest killed her, I might've left TFU.

He didn't. He slept with me instead. Decided upon cruelty mixed with tenderness when taking my body for himself.

Because of that, we're both left clueless about what to do next.

25

ARDYN

I've somehow collected my bearings enough to pull my wet hair back, get dressed in a denim maxi skirt and top, and wander into the campus clinic to purchase tampons, chocolate, Coke, and a non-descript emergency contraceptive underneath. My obvious disguise is unnecessary—the check-out lady doesn't even blink. While I'm there, I also make an appointment with the ob-gyn to get tested and checked out.

I'm nothing if not prepared. *After* the fact.

Tempest's caused all sorts of idiot moves on my part. The worst part? I want him to do it again. And again.

Once finished, I make it to occult studies with two minutes to spare.

Clover's already in her seat, and I fight against the blush of shame creeping along my cheeks as I sit next to her and use all my concentration to take out my notebook.

If only my butt would cooperate. My dirty deeds are outed when I plop down with a wince.

"You okay?" she asks like any good friend would.

I suck. I'm a sucky human being. A terrible friend. I should tell her the truth. "Yeah, I decided on a quick yoga class at lunch, and I think I'm regretting it."

Sucky. Friend.

"Omigod, really? Text me next time. I'd love to join."

Nodding enthusiastically, I try to find a more comfortable position without being obvious.

"Greetings, my disciples!"

Professor Morgan breezes in, his angular face flushed from the outside wind. Clover, me, and the rest of the class greet him with quiet hellos and too wide smiles. His charisma and passion for occult and Wiccan culture are charmingly addictive.

His boyish good looks mixed with an insane amount of tattoos doesn't hurt, either.

Clover rests her chin in her hand and sighs as he approaches the table, and I stifle the urge to smack her on the back of the head to snap her out of it. The image stays in my mind, however, and I can't help but laugh at the abject horror that would cross her face if I actually did it.

"Something funny, Ardyn?"

My cheeks heat with more shame when Professor Morgan closes in. When I meet his eyes, though, I don't see anger, but mirth, instead.

"Do let us in on the joke," he says.

Clover turns her head toward me inquisitively. I cough. "Oh—no. It's nothing. Really."

Dear floor, swallow me whole, now please.

"No? I assumed it was due to your uncontainable joy in coming up with the perfect topic for our main essay this semester."

"Of course!" I say, showing my teeth with a pained smile.

He tilts his head, his amber irises glinting with gold behind his glasses. "Might you let us in on your exemplary idea?"

"Well..." I draw out the word, scrabbling for something to say.

"Ardyn and I have decided to join forces," Clover says beside me. She rests an arm on the back of my chair, leaning toward me with the likely intention of off her cleavage to the professor.

Morgan raises his brows and falls back on his heels but doesn't deny us.

"We want to learn more about the Anderton witches," Clover continues.

"We do?" I whisper.

Morgan's impressed brow-rise lowers. "Hmm. I can't say that the idea's a creative one."

"Well—we wanted to explore the prevalence of prejudice against women against the backdrop of witchcraft in the eighteenth century."

"Again." Morgan turns away from us and sits at the head

of the table. "Not the most imaginative topic I've heard, especially at Titan Falls. The next thing you'll tell me is that you're looping in the Salem witches in your research, too."

Muffled laughter from the rest of the class follows.

Clover sears them all with a targeted glare.

Morgan opens his binder and clicks open his pen. "Now, if anyone else has—"

"Sarah Anderton and her daughter were executed for assisting noble wives in poisoning their husbands. How do we know her clients were *all* female?"

Morgan slowly raises his head from his notes, regarding Clover with the same oddly cold stare my cat gave me a few hours ago.

Bolstered, Clover adds, "Certain texts that I found in TFU's library indicates some of those clients were men wanting women in their lives dead. These men buried the Andertons under the guise of witchcraft yet used those same witches to meet their own dark desires. I'd like to explore that more thoroughly. *And,*" Clover adds when Morgan opens his mouth, "I'd like to argue that Sarah Anderton's daughter was deleted from all known texts by these same men, as she was the one who predominantly worked with them in offing their female loved ones."

Morgan purses his lips. "You have my attention."

"Good." Clover sits back, a confident smile lifting her lips. She holds his stare a little too long.

My gaze bounces back and forth between them, waiting to see who will break first.

"I also want to unearth her name."

Now my brows jump. "What?"

"The daughter's name. I want to be the one to discover it." Clover lifts her brow at Morgan. "Is that interesting enough for you, professor?"

The other students murmur their disbelief with their neighbors. I regard Clover with an uncomfortable mix of pride and dread. I'm not sure I want to know how she means to figure out the daughter's name and what part she wants me to play. Probably none of it will be good.

And probably karma for what I've done behind her back.

"Oh, you hold my interest, Clover." Morgan's dimples flash. The girls around me bite their lips, but Clover just sends him a cocky grin. "I'm more than looking forward to reading your paper on the subject. Both of you." Morgan shakes his head, laughing at some internal thought. "I can't wait to see what the two of you uncover within these walls."

His words carry a curious undertone, but I'm jostled out of my focus when Clover elbows me and whispers, "He'll be so fucking turned on by my work, I'll have him between my sheets by the end of the semester."

Choking on nothing, I try to cover it up by rustling my loose papers.

Clover giggles, and I spend the rest of the class pretending to pay attention while daydreaming what it would be like to have Tempest between mine on a regular basis.

"Okay, hear me out," Clover says, perching on her bed and facing me while I sit on mine. My knees are up with an open notebook resting on my thighs.

I don't look up from my handwritten scrawls. "Nope."

"But *whyyyyy*." Clover flops to her back, rolls, then cups her chin in her hands and flutters her lashes. "Once. That's all I ask."

"Hang on." I rest my pen under my jaw and stare at the ceiling as if pondering. "Still nope."

"It's the one way I can think of to impress Professor Morgan. Otherwise, he'll fail us."

"That's a bit dramatic."

"It's one séance. You don't even have to say anything. I'll be the one summoning the Anderton daughter." Clover sticks out her lower lip. "Besides, I thought you don't believe in spirits, so why does it matter if you sit across from me while I chat to them."

"It's not the why." Sighing, I lower my knees. "It's the where. I'm not comfortable sneaking into Anderton Cottage."

I rub my lips together to prevent anything more from coming out. Further explanation would require mentioning Tempest's name and calling him out loud has the same effect as summoning a dark spirit. All my sins would come to light in front of my best friend and his sister.

Ironic, considering what Clover's trying to convince me to do.

"Which is why I asked you to hear me out. Again." Clover scoots to a sit. "I have it on strong authority that all three residents—Tempest, Rio, and *sigh*, Professor Hunter…"

I snort. If Clover could manifest heart eyes on her face, she'd be doing it right now.

"…will be off the premises in a week. They're going out of town."

"Why?" The question comes out before I can stop it. The thought of Tempest leaving the area—leaving *me*—forms a small pit in my stomach, rough and hole-filled like a stone fruit. Ridiculous, considering I have no right to ask where he's going or what he's doing.

Or who he's meeting.

If it's another girl, I might vomit.

"Some kind of boys' trip." Clover shrugs. "I guess grading papers and generally being on leashes with other professors is too stressful for my brother's fragile state." Clover cackles at her own joke. "Honestly, they just probably want to get laid without getting in trouble by sleeping with one of the students."

I knew it. My stomach sinks to the floor.

"Anyway, it means the cottage will be vacant for a while, and you have to agree that if I'm to attempt it, it's gotta be there. She was tortured there, killed there, and if she's haunting the place, she won't be straying far from where it all went wrong. And even if she doesn't come and I get nothing—" Clover points at me, shutting down any argument I was about to make—"you have to admit it'll be a fabulous addition to our thesis. He'll be so proud." She ends her speech with a toothy grin.

"Or he'll kill you for sneaking into his room when he's not around."

Clover throws a hand on her chest, feigning innocence. "Who says I'll be snooping around his bedroom?"

I laugh. "You don't need to say it for me to read your dirty thoughts."

Clover huffs in agreement. "You know, you're more clairvoyant than you let on. You *need* to come with me."

"Why can't you use someone from your study session? I hear you're acquiring quite the fan group." I waggle my brows comically.

"Oh, fuck off." She rolls her eyes.

During one of my quick trips through the library, I spotted Clover at a table with four other guys, Clover poring over her textbooks while the guys drank in her cleavage. She enjoys toying with men and always has, especially when they're intelligent, witty, and able to keep up with her.

Something tells me these boys won't.

"They help pass the time during the mandatory equations and statistics I have to do to qualify for a respectable psych degree." Clover twirls a piece of her hair around her fingers. "Morgan's class feeds my id. And you need to step out of your bubble. Come on, try it with me one time. Like I said, if you hate it, I'll never ask you again."

Clover clasps her hands in front of her, her pleas sincere and resounding in my head. I almost agree with her right there but scrutinize her further. There's no indication she's attempted to summon Mila. Even if she has, I doubt she'd tell me. And I'm certain she respects me enough not to do it with me around—no matter how often I say I don't believe.

I don't want to go back there. I don't want to do it on Tempest's turf. And I don't want to remember any more about what broke me than I already do.

I'm not sure how to explain my worries when all Clover desires is to discover the name of the Anderton daughter.

"Clover..."

"Pleaaaaase?"

Exasperated, I rub my forehead. "Fine. *Fine.*"

"Yes!" Clover claps.

"But only if you figure out a fail-safe way so we won't get caught."

Clover nods eagerly.

"*And* we search for actual artifacts at the cottage. Things we can actually use to prove our theory of misogyny killing the Andertons."

"Absolutely." Clover ends our chat with a resolute nod. Or so I think. "I hear their skulls have been dug up and are on display in a hidden room."

"Jeez, Clo." I throw a pillow at her. "No more morbid talk. I'm ending this discussion."

Clover laughs but bends to pick up one of her books from the floor, joining me in homework.

Until I hear, "Will we succeed in our search for the Anderton daughter?"

I roll my eyes up to the ceiling but end up glancing over.

Clover flips three tarot cards faceup on her comforter, then winces.

Curious, I tilt my head to better see. The first card I notice has a man with plenty of swords digging into him. I point at it. "What does that mean?"

"Ten of swords." Clover swoops her hand over the rest and returns them to the pile. "Apparently, we're about to suffer an unwelcome surprise in the future."

I draw away, but I'm unable to delete the image of the man with ten swords stabbing him in the back from my mind.

"It's not like it affects you, right?" Clover says, though her tone doesn't sound convinced. "You think this stuff is a bunch of hooey, anyway."

26

TEMPEST

The numbers blur on the screen before me, and I shut my laptop with a hiss.

Even without her anywhere near, I'm thinking about Ardyn. A week has passed without exchanging a single word with her, yet I find myself staring at her profile in class, the straight line of her nose and the pillowy curves of her lips as she takes notes during Miguel's lecture, her brows pinched in concentration.

At one point, the setting sun through the window outlined her in a lovely glow, her blond strands catching fire and her skin turning gold under Midas's touch.

She is breathtaking, this girl, and the thought that I dirtied her up with those same Cupid's bow lips wrapped around my cock and her swan-like neck under my hand... I nearly came in my pants twice in one lecture.

The fragility she casts is less breakable than I initially

thought. Ardyn's stronger than I predicted, but she *cannot* be strong enough to crumble my walls.

Her presence threatens the four years I sank into this shithole and the coup I joined Miguel in planning. I saved her life back when I had no idea what I bargained her for, and now it's become all too clear.

What am I doing, exactly? Making her fall in love with me so she'll willingly keep any recollections she has a secret? Turn her into an adorable sex slave who will spread for me, suck me, and moan my name whether awake or asleep?

It's a useless endeavor. I see how she studies me when she thinks my attention is elsewhere. The softness creeping along her eyes, the parting of her lips as she reminisces on our fucks and wishes for me to take her again. I've piqued her curiosity, released a lioness, and fuck, if I know what to do with her now.

Weakness is the worst trait I could acquire. Affection is even lower on my priorities. I cannot allow Ardyn to keep affecting me like this. I can't keep treating her like a precious artifact I'd love to smash against the floor and put together again, piece by gorgeous piece.

"Are his holdings that annoying?" Rio asks as he wanders into the den and sits across from me.

I push the laptop off my legs, reaching for a crystal tumbler of whiskey instead. "He's moving money around. A lot of it."

Rio hums his concern. He eyes my whiskey, then rises to

make himself a glass. "That's not new, is it? The laundered money must go through plenty of channels."

"Yes, but not this much, this often."

I don't say what's heavy on my mind, but I don't have to with Rio. He's aware as much as I am that our boss, our capo, is making the type of moves one makes when he believes he's being targeted.

"Have you notified Miguel?" Rio asks, returning to his seat, tumbler in hand.

"Not yet."

"Think of it this way," Rio muses. "If Marco Bianchi doesn't know that Miguel killed his brother, he probably has no idea Miguel's aim to take over the Outfit."

Marco Bianchi and all his made men also have zero clue that I'm monitoring their transfer of funds daily. If you want to know what a man is planning, look at their bank account. After I was dropped off at Miguel's feet by my father, he made quick work of my skills and demanded constant access to Bianchi's inner workings.

Miguel worked his ass off for Bianchi, but as a man of only half-Italian descent, Bianchi made it clear Miguel would never rise in the ranks. He was good, though, too good to have around for long without worrying about Miguel's influence over actual made men who could take over the Outfit one day. Under the guise of a mistake, of which Miguel doesn't make any, Bianchi had Miguel ostracized to TFU, where the other lesser men and screwups of the mafia go to rot.

If anyone fucked up, it was Bianchi. Miguel quickly

disposed of the exiled men he found useless and began training the ones he saw potential in—like Rio and me. We made a name for ourselves, and soon, Bianchi sent VIPs and other important debtors to be made examples of, and the Vultures were born.

Bianchi couldn't very well dispose of Miguel without causing questions, so in an act of good faith (or fakery), he sent his nephew, Hunter Morgan, to be trained in the types of skills the Vultures were acquiring in "information retrieval" and disposal. Morgan, like Miguel, is half-Italian and not qualified to ever become an underboss or boss. His father, however, was.

Until Miguel killed him one night—*the* night—under the guise of an art theft gone wrong.

Ever so efficiently, Miguel is turning the men he needs and initiating hits on the ones he doesn't, all without Bianchi's knowledge. When Hunter was sent here, that put a damper on things, but Miguel is never one to give up. Personally, Hunter's presence acted like a trigger for me, fueling my desire to fuck up this underworld even more than I already did.

But when Ardyn arrived next, *that's* when I became fucking concerned.

I'm not meant to be here doing this shit. My escape from Briarcliff Academy was meant to prevent any more chains from wrapping around my neck. My best friend, Chase, made it out. Why couldn't I?

If my father weren't so callous, so manipulative, so

willing to cast off his only son into a forest haunted by witches and tainted with screams…

"Keep an eye on how much money is going to the Caymans." Rio cuts into my thoughts. "It's all we can do when there's important business to dispose of tonight."

I massage my brows. Thank God for Rio, who'd follow me to the ends of the earth if he had to. Fuck, he already has. He doesn't have to be here. It's only because of me.

"Yeah. I've told Clover we'll all be out of town for a few nights, so she shouldn't bother us."

"That's unfortunate."

"What'd you say?" I slit my eyes at my friend. If he so much as gives me an eye twitch relating to my sister…

"Nothing. Never mind. Not like anyone wants to visit us in this ghost house, anyway."

"That's deliberate."

"Yeah, yeah. You know who we're getting?"

I nod curtly.

"It's a couple," Rio adds unnecessarily. "A chick is going in that basement, T."

"I know."

"I don't know if I … the last girl we had to off—"

"You mean *I* had to off."

"Was Mila."

"I *know*."

Rio studies me intently. I shift, then smack the arm of the chair and push to my feet, aiming for a refill. I hate being studied like there's something wrong with me. As if there's an emotion I shouldn't be showcasing.

Damn you, Ardyn.

"Can we handle working over another woman?" Rio asks my back.

"Doesn't matter." I lift the crystal decanter, the rim clanking dangerously against my glass as I pour. "If you don't have the stomach for it, you know who does."

Rio releases a disgusted sigh. "Hunter."

"Yeah," I reluctantly agree. "Hunter. And if it's all the same to you, I'd rather not be there to watch him cut out another heart. Let's kill her quickly."

Rio mutters his agreement, burying the rest of our debate into his whiskey.

27

ARDYN

One week.

An entire week passes by with bare-bones glimpses of Tempest and one-second meetings of our eyes in class.

I'd spent those seven days holding on to hope, going so far as to keep my ob-gyn appointment and go on birth control ... and for what? To deepen my already unrealistic expectations of a relationship with him? To somehow assume that he'd want to sleep with me again, maybe in a bed this time, maybe with gentle love-making?

Dammit, my therapists would have a field day if they were aware of what I'm doing. I'm avoiding those bi-weekly calls in the same manner I'm avoiding my parents'. Shooting off short texts of, **having so much fun!** and **I'm totally fine** have satisfied them so far. It won't last for much longer, especially if I continue down the delusional road of *Tempest likes me*.

No, he doesn't. He never has. I dangled sex in front of him, and he took the bait. Now I'm left to pick up the pieces of my pride, all while looking Clover in the eye and pretending I've never seen her brother's penis.

And here I thought I was doing better.

"Are you ready?" Clover asks behind me.

I tear my gaze off our droplet-splattered window (of course it's raining on a night like tonight) and turn to face her. She's dressed in an all-black ensemble with a Henley shirt, a lace skirt, and leggings capped off with Docs platform boots. She grabs her leather jacket off one of her bedposts, sliding it on, then pulling her ebony hair out from under.

I look down at my chosen outfit of boyfriend-cut jeans and a V-neck T-shirt knotted off at the waist. "Am I dressed right for this?"

"Meh, you'll be fine." Clover tosses me my wool peacoat. The nights are progressively chillier as we approach October. "No one's at the cottage, and in this weather, only morons are out walking."

"We're the morons."

"Yes, but with umbrellas!" She tosses me one of those, too. "Come on, we need to get moving before it gets worse. But holy *shit*, I'm so turned on. A thunderstorm is literally perfect for a séance."

"Yaaaay," I murmur but follow with Clover's duffel bag of goodies like a good little séance partner.

We reach the bottom floor and push through the doors, stepping into the relentless wind and sideways-driven rain.

A flash cuts through campus the minute my shoes splash into a deep puddle, outlining the quad in stark white and black.

Clover shrieks with glee, and I'm left honestly wondering if she should've joined me in my institutional retreat.

We put our umbrellas together and start running, our legs soaked through within seconds and our path dictated by the sputtering glow of streetlamps and streaks of lightning. Now would've been a good time to ask Clover if we could drive. Still, I'd spent the afternoon nervously researching Anderton Cottage. One of the perks of living there was that it was off-road and impossible to get to by vehicle.

We're the sole morons sprinting through the quad, past the shut-off fountain, and into the woods, trading asphalt for a sodden, muddy trail. This was the way we took on our first night at TFU, when freshmen were trading wishes for their blood, and Professor Morgan was strangely taking part in it.

Professor Morgan and his class requirements draw more questions than answers, but I'm the only one who seems to be confused. Clover's absolutely in love with his theatrics, so I guess it's safe to say that I'm the odd one out of how we earn a Titan Falls diploma.

The forest's thick canopy shelters us from the worst of the rain. Clover turns on her phone's flashlight and gestures for me to do the same. Soon, our bouncing circles of white light join in the sporadic mapping of our way to the cottage.

Rain should provide a soothing white noise. It always does when I'm lying under the covers and reading a good book. Here, though... I'm not at ease. Any animals living nearby have taken shelter. There aren't any owls out to cast their mournful calls across the sky. Only the trees left to fight through the night, their gnarled trunks and twisted branches guiding us to our destination like skeletal arms and hands.

"I don't like this," I say.

"We're almost there. Don't wimp out on me now."

"It's too quiet."

"It's raining. There are thunderclaps above us. It's not too quiet."

"Doesn't something feel off to you?"

"Other than my socks squelching in my boots? Nope."

Taking a deep breath and feeling stupid, I let Clover take the lead.

A noise travels through the shadowy gaps of the forest and into my ears. A wailing of some kind. No—a keening. "What's that?"

"Probably nothing. Or a wolf wondering where his next meal is."

"Do *not* joke about that right now."

Clover chuckles, then seems to feel bad about it. She slows down and wraps an arm around my shoulders, our open umbrellas tangling. "I promise it's just a little bit farther. I'll even throw in one of Tempest's espressos from his fancy coffee machine. Or how about hot chocolate?"

Clover knows exactly how to melt my insides. "Extra marshmallows?"

"You got it. C'mon, I'll race you!"

"Clover—no!"

She releases me and races off, her dark clothing becoming one with the forest in too short of a blink.

"Clover?"

Her fading laughter follows.

"Clover! Don't do this!"

My breaths become small. Rain patters against my umbrella, insistent and relentless. I squelch my way forward with careful steps, wary of fallen branches or—oh, God—snakes.

"Over here, Ardyn!"

Clover's voice is closer than I thought. I gasp in relief, picking up my steps and highlighting my way with my phone in a shaking hand.

She appears as if out of nowhere, standing in front of a clapboard house with a red front door sprouting out from the ground as if planted there by a mischievous fairy.

"That wasn't funny," I heave out.

"It was only a few steps." When I don't respond, Clover's face falls. She steps off the porch. "Shit. I'm sorry, Ardy. Sometimes I forget what you... I shouldn't have done that. I was playing around, trying to get you to loosen up..."

Pity is even worse than shame. I shake off her sad

words. "You always were the bitchiest of us three. You just hid it better."

Clover barks out in laughter. It cuts off abruptly.

Both of us realize what I said.

"Wow. Now I'm the one who's sorry." I shake my head while she takes us to the porch. "I can't believe I said that."

"It's this forest. This house. I've heard it acts like a truth serum because of a curse put on it by the Andertons before they died."

"That's impossible," I scoff, but eye the bright red door more warily.

Neither of us wants to enter into a conversation about Mila. Clover jostles my side, fishing through the duffel's front pockets. She raises her hand, clutching something that glints silver.

"Are those house keys?" I ask dubiously.

"Tempest likes to think he's the sole brains of the family. I prefer to see it as his overinflated ego preventing reality from smacking him between the eyeballs. I stole his keys a while ago and copied the one to Anderton Cottage."

At my wide-eyed stare, she jangles the keys at my eyeline. "As if I'm not going to want to explore a witch's cottage! He really should've seen this coming."

I'm forced to agree. "How did you manage to do it without him noticing?"

"He hates summers at our home in Manhattan and spends most of his nights drunk off his ass and bringing girls home. All I had to do one time was sneak in while he was snoring with two girls draped on top of him and go through his pockets. I'm sneaky when I need to be."

The unwanted image of Tempest entertaining orgies should be enough to shake off any excess feelings I have toward him.

Sadly, the twinge in my middle isn't growing hatred. It's *jealousy.*

"Has he done that recently?" I ask as casually as I can.

"Don't know, don't care. I got what I wanted."

Clover's shoulders open the door, ending further questioning. I walk in behind her, the room we enter dark and silent.

She curves around me and shuts the door, leaving us in utter black.

"Um. Clover?" I ask.

In answer, her flashlight app flicks on. "Can't risk turning on any lights. Someone could be bored and looking out their window. It'd be my luck to have some dumbass at Meat House notice a light at Anderton Cottage when no one is supposed to be home. I'm daring when it comes to pissing off my brother, but I'd really rather do it only when necessary. He considers being an asshole as qualifying for a good mood."

"Don't I know it."

I stiffen, thinking I've given too much away, but Clover doesn't blink. Instead, she's routing our way deeper inside. My flashlight app joins hers, and soon I can make out worn-down wingbacks framing a thick wooden coffee table and long maroon-colored couch.

A free-standing fireplace with stonework up to the thatched ceiling is next. I walk around it, admiring the stones that had to be stacked by hand a long time ago.

Clover's light darts across an entire wall of bookshelves with an archway in the middle, leading to another room. She pauses on a wooden staircase in the corner leading upstairs.

"Where do you want to do this?" I whisper, overcome with a desire to stay quiet and unnoticed even though no one's here.

"This coffee table should work."

"Really?" I stop in surprise. "I figured you'd know of a secret room or the actual spot they died in."

"The records of this cottage are sparse. The second floor is a modern addition, and so is the kitchen. As far as I can tell, this main room is the only original survivor of renovations."

I nod along, as my own research brought up the same thing. But knowing Clover, she would have found a workaround and unearthed any secret crawlspaces Anderton Cottage swallowed up. I'm not sorry to admit I'm relieved that all we'll be doing tonight is sitting around a coffee table calling for a ghost that doesn't exist.

What was I so afraid of?

I shoulder off the duffel and assist Clover in taking out her supernatural wares. I spot a few crystals, candles, and incense sticks—all tools I expect from her.

Then she pulls out a Ouija board.

"Wait, seriously?"

Clover pins me with a look across the coffee table before she squats down and centers the board. "Be useful and light some candles."

"You know the Ouiji isn't real. A million articles prove that we move the draggy thing through muscle memory, not spirits from another realm."

"I'm well aware of nonbelievers, thank you. And no, I don't think it's the answer to summoning Sarah's daughter. What I do believe is that it adds to the atmosphere, centers our concentration, and, if an Anderton so chooses, will be useful in their communication to us when they use our bodies as vessels."

I give her a dead-eyed stare. "I hate you."

"You'll hate me less if you stop being obnoxious and entertain my spiritual whims long enough to grant you an escape." She sits on her haunches, pleased with herself. "Light the insense, please."

I do as she asks, finishing off the triangle of wax candles, setting the incense stick in its holder and lifting the lighter to it. While I'm doing that, Clover takes a plastic bag out of the duffel, tears it open, and starts distributing what looks like salt around us.

I don't even want to ask.

A scent hits my nostrils, saving me from speaking. Pine. Woody and earthy.

My heart shoots up into my throat—*it can't be him; he's not here*—until a less recognizable scent hits the back of my nose. Citrus?

Clover notices my nose wrinkle. "Frankincense. One of

the oldest magical resins harvested from trees. It's been used for over five thousand years in rituals for cleansing a sacred space or purification." She lifts her chin in my direction. "Look it up in one of your science articles if you don't buy what I'm saying."

I laugh under my breath, proud of my friend for holding on to her passion and maintaining it despite constant pushback. "I don't have to. I believe you."

The smell, in such an unfamiliar environment, calms my nerves.

"Reduces anxiety, too," Clover adds pertly.

"I'm ignoring you now." I close my eyes, pretending I'm back at the dorms with Hermione warming my feet.

A few minutes later, I hear Clover huff, "Okay, the circle's complete."

She returns to the coffee table and centers the Ouija's planchette on the board, then plops a small stack of papers beside it with finality. At my raised brow, she explains, "Copies of the Andertons' trial transcripts. I found them in the occult section of the library. Sarah's daughter's name has been obliterated on every page, of course."

"Oh. Cool." I lean forward, my love for historical artifacts overriding the creepy reasons we're here.

Clover slaps her palm against the stack. "Read later. Now, we start."

I lean back with a long-suffering sigh. "Okay. What next."

"Place your first two fingers of each hand on the

planchette. *Lightly*. I'll know if you're fucking with me and moving it."

"Clo, I'd never do that."

Clover pushes her lips to the side. "Sorry. I can't be too careful when my entire life boils down to defending my beliefs."

Guilt worms its way through my rib cage. "You're right. I'm the one who's sorry. I'll take this seriously from here on out. There. Fingers on planchette."

Clover gifts me with a small smile and nods. She rifles through the duffel again, pulling out an item with a similar metallic glare to the house keys.

It gleams between us, and when I register what it is, it takes an unordinate amount of effort not to beetle away. "Clover, is that a *knife*?"

"Just real quick." She opens her other hand, exposing her palm, dragging the tip of the knife across it before I can stop her.

"Clo, *what the hell?*"

Droplets of her blood splatter onto the Ouija board.

"It's just a little cut! Don't freak, Ardy. We're summoning some angry spirits, and they require sacrifice. It didn't even hurt."

"That was—you didn't tell me about this part."

She levels me with a look over her blood stains. "For obvious reasons."

I still haven't collected myself.

"If it bothers you so much, close your eyes. I don't need your vision for this part."

I'm all too happy to comply. With my eyes closed, Clover returns my fingers to the planchette. I assume she does the same when she murmurs into the room, "Are any spirits here?"

I peek with a slitted eye. The planchette doesn't move.

"Hmm." Clover's eyes bounce between where our fingers rest and the trial transcripts. "What if we…?"

She dips her fingers in her blood, then smears it over the papers. They're photocopies, but still, I can't hide my pained grimace.

"Put your free hand in my blood on the papers." Clover asks it of me like she's requesting I pass her the butter over dinner.

"Clo, I am *not cool* with this."

"You don't believe in this shit, remember? And we're practically sisters. Touch my damned blood, you pussy."

My sigh has sound, but I do what she requests. The easier to get this over with and leave. With one side of my face screwed up, I rest the tops of my fingers on the cold, wet patch of blood.

The planchette shoots to the side under our fingers.

Y can be read through the circular window in the planchette. I whip my fingers off that plastic faster than I thought possible.

"Clover, did you move—?"

Our triangle of candles is snuffed out.

"*Clover*. This isn't funny!"

"It's not me!" she says through the darkness.

I can't see her. Without the candles, I can't see

anything. Belatedly, I feel for my phone, trying to remember where I left it.

A bang reverberates beneath my feet. A hollowed-out, torturous wail follows, high-pitched and mirroring the one I heard when stumbling through the forest.

"Clover, stop this now. I'm not kidding."

"I swear it isn't me!"

There's a tickle at the back of my neck, morphing into a bone-deep chill as it travels down my spine in a playful staccato. Something is using my spinal cord as their piano.

"*Clover!*"

"What's happening? Are you okay?"

A small flame illuminates the table between us and parts of Clover's face. She's lit one candle. We face each other across the board, catching our breath.

She doesn't see the shadows take shape above her head, forming into shoulders, into arms, and then into black, elongated talons darting for her neck.

"Clover." Her name comes out as a croak.

Clover's eyes widen. "What?"

"*B-*" My voice hovers above a whisper. "*Behind you.*"

28
ARDYN

Clover screams. Or is it me?

"Run!" I shout, then bolt off the floor.

Ghosts aren't real. I never believed in untethered souls trapped in the land of the living. So why am I stumbling blindly through a cottage I don't know, a house filled with horrors, with the certainty that one is clipping me at the heels?

A beam of light arcs over my shoes, and I dive out of it, my manic sense of survival egging me on that this is Sarah Anderton readying to deliver evil by searing my flesh off my ankles.

"The *fuck* is going on?"

It takes a second to register the voice. I've burrowed somewhere between a chair and the bookshelves, huddling into a ball and burying my face in my knees. *It's not real. It's not real. It's not real...*

"Clo, please do me the honor of telling me what the *fuck*

I'm looking at," the voice growls, so low it sends vibrations into the soles of my feet.

A light flicks on. The side lamp by the couch.

Through the gap between the floor and the chair, I watch the clomp of boots come out of—the bookshelf?

I'm able to study the first few steps of a descending staircase before that stupid sense of survival overtakes me again, and I slip through the gap before the hidden door is slammed shut by an angry hand.

Tempest. It was Tempest who came through this door, shouting at his sister. He can't catch me here at the cottage. He can't find me at *all*.

I've been humiliated by him more times than I can count. If he figures out I came to his house like an abused puppy, hoping for a glimpse of how he lives or what his bedroom looks like, I'd be mortified. He'd think me a stalker. Worse, a clinger. I'm meant to be as unaffected by our time together as he is.

There's no *way* he's allowed to learn I used the excuse of a Ouija séance with his sister to break into his house and get a peek at his private life.

Just the thought of being caught under his cold scrutiny prickles my skin. I hope to all of Clover's Wiccan goddesses that she doesn't out me. She can handle her brother just fine. Me, on the other hand...

"Tempest? What the hell are you doing here?" Clover's muffled voice filters through.

I push my ear against the bare concrete wall. This side of the bookshelf is paved smooth.

"I *live* here."

"You're supposed to be out of town—"

"And that gives you permission to break into my house and what, talk to Casper?"

"Sarah Anderton, actually."

I can picture Clover's stance perfectly as she faces off against her brother. Tall, chest out, arms folded defiantly. Exactly like he'll be regarding her.

"Clo, how many times do I have to tell you this cottage is off-limits?"

"But why? You *know* a place like this is like catnip to me. If anything, it's your fault for deciding on this cottage as your home. If you were in any other dorm, you wouldn't care that I came here to summon the dead."

"Do you hear yourself? Really, I'd love to know."

"Why does it matter to you so much that I want to use a Ouija board on your coffee table? You're always so annoying, Tempest! I'm not hurting anyone."

"Get out, Clo."

"No. Not until I finish listening to what the Andertons have to say."

"Do not make me force you out of here."

"Do *not* make me drop-kick you in the balls if you try to touch me."

"Clo, I swear to God."

"There are no gods here. Just me, you, and the spirit of Sarah Anderton that you scared away."

I sag against the wall in relief. She's not telling him I'm here.

"Jesus Christ, is that your blood on my table?"

The siblings erupt into a passionate argument, fading as Tempest moves from the hidden door and presumably toward his sister to push her out of the house. It dawns on me I'll have to wait for an opportune time to escape unnoticed, and so far, the only other option is ... down.

A small bulb on a chain illuminates the descending staircase, still swinging with the force of Tempest's slam.

I take the steps on the tips of my toes, somehow confident that any noise I make will reach Tempest's ears. He'll be back any minute, too. I can't very well stand here and wave when he opens his secret door and sees me on the other side.

If I thought he'd be mad for exploring his bedroom...

Gulping, I take the next few steps. So far, so good. The walls on either side end at the bottom of the stairs, opening up to what I assume is a basement. It occurs to me this could be the same room Tempest trapped me in last week. I didn't get much of a glimpse when I was here last, what with Tempest's naked body encompassing my entire world once he removed my blindfold.

Interest piqued, I take the rest of the stairs with faster steps.

"Do you think he's done?" a baritone voice asks.

I freeze.

"Whatever. It's his fucking problem for giving his sister so much leeway in the first place. Storm Cloud acts like such a badass when in reality he's a pussy for pussy. Even ones he's related to."

The second voice is instantly recognizable: Professor Morgan. What makes my brows lower is the way he's referring to Tempest, so casually and with such heated dismissal.

"Thanks for making the decision for me, then, Hunter, because I'm not going to listen to you bash the man who could kill you while you busy yourself with ... whatever this is."

That voice is also familiar but recognizable from the past. It brings back memories of sneaking under the dinner table with Clover as we tried to eavesdrop on what Tempest and his insanely hot friends were talking about when they took brief trips home for the summer. It's not Chase, the godly blond, or James, the curly-haired asshole.

It comes to me. Riordan Hughes. Rio.

A sound from above snaps my chin up. Tempest coming down.

Shit!

I scuttle to the bottom and do a sharp U-turn in hopes I'm not exposed to the two men hanging out in the basement. I duck into the crawlspace under the stairs without issue, rounding my lips and blowing out a relieved, silent exhale as I crouch in the darkness.

Tempest's steps thud above me.

"Good," Rio says. "Remove the tape."

A rip sounds. I peer through the sliver of light I'm granted in my hiding space.

I swear I hear the same despondent wail that echoed

through the woods in our trek over here. It cuts off, and a gurgling, choking sound follows.

My hand goes to my mouth, but I can't unsee.

Rio and Professor Morgan circle a wooden chair in the middle of the room, surrounded by items I recognize from last time.

The same chair Tempest used to tie me up and have sex with me.

And in that chair is ... another woman.

29

TEMPEST

Today is *not* the day to fuck with me.

Our assignment was going perfectly. Rio secured our targets by injecting top-level ketamine into their necks and transferred them to us in his Sprinter van. It took a day or two, given where they were located. Hunter assisted in propping them up in their assigned seats underneath Anderton Cottage, and I got to work.

What I do not expect, want, or need is to have my phone go off mid-garroting on CFO Steven Charles, alerting me to motion upstairs.

Unwinding the garrote from his neck, I step back and pull the phone out of my pocket. Imagine my annoyance when I witness two bobbing flashlights through our camera's night vision mode and the shadowy outlines of the figures behind them.

They were women, easily. The long, dark hair was quickly attributed to my wonderful, harebrained sister.

The second body could only belong to one girl.

"Fuck."

"What is it? Why'd you stop?" Hunter pouts nearby, put out that I didn't allow him his full, fucked-up ritual killing.

"We've got ourselves some visitors."

"The hell?" Rio straightens from his recline on a spare chair. "I thought we made sure no one would come by these next few days."

"Yes, well, people are anything if not stupid."

"Who are they?" he asks.

It pains me to admit, "My sister and her friend."

"Friend?" Hunter pops a brow. "As in..."

"Don't fucking say her name," I warn. "I'll take care of it."

"You'd better," Hunter says. "Bossman won't be too impressed to know your kid sister's at it again."

"We'll hold it down here." Rio straightens and grabs the roll of duct tape sitting on the apothecary cabinet.

The man in front of me tips back in his chair, of the school of thought that simply by reeling back, he could avoid further torture. The woman beside him—Marnie Charles—screeches and pleads, her shirt torn at the shoulder and bright red ribbons of blood dripping from her neck. I'd used the tip of my knife on her throat to draw out information from her husband.

"Or hey," Hunter says, "bring her down here. We have

an extra chair, and I'd love to see Clover Callahan in all her raven-haired glory...."

"Keep going, and I'll cut out your tongue." I say it offhandedly, overly used to the ways Hunter enjoys riling me up.

"Only if I can suck on hers first."

My exhale calls for calm. My fists *thrum* for revenge. Rio clasps my shoulder, muttering, "Deal with the important shit. I'll handle him."

Nodding, I sprint up the stairs, leaving Rio to use his finesse in reining in the loose cannon that is our capo's nephew, who I can't very well kill on the spot, as much as I'd love to.

I deal with Clover as expeditiously as she allows, which means a fuck-load of frustration and insults. I'm all too aware of the missing body in the room. I'm able to sense Ardyn's presence within seconds, her scent like a caress that ties a loose knot around the organ that is my heart. I don't have that tug now.

After wasted minutes of threatening Clo, she eventually tells me Ardyn was the first to race out of the house as soon as Sarah Anderton came calling—whatever the fuck that means.

Raising my eyes skyward, I shove the door shut on my dear sister's face and return to the main room, where I pull back a framed painting of a map of Titan Falls in the 1700s, enter a code on the keypad behind it, and watch with impatience as a seam cuts through the wall of books and the hidden door swings open.

I'll deal with the two Nancy Drews later. Right now, I have to complete this goddamned assignment.

I'm relieved to see everyone in their proper positions when I get to the bottom of the stairs. No rebellion from Hunter's part means we might just be getting him on our side, or at least blinding him enough so that he's not suspicious.

He hasn't questioned our reasons for kidnapping and interrogating this couple, too in the throes of torture, and I plan to keep it that way.

Without another word, I pick up the discarded garrote and wind it around Steven Charles's neck.

He can't fight me. I almost wish he would. I greatly dislike disarming an opponent to the point there's no retaliation or attempt to survive. This is how Miguel wants it, however, assuring decisive kills with no mistakes.

I'd hate to tell him that no matter how much a man fights back, I'll always take him down. All Miguel's doing is removing all the fun.

The wife screams as she watches her husband die beside her. I glance over while Steven's head digs into my rib cage. "Perhaps if your husband didn't skim off the top of the Outfit's funds, you two wouldn't be in this sorry state."

"B-But I don't know what you're talking about! Steven's a good man. He'd never—*please*, let him go!"

"Mm, a good man doesn't work for men like us, sweetheart. Sorry to say." I pull the garrote tighter.

Marnie shrieks. Steven's struggles weaken to flails, then slacken into nothing.

"No," she sobs. "Nooooo!"

"Can I have her?" Hunter practically jumps with glee at the thought of gaining access to our final victim.

"No."

"Why not, man? I have my tools ready. She's second-best, anyway. You got the information you needed."

"Not quite." I release Steven's neck, his head sagging backward and staring vacantly at the ceiling. Rounding his chair, I then face his wife, leveling her with a *do not fuck with me* look.

"My research tells me you're not innocent in this, Mrs. Charles."

"I-I-I have no idea what's going on." Snot drips onto her tremulous lips. "I'm j-just his wife. I'm on the board of charities. I raise funds for education. I go to banquets with him and talk with his c-co-workers, but that's all I know about his b-business..."

"The only people I dislike more than embezzlers are liars."

"I'm telling the truth!"

"Are you?" I tilt my head. "Or are you his teacher on how to skim off funds without getting caught? Tsk, tsk, Mrs. Charles, you got greedy."

Her eyes widen with innocence, but I catch the flash of temper before they do. "I told you what I am. I participate in social outings, that's all."

"Hmm. Rio." I jerk my chin to my friend. "Finish her."

"What? No!" she cries.

"Aw, really?" Hunter says. "Can't we strip her, enjoy the view, and *then* kill her?"

I clench my jaw, then glance back at Rio. He nods in understanding. Ever since Mila, I haven't been able to kill a woman, even quick and efficiently. There's something about their eyes, the abject fear and plea in them. The men possess the same look, but when it comes to females, all I can envision is Mila, and then Ardyn takes her place...

And it becomes a complete fuckup.

"Make it quick," I say to Rio as he takes my position.

"No! Please! I'll tell you everything." Marnie struggles against her restraints. "You're right. It was my idea to skim off the top of the laundered funds that came through our business. But it was only under the request of Marco B—"

I give a sharp look at Rio, and without hesitation, he shoots her in the middle of the forehead with his silencer.

She flops forward, the opening at the back of her skull spraying blood and brain matter over the walls.

Hunter clucks his tongue. "Now that's gonna be a troublesome cleanup."

He is correct, though I won't tell him. Rarely do I approve of the use of guns down here, even silenced ones, because of the mess they make. Unfortunately, they're also the most effective with instant death, and with Marnie Charles, she needed to be dead immediately while Hunter was in the room.

A sound close to a kitten's whimper comes from my right. My head snaps in the direction of the sound. I catch movement in time to notice one filthy white sneaker slide into the shadows under the staircase, along with a flash of blond hair.

Fuck.

My jaw clenches.

"All good, T?"

I force a nod.

"Well, you two have fun!" Hunter waves in the direction of the bodies as he waltzes toward the stairs.

Normally, I'd stop him and chain him to the walls if I had to in order to secure his help, but I let him go.

Rio's gaze slits in suspicion. I respond with a single headshake so he doesn't vocalize them.

As soon as Hunter's footsteps fade and the door upstairs clicks shut, I snarl, "Get out."

Rio cants his head. "Huh?"

"Not you." I step back from the growing pool of blood at my feet and stalk closer to the staircase. "She knows who I'm talking to. Get the *fuck* out before I drag you by the hair."

"T, what are you playing at..." Rio trails off when he hears a scuffle in the shadows, then a small, "Please. I didn't mean to be here. Don't hurt me."

Rio's eyes go wide. "Oh, *fuck*."

This is the last thing I need. The very last problem I want to deal with. After a long, cleansing breath, I duck under the stairs and haul Ardyn out.

She squeals, but I nip that sound in the bud by covering her mouth with my hand. The girl fights in my grip, despite just witnessing what a great shot Rio is and how cold I can be when ordering an execution.

"Want me to grab her … somewhere?" Rio asks, his hands splayed as he tries to get the right angle to hold her down.

"Jesus, it's like I've put a squirrel in a bag," I grunt, shuffling us to the middle of the room.

Ardyn's teeth gnash against my palm. She's already soaked my hand in her tears.

Rio gives up his attempt to assist. "What are we going to do with her?"

I don't know. "You have any K left?"

"Not on me."

"Shit." I don't want to do it, but she's left me no choice. I put Ardyn in a headlock, pressing against her windpipe until she falls unconscious.

She goes limp in my arms, her knees buckling. I follow her body's sag to the ground, gently laying her on the floor, well away from the blood spread.

"This is bad, T." Rio begins pacing the room. "So fucking bad."

"I know."

"If Hunter gets wind of this—"

"He won't."

"How do we keep her silent? If we let her go, the first thing Ardyn's going to do is alert the authorities."

Standing, I run a hand through my hair, staring down at her. She's beautiful in repose, her soft features stark against the cracked stone floor. Her hair has become a halo around her head, waves of innocence mere feet away from puddles of blood.

"I can't hurt her."

"What?"

I didn't realize I said it out loud. Inwardly cursing, I add, "I can scare her into staying silent."

"For how long?" Rio comes to a stop on the other side of Ardyn's supine form. "She witnessed us kill two people. Our covers are blown. If Miguel gets even a whiff that we're compromised—"

"He *won't*."

"How can you ensure that? This is my life, too. Fuck, even Hunter's. Years of our training, of Miguel's planning, have gone out the window."

When all I do is work my jaw while staring at Ardyn, Rio keeps going. "We were promised freedom in return for our cooperation, remember? *Freedom*, T. We haven't had that kind of life since we were fucking fourteen. We can't throw it all away for a girl. You were able to get rid of the other chick, Mila, and your sister recovered okay. We can do the same with Ardyn—"

The roar fires into my throat and coats my teeth before Rio can blink in shock. I vault over Ardyn and slam Rio—my friend, my supporter, the man who'd do anything for me—against the far wall, my hand on his throat and the gun I tore from his grip digging into his temple.

"I will not kill another girl again," I seethe into his face.

Through forceful breaths, he responds, "Then let me do it."

"*No.*"

"You can't expect me to bet my life on your word that you'll keep her quiet."

My finger strokes the trigger. "I expect you to trust me like you always have."

"T…"

I press harder into his neck. Rio grimaces.

"Ardyn's impressionable. Unstable. I can make her believe the worst in herself and the best in us. Give me time."

Rio thinks this over, the skin around his eyes reddening and veins protruding from his forehead. "A day."

"Fine." I bend low until we're nose-to-nose, then release my hold on him.

His top half crumbles, his hands on his thighs as he coughs.

"Go upstairs," I tell him. "Make sure Hunter's nowhere near. I'm carrying her home."

Rio straightens, wiping the back of his hand on his mouth. "Whatever, man. This is on you."

But like the good comrade he is, Rio does as I ask and clomps up the stairs.

I spin on my heel, returning to Ardyn and lowering into a crouch.

"Princess, what the fuck am I going to do with you?" I murmur, then take her in my arms and carry her upstairs.

Rio gives the all clear, and I quietly maneuver through the room without turning on any lights and out the front door. Thankfully, the worst of the rain has passed, and I take the trail to campus with careful but sure steps. Ardyn's hair trails down my arm, her strands tickling my exposed skin. She shifts, then moans, burying her face in the crook of my neck and awakening her sweet vanilla scent.

My nostrils twitch. Her smell is a welcome reprieve from spilled blood, sweat, and gunpowder. It's also a terrible reminder of what I am compared to her.

The forest accepts our entrance with its similar black heart, blanketing our forms in colorless, inky grays. A howl unleashes somewhere above us, the hoot of an owl soon after. The nocturnal creatures are awakening after a bucketing storm, and I prowl with them, my prey firmly clamped between my teeth.

What am I going to do? I ask myself again and again. I'm always so sure of my next move. We were successful in our task that I was in charge of tonight. So much so that Miguel will be in a rare, agreeable form.

We all but confirmed Bianchi is acquiring a personal stash on top of the money going into the Outfit. He's securing enough secret funds to pay for a large-scale maneuver. My monitoring of his bank accounts proves as much.

Marnie and Steven Charles were brought here for a double confirmation. Miguel will be satisfied with the evidence we've obtained but frustrated at Bianchi's accurate prediction that he needs to start protecting his assets. *Because he's suspicious.*

Dammit all. There goes Miguel's agreeable state.

"You've truly fucked me over, princess," I mutter, deftly avoiding a fallen tree branch.

Ardyn stirs. I shush her by rubbing my nose on top of her head, inhaling deep and capturing more of that angelic scent.

I make the mistake of closing my eyes and fully immersing myself in Ardyn's captivating freshness, perhaps not realizing just how much I needed it. It's almost enough to make me less pissed off at her foolishness.

Ardyn bucks in my arms.

It's so sudden, she tears from my hold the moment I register she's awake. She stumbles a few steps, rights herself, then disappears into the trees without a single glance over her shoulder.

I come to a stop, staring at the canopy above and massaging the back of my neck.

"Oh, *fuck* me," I snarl, then crash into the woods behind her.

30

ARDYN

I'm not adept at eluding capture. I don't know these woods at all, and even if I did, what would I do once I broke through the trees and landed back on campus? Go to security? Alert the chancellor of the senseless, violent murders occurring under his nose?

I'm also not entirely stupid. The chancellor might be well aware of the viciousness going on, and all I'll do is alert *him* of my unwelcome knowledge.

All I can think to do now is escape Tempest's clutches. Dry, brittle branches whack me in the face, and upturned roots trip me up more than once. The twisted path in front of me is curtained by internal visions of Tempest ordering Rio to shoot that woman. Of the man lying at their feet, gored and vacant, his soul departing his body through Tempest's hands.

Tempest did this.

The boy I crushed on, my best friend's older brother,

who was so dismissive of our antics it was almost cool to watch, his air of mystery and aloofness, even among his three closest friends. The four of them, Chase, James, Rio, and himself, heads always close together, brows constantly pinched in thought, the grim lines of their lips too mature for my eyes and their age...

How long has he been doing this?

Since high school? *Before* it?

As another branch scrapes along my cheek, claiming pieces of my skin, I realize his length of experience doesn't matter. He's coming for me either way.

At first, I heard him plow through the forest like a construction roller, seemingly three steps behind me and close to pouncing. Then ... it stopped.

The only noise coming from this forest are from me, slipping on wet leaves and ricocheting off tree trunks, causing birds to shoot from their chosen places of slumber, their wings flapping angrily into the air.

Veering to the left, I fall into a crawl, weaving my way blindly through ancient oaks and skyscraper evergreens, aiming for a place to hide. If I'm to make it until morning, I have to be as silent as he is.

The thought of Tempest killing me, of him using that same gun on *me* that Rio did to that poor lady, oh my God. *Oh, my God.*

My heart lurches into my throat, bile surging behind its flight. My ears burn with acid, my tongue becoming raw with it. I'm so scared that my insides are liquid.

I haven't been this frightened since I was taken, and even then, I didn't have the sense of betrayal that I do now.

Tempest was inside me. He made me trust the pain and taught me how to embrace and mold it into pleasure, to take control back. He's the only one who chased away my nightmares after years of torment.

How could he? *How has he been able to hide the killer inside him so well?*

Cowering against a large, overgrown root, I attempt to make myself as small as possible, covering my mouth to stifle the sound of my panicked breaths.

Tempest is somewhere close by. He won't give up so easily. I'll wait him out if I have to.

And I have to.

More time goes by. The forest quiets with the slowing beats of my heart, the birds coming back to rest and nocturnal predators pausing in their hunt for prey.

I scrunch my eyes shut, urging the woods to tell me where Tempest crouches, so I can run first.

Is this how Sarah Anderton felt when she tried to escape her fate? Did she drag her daughter along with her or hold her close while the pick-axes fell upon her head? The daughter's age was never written down. In my head, she's ten years old, cowering against her mother's chest, crying for help.

She was a killer, too. Sarah molded her daughter in her murderous image. Why my mind conjures these women while I'm hiding from Tempest is a puzzle for another time because now I need to figure out a way to survive, make it to the dorms, and warn Clover.

Unless Clover is well aware.

Conspiracies shoot through my head like a swarm of wasps. Reality and paranoia are interchangeable at this point. But I know what I saw. It was real. Tempest snapping a garrote between his hands, the strangling of that man, the shooting of that woman, man and wife dying together and under the direct torture of Tempest, Rio, and Professor Morgan.

Except the ghost I thought I saw behind Clover takes Tempest's place. Transparent claws, shimmering through shadow with the rainbow colors of the darkest onyx, reach for the man's throat and swipe at him until his skin splits open.

"*Boo.*"

The whisper caresses my ear like a soft summer wind. I spear out of my huddle, choking on a shriek.

Tempest catches me mid-leap by weaving his arms around my torso and tossing me to the ground.

My back smacks against the uneven forest floor, my head crunching against it soon after. Blurry stars interwoven with a canopy of trees and black, black night make it hard to gain my bearings and allow Tempest the advantage he needs to flatten himself against my body, his features overtaking the sky.

"Did you honestly think you could run from me, princess?" he purrs.

Both my wrists slam against either side of my head,

held firm by him. His groin rubs against mine, calling for the heat with a demon's expertise. The whites of his eyes, two moons bright against the gruesome aftermath of my memories fight for dominance and demand my attention.

It dawns on me Tempest might've done this before. Chased women into the woods, jumped them, assaulted them ... murdered them.

His teeth gleam through the night, enjoying my struggles and the useless kicks of my knees against his well-honed, muscled thighs.

Tempest is bigger, fitter, and crueler than me by a record-breaking margin. I have no hope of fighting him. He probably likes it when they do.

An idea takes shape in my head, one that sickens and arouses to the point of confusion. My stomach twists into excited knots. The fact that I'm looking forward to what I need to do next ... am I drawn to depravity like Tempest is?

No. *No*, I'm eager for control. And I'm pretty sure how to get it in this situation

So I tip my head back and moan.

Tempest stiffens above me. His grip doesn't loosen, but his jaw sure does. "What are you playing at?"

I wriggle underneath him, not in protest, but to get closer to the hard length pressing into my belly where my shirt's risen up, and the cold button of his jeans quickly warms with my heat.

"I want you," I say.

There's enough moonlight through the break in the trees to see his brows come together. "You're fucking insane if you do. Are you sure they let you out at the right time, or did you escape?"

His dart is a direct hit. Any mention of my time at Cedar Springs is a hurtful reminder of what I've been through and how I'm unable to handle tough situations. There are events that test a person's stamina or break them altogether. I'm so *tired* of shattering.

"The person I saw back there," I begin carefully, "that man, it's not the real you, is it? I've had the true man. I've tasted him, and I want to remind myself you're still in there."

Tempest pulls his lips in, conflict rippling across his features as he probably wonders whether I'm fucking with him or being honest. With my history, it's hard to be certain.

I hate to admit, I'm not so sure myself because what I'm saying is true. I want to believe the Tempest who hurts and pleases me is the stronger one.

"All you want me to do is to get off you," he responds. "And you're willing to say anything to make me."

A sifting of disappointment occurs in my gut at how fast he came to that conclusion, but what did I expect? He's expertly hidden a terrible secret for years. Tempest knows how to read people in their most desperate situations. "I can't fight you, it's true. But is the time you spent with me a lie? Did you have sex with me as part of a more sinister plan? Tell me, Tempest. You can't make this night any worse if you explain why you chose me."

"I..." For the first time, he's at a loss for words. "No. You weren't meant to be a part of this. I'd planned to keep you separate, but then you had to go and break into my home and sneak into the basement. Why did you do that, Ardyn? Fucking *why*?"

"I thought I saw something," I whisper, meeting his eyes through the moonlight. "I swear, I thought I saw something behind Clover, and I ran. I never expected to find —I didn't climb down those stairs knowing you had h-hostages there and were..."

"I don't know what to do with you." Tempest's voice lowers to a rasp. "I'm at a loss, and I wish you never made the decision to creep through that door."

"Me, too."

Tempest grows serious. At his expression, a dire warning flows through my center. "I can't let you go."

"I don't want you to," I say as fear claws its way into my throat. I press my hips against him, my core warming against his length despite the real danger he poses. But my plans haven't changed. The only way to get him to release me is to lower his barriers.

"Please," I beg. "Please, I need you now more than ever."

"You don't."

Lifting my head, I coax his lips to mine, sucking on his lower one gently and kneading the soft, silken interior with my teeth. He groans, and I drink it up eagerly.

Tempest captures my lips, transforming my gentle exploration into vicious pursuit. There's a sting in my lower lip, and a hot, metallic taste covers my tongue. I grunt at the pain, instinctively drawing away, but he pushes my head to the ground with his lips, forcing me to open, sucking my tongue inside his mouth and biting down on it.

Not enough to draw more blood, but to make it clear who is in charge.

I won't let him.

As I clamor for the upper hand, my tongue wars with his, drawing it out, our saliva mixing, spilling like the nocturnal animals we've become. I take his tongue in my mouth, and I bite it, too, aiming for blood.

He grunts into my mouth, then tears away. Streaks of red and shimmers of our saliva frame his lips. "You're a fool."

Panting, I collect every ounce of bravery I have left in me. "I told you. I'm not afraid of you. I want you." While I watch the determination waver on his face, I heave out, "I want to taste you again, Tempest. Let me... let me suck your dick. Please."

My sudden, dirty request has the intended effect. His fury falters, dumbfoundedness taking its place. I'm not like most girls he chases, and I'm definitely not like his victims. Meaning, I'm not nearly as predictable.

I'm banking on that.

And I hold on to that certainty as one corner of his mouth quirks, and he comes to a decision. "All right, princess. You can have what you want. But you'll be staying flat on the ground because I'm going to lick your cunt while you do it, and there will be no chance of your escape."

31
TEMPEST

I crave her.

After a kill, I always contend with a flurry of emotions—adrenaline, satisfaction, shame, certainty, and need, to name a few. I've never been able to release them efficiently, turning to running myself ragged at the gym or collapsing in a cloud of weed. I've tried sex, too, and while a nice release happens in my balls, my mind continues its fucked-up adventure from my nightlife into the day, never truly knowing where one ends and the other begins but having to play the part anyway.

Tonight is different. This time, Ardyn writhes underneath me with the movements of a caught selkie dragging herself across the forest floor and into my arms.

She could be up to something, my Ardyn, but my warring emotions don't seem to care. She's offering up her mouth, and so, to be sure she doesn't bite off my dick, I'll offer up mine.

Seems fair.

It's effortless to keep her flat while I maneuver so my dick is near her face and mine close to her pussy. If she tries to rear up, she'll have a nice meeting between my thighs since I've blocked her in with my knees on either side of her head and my elbows at her waist.

I'm a cage of bones prepared to lock her down until her screams die out, but Ardyn doesn't fight me. She hesitantly reaches for the zipper of my pants, instead.

Fuck, this girl. She'll be the reason I die. I'm certain of it.

What Ardyn should fear, she runs to. The things she witnesses should make her crawl into a haven and never want to come out. A private facility was the best place for her—or so I thought.

Tonight, she's making me think *I'm* the best place for her.

I'm a skeleton without a heart. My bones are yellowed with too-old experiences and scarred with battles she should never have to see.

She did. And she's here, anyway.

Ardyn's tentative tongue rips me out of denial and to the sensation of my dick being freed into the air and entered into slick warmth. Her lips are tight around my tip. I'm reminded of how small her mouth is compared to my size. All it would take is one full thrust to crack her jaw and suffocate her breaths.

A sudden scraping against my sensitive flesh makes me jolt. "No teeth, princess," I hiss.

She does as requested. It's her sweet attention to the

direction that makes me gently push into her mouth instead of savagely staking my claim and cementing just how bad I am for her.

A tight, hot feeling rushes into my center. Not an orgasm—never this soon—though its heat is similar. This is more akin to jealousy, possessiveness, a strange pride that I am the only dick she's ever had in her mouth and—

ever *will*.

That certainty pulses into my cock, and I force her to swallow more of me. Ardyn's jaw unlocks when I hit the back of her throat. She makes strangled noises while I fill her, her fingers digging into my ass as she both pushes and pulls at my pants.

To relax her, I unzip her and draw her pants down past her hips. I'm not about to relieve the pressure in her mouth. She has her nose for that, and instead, I play with her perfect, fuzzed-over folds that glisten under the moonlight.

The scent that comes from that glisten is pure ambrosia. I bury my nose and mouth in her, unable to play and string her along like I planned. I want to consume her, I want Ardyn to become a *part* of me, and that notion has me baring my teeth and plunging my tongue deep into her hole, basking in her heated want. For *me*.

Always for me.

I feel her moan against my dick, and the gorgeous picture of her reddening face with streaks of drool and tears sparkling under the moon nearly makes me come. I match my licks to my thrusts, drawing all the way out of her mouth, then plunging back in, my balls smacking against her nose. The sound of my retreat and wet reentry overtakes the forest. I moan into her pussy, using the pad of my tongue on her clit, and then, feeling creative, I push one of my fingers into her ass.

She jolts, her cheeks clenching before I stroke her back into submission, collecting her wetness like a lubricant and spreading it all over her, painting my mouth with it.

This was meant to scare her into silence. Still, I'm so immersed in her body and the way it responds to me, how her inexperienced mouth delicately tries to suck. At the same time, I ram into her and make her head bounce off the ground with my force, that the orgasm is inevitable.

I refuse to come undone alone. I stimulate her clit to the point of severity, and she has no choice but to follow. Nor do I pull out, choosing to spurt down her throat and enjoy the sounds of her choking on my salted taste.

Ardyn's coaxed out an abnormal amount from me, and I withdraw so I don't kill her, spurting the rest of my ecstatic release on her face, my cock jerking as her hands try to contain me.

She bucks underneath my ministrations, my fingers soaked by her. Ardyn's trying to swallow while orgasming at the same time, causing these gurgling fits of noise that almost have me chuckling with pride.

I come up on all fours, more out of breath than I care to admit and needing a few moments to collect myself. Ardyn squirms but doesn't squirrel out of my hold, her limbs slackening as she attempts to calm her own haggard sounds.

Using our moment of weakness, I turn until my face looms over hers. It's a pleasure to notice the smear I've left on her flawless features, the strings of cum on her cheeks and arcing over her nose. Ardyn makes no attempt to wipe it off as she stares up at me, showcasing the same amount of pride I was reluctant to admit possessing mere moments before.

I curl my upper lip, wishing for the strength to dominate her in the purest form by sinking my dick inside her and reminding Ardyn, who is in control of this situation, but unfortunately, I cannot.

Because she's more in control than anyone has ever achieved over me, and that shakes me to my core.

"You can't keep me here forever," she says, her unblinking, ethereally bright eyes boring into mine.

"True. I can move you into the basement permanently."

Her gaze shutters exactly like I predicted. What I didn't expect was a dried clump of shame to fall from my heart at the sight of her fear. Fear that I'm supposed to be heartlessly causing.

"You don't need to do that," she says.

"No?" I angle my head. "You're an unfortunate witness to an underground crime ring you had no business unveiling. I don't leave any loose ends. Ever."

"You don't need to worry about me."

Ardyn rises to her elbows, signaling for me to move off her and doing it with a deadened stare, indicating she's not about to run.

I was not confident when I started to read her so well,

but now is the best time as any to test that theory. Carefully, I maneuver off her so she can sit.

"Two people were brutally killed by my friends and me," I say as I watch her drag up her pants and come to a curled-up position, wrapping her arms around her legs. "Tell me, why shouldn't I worry about you flipping out and telling the next person you see?"

"I'm not reliable." She ticks off her fingers. "I have a history of instability. I'm constantly medicated. My one alibi is your sister, who, as far as I know, has no idea where I am and can't—or won't—back up my story because of her relation to you, and I thought I saw a ghost right before you strangled a man and Rio shot a woman."

I raise my brows at that last part, then decide to address the points I can. "Clover has no idea what I do. What I've done. I've protected her for most of my life." The mention of my sister draws me into a past I'd rather not visit. I detest Ardyn's ability to take me there. Raising hardened eyes, I say to her, "Congratulations, princess, you've brought up the one bargaining chip you have. Are you sure you want to use it now?"

"Would it even be possible to barter for my life, or have you already determined I should die?"

Ardyn asks it without a tremor.

"I'd rather not kill you," I say honestly, though I'm not about to get into the reasons. *Because you intrigue me. Because I'd miss you. Because no other woman will have your scent, your sound, your presence.* "But my men will expect me to take care of this. Rio saw you."

"Professor Morgan didn't."

I arch a brow at her point.

"He seems to be the one who'd expect you to get rid of me. Riordan, he'd follow you to the ends of the Earth. I don't ... you probably don't know this or care, but I've watched you and your friends for a long time. You didn't come home much, but when you did, you always brought a friend. Chase or Riordan. You're relaxed with them, more at ease than you were with your own family."

Not once did it ever occur to me that Ardyn could read me as well as I could read her. It irks me, and I snap, "I have a lot of trouble believing that a recently ransomed ten-year-old would have any idea what was expected of me or what I endured."

Ardyn continues undeterred as if she's experienced a thousand insults regarding her kidnapping, and now they no longer stick. "Clover and I would sneak under the table when you hung out with them in your drawing room. Did you know that? We'd discuss who was the cutest of your friends and listen in on the one we liked the most. I never admitted to her that it was you, always you, who I wanted to understand. You started off bright."

My tone lowers in warning. "Excuse me?"

"Like me," she says. "You were handsome, and enjoyed the world, and loved every second of sunlight. Then you were sent off to boarding school, and I was ... well, taken, and when we both returned to each other's lives, we had a grayness. It's most prevalent behind your stare. When you look at people from a certain angle, I can see it. It matches mine. I don't know what you went through when you enrolled at Briarcliff or what happened after to make you come here and do this, but I do understand what it's like to become a person you never wanted to be."

"Stop." My throat has become thick. "You have no fucking clue what I've done. If you did, you'd—"

"What? Hate you?" She moves until she's sitting back on her calves, tucking her feet beneath her. "Don't you think that should've already happened? You killed innocent people."

"They weren't innocent."

Ardyn cocks her head, her gaze turning wizened. I'm growing uncomfortable under her owl's stare. "Whatever they were, they probably didn't deserve to die."

"None of my victims do, if you boil it down."

"Then why do you do it?"

The muscles in my cheek tick under her scrutiny. "Because I was trained to. What was it like being held against your will?"

She startles.

"If you're here to ask me the hardball questions, expect a fast return."

"Well." Ardyn clears her throat. "It was terrible. I was positive they were going to kill me."

"Did they hurt you?" My voice takes on a slow, careful tone, usually used once before I go in for the kill. I don't even realize I'm doing it until Ardyn's lashes flare, then settle as she studies me with interest.

She's not meant to be intrigued by me. The girl's supposed to live in constant *fear*.

"No," she responds, "they used threats, constantly told me they were going to cut me to pieces, but they didn't ... they never..."

"I'm aware of that part," I say dryly, "since I'm the one who had the privilege of shredding your hymen."

Yet the thought of a man even hinting at raping her sets my ears on fire and produces an unyielding ringing in my head. My fists ache to do some permanent damage.

Ardyn snorts in disgust. "Leave it to you to ruin the moment."

"What moment?"

"The few seconds when you actually cared about my outcome."

"At no point have I given a shit about what happened to you," I lie. "I read the news as a favor to Clover and was curious if the press got it right. I guess they did. You were damaged but whole until you were splattered across asphalt next to your dead friend. Cue another mental breakdown."

My words hit their intended mark. Her features darken, half her face highlighted by the moon, the other consumed in shadow. My soul, everyone, in the shape of Ardyn Kaine.

Except for this time, I don't like the taste of my insults. Bitter, acidic, and tough to swallow. Probably because I'm the one who caused the mess this time and forced her to live with her pain.

Ardyn, the sweet girl, wisely changes topics. "Why did

you choose Titan Falls? Why with Rio? And why that couple?"

"That information is way above your business, princess. We're still needing to discuss our next steps when it comes to *you*."

"I won't say anything."

"And why should I trust you?"

"Because of Clover."

Ardyn doesn't flinch. I do.

"And there it is," I say. "You've discovered the one reason I have to live."

There's a twinge in my gut following those words since they're not altogether true. Ardyn is fast becoming another excuse not to die, a fact I can never voice because it won't do either of us any good.

I am a weapon of Miguel's, a tool for Bianchi, a piece of trash to my father. Ardyn deserves better.

She deserves a man who didn't kill her best friend because he was ordered to.

"If what you say is true and she has no idea, if I go to the police, I'll destroy Clover," Ardyn continues. "I missed out on a lot of her life, but if these past weeks with her have shown me anything, it's that she's had trouble processing Mila's death the same way I have."

It takes every ounce of training I have not to react to her words.

"Clover's buried herself in magic, crystals, witches. I've deleted my memories. We're both shells of who we used to be. I don't want to do worse to her. I want..."

I resist the urge to draw closer. "Yes?"

"I want it to be different." Ardyn sighs, chasing the tightness of her features by rubbing her hands over her face. Then seeming to realize I was still all over her, she lifts her shirt to wipe the rest of the mess away. I track every exposure of skin, from the lines of her torso to the perfect divot of her belly button. "No one will believe me. It'll be my word against yours, and to go up against a teaching assistant to a respected, tenured professor ... no, I'm not stupid."

"You took the very words from my mouth."

"Yeah." She slumps. "I know."

"I can't kill you. I've already tried once and failed."

I say it softly, but she perks up nonetheless.

"If I have your word you'll stay silent."

Ardyn nods. Not eagerly, but she does enough of an up-and-down motion for me to take it as agreement.

"You're right about Hunter. Professor Morgan. He doesn't know you were there, and I can entrust Rio to silence."

"On one condition."

My chin jerks back. "You realize you're in no position to dictate terms."

She meets my eyes again. "All I want to know is how. *How* you got into this. I know why my world became colorless," Ardyn adds. She must notice the tight pinching of my features. "But I have no idea why yours went black. Please, just tell me. I've given all of myself to you. I want to know."

I shake my head. "Giving me your virginity does not also give you the right to ask for something in return."

"I'm not asking you. I'm asking the boy I knew, the one who played in the sun. The one who I watched from dark corners, who caught me once and gave me a dandelion in my hiding spot. That impish jerk who blew the seeds in my face as soon as I reached for it."

"He's dead."

"Then tell me how he died."

"Ardyn…"

"Clover always told me how funny you were and that you made jokes out of every situation. I used to pine for a brother like you until I was old enough to realize people aren't attracted to their siblings, and I was *desperate* for you. The meaner you were, the more pranks you pulled on us, the more I wanted you. I noticed so much about you, Tempest. How you prefer cucumbers in your sandwiches instead of tomatoes. How you could lower the room temperature in any tense situation between your parents by making some sly remark. Your preference for a tailored uniform you always kept impeccable and your messy, tousled hair. Your utter confidence while walking into an unfamiliar room. Your complete, *undying* loyalty to your friends. God, how I wanted to be your friend."

I'm holding my stomach muscles so still that they ache. My face begs to be loosened from the vise-like, emotionless weight I'm forcing it to endure. Every sentence leaving Ardyn's mouth flays me open like a bullet, small in the front, and a total, explosive mess in the back where she can't see.

I had no idea she saw me that way; that the little pimply tyke saw me in any way. She was a figurine, delicate and fragile, that I was expressly forbidden to touch. I fucked around with her and Clover—what self-entitled big brother wouldn't?

I told myself it was her kidnapping that changed my behavior toward her. I've never considered how closely tied our severed childhoods are until now.

I'm able to scratch out, "Is this your way of breaking down my walls, princess? I gotta say, you get an F."

Ardyn draws in a deep breath. "If you won't explain to me why you killed those people back there, help me understand why you destroyed the best parts of yourself."

I sigh. Stare up at the canopy of skeletal branches, then scrape a hand down my face in a bid to bring myself back to center. Ardyn's tilted me too far over a precarious edge. "Are you sure you want to know?"

"I've wanted to understand you since the day I met you. Yes. I want to know."

"Fine."

32

TEMPEST

Five Years Ago

The rubble that was Briarcliff Academy's best-kept secret shrinks in the rearview window, the car's engine providing an appropriate roar to the disappearing castle the farther we crest away from it.

"Unbelievable. Fucking *unbelievable*." My father slams his hands against the steering wheel, beating it again and again as he belts out curse after curse.

"Dad." I'm switching my focus between him and the road in front of us, bouncing between them at a faster rate. Dad isn't slowing down, and the asphalt underneath the McLaren is a blur.

"The amount of time I put into those people, the blood,

sweat, and *money* I invested to keep their riches afloat, and they let a girl destroy hundreds of years of work? A teenaged *cunt*? I won't fucking have it!"

"Jesus—Dad!" I grab the wheel as he swerves, streetlights being a thing of imagination in this area of Rhode Island. A moonless night adds to the shit-tastic shitfest that occurred on school grounds, and I'm not confident Dad won't see a deer and aim for it.

"We got away," I assure him. "No one knows we were there. And Chase, he'd never surrender our family."

Dad cackles. Laughs and laughs until tears escape from the corners of his eyes, streaking down the curves of his cheeks and dropping onto his thousand-dollar suit.

"Don't you speak to me, son, like you had nothing to do with their downfall. You played your part well like I taught you, but know this—I am well aware of how deeply you betrayed my honor."

My shoulders press into the bucket seat, the engine seeming to come alive in my veins as Dad directs its thrum. It takes mere seconds for my fear of him driving to morph into thankfulness. It means, for the moment at least, he can't use his fists on me. "I've always been loyal to you, Father."

"You're an excellent liar, Tempest. Hone it well because I assure you, you'll need it for where you're going next."

"We're going home." I lift from my seat. "Aren't we?"

Dad's lips thin. He steadies the wheel until we're coasting at an excess rate of speed but in a straight line.

A pit opens in my gut, deep enough to fill with dread.

"I've done everything asked of me, Dad. Since I was fourteen, you stuck me with these rituals, made me perform these stupid fucking ancient tasks, like wear cloaks and exchange blood and basically bond with the elite through orgies and prostitutes. And I did it *all* without saying a damn word. You can't blame me for their destruction simply because I was there to watch it fall!"

"Son, I'd be careful with your words."

"It was their arcane rules that broke them and overinflated, criminal egos that destroyed your sacred brotherhood. You wanna get behind sex rings and high school crypt ceremonies? Fine. I, for one, am done with that shit. I'm glad we were forced out of there because frankly, Dad, thinking of you fucking fourteen-year-old girls—"

My head cracks into the passenger window. Fire spreads across my cheek where his blow landed. Working my jaw, I feel around the area where his raven signet ring split my skin open.

"Oh, I'm sorry, Dad. Did I get it wrong? Was it little boys you were after?"

"You fucking *waste!*" The car swerves when Dad attempts another swing. I duck and grab the wheel, swerving us in the other direction on the two-way road.

"You want to kill us?" I roar. "Then do it! End your legacy by taking the coward's way out!"

"I won't stand for your insolence, you son of a bitch." Dad's face bloats with rage, his skin red and his features almost beyond recognition. He clamps his hand down on the back of my head and rams me face-first into the dash until I can't see anything but black.

When I come to, the world is too bright, but the smells are familiar. The ticking of a cooling engine and the fragrant scent of leather gives me enough of a clue that I'm still in the car.

I come to slowly, my head pounding and my vision blurred. Squinting, I notice stadium lights outside the window, so bright they white out the night sky.

It's still night, though. One check of the car's clock through pinhole vision confirms it's 3:00 am.

The door on my side opens so abruptly, I nearly fall out.

"Come with me, boy."

"Huh?" Smacking my lips, I collect the drool that accumulated there during my nap. "Where am I?"

"Private airfield. Get out."

I look up at the figure looming over my vehicle. "I've been taught not to go anywhere with strangers. Or my father, actually. Have you heard about his preference for dick? I'd rather he not sell me to one of his friends with the same fetish. I have a really good-looking cock, after all. Many have wanted it, yet few have succeeded."

"Funny." The dude grips me by the elbow and jerks me out.

Cursing, stumbling, I land against a brick wall of a chest before I skip back a few steps and straighten. A tall, olive-skinned man with black-centered eyes and salt-and-pepper hair glares down at me.

I study him as my world sits back on its axis, and I gain

some clarity. "Hm. If I were into dick, you'd come in the first place."

He's a handsome bugger if one enjoys a large expanse of chest and long, flowing, cover model hair. Like I said, I'd be into him if I didn't prefer to place my dick in female cavities.

I give him a mock frown. "Sadly, I don't have an age-gap fetish."

Those bushy brows come down. And he plows me directly in the nose.

"Ah! Fuck. *Fuck!*" I hop from foot to foot while clutching my nose in a weak attempt to stem blood flow.

"That's for insinuating I have an underage fetish."

I curse. "Why are so many old men trying to fuck up my face tonight?"

The man brushes his hands together in an impatient gesture. He waits for me to crack not one but two eyes open.

"I'll give it to you straight, boy. Your father did sell you."

An uneasy weight nestles behind my rib cage. "At least tell me how much I went for."

"You're a debt. Mr. Callahan got himself into a rotten pickle and was banking on the help of Daniel Stone to front him the money and get him out of it."

"Chase's dad? Jesus, he should've talked to me before he sold me." I roll my eyes comically though my insides are churning. Dad and I, we weren't able to talk much before he tried to burst my face open. "Listen, Chase doesn't give a shit about my dad, but he's loyal to me. He'll pay you anything you want. If you'll be so kind as to allow me the…"

I feel around my uniform pockets for my phone, finding none. "Uh, where the fuck's my phone?"

"Gone, along with your father."

"You killed him?" My tone doesn't come out as shocked as it probably should.

The dude regards me with an amusing slant to his lips. "He's very much alive, now that he's used you to settle his debts. You're to come with me as a new soldier for the Vultures."

I stare at him for a few beats. Then say with a nice *pop* at the end, "Nope."

"Come again?"

"Buddy, I just got out of a FUBAR situation like you wouldn't believe. I'm not about to go into another secretly named circle jerk and do their elitist bidding. I am *out*." I salute him as I turn on my heel. "Sayonara."

Paved road spits against my ankles after a loud *crack*. I freeze where I stand, then slowly raise my hands.

"I tried to be nice," the man says behind me, his voice coming closer. Something cold hits the back of my neck, and I close my eyes in defeat. The nozzle of a gun. It burns where it hits my skin due to its recent discharge.

"I felt sorry for you, boy, given how easily your father produced you when he could've protected his family by surrendering his own life. But like you said, elitist, *circle jerk* men like that aren't the first to offer themselves up for the greater good. We are secret, yes, but we are also deadly weapons. I'm tasked to train your sorry ass into becoming a cold-hearted, emotionless killing machine, and I'd really prefer not to start by blowing off your head. Either you come with me, or you die. Your man Chase isn't around to save you."

I know a rock and a hard place when I see it, so I lower my arms in answer. The man makes a satisfied sound, grabs my elbow again, and twists me toward a plane waiting on the tarmac.

"I'm not sure you'd enjoy a protégé like me," I say once I get my voice back. I will never admit that this man managed to shrivel my balls, but he sure as fuck did. "I'm poor with instruction, get bored easily, and generally prefer my plans to anyone else's because they're always smarter."

"Because you come out clean?"

I grin. "Exactly."

"Not this time, son."

I frown at his use of a term I've heard too often.

"My name is Miguel Rossi, and as a sign of good faith, I'll allow you to keep your name. You will come to my university, attend classes, and show me that you're smart enough to obtain a perfect GPA. Otherwise, you'll be punished in the worst of ways. Starting with your fingers."

"Uh, what?"

We reach the plane's steps, and Miguel shoves me to take them first.

"I find the easiest way to test a man's longevity is to have him kill immediately," Miguel says.

I try to pierce him with a look over my shoulder. "Dude, what are you *talking* about? I'm an asshole, sure, but I don't kill people for the fun of it. Never have."

I catch Miguel's grin before he pushes me up the rest of the steps until we reach the cabin.

Miguel's gun digs into the small of my back when I stumble to a halt at the front of the aisle.

It's a private plane with six seats, three on either side, and two of them are occupied.

An elderly man and woman, tied, gagged, and bloodied from previous beatings.

"I don't understand..." My voice is small. I hate myself, fucking *hate* myself, but suddenly, I'm scared.

"I think you do, boy. I'll even allow you the choice." Miguel moves in front of me, a gun in one hand and a knife in the other. "It's their plane. Bianchi doesn't give me enough money to properly secure more men, forcing me to figure out more imaginative ways of success. What was it you said? You're poor with instruction? Let me make it easy for you. I don't have many men under me because I'm forced to kill most of them after they prove how short-lived they are. Are you a coward, Tempest Callahan, or can you be my Vulture, pecking at dead meat, allowing your victims to rot and circling the men I tell you to?" Miguel brings his face close to mine. "Will you be a good little baby bird until you earn your black feathers, or should I just kill you now and save us both the trouble?"

I gulp. My eyes are hot and too wet, and my fingers tremble at my sides.

"Choose, Tempest. Or, I'm told, Mr. Callahan is more than happy to offer up his daughter if you fail."

The couple whimpers behind him.

Then do it! End your legacy by taking the coward's way out!

Those were the last words I said to my father before he sold me to a madman, and that is exactly what I should do now.

Allow Miguel to kill me.

End the Callahan line for good and get back at my father that way. Protect my sister. *Protect my sister from all of this.*

She knows nothing of this life, my success in my father's realm enough to convince him to send her to a Manhattan school and nowhere near Briarcliff and keep her sequestered. She's grown up normal. Clover has weird friends and is a little too invested in ghost stories and true crime, but she's happy. Acclimated. Enjoying being a teenager.

I cannot be the reason she's thrown into this life.

But I also ... "Can't do it."

"Excuse me?" Miguel asks with deadly calm.

"I can't do it. Sir." I swallow reflexively. "Please don't make me."

Miguel veers toward the man, knife held high.

It's messy, the stabbing. Brutal and filled with screams —both the man and his wife's.

To prevent me from throwing up, I think of Dad, how he molded me in his image, expected me to take on the title of cruelty with no pushback, then cast me over to a vicious undertaker when all I did was hurt his pride. And his willingness to sell Clover, the heart of our family because I'm not evil enough for him, and he'd like to poison her innocence next.

When he finishes, Miguel turns to me, wiping his blade clean by using my shirt.

"That is how it's done. Now be a man," he seethes, "or join *that* man. Here. I'll even let you be a pussy about it."

Miguel shoves the gun into my hand.

The fury of the last four years, the amount of survival I had to learn when I hadn't grown pubes yet, the rage at being left behind by my friends, my family, and my complete lack of control over my future give me the strength I need to shoot the woman.

To prove my longevity.

"Very good," Miguel croons behind me. "Now. Let's move onto the pilots and ensure they take us where we need to go."

33
ARDYN

"So ... that's it." I hold my bent knees. Tightly, like I'm holding him.

Tempest leans against a gnarled tree root, the green of his eyes brighter than the somber forest surrounding us, changing colors and dying with the season. His haven't transformed since he was a boy—always heavenly, despite the horror he describes.

"I'll never give you everything," he says. "But that's a large reason I've become the creature I am today."

"The Vultures." I test the name on my tongue, my chin bumping against my knees.

"We're the cast-offs of the Mafia. Failures lucky enough to be given a second chance instead of dying on our knees in front of the *capo*."

"You. Rio. And ... Professor Morgan?"

Tempest casts his eyes skyward. "Yeah, him. He's a

different story. Like me, but unlike me. We didn't fail at becoming a soldier and therefore were exiled to the Vultures. Nor were we ever eligible to be a made man—both our parents have to be Italian to move up the Mafia ranks. I'm neither. He's half. We just have fathers and family who decide our destiny. My father sold me as a debt. Miguel, Professor Rossi as you know him, saw the potential in me because of my history, and Hunter's dad was—"

He stops abruptly.

I lean forward. "What? Professor Morgan's dad was what?"

Sensing more than seeing Tempest's closer scrutiny, I hug my knees tighter to my chest. He waits among the dying trees and leafless branches, sitting in the decay of summer flourish as if waiting for me to join him there. I have the feeling I'm supposed to find importance in his sudden silence because he almost told me something but didn't.

For the life of me, I can't figure out what it is.

"Hunter's dad is the nephew of the *capo*," he finishes quietly.

If Tempest was fearful I'd react in a negative way to that, he's sorely disappointed.

I blink. "And the *capo* is what? The king of the Mafia?"

His teeth flash. "You can put it that way. The highest-ranking official."

"Okay. Is Professor Morgan being punished? As a nephew to the capo, you'd think he'd be much higher up than the Vultures."

"Mm. Good girl."

Thank God, he can't see me. I almost preen under his praise before remembering why I'm sitting in the rotting woods with Tempest, and he's confessing to me in the first place.

"Hunter has fetishes that make most of the made men uncomfortable. As a boy who can't inherit or earn the *capo* title, they weren't sure what to do with him, especially after he unveiled his preference for witches and wizardry."

I watch the whites of his eyes practically roll back into his head.

"If I have this right..." I hold out one hand, counting off my fingers. "You were put into the Vultures against your will but trained under Professor Rossi's—sorry, Miguel's, skilled eye. Hunter Morgan was put here because they didn't know where else to assign him and wanted to teach him skills other than the dark arts hoping he'd become useful one day. And Rio...?"

"Follows me anywhere. He's a good friend."

Tempest's curtness after choosing to be surprisingly open is enough of a clue not to pursue Rio's reasons. I don't mind since I have about a million other questions.

"What's Professor Rossi's story?"

Tempest lifts a shoulder, a sliver of its movement caught by the moon above. "He prefers an air of mystery."

"Well, I prefer my professors not to be murderers, so you'll have to do better than that."

"You're getting more than anyone else ever has who isn't part of the Outfit, princess."

"Why is that? Do you think all this information will scare me into silence?"

"You've said you'll keep my secret for Clover's sake. And I feel like you deserve an explanation for what you witnessed." Tempest clears his throat. He's uncomfortable with the subject of opening up to me. I quite like it. "Do I have your word you won't tell anyone? It would only end up bad for you."

That angers me. "I've given you so much slack, Tempest. I'm surprised I'm not mummified. Even after what you've told me and being introduced to your terrible memories, no, I won't tell another soul." Rising, I brush twigs and leaves off my pants. I've given up on my hair. "Your memories are worse than mine, and that's saying something. I can only be certain your nightmares are worse, too."

An inscrutable tenseness crosses Tempest's features before he stands, too. "I sleep just fine."

"Good to know." I fold my arms over my chest, cold now that I'm moving. My face is tight and sticky with his cum stains. I couldn't dry completely, and suddenly, I feel like a fool.

For a brief period, I felt triumphant. Earning information from Tempest was unexpected gold—fool's gold. Because he's still a killer, my professors trained him, and this campus is a farce. People die here for reasons only benefiting criminals. Tempest has allowed his sister to enroll here, knowing the dangers. *I'm* here when all I wanted to do was escape the darkness.

And I ran straight toward it.

Facing him in these grotesque woods, I'm not running when I should be.

"You're safe," Tempest says, reading my thoughts. "I won't allow anything to happen to you."

I nod, then try to walk around him.

He catches me by the crook in my elbow. "Are you all right?"

I'm stunned into silence by his question. I never thought he would care. "Yes."

"You're not ... seeing things? Feeling unhinged? What you saw back there is similar to—"

"I know what it resembles. And no, I'm not crawling deep inside myself and refusing to come out. I've..." *Become stronger since meeting you. Understood the cracked pieces of myself better after you stoked those embers into the fire. Drowned in confusion whenever you aren't nearby because I shouldn't need a reluctant hitman to heal me.*

I've become as fucked up as you.

Tempest releases my arm, nodding. "Good. Next time, don't break into my home thinking you'll find memorabilia from the boy you knew."

I glance up at him once more as if in search of the lost boy behind his eyes. He's not there. This Tempest is harder, hewn sharper, and has given all the softness he can in these secluded woods.

"Believe me, I'll never take a trip to that cottage again." Shuddering, I move past him. "Clover will be looking for me. I have to go."

"You'd better," he agrees, allowing us space. Then he says to my back, "Because now I've tasted your fear, princess, and unfortunately for us both, I fucking love that kind of seasoning on your cunt."

34
TEMPEST

Ardyn's avoided me for three goddamn weeks.

This is a good thing. I spent most of those days stalking her, ensuring not a whisper of my secret life left those delicate lips. Not to Clover, not to campus security, not to any-fucking-one, no matter how low in the hierarchy at TFU, because I truly did not feel like killing an innocent to keep her—and them—quiet.

The deaths of the Charleses sit heavy on my chest, an anomaly after four years of hardened hits. I came to the reluctant conclusion it was because of my princess. She was my innocence, a sweet, glorious seashell I was eager to rip from her solitude and force into darkness, but on my terms. Not under hers. She gained unearned insight into my darker tendencies before I was ready, and now I'm a walking contradiction.

Hating what I am, doing what I must, stalking when I shouldn't.

"Yo, you there, man?"

Rio's question draws me into the present, and I look from the fountain to him. "I was thinking."

"Hard, it would seem, considering this is the last day we'll see skirts for a while."

The air around campus has cooled considerably, with surprising, minute pieces of ice if one breathes too deeply. Students are dressing in puffed jackets, fake fur, and bomber coats, some adding boots while others stubbornly wear open-toed shoes until snow actually falls on the ground. I'm eyeing a particular girl in a white down coat picking her way across the quad and talking closely with my sister.

Rio follows my line of sight and sighs. "I'm not sure that was the best idea, letting her go."

"It was either that or mess with my sister's life further, and I'm tired of picking up her pieces."

"Are you sure that's all it was?"

I tear my gaze off Ardyn's blowing strands long enough to glare at him. "Know your place."

"My place is to protect you, and I'm worried you've developed feelings for that girl."

"Your worries are unfounded."

He studies my profile, his stare causing annoying prickles across my cheek. "Nah. I don't think they are."

I respond mildly, staring at Ardyn while setting fire to Rio's feet in my head. "You're a man of many talents, Rio, but mind reading isn't one of them."

"I've wondered about that night when Mila died."

I look at him sharply.

"You gotta admit, T, you've had an unhealthy obsession with Ardyn since."

"And how would you know that?" I ask through my teeth.

"I'm not trying to snoop, but sometimes, your computer screen is noticeable, or I hear your side of phone calls. You were keeping tabs on her. A hell of a lot more than necessary to ensure Mila didn't have the chance to tell her what she saw before she—" At my level glare of death, he amends, "Before she was killed in that car accident."

"And?"

Rio clenches and unclenches his jaw, deciding whether to continue this path of self-destruction. "And a hell of a lot longer than necessary. Unless…"

"Be very careful," I warn softly, "with what you say next."

"Unless it wasn't Mila who saw Miguel kill Nico Bianchi in the first place."

"Fuck, you have a death wish." I stand with all intentions of storming out of the center of the quad.

Rio doesn't take well to my efforts to save his life. He catches up to me. "Tempest, you're playing with fire. And not a camp one. I'm talking about those out-of-control brush fires they have in California and Australia. Miguel won't stand for this. He'll—"

I whirl, catching Rio by surprise. "He'll never *know*."

"Jesus, T! If she saw that, and then she saw *this*, we're

done for! Do you really want to put your life on the line for her? *Mine?*"

"She doesn't remember!" I hiss. "None of it. Not running behind the stage, not the shooting, not the race out of the art show. Not even borrowing Mila's fucking jacket! You wanna know why I was so on top of her treatment? It was to ensure she was so heavily medicated she didn't know up from down or reality from fantasy. She can't trust herself, Rio, which is why she hasn't said anything about what happened then, and she won't say anything now."

"Why go through all the effort in the first place?" He won't let up. "Why did you kill the wrong girl?"

"*I don't know!*"

My roar draws the attention of any student within a thirty-yard radius. Groups pause. Eyebrows shoot up.

Ardyn glances over.

Our eyes meet across the quad, hers disturbingly steady on mine.

What are you thinking, princess? Are you wondering when I'll take you into the forest again? Do you still taste my stains on your lips like I do you?

Do you hate what I've become?

Do you despise me?

I can't read anything in her expression. Sadly, all I've accomplished is teaching her how to be a better liar.

Clover also looks over at the scuffle. When she notices the source, she rolls her eyes so hard her head nearly falls off, then pulls Ardyn away.

I wait for her to look over her shoulder as they show me their backs.

She doesn't.

"Oh, we are so fucked," Rio curses beside me.

"No," I respond to him while keeping my attention locked on Ardyn. "I'll prove it to you. I'll show you that you have nothing to worry about, and I have her under control."

"Care to give me more information other than that cryptic sentence?"

"You still like to watch, don't you?"

Grinning, I spin toward the STEM buildings, knowing Rio will follow.

35

ARDYN

Twenty-two nights.

The number of evenings I've spent restless, soaking through my sheets with sweat and triggered by nightmares, then soothed by memories.

The terror of watching Tempest kill.

The rapture of Tempest's tongue on me, sipping, branding, calming me with pleasure.

Blood splattering against a wall.

Tempest groaning as I take all of him in my mouth.

Having to touch and bring myself to orgasm to escape the carnival of madness lining my dreams.

And then I open my eyes in shame.

I'm not a good person. I *can't* be a good girl if this is what I think of.

This isn't like before, when I was forced to endure the worst aspects of humanity. Abduction, death, the loss of a friend... I wasn't able to handle those tragedies, and any of my therapists would be shocked I'm functioning now.

Unless I don't believe myself? Is that it? I'm not trusting what I saw at Anderton Cottage?

If that's the case, I can't trust my experiences with Tempest. They could all be in my head, and I'm still a virgin wishing for my best friend's brother to fall in love with me.

It's for these reasons I'm staring vacantly into my bathroom mirror after a scalding shower, my skin red and puffy, my eyes bloodshot.

We've just escaped Tempest glowering in the quad, arguing with Rio. I'm not so arrogant to think they were arguing about me, but ... I feel like they were arguing about me.

Rio probably wants me dead. Tempest, for his own selfish reasons, wants to keep me alive.

And I want to be alive with him.

Disgusted with myself, I smear my hand over the condensation on the mirror and turn away, wrapping the towel tighter around myself.

"Hey."

I squeal, flying against the open bathroom door.

"Yikes, did I scare you?" Clover sits on her bed, idly flipping through a textbook. "Sorry to inform you, I live here."

"Yeah, I—" Shaking my head, I push off the door. "I don't know what's up with me lately."

Lie. I know exactly what's up.

Clover not-so-subtly eyes the meds lining our bathroom counter.

"I'm not skipping doses," I mumble, padding over to my side of the room.

"I wasn't thinking that. If I didn't know better, I'd say you were experiencing heartbreak."

I stiffen in front of our shared closet, then give an Oscar-worthy snort. "That's impossible. I don't talk to anyone but you."

"Not entirely true. You talk to my brother occasionally."

If my spine could turn into a solid stick of metal, this would be the time. "Only when he forces me to."

"Mm-hmm, his social skills are totally on point. You almost ready?"

Clover's excited to present our progress to Professor Morgan in class today. Clover was undeterred by our botched séance and moved us into TFU's library instead. I was relieved to take up residence in the occult section rather than suffer through another attempt at contacting a dead Anderton—or figure out an excuse not to go back to Tempest's house. Ever.

We pored over the joke of a trial the Andertons endured and were fascinated by the sketches of Sarah Anderton. Her daughter was drawn with a blank circle for a face. I stared at that white space for what seemed like hours, imagining my features with Tempest as the judge, sentencing me to an eternity in hell.

But I'm not a child anymore, and I can't hold anyone else accountable for my actions. With my kidnapping, I could. With Mila's accident, I could. With what I discovered about Tempest and my professor, I only have myself to blame for any consequences.

"Ardyn? Did I lose you again?"

"I'm here." I pull down my shirt and finish buttoning up my jeans. "Let's go."

Clover doesn't move.

"Aren't we going to be late?" I ask, grabbing my packed bag off my bed.

"Not until you tell me the truth."

I play dumb. "Sorry?"

"You've been acting weird, Ardy. Weirder than normal. Spacing out and withdrawn and ... keeping secrets. Is there something going on you're not telling me about?"

So much. It's so wrong of me to debate which is worse: telling Clover her brother isn't who she thinks he is or confessing I've slept with him. If I can't be straight with her, I should at least be honest with myself—I'm being selfish.

"Are you reliving your past again? I hear you at night, crying out." Clover leans forward, clasping her hands on her lap. "Talk to me. I'm worried about you."

Clover has unwittingly given me an excuse, but I'd hate myself even more for using it. "I'm adjusting to this new, independent life at college. It's been hard, I'm not going to lie." *Liar, liar, liar.* "But you've played a big part in keeping me sane."

Clover straightens but doesn't take her eyes off me as she rises. "You were gone a long time when we were separated after our séance."

"I told you. I got lost trying to get back. The only reason I made it to the cottage was because you were leading us."

"Uh-huh." Instead of moving with me to the door, Clover opens her bedside table.

"Clo, do we really have time for this?"

"Always." She pulls out her tarot cards, closing her eyes and shuffling the deck. "Is Ardyn lying to me?"

"Clo—"

"*Shh.*" She lays out three cards.

Despite my realism and certainty that none of this matters, my stomach clenches as I wait for her to read them out loud.

"Death, the past. The devil, present. And the three of swords, the future."

My answering swallow is forced and dry. The names of the cards alone are enough to paint me as a traitor.

"Death is the ending of one phase of your life that could bring about a positive change. Not so bad. The devil—"

Is your brother.

"—means you currently have an unhealthy addiction. Or it can be fear-based. Something's holding you back. It's essentially a warning to change your life."

All too accurate.

"And the three of swords"—Clover runs her fingers down the intricate drawing of blades that look like they should be held by medieval knights—"means loneliness, betrayal." She meets my eye. "Heartbreak. You're lying to me, Ardyn."

My gaze bounces between the benign cards laid out on

her bed and her searching eyes. I scoff, flapping my hand at the cards like they're nothing but child's play. "You're going to take the word of your cards over me?"

She doesn't blink. "Yes."

I want to scoff. Act outraged. Convince her I'm innocent.

I can't.

"Let's go, Clover." I turn the knob.

She says to my back, "I suppose I should be happy you're giving me enough respect not to keep lying to my face."

I don't respond as I head out into the hallway, and our walk to class is tense and silent for the first time since I came back to her.

Everything I've learned over the past few weeks has me on edge.

The Anderton witch hunt, Tempest's macabre basement, and my own recollections, gnarled and unsure.

When Professor Morgan begins the class, my teeth clank together. Clover resumes her heart-eyed stare as he reclines in his seat and listens to each pair of students discuss their thesis. When he gets to us, my jitters are more difficult to control.

I watch him for the same tells, like the tic of an eye or a lowered brow of suspicion as I get up from my seat along with Clover. Throughout our speech, Morgan doesn't bat an eye, his expression as interested as it ever was when it comes to occult history.

... after he unveiled certain fetishes for the dark arts ...

Tempest's revelation swirls in my head, a laughing, screaming banshee as I outwardly pretend to be like every other student here. Ignorant of what's hidden at this university.

I should be elated over Morgan's dismissal. He doesn't regard me unusually or do anything to indicate I'm on his watchlist. I'm not.

Because he only has eyes for one female in the room, and it isn't me.

It's Clover.

She finishes our update, and Morgan makes a humming sound of approval.

"Good work, girls," he says before moving on to the next pair.

Clover's harsh whisper tickles my ear. "That's it? *Good work, girls?*"

I try for an understanding shrug, whispering back, "We haven't handed in the full paper yet. Maybe he's keeping his grading close to his chest until he reads our conclusion."

Clover grumbles but doesn't force the issue, slumping in her seat for the remainder of the class.

"Excellent work to all of you, I must say." Morgan pushes up from his seat. I watch how his tattooed fingers splay across the table, picturing them dipped in blood and drawing runes around dead bodies.

A white flash bursts into my eyesight, then a falling

sensation, like I've lost the back of my chair. I land in a windowless hallway with nothing but a cracked-open door ahead.

In it, I hear a male, baritone voice order, "*Turn around.*"

Terror surges from my belly to the tips of my fingers and toes, freezing me in place.

Then Tempest steps into my view. "What are you doing here, princess?"

What?

I scream, slamming my hands against the wood.

"Ardyn. Ardyn!"

A hand shakes my shoulder.

Blubbering, I scrunch my eyes shut, then open them again to a classroom of wary, suspicious gazes.

Long, dark brown hair curtains their judging faces, and Clover's concerned one replaces them.

"Are you okay?" she asks. "What's going on?"

"I don't ... I don't know."

"Ardyn? Do you need to go to the clinic?"

Morgan's parental concern somehow makes it worse.

"No." I stand too quickly, making myself dizzy.

"You sure? You don't look okay. I'll carry you if I have to."

"I don't want you to touch me."

"*Ardyn,*" Clover hisses when I lean on her instead. "I love you, and I'm concerned for you, but you're being rude."

"I don't care. Get me out of here."

Clover mouths, "*I'm sorry,*" to Morgan as if I can't see, then directs me out of the class. Nobody says a word until the door shuts behind us, then I hear Morgan say something that has the rest of the students easing up and laughing.

So affable, that guy.

So psychotic.

"I'm totally attempting to understand why you were such a dick to Professor Morgan when you practically fainted in his class, and all he wanted to do was help—"

"Stop, Clover, please."

"No, not anymore. I've given you enough benefits of the doubt. What the hell is going on to disturb you so much? You were doing so well. Should I—do I need to call your parents? I want to help you."

I bring us to a stop in the middle of the deserted hall. "Don't bring my parents into this. Please."

"Okay." She rubs my back at my stuttering tone. "I won't. But talk to me. All we want to do is help."

I raise my head. "We?"

"Well—Professor Morgan back there. You shut him down as efficiently as you shut me out. I wish you would open up—"

"Stop talking about him."

"Who? Morgan?"

"Yes." I reach up to rub at my temples, staunching the growing headache. "I see the way you look at him, Clo. And how you're defending him now. Aren't you wondering *why* I dislike him so much?"

"I dunno. Are you actually going to explain it to me, or will I get your zipped-shut mouth again?"

Shoot. She has me there. All I can come up with on the spot is, "I've heard the rumors about him, okay?"

"So have I, and guess what?" She leans in close. "*I don't care.*"

"You haven't heard the truth!"

"Yeah? What is it then, Ardyn?" Clover pushes her chest out and crosses her arms. "Give it all to me."

"He-he worships dark things, plays with magic in all the wrong ways, performs creepy rituals—"

"I do all those things." Clover points at her chest. "*Me.* Does that mean I'm creepy? That I devil-worship?"

"No! But you also don't have orgies with co-eds and drink blood and-—"

"You don't know what I'm into! You never try to understand! I *like* orgies, Ardyn, and I *love* the dark aspect of magic. It's as important to me as the light, and if you tried to understand anything about me rather than retreat into your hidey-hole of deniability—"

I suck in a hurt gasp.

"—then maybe you'd figure out I'm perfect for that man in there."

"You're not." I shake my head, horror coating my words. "You're so much better than him."

"And you're no better than the townspeople who ripped out the Andertons' tongues and chopped off their fingers before hanging them."

My mouth drops open. "Clover. You did not just compare me to a rabid mob. And those women—"

"*Witches.*"

"Those *witches*," I amend, "committed murder themselves. They were serial killers and were caught."

"So they deserved torture? What if I told you their victims were scum? That they were doing their town a favor by getting rid of pedophiles, abusers, killers of innocents?"

"I am not getting into moral code with you."

Because you're a hypocrite, I chastise myself. If I can stay silent over Tempest's behavior, how can I possibly argue against the Andertons' choices?

"You also don't get to decide who I crush on. I like Professor Morgan, I *love* the rumors that he hooks up with students, and I can't wait to see him naked!"

Her voice turns so shrill that I wince, her stubbornness smacking into me like bullets.

I open my mouth to return the favor when someone clears their throat behind Clover.

Stepping out from in front of her, I notice who it is. My shoulders slump.

"Excuse me, ladies. Everything all right?"

Morgan leans out of his classroom, his mouth curved in concern, but his eyes glinting with what he overheard.

Clover cuts her eyes from me and twists on her feet to face him.

"We're doing terrific, Professor. Thanks for asking," she says. "I'm taking Ardyn to our room now."

"Good," he says, a slow grin creeping along his face. "I'd hate to have such an interesting project derailed by a fight over a ... boy."

"Not at all, Professor." Clover gives him her best smile, disarming and beautiful. "Just friendly concern over here."

"Okay, then." After a brief nod and a lingering study of Clover, he dips back inside.

"Shit," I mutter.

"Your shit," Clover snaps. "Not mine."

She swings her arm through mine and pulls us to the exit.

I let her and deliberately stop engaging in conversation.

Because I know what my next steps are. What I have to do.

I have to let Tempest know about Professor Morgan's interest in Clover.

We have to protect her from becoming like me.

36

ARDYN

I told myself I'd never return to Anderton Cottage.

As I stroll through the woods outside campus, I assure myself that it's daytime and too cold for any predators to be out. I'll only stay the five minutes necessary to inform Tempest of the danger to his sister, then I'll run in the other direction.

I'd text him if I could, but I don't have his number, and after this one errand, I don't intend on keeping him as a contact.

A *snap* echoes off in the distance. I press myself against a tree, the rough bark scraping against my cheek while panicked, white tufts of air escape my mouth.

I can do this. This is the bravest I've ever been, willingly returning to the scene of a crime. If I had a minute, I'd ponder the advances I've made since the first time I endured the most terrible. At no point did I believe in the fortitude to retrace my traumatic steps.

Blood sprays across my vision until I blink the memory away. It's coming more often, a violent splatter against gray concrete, then black paint. Shelving with strange items being showcased, like a piece of pottery splashed with blood, swirls into the scene, then disappears. A man on his knees, then another man tied to a chair. A woman beside him, then a sole victim facing the end of a gun, begging for his life.

That couple was killed in front of a bare wall, trapped by Rio and Tempest. There were no art pieces in the room or a single gunman coldly lowering his weapon to a cowering form. Mila doesn't scream for them to stop.

I can't trust my visions any more than I can trust Clover's damn tarot cards. I just wish they'd stop using my head as a garbage disposal.

Pushing off the tree, I resume my walk, using my phone as a compass. I left Clover in our room, excusing myself after classes were finished to go to the library. We've entered into a truce of sorts, meaning we're not saying much to each other, so she let me go without a problem.

If she knew where I was *really* going ... if she knew who her brother *really* was ... if she knew she crushed on a dangerous killer...

Okay. That last one is a little hypocritical of me. I file those arguments away and hum an off-key tune until I reach the familiar, winding dirt path up to a wooden front porch and farmhouse door.

I stand in front of the closed door, counting the peeling strips of red paint, waiting to drum up the nerve to knock.

It never comes, so I force myself to do it anyway.

Less than two seconds pass before it swings open, and those inhuman, brilliant green eyes stare down at me.

"Ardyn?"

The surprise on his face is palpable, rippling through the air between us and numbing my lips.

"I'm not staying long," I manage to say.

Tempest steps aside. "Come in."

"I'd rather not."

"If you come to my house, I'm treating you like a proper guest. Get the fuck in, Ardyn. It's cold out there."

"There's no need. It's about your sister. She—"

"If Clover's involved, you're absolutely telling me over a shot of whiskey."

When I don't move, he sighs, then twists on his heel and disappears into the shadows of the house.

"Tempest!" I curse his retreating form.

He's left the door wide open, so I move over the threshold and shut it behind me. Refusing to take off my jacket, I follow his footsteps into the main area. He's lit a fire, the crackling, flickering flames bouncing across bookcases, heavy wooden furniture, and two wingback chairs that are unfortunately occupied.

I grind to a halt at the sight of Professor Morgan and Rio.

"Ardyn, what a lovely surprise." Morgan removes his glasses and lowers the pen he was using to mark his papers. Piles of them are strewn across the coffee table.

"I'm not staying," I say, wringing my hands together. Where the hell did Tempest go?

"Good."

Rio mutters it from his seat, keeping his nose in his book and refusing to acknowledge me.

I'm not insulted because, in all fairness, I'd rather a deadly marksman *not* care that I'm in the room.

"How's the thesis coming along?" Morgan tries for conversation. I wish he knew I'd rather slit my own throat than discuss the mundane with a bloodthirsty killer.

"Fine. Clover's working on it now."

"She has so much passion, that girl. I love setting it alight."

Even Rio glances up at the thickness in Morgan's tone.

So I didn't imagine it then. Morgan has an unnatural fondness for Clover. It's both unsettling and a relief, knowing that my reluctant trek to the cottage won't be fruitless.

Now my big worry is what Tempest will do with the information.

As if summoned by my thoughts, he reappears with two highball glasses in his hands.

"Drink?" he asks me.

"Uh. No."

Unperturbed, he hands the second one off to Rio. "So. What did Clover do now?"

Amazing how this man can talk to me like I haven't witnessed the worst of him or experienced *all* of him. It irks in a way it's not supposed to, the way he regards me so blandly. I've been avoiding him for weeks—I would've expected more curiosity at my reappearance, or at least suspicion.

Not *nothing*.

"I'd rather talk to you in private," I say.

Tempest quickly glances over at Rio and Morgan, then directs me to the other side of the fireplace, where a large, heavy wooden dinner table acts as the centerpiece.

"No, I mean, *really* private," I add.

Tempest's brows smooth as he processes my meaning. Morgan and Rio are still within hearing distance. He jerks his head to the staircase. "My bedroom, then."

My insides recoil.

"Unless you prefer the basement?"

"Bedroom's fine." Stuffing my hands in my coat pockets, I lead the way up the stairs to the second-floor hallway.

"The door straight ahead," he murmurs near the nape of my neck.

My baby hairs tickle my skin. Shivers cascade between my shoulders. He breathes out, and I'm engulfed by warm cloves.

Snap out of it. I force my feet forward until I come to the closed door. Tempest reaches around me and opens it, his arm brushing against mine.

There is at least an inch of down between his skin and mine, yet goose bumps spread across my forearm like he just stroked it with his tongue.

Sending a sharp look over my shoulder for him to knock it off, I walk in, flipping on the light switch next to the door.

I'm hot—too hot—but I will *not* unzip my jacket.

His room is what I assumed it would be—bare except for the essentials and decorated in blacks and grays. A queen-sized bed with a black, quilted comforter is centered perfectly under the angled roof. My mind immediately questions how many women have felt the soft fabric between their legs after rubbing up against Tempest.

"I don't bring any girls here, if that's what you're wondering."

My hands clench in my pockets. I hate that he knows what I'm thinking.

Tempest strolls past me and makes himself comfortable on his window seat, sipping his whiskey. He watches me over the rim, unblinking and consuming.

Like he wants to eat me.

Maybe he does.

I clear my throat. "I think Professor Morgan's developed too much of an interest in Clover."

His lips freeze against his glass. "You think?"

"I know."

Tempest's gaze swings to the floor, contemplative.

"What's worse, Clover likes him, too."

His eyes snap back to mine. When he doesn't move an inch, or a muscle, or even twitch in anger, I ask, "Aren't you going to do something about it? I didn't want to come here, but I couldn't figure out another way to keep them sepa-rated. I'm scared he'll introduce her to this world."

"I'll take care of it." Tempest rises. I note how his fingers clutching the glass have turned white. "Not to worry, princess. I'll make sure she doesn't suffer the consequences of this life like you have."

I take it for the backward compliment it is. "Thank you. I'll see myself out."

He catches my hand as I turn, his cold fingers squeezing like he's trying to pump my blood into his. "Have I made you suffer, Ardyn?"

Without turning back to him, I lower my head and close my eyes. "Unbelievably so."

"I apologize for that. I really do. Answer one question for me."

It's not a request.

"If you hadn't seen what you did or considered what I'm capable of, would you still have allowed me to do this?"

Confused, I turn my head to him. "Do what?"

He whips me toward him, my chest crashing against his. I gasp when my forehead nearly hits his nose.

Tempest twists my arm around my back, holding it firm, and tilts my chin up with the other. "You weren't supposed to be so all-consuming, princess. You saw what I am, and my next logical step is to get rid of you."

My heart thuds in my ears, but I meet his stare. "Then why didn't you?"

He angles his head. "Probably for the same reasons you're not disgusted by me."

"I am."

Tempest's mouth lifts in a cunning smile. "If I'm so vile, why is your pussy drooling for me right now?"

My lips fall into an *O*. I push at his chest with my free hand. "Bastard. I'm as dry as this dead witch's room."

Tempest's brow quirks, impressed with my insult.

It only spurs me on. "If I'm disgusted by any part of you, it's your sheer arrogance—"

He unzips my jacket, pulling the collar down until both my arms are pinned against my back.

"Tempest—what do you think you're doing?"

Tempest looks me over, pausing at the V of my shirt and licking his lips. "My innocent Red Riding Hood, you should not have come back to Grandma's house."

A thrill shoots through my center. I staunch that unacceptable response as fast as it comes.

"Let me *go*."

"You should've requested that before you dared me to check to see if I was right. Is your pussy wet for me, princess?"

"I told you. You're out of luck."

"Mm." With a flick of his wrist, Tempest unzips my pants and pushes me onto his bed.

With my arms pinned underneath me, all I can do is buck my hips and kick, which he dodges with ease, nestling into my spread legs at the foot of the bed and peeling my pants from my hips.

"You jackass! I came here because I was worried about Clover, not for you to take advantage of me!"

"Not the best time to bring up my sister, princess." Smiling that irresistible smile, he scoops into my panties and plunges his fingers in.

He doesn't waste time. Tempest begins playing my clit like his custom instrument. My head drops back, and I immediately see stars.

"That's right," he says from above. "Give in, the same way I can't stop myself from giving into you every moment we cross paths."

"I ... this isn't ... right..."

"You're a sorceress, Ardyn. You fucking have me under a spell." His fingers swoop and swirl, and after a masculine grunt, he gets to his knees and buries his tongue in me.

"Oh, my God," I whisper through the intense, wonderful swirls of pleasure he cascades into my body. "I'm such a hypocrite. I can't ... do this ... to Clover."

"What did I say about my sister, princess?" He nibbles on my clit in warning, making me squirm and clutch the bedcovers under my body.

My hands fall asleep from the weight on them, but I don't care. I'm starting not to worry about repercussions, either. Or what I'm doing to myself by submitting to him.

When he stands, hungrily eyeing my spread center and removing his pants, my muscles loosen to accept him.

When he pulls my shirt up to expose my bra, then yanks my bra up to my neck, I moan with excitement.

Who am I? What is this girl doing, knowing she's getting in bed with the worst of humanity?

But he smells like the boy I obsessed over. He grins like him, too. And the sex ... the sex is all I dreamed of and then some.

He frees his dick, thick and winding with veins. I've

never seen him in daylight, and when he rips off his shirt, I'm flabbergasted as to why I denied myself the pleasure for so long.

"My God," I say.

A shadow of a smirk crosses his face. He wraps a firm hand around himself, lining it up with me.

"I'm on birth control," I blurt.

His eyes flick to mine, his pupils blown out and his burnt chestnut hair fragmenting the fire of his stare.

"I-I took an emergency contraceptive the last time. I thought you should know. In case..."

He quirks a brow. "Did you think I'd be upset about putting my baby in you?"

"Well, I sure would be."

His lips twitch. "I should be, too. Fuck knows I'm supposed to do everything possible to stay away from you. At least one of us is being smart about this."

I bite my lower lip. Tempest seems to enjoy that and grunts in approval. "Do that again."

I do.

He lowers down, moving to free my arms and toss my jacket to the side.

"I want you to pinch your nipples while I fuck you. Hard. Twist and abuse them, princess, the way I'm about to split your cunt."

I should be appalled by his language. My mind sure is. But my body simply *thrums* with expectant pleasure.

And I do as he asks.

I'm depraved. Wanton. Screwed up in the head. But

Tempest has given me the one thing I can hold on to to keep my pride—control. I'm in charge of the pain.

My nipples have hardened to peaks making them easy to latch onto. I flinch at my first testing pinch until the pleasurable stimulation blankets the zing of hurt. Bolstered, I pinch harder. Twist more aggressively.

Tempest watches every emotion flutter across my face with predatory alertness. I wiggle, moan, and shut my eyes to fully immerse myself. Unwittingly, my butt scoots toward him, begging for him to fill it.

His rough, velvety voice whispers its seduction. "Very well, princess."

And he buries himself so deep that I feel the tightening of his balls.

Tempest's rhythm is hard and unforgiving. He commands me to keep my hands where they are, though I ache to scrape my fingers down his chest or dig my nails into his back. I want him close, I want him ruthless, and I want it *all*, my hips meeting his, my stomach clenching with effort as I lift and attach his mouth the way he's savagely taking me.

His growl tickles my throat as I suck it back. Tempest reaches around me and holds me against him, then flicks one of my hands away and commands the line between pleasure and pain himself. His pinches are harder. I yelp when it feels like he's about to tear my nipple from my breast.

"Come all over my dick, baby," he groans into my mouth. I narrowly avoid him biting through my tongue, but

I love the chase, the thrill of avoiding his danger and hazards.

It gives me the confidence to return the favor.

Chuckling darkly, he allows me to try.

My core tightens, suctioning his dick. The pleasure mounts and explodes, rendering me weak. Tempest leaves room for one more unforgiving thrust, then releases himself and lifts me until he covers a nipple with his mouth and bites down.

Screaming, I experience an orgasm through pain. I cover my mouth to stifle the piercing cry I unleash.

Shaking, trembling, I hang onto Tempest's shoulder for dear life.

He lowers me onto the bed, sweat-slicked and shuddering, licking my nipples and massaging my breasts in a soothing, circular rhythm.

"This. Just this." Tempest lays his head on my chest, breathing deep. "You bring me a calm like I've never known."

"A calm *after* the storm," I joke, but stroke my fingers through his hair.

His throat vibrates with agreement before rolling off and bringing me with him, tucking me against his chest.

"What are we going to do?" I ask.

Tempest cups my breast, stroking, alleviating the sting and angry swelling.

"The very thing we shouldn't." He nips at my earlobe. "I don't want to free you, princess. I'd prefer to keep you isolated in my castle walls, trapped and touched by no one but me."

I flip to my back to face him. "I didn't escape one king to fall into the hands of another."

"I'm aware." Tempest strokes a finger down my cheek. "Never said I was a king, though."

"So you'll contain me like everyone else in my life, enemy or friend?"

Tempest's lips flatten into a single line. "I prefer to call it protection."

The excited breath I'd been holding billows out in a disappointed cloud. I sit up, combing back my hair and scanning his room for my clothes. "I was hoping you were different."

He sits up with me. "I'm a far cry from anyone you're trying to compare me to in your head."

I twist to meet his eyes. "Are you, though? My father, my therapists, my doctors, my *abductors*. Everyone wants to keep me locked in a cage."

"You preferred it that way, once upon a time."

I slide off the bed. "I'm different now."

"I wouldn't be so sure. You're still afraid of the dark, aren't you?"

After pulling on my pants and sliding through my shirt, foregoing the underwear I can't find, I pause at the foot of the bed. "You are the dark, Tempest, and I'm not afraid of you."

He smiles, in beautiful repose, naked and restful in bed. "Maybe you are progressing."

Or maybe I'm declining. I shouldn't love the man you've become.

"I came to tell you about Clover, and I have. I'm … gonna go."

His features war with one another, debating whether to stop me. With Rio and Professor Morgan downstairs, it's unlikely he will. After all, Tempest isn't supposed to want me any more than I want him.

"Goodbye, Tempest."

"Princess," he demures, then strokes a hand up his hardening dick, telling me what I'll be missing.

I pulse, swell, and ache from his love bites and thrusts, yet I salivate for more. Spinning on my heel, I get out of there before my body gets any more ideas.

The cottage is as quiet as I entered it, my footsteps clomping down the stairs and into the main area. Rio and Morgan have left.

Telling myself this is the *final* moment I'll spend in this haunted, violent home, I take my last look, ingraining Tempest's comfort zone in my mind for later thought.

The hearth, spitting flame. The wingback chairs and extensive library. The coffee table where Clover and I asked the restless spirits to wisp through the cracks. Picture frames adorn the small tables by the chairs. I never took Tempest or Rio for family men. Curious, I move for a closer look.

Tempest said Professor Morgan was from a mafia family. The nephew to a kingpin. The gray-haired man with his arm slung around a young, un-tattooed Hunter doesn't look anything like the fat, balding men in sweat-soaked suits ordering hits from a city steakhouse.

Squinting, I pick up the frame.

He looks familiar, though. Weirdly so. I don't recall ever meeting Hunter's family before. My father kept me mostly sequestered from any business with other powerful men.

But...

The flash of white, a lightning crack of clarity, cuts through the center of my skull and burns the backs of my eyes.

Oh, my God.

Oh, my God.

I know this man.

I know him!

Because I saw him die.

37

ARDYN

A fractured, broken sound ricochets through the den. I've dropped the picture, the glass shattering at my feet.

I can't breathe.

My chest tightens. I clutch it as I stumble back. The walls are moving, creeping closer, locking me in a tomb.

I can't breathe.

The ceiling whirls, centers itself, then whirls again. I spin around, expecting to see the door, *freedom*, but instead, I see Mila.

She's not the Mila I remember. Skin peels off her skeleton as she reaches for me. Her face concaves as I watch, decay giving her a grayish-green cast. She tries to speak to me, but all I see is a gaping black hole where her tongue should be.

"*Mila.*" Her name comes out of me in a gasp.

She unhinges her jaw, her eyes melting from their

sockets and a ghastly skull taking its place. Yet I can hear the words as if she speaks them.

"Please. Help us."

Black combat boots step up to her as she tries to crawl out of the wreckage.

"I think Ardyn's still breathing, but I can't check on Clover. You have to help us!"

The form standing over her doesn't move.

She tips her face up as much as she can while splayed on her stomach. "What—what are you waiting for? Help me! Call someone!"

Pants move into view as he bends, resting on his haunches.

I blink into black but force my eyes open, hanging upside down, trying to move my lips, to form words, but I'm sick, so sick with nausea and just want to escape...

"Tempest, what are you doing? Stop!"

Choking sounds. Mila can't breathe.

I have to keep my eyes open.

In half-lidded, upside-down crescents, I see familiar hands wrapped around Mila's throat, and then they twist.

Snap.

That same murderous hand strokes back Mila's hair from her slack, vacant face. "Sorry, darling. It had to be done."

NO.

The ceiling whirls again, bile collecting in my throat, and I'm dumped in the back of an auction house, watching Professor Rossi—*Miguel Rossi*—pull the trigger into the forehead of the man hugging Hunter.

The man.

The father.

Professor Morgan's father.

The intricate web of lies unspools from my head with the force of projectile vomit. I drag my body to the front door, using the wall to steady my sickly escape.

Tempest killed Mila.

Professor Rossi killed a man I wasn't supposed to know about.

And the most awful thing, the most soul-destroying of it all, is that I was well aware of Tempest's true self before I ever remembered he killed my friend.

"Ardyn?"

Tempest's concern plops into my consciousness like a pebble being thrown in flat water, rippling out its impact.

I fall into the door, clutching the handle. *"Don't touch me."*

"What's wrong?"

He's on me in three strides, cataloging the scene in front of him with expert alertness. The broken frame. The people housed in that photo. My bloodless face.

Tempest stops short of grabbing me. "You've remembered."

Through chattering teeth, I cry hoarsely, "You murdered her!"

He doesn't deny it.

That somehow makes it worse. The tears I'd held back poured freely down my face. "You bastard."

"It was either her or you, Ardyn." Tempest's expression is too impassive. Too controlled. Like he's afraid to emote or give me any clue about his feelings on the subject.

"Then it should've been *me*." I slam a trembling hand against my chest. Turning, I open the door. Tempest palms the wood above my head, slamming it shut.

"I can't let you go until we talk about this."

"There's nothing for us to discuss. You *killed my friend*!"

"Because of what you saw. Don't you get it? Miguel saw you, or someone who looked very much like you, kill the heir to a Mafia empire. He couldn't let that go, and I had to follow orders."

"Follow *orders*?" I stare at him through a blur of tears. "You knew her, Tempest! She was Clover's best friend!"

"She was my preference over having to kill you."

Tempest doesn't move a muscle. Just stares down at me as if waiting for the moment I will—"Do you expect me to thank you for sparing my life?"

"No. I wouldn't ask that of you."

I have no idea if he's being sincere or not. "I thought I could understand the monster behind your eyes because I've met a lot of monsters in my life. But I'll never understand this."

"You have to. I can't let you leave until you promise me your silence on this."

"Are you crazy?" Then I laugh. "Wait, no. I'm the crazy one. The locked-up one. The unstable one. Even though everything I witnessed was true!"

Tempest hooks my biceps, shaking me. The control he'd grasped slowly slips from his stoic, shaking features. "Is that what you want to hear? That you're not crazy? Fine, Ardyn. You're worse. Your life is in constant danger, and I did everything in my power to save you. I'll keep doing it now. You cannot tell Clover. You can't discuss this with *anyone*. Not if you want to live."

I heave in his arms, staring at him, not knowing him, not understanding myself.

"Do you hear me?" His eyes sear my skin, green toxins slipping into my veins. "I've spent the past four years deleting you from Miguel's memory. Then you fucking show up at this school! We've never been so close to death as we are now, so if you won't do this for yourself, do it for Clover."

My lips curl in disgust. "Damn you for using her like this."

"You know I'm right."

I rip out of his hold and glare with all the energy I have left, which isn't much. I'm destroyed inside. "I'm not the person who killed her friend. *My* friend."

"She was a vapid, ignorant, jealous girl, and she would've screwed you over a thousand times by now."

I pull my features in, staring at him with wide eyes. "I can't believe you. Whatever her personality was, she didn't deserve to die."

"Jesus, Ardyn." Tempest rubs a hand down his face. "Sit down. We can talk about this. I don't want you running through the woods in this state."

"Oh, so now I'm a hysterical woman who can't get home by herself because I'm horrified over what you've done?" My words are enough to bolster the fury to rip open the door and storm out.

"Ardyn!"

I throw myself into a full-on sprint into the forest.

Tempest could easily outrun me. He's proven it once. But as the afternoon darkens into evening and the woods fall over me like a cold blanket, Tempest doesn't come looking.

He lets me go.

38

TEMPEST

Ardyn isn't in class the next day. Or the next.

I send a text to Clover, asking how she's doing and discreetly asking after Ardyn, to which she replies: **since when do you give a shit what we're up to?**

I assume that means they're both fine, and Ardyn hasn't confessed any dark truths to my sister.

Thank fuck.

That bought me forty-eight hours to figure out how best to navigate our future if we're to have any.

I kept a straight face around Miguel, updating him and maintaining my duties. An amazing feat, considering I was in a foul mood. The students didn't fare nearly as well. I bit their heads off if they so much as moved their lips to form a question and weighted my grades heavily on whether or not I thought they were obnoxious, intolerable, or both.

Needless to say, my office hours weren't filled.

I spent that free time mulling over the consequences of

choosing Ardyn over Mila all those years ago and why I did it. I still can't figure it out. All it's done is make my life harder. Worse. Complicated and crazy. I crave her and want to escape her in equal measure. I'm hoping she's busy packing and praying she doesn't want to leave. I'm lighter now that she knows all my secrets but weighed down by how much she must despise me now.

And why the *fuck* do I care that she hates me? I've never cared what anyone thought before. It's a gross, annoying feeling that I wish would just fuck right off.

A knock on my doorframe sends my head up. I glower at the figure filling up my doorway.

"I assume that means come right in?" Rio asks with a lopsided smile.

I'd like to smack it off his face. If only he were close enough.

Without waiting for a response, Rio strolls inside, shutting the door behind him.

"What do you want?" I ask.

"Join me for a drink, will you?" Rio helps himself to my bar caddy, uncapping a crystal decanter of whiskey.

"I'm on the clock."

"Since when has that stopped you?"

"I'd prefer not to be inebriated at the moment."

"That's your choice." Rio pours himself a healthy three fingers, takes a deep swallow, then sits across from my desk. "I'll just sit here enjoying your top shelf while you laser into your desk using your eyes."

"Have you stopped by to annoy me? I have a lot of work to do before tonight, so if you don't mind—"

"How did she remember?"

My head snaps up. "Excuse me?"

"Ardyn." Rio licks a droplet of whiskey from his lower lip as he stares me down. "How did she figure out you were the one who killed Mila?"

I lean back from my desk, slowly and with careful consideration. "You're lucky I sweep my office for bugs on a daily basis."

"You're my best friend. Of course, I know that, about as well as I understand your moods, and you've only been like this once before."

"Oh?"

"Yes. When you decided Ardyn should live."

My lips turn way, way down.

"It's the one moment I could honestly agree with Hunter that your nickname should be Storm Cloud. Don't get me wrong," Rio adds over my warning growl, "you're the Zeus of all storm clouds, but you're usually able to contain your miserable anger a lot better than you are now. As much as you're trying not to show it, I'm here to tell you people are noticing. Hunter, for one."

"Hunter can go fuck a forest animal."

"He's crucial to keep on your side, Tempest. Don't forget that."

"I'm not. I'm only..." I scrub my face. "I'm in a bind."

"I know it."

"So are you here to offer friendly advice, then? Because I have to tell you, I need a lot more than that."

"Look, you dug your grave. You chose Ardyn, and I'm having trouble believing that you still don't know *why* you kept her alive. Same as now—how can you not see why you're so miserable?"

"She's my sister's best friend. The only friend Clover has left. As much as Miguel wanted me to, I couldn't kill both her friends that night."

Rio sits back, tonguing his cheek. "You believe that?"

"It's true."

He makes a noncommittal motion with his head.

"The fuck that's supposed to mean?" I ask him.

"Don't make me say it, man."

"Say *what?*"

"Dude, if you make me spell it out for you, I'm only going to make your life more complicated."

I grind my molars together. "I dislike riddles."

"Fine." Rio sighs. "You're in love with her."

Piles of papers tremble as my fists hit the desk, and I stand. "I am *not* in love with Ardyn Kaine."

"What do you call this then?" Rio motions up and down, taking into account my vibrating body, snarling mouth, and burning stare. "A regular day for a storm cloud?"

"Fuck you." I point at the door. "And get out."

"Not gonna happen."

"Then allow me to punch you out."

I round the desk. Rio, not a stupid man, leaps from his

chair and puts my bar cart full of thousand-dollar whiskey in front of us.

"Hear me out," he says, his voice calm. "You love her, and you need to start accepting that so we can make proper plans moving forward. Your life is in danger. Mine. Hers. You need to guarantee her silence."

I respond with deathly quiet. "I am not killing her."

"I'm aware. But the fact is, you being in love with her is a *good* thing. That's all she's wanted from you, T! Since you were kids, and she was that weird ghost girl who hid under tables and eavesdropped on us. It's why, when she was unconscious in that car wreck, you couldn't finish the job, and it's why you're in such a sour mood now—because she knows who you really are, and you hate that she thinks so little of you now. Am I right?"

I cross my arms and glare.

"I'll take that as a yes. If you tell her you love her, we might get out of this unscathed and finish up our plan to freedom. Ardyn wants your love, Tempest. That is the answer you've been looking for these past few days but haven't been able to find."

"Bullshit." Giving in, I pour myself two fingers from the bar cart between us. "It can't be that fucking easy."

Rio shrugs. "Love isn't complicated, dude. It's only hard for people like us who've never experienced it. I still know it when I see it, though, which is more than I can say for you."

"I'm incapable of such a useless—"

Ardyn, in my bed, wrapping herself around me. Ardyn, listening to my truth with palpable sentiment in her eyes, like she hurt for me, with me. Ardyn, cheeks flushed and words harsh as she stood her ground, stronger with experience, heartier with courage. Ardyn, who will keep my secret even though it pains her because she's loved me from the time I was an innocent boy.

"Fuck." My glass shatters to the floor.

Rio smirks.

His face is saved from serious marring when my phone goes off. I snap it off the desk, reading the text.

Clover: YOU SLEPT WITH MY BEST FRIEND??????

39

ARDYN

I haunt the halls of Camden House for two full days.

Or maybe haunt is the wrong word since even ghosts have reasons to stay behind and turn away from the light. Their hearts are broken, and I'm no longer certain that I have even that.

I didn't think it was possible to be worse than broken, so shattered as to be irreparable, yet here I am, still functioning at a basic level but not nearly enough to still be considered human.

A hollow ache replaces my heartbeats, burning fire substitutes for my tears, and a nonstop, thunderous rumble scars the void that once housed my mind.

I'm aware of the one person who could stun me out of purgatory, but I'm terrified to run into him. Tempest would awaken sections of my soul, but not the right ones. Not the good, moral ones that understand right from wrong and always chooses mercy. No, he would summon the poison in my blood and turn it as black as his. I'm horrified that I might accept it.

That is how deep my love for him runs—obsessive, unhinged, unhealthy. I cannot love a killer, yet I do. I'm heartbroken, fearful, empty, and desperate for him.

I'm better off staying in bed.

"Hey. Sleep monster."

Clover jostles my shoulder through the layers of bedcovers.

"Time to get up. You've taken pathetic to a whole new level."

I mumble, "You don't understand."

"Because you won't tell me."

I can never tell you. If one thing has been constant in my mind, it's that. Clover can never know what her brother did. I can't put her through what I'm being forced to endure.

"I'm sorry for what happened between us." Clover's voice comes out quiet. "Maybe you were joking about Professor Morgan, and I took it too seriously. You were looking out for me, and I'm *told* I can be overly sensitive..."

I stiffen underneath her hand, clamping my lips shut.

"I never want a guy to come between us, Ardyn. And I never want you to think you can't talk to me. The way you've been acting these past few days ... If you need to talk to someone, I'm here."

"I can't talk about it with anyone." My voice comes out as a pained whisper.

Clover sighs heavily. "It's my brother, isn't it?"

I freeze, then unfreeze enough to draw the covers down from my head and peer at her.

She gives me a sidelong look. "You and I, girl, we don't talk to many people, but I watch enough k-dramas to recognize what not showering and sobbing into your pillow every night means. You've got a broken heart, and since Tempest is the only other person of the opposite sex I've seen you talk to..."

"You're not mad?" I croak.

Clover's eyes widen. She leaps from the bed, splaying her hands out and shouting, "What the fuck? I was right?!"

I shoot upright. "You just said you knew!"

"I didn't think you'd agree with me! I thought it would disgust you enough to shake you out of this funk and tell me what's really going on with you!"

"Oh." I shut my eyes with a pained grimace. "Well..." *If only you knew the rest.*

"Did you sleep with him?" Clover's question is cold.

My heart, what little there is left of it, plummets. But I can't lie to her. "Yes."

Silence.

"Why didn't you tell me? I thought you were my friend. How long has this been going on? You've been sneaking around behind my back? When were you—?" Clover spins with the speed of her questioning. "Were you ever going to say anything? What if I hadn't guessed right now. Would you have just laughed at my expense forever?"

"No!" I push the covers off and get to my feet. "Clover,

no. I was trying to figure out the best way to tell you, but there's so much going on, so much you don't know, and—"

"And here I am, being a good friend and trying to cheer you up. Meanwhile, you're fucking my brother—who is a *bonafide* sociopath, by the way—and *God,* Ardyn, I felt sorry for you! I pitied you and hated all the pain you've had to endure, and this is your thanks? Lying to me?"

"It's not like that." My defense comes out as a squeak.

"It's pretty fucking simple, don't you think? Me fuck best friend's brother, me tell best friend. See? Even a caveman can do it."

"You're right." I lick my lips.

"Then why didn't you? How could you let me play dumb for this long? When did you start? This summer? Before then? During your stay at the funny farm?"

My eyes shoot to hers. "Don't."

"I think I've earned the right to insult you, Ardyn. You can't go around playing innocent and then be conniving at the same time. It can't *all* work to your benefit."

"Stop it."

"You can't avoid it this time. I'm *pissed,* and you're not giving me a good enough answer." Clover pulls her phone out of her pocket.

"What are you doing?"

"Texting Tempest." Her thumbs start flying across the screen.

"*No!*" I pounce on her, grabbing the phone and flinging it clear across the room.

Clover watches its flight, stunned. "What the hell?"

"I understand you're upset, *but so am I!*" I scream. "You think I wanted to fall in love with him? I know he's bad for me. I'm so aware of it that I get sick to my stomach every time I think of it, but I can't stop it if I try, okay? He is the one for me. I don't know why, how, or what fucked-up fate decided to have me fall for a villain, but here I am, wasting away in my *fucking bed* because I can't stand the thought of him. At the same time, I can't stop thinking about him!"

Clover's mouth drops open.

"I feel terrible that I betrayed you, Clover, and I am truly sorry you found out like this. If I had it my way, I would've asked you about it first before pursuing him, but it didn't—couldn't—work like that. You know why? Because we were an explosion. I didn't see it coming. One minute, I'm yelling at him and hating the very ground he walks on, and the next, I'm in his arms, and he's kissing me, and he's showing me parts of himself that I can't ever explain, and I should hate him. Oh God, I should want him to suffer for all the things he's done. And maybe one day he'll pay for his sins, but I'm not going to stand on the outside and watch him go down in flames. I want to be beside him when he burns." Tears roll down my face. "I want to protect him and show him the good that's left inside him. I know it's there. I've seen it, and I feel like, without me, he'll extinguish it forever. I want to be what keeps him good, Clover." I inhale deeply, my breath shaking and my lips trembling. "I want it to be me."

Clover blinks.

I shut my mouth. Swallow. But I won't look away from

her. Not anymore. I'm standing my ground, facing the truth of my actions, and I'll take the consequences, no matter what they will be.

I'm not running again.

"Wow," Clover says.

"Do you hate me?" My voice is hoarse.

"No." Clover runs her tongue over her teeth, thinking. "Actually, the opposite. Nobody has spoken about my brother like that before. Literally no one."

I sniff. "He's not really the welcoming type."

Clover snorts. "Definitely not." Then she looks at me more closely. "Are you sure this is what you want to do? Love him? He's a huge asshole."

"I know." I shake my head, amazed at myself for coming to this decision. "But he's my asshole."

40

ARDYN

By Thursday, I'm able to make it out of my dorm and into the outside, fully dressed and showered with Clover at my elbow.

She's forgiven me, in a way. After our blowout, she consulted her cards to ensure our friendship could withstand this kind of curveball. This made me nervous. Her cards aren't known to be kind to me. Thankfully, her cards read true. I knew in my heart that we could withstand anything, even this, so maybe there is something to her cards, after all.

Clover and I aren't perfect, and we still have a lot to catch up on with each other and how we each grew up during those missing years, but what's important is that we *are* working on it, and at least the truth of my feelings for her brother is out in the open.

The other stuff, however...

I'm still sorting through it in my head.

The best course of action would be to talk to Tempest and sit Clover down together, but we all know how that suggestion will go down. It also means I'd have to face him, and with my confession to Clover coupled with the knowledge that he's responsible for Mila's death ... I can't. I can't process it, and I'm at a loss on how to move forward.

I'm seriously hoping I don't run into him today. It's pure denial, but continuing to put distance and space between him and me has to help me come to grips with all these explosive confessions. Right?

Clover's tarot cards are definitely reading right today because I get through my classes without one sighting of Tempest and spend the rest of the evening in the library catching up on my missed assignments undisturbed.

The lights flicker, indicating closing time. I'm the last person in here. I stand and collect my books, satisfied with my progress for the day. The last thing I need is for my private life to bleed into my schoolwork and make all my progress obsolete. It doesn't matter that my private life includes murder, betrayal, mafia rings, and hitmen; my parents are looking for any excuse to pick me up and cart me off. If anything, I'm rather proud of myself for remaining upright all day.

"Ardyn."

The voice comes from behind me, but I'd recognize it if it were across the room. Across the globe.

With goose bumps prickling my neck, I turn.

Tempest stands near the entrance, dressed in black, the green of his gaze in startling contrast as he targets me. "I have no right to ask this of you, but I need you to come with me."

I shake my head while my heart cries, *yes!*

"Please."

Tempest never begs. Please doesn't leave his lips. He forces them out of victims. I know how much it must take for him to utter that word to me.

"I can't forget what you've done," I say.

He nods. "Then at least let me try for your forgiveness."

"I don't think that's possible."

Tempest holds out his hand, beckoning. "Come. Please. Don't make me say it again."

My eyes dart right and left. I'm not sure what I'm looking for. It's not like a librarian will successfully shoo him away. It's also unlikely I'll escape him. Tempest will figure out another way to make me go with him, a lot more forceful than this. If Tempest has a point to prove, he will not relent until he proves it.

"Fine." I sigh. "Let me drop off my stuff at the dorm and—"

"No time. Leave it here. I'll send Rio to grab your stuff."

Frowning, I do as he asks. As I walk toward him, I'm not ignorant enough to believe that the lightness in my shoulders isn't solely due to the lack of a backpack. It's *him*. He's back, Tempest is near, and I feel better already.

What does that say about me?

I lift my hand, enfolding it in his. Tempest's grip is powerful, but he holds me with great care, leading me out of the library without another word.

Tempest takes me into the woods with moonlight guiding our path. He doesn't pull out his phone, and I don't ask questions, knowing where he's taking me.

Trust is a fragile trait and an even more tenuous gift, but I can't convince myself to run in the opposite direction. Maybe it's because he's saved me once, twice, a countless number of times. Maybe I think that with me, he inflicts pain only so he can enjoy giving me comfort after—a habit he reserves only for us.

Either way, I go with him.

Anderton Cottage is dark as we approach. Rio must be somewhere else if he's picking up my things, and I've sensed hostility between Tempest and Professor Morgan, so I doubt he's sitting comfortably in the dark while Tempest unlocks the door and ushers me in.

I follow him through the home. He doesn't turn on any lights, and when he pushes aside a painting and enters in a code, I show no surprise when the bookshelf swings open and we step through.

Tempest takes the stairs first. He stops at the bottom, waiting for me.

The gloom of the stairway doesn't detract from the intensity of his stare as he watches me descend. His eyes are brighter than usual, more fervent. Muscles in his cheeks tic as he debates what to say.

When I join him on the bottom step, he takes both my hands in his, and says solemnly, "This is for you."

Tempest flicks on the light.

I stare into the room and scream.

41
ARDYN

Three men are bound to three chairs, struggling in a neat row as they moan and plea through gagged mouths.

"Oh, my God," I whisper after collecting myself.

Tempest strolls to the middle of the room. "You recognize them?"

"Yes. They're my captors."

"Out on parole, the lucky buggers. Amazing how scared they are now, right? Considering they bound, gagged, and tortured a little girl in much the same way. How does it feel to have a grown man tower over you with a knife in his hand, hmm? Would you like me to scar you in the same way you did her?" Tempest turns and lifts up a wooden paddle. "Or should we go straight into sodomy? I never believed in an eye for an eye. More like a head for an eye."

The man closest to him moans. He's so frightened that his eyes roll into the back of his head.

As his head tips back, I notice the knife marks.

"You've been torturing them." Carefully, I make my way to Tempest to get a closer look.

"I tried to wait for you, but they're such fucking assholes, I had to make my position known." He clucks his tongue as one kicks out at him. "Aw, you're just angry I interrupted your Powerpoint presentation to each other." Tempest looks at me. "They were planning another kidnapping, princess. Another child. A girl."

I suck in a breath. My face goes numb.

"And this time, they weren't going to let her go since it went so wrong the last time, and you identified them. They just don't learn, do they?"

Tempest thumps the paddle on one of their heads. The man shrieks behind his gag.

My throat burns. "Nicholas Brewster. Terrance Smith. Micheal Krakowski."

"My girl always remembers the names of those who hurt her." Tempest straightens.

His use of *my girl* rings in my head ... not as an alarm. As a ring of truth. Without considering what I'm becoming or who I should be. Instead, I nod.

I'm his.

"Tell me, baby, which one do you want to suffer the most? I can make it happen for you." Tempest gifts them each with a saccharine smile.

I go to Tempest's side. Stroke down his arm. And consider each man. Each *assaulter*. "I could ask you to start with Nick first. He held me down and pulled up my shirt. Squeezed my barely-there breasts. Spit on them."

Tempest's arm hardens in my grip. To prevent him from springing, I continue, "or Terrance, who pretended to be my friend. He'd get information from me, like my favorite kind of ice cream, the best hamburger I've ever had, and my beloved stuffed animal, and then he'd torture me with them. Setting them down just out of reach from where they chained me."

Tempest sucks on one of his canines. "Psychological warfare. I could work with that."

"And then there's Micheal. Never Mike. Every time I shortened his name when I pled for my life, he'd slap me across the face until either my lip or the skin under my eye split open. Then he'd lick my blood off his fingers."

"I think I'd like to start with Nicky by cutting off his nipples."

"Still sore about that, are you?" I ask.

Tempest awards me with a sidelong glare. "I meant when I said don't ever mention his name to me again."

I purse my lips, properly chastised.

"Then perhaps I'll move on to *Mike* and make a necklace out of his teeth and his tongue as my pendant. And Terrance? I could easily leave him for Hunter." Tempest's bicep pulses under my hand. With whitened lips of fury, he turns to me and adds, "Believe me, you'd witness just desserts if I let him loose."

The three men moan and struggle as they process Tempest's words. With his stone-hewn expression, there's no doubt Tempest lives up to his promises. I take in each man, noting the tears coursing down Nick's face, the splotchiness of Terrance's, and the sweat-soaked Michael.

I consider each one of them, taking my time. Tempest waits beside me, if not patiently, then out of respect for me in facing my captors for the first time in almost a decade.

Stepping forward, I pull down the gag of the one closest—Micheal.

"P-please," he begs hoarsely. His brown eyes stare into mine. "I have a family now. Children. I'm a changed man."

"Is one of them a girl?" I ask, my lips scarcely moving.

"Yes." His answer comes out as a sob.

"How old is she?"

"E-eleven."

"Do you know what I was doing at eleven years old?" I fold my hands in front of me. "Sleeping under my bed. Eating under it. Scratching and biting anyone who came near me. Every time my mother wanted to bathe me, they had to sedate me. A nurse would grab my ankle and drag me out from under, stabbing a needle into my arm until I stopped fighting. My parents would stand by and watch, my dad not able to stand it, my mother falling to her knees and sobbing. You did that to me."

"I'm sorry." Tears roll down his cheeks. "It was wrong of me. To imagine my baby girl going through that—I'm sorry. I'm so sorry."

I worry my cheek, staring at him. It would be so easy to give Tempest the nod, to watch them all burn where they sit and feel better about myself, knowing these men aren't out there haunting my every step anymore.

But then I think of Mila. What happened to her wasn't due to these men. Tempest took an order and morphed it into his own vendetta, to sacrifice her in order to save me. Here, he wants to do it again.

I like to think I've learned and lived through more than the average nineteen-year-old. Having that knowledge comes with a duty to use it, and if I don't consider my next decisions wisely, then what the hell was the point of living through death and struggles and sickness if I'm just like the rest of them?

If it was wrong with Mila, it is wrong now.

I turn to Tempest. Move in front of him. Rest my hands on his shoulders. "No."

He cocks his head, his eyes slitting. "No?"

"I don't want this. More suffering. It's not going to grant me my childhood back, and it won't gain you any favor in a life you're already fighting for survival in. It's not worth it."

"They marked you. Scarred your mind. Blackened your soul. All of that gives me ample permission to tear them to pieces and scatter them across the burned ashes of their homes."

"You hurt me, too."

That gives him pause.

"I'm starting to understand you, Tempest, as much as I fought against it. You equate pain with love, don't you? I'd like to show you that the two don't have to go together. I can love you and not require torture, at someone else's expense or at mine. I can touch you like this..." I lay a hand on his cheek, scratchy with day-old scruff. "And leave it at that. No pinch, no slap, no unkind words. Just this. A gentle touch."

Tempest's brows crash together, his eyes searching mine. He wars inside his head, coming to terms with the cease-fire I'm requesting. He doesn't flinch away from my hand or slap it away. He turns immobile, his lips parting in shock, or question, or both.

The corners of my lips pull up. Tempest has no idea what to do with himself.

"Tempest, I love you. Since you were a boy, and then a bully, and even as the man you've become. I don't love what you do—I'm not sure how I'll ever wrap my head around it—but I *do* know the prospect of living without you, well..." I glance over my shoulder to include my captors. "...I'd want to tear anyone who comes between us to pieces and burn down their homes, too."

Tempest catches my wrist, and my gaze shoots back to him.

"I'm not a good man. I can't stop what I do. There's a plan. Rio and I have a plan, and I can't take your hand and walk off into the sunset."

I nod, keeping my expression soft.

His tightens. "I've become a demonic version of the boy you first met. I'm nowhere close to the prep school kid playing around with secret societies that you tried to catch glimpses of at our summer homes. And I ... I can't change anymore, princess. I'm so fucking tired."

"I'm not asking you to change."

"Then what do you want? You must require something to accept this much of me without blinking an eye."

"I want you to love me," I say honestly. "And I want you to listen to me. To take my opinions into account whenever you are thinking of doing something ... controversial. Like Mila."

One of his eyes tics. The mention of her name still affects him.

"I don't want to be put in that position ever again," I continue. "I mean it. Don't blindfold me. If your plans with Rio affect Clover and me, then we deserve to be made aware of it *before* anyone has to get hurt. Or killed."

"I will always protect you," he says. "No question. You and my sister are the only people keeping bits of my heart red and beating."

"Tempest."

"I understand what you're saying. Protecting you also means not hurting you, ever. Anymore."

"I meant what I said—I can't forgive Mila, but I can understand why you did it. I wish I hadn't seen what I did, that I could rewind—"

He cups my cheek. "It's not your fault."

I still in his hand, closing my eyes, enjoying the feel of his fingers whispering against my temple. "See? A gentle touch is all it takes sometimes."

Tempest makes a sound in his throat, sounding vaguely threatening. My eyes spring open.

As soon as I meet his blacked-out stare, his pupils overtaking his irises, my middle starts tingling in anticipation.

"I'll grant your wish, princess. These men can live. Now grant mine."

"Which is?"

"Upstairs." Tempest lowers his voice ominously. "Now."

He lifts me by the backs of my knees and sprints out of the basement while I wrap my hands around his neck, squealing.

And without a backward look at my captors.

Or my past.

42

TEMPEST - EPILOGUE

Only Ardyn could take a torture scenario and cast a lovesick spell into the atmosphere, blotting out all hate and forcing introspection instead.

Her delighted shrieks tickle my ear as I carry her through the bookshelf and kick it shut with my feet, then take the stairs to the second floor two at a time, my princess tight in my arms.

"I want you naked," I growl into her ear, snapping my teeth near her lobe.

She trembles at the cascade of breath down her nape and across one shoulder.

At the entrance to my bedroom, I set her on her feet. Ardyn spins, light on her toes, pulling her shirt up and tossing it aside. I make quick work of my clothes and by the time I'm naked and standing before her, she is, too.

"Breathtaking," she whispers, her eyes trained on my cock, before she enters into my arms.

My immediate reaction should be to throw her on the bed and spread her legs, biting the inside of her thighs until she trembles and sweats.

Instead, I'm struck by the need to hold her. Just hold her.

Our warmth intermingles, her hair a blanket of silk between my fingers. I burrow into her nape, inhaling a scent that is only Ardyn's, sweet and pure.

She runs her hands down my back, scraping delicately and drawing concentric circles. Soon, our breaths match, our chests rising and falling together.

"I could stay like this," I admit, swaying with her in my arms.

Ardyn raises her eyes to mine, our noses bumping. "Then we should."

This close, I notice how her lower lip is bigger than the one above, a sensual curve with an ombrè hue of pink to rose. Unable to resist, I dart out my tongue, tasting the center.

She melts into my chest, her tongue brushing against mine.

That's all I need.

I lay her on the bed—gentle now, trying to be oh so gentle—trailing my fingers between her breasts, over her belly button, and into her folds.

Ardyn arches into my fingers, her eyelashes fluttering as she attempts to maintain her stare on mine.

"Give in," I say, shifting to better accomodate my raging boner.

She lifts her hips, allowing me deeper access. I curve my fingers inside her, prodding and coaxing, but it isn't enough. It never is.

I shift until I'm between her legs and my mouth takes over. Her taste explodes on my tongue. Ardyn yelps her hands knotting the sheets as she humps my face. I groan into her softness, the desire to stain my face with her forever spurring my tongue forward, driving it as deep as it can go.

It's no replacement for my dick, so when I have her on the brink, I lift my head, running my tongue across my lower lip.

"Why'd you stop?" she pants, squirming uncomfortably.

I say simply, "Because I want to see you every time you come undone for me."

Her legs fall to the sides as I slip in between, rising above her and slipping in where I've always belonged. I've shaped her for myself, and I can honestly admit, I'm happy to call Ardyn my forever home.

The men downstairs still must die, obviously. They touched her—they messed with my home, and I will never let them experience a safe space again.

To Ardyn, they will just disappear from her life and she won't give them a second thought. As I run a finger down the angles of her cheek, nestling into the corner of her mouth, I vow to make her forget every single bad thing that happened to her—except for me, of course.

I'm the only bad that will ever be good for her.

Ardyn accepts my finger and sucks it into her mouth, down to the knuckle. She thrusts against it with her tongue, mimicking what she wants me to do with my dick.

I smile.

"You're mine," I say to her before pulling out, then slamming in. "You're fucking mine."

"I'm yours," she agrees with a heavy-lidded stare, her body wide open for me. "I love you. I love you, Tempest."

"I..." Groaning, my head falls forward, my balls tightening as she clenches and seals me inside. "I don't deserve you, but I fucking love you, too."

It isn't until later, after Ardyn fell asleep, that I sneak out and dispose of the bastards downstairs. I return, slipping between my sheets that Ardyn's kept warm and spoon her into my chest, and I murmur into the night, into her ear, "I'm only ever yours, princess. I hope you'll keep me."

Her mouth curves in sleep and she rolls over, nestling closer to where she belongs.

Thank you so much for reading Cruel Promise! Clover's book is up next:

. . .

Forbidden love, a mafia group on the hunt for a witch's hidden treasure, and a young woman torn between them all. Experience the gripping tale of Clover Callahan and the Vultures in BROKEN BEAUTY, a heart-stopping romance you won't forget.

Get it now.

A Note from Ketley

Hello, my lovely reader!

Thank you for reading this series all the way to the end! I love my stories, but it always feels so nice and surprising that other people love them, too. If you have the time, **I'd be grateful if you left a review** on your preferred platform. Those golden little stars are what drive me to keep writing.

Thank you for going on Tempest's final journey with me! Are you interested in his role at Briarcliff Academy? **Start with Rival** and get a first look at how Tempest came to be the man he is.

Keep an eye out for Clover's story, coming Spring 2023 in the Titan Falls world and continuing the mystery of the Vultures.

You can also join my readers' group, **Ketley's Crew,** on Facebook, to talk more Tempest and Ardyn! Did you love them? Want Tempest for yourself? Let me know! I'd love to meet you!

xoxo, Ket.

all in kindle unlimited

If you want more bullies and secret societies, read:

Rival

Virtue

Fiend

Reign

If you like your bad boys and bullies as standalones (no series, one book, a happy ending), read:

Rebel

Crave

If you like mafia men, read

Underground Prince

Jaded Princess

If you like a grump turned into a protector for his woman, read:

Rock

Lover

If you like your playboys with tormented hearts and scars, read:

Trust

Dare

Play

If you like crime with your romance, read:

To Have and to Hold

From This Day Forward